About the Author

Mark Hayden is the nom de guerre of Adrian Attwood. He lives in Westmorland with his wife, Anne.

He has had a varied career working for a brewery, teaching English and being the Town Clerk in Carnforth, Lancs. He is now a part-time writer and part-time assistant in Anne's craft projects.

He is also proud to be the Mad Unky to his Great Nieces & Great Nephews.

NINE OF WANDS

The Fifth Book of the King's Watch

MARK HAYDEN

PAW
PRESS

www.pawpress.co.uk

First Published Worldwide in 2019 by Paw Press
Paperback Edition Published 2019
Reprinted 11 June 2021 with minor corrections.

Cover Design – Rachel Lawston
Design Copyright © 2019 Lawston Design
www.lawstondesign.com
Cover images © Shutterstock

Paw Press – Independent publishing in Westmorland, UK.
www.pawpress.co.uk

ISBN: 1-9998212-5-4
ISBN-13: 978-1-9998212-5-8

For Suzanne

Physiotherapist Extraordinaire

NINE OF WANDS

A Note from Conrad...

Hi,

Some of you have said that it might help if there was a guide to magickal terms and a Who's Who of the people in my stories.

Well, I thought it might help, too, and my publisher has been kind enough to put one on their website. You can find them under 'Magickal Terms (Glossary)' and 'Dramatis Personae(Who's Who)' on the Paw Press website:

www.pawpress.co.uk

I hope you enjoy the book,
Thanks,
Conrad.

Prologue - A Taste of Paradise and Things to Come

'Can we stay here for ever?' said Mina.

She ducked under the parasol and put down her drink. 'Budge up. There's room for a little one.'

There was room, if I shuffled dangerously close to the edge of the sunlounger. I shuffled, and she snuggled. I put my arm around her. It was hot, here under the parasol, and roasting outside its patch of shade. Definitely time for a siesta.

'How did it go?' I asked.

'Your mother says that I have potential but I jump to conclusions. She may be right.'

We'd arrived at my parents' villa on Saturday afternoon, and it was now Wednesday. Since Sunday, Mother had been teaching Mina how to play bridge in the mornings while I went walking with Dad or practised yoga at the gym in town. My Spanish may be (very) limited, but I now know my *Postura de la Silla* from my *Perro hacia abajo*. Mina was doing much better with her bridge than I was with my *Postura del Puente*.

Bridge is an intense game, and Mother can be an intense teacher, so afternoons were for siesta and evenings for leisurely Spanish dinners – here at the villa, down in town or over at their friends' houses. It *was* pretty much Paradise, and exactly what we'd both needed, given recent events.

Last week, I'd been attacked by a Black Unicorn, and Mina had still been banged up in Her Majesty's Prison Cairndale. No wonder she wanted to stay here forever.

She adjusted her ponytail and nestled her face against my chest, nudging me with her pointy nose in a subtle effort to get more space on the lounger. 'Who are we seeing tonight?' she murmured.

I moved an inch and gathered her closer, feeling her warmth through the cotton dress and running my fingers up to caress her neck. 'Didn't Mum tell you about them?'

She moved her hand and slipped it under my shirt. 'I know all about Isabella's tendency to over-bid No Trumps and Juan's general uselessness in following his wife's lead, but absolutely nothing about who they are.'

'Dad calls them *Very Important Locals*. Juan is the town mayor, amongst other things. They're nice.'

Her hand shot out of my shirt and she opened her eyes. 'What? The *mayor*? Why didn't anyone tell me?' She swung her legs on to the floor. 'Am I supposed to lose? Do we butter them up? Will Juan arrest your father if we beat them?'

I rolled on to my back. For once in our relationship, I was looking up at her physically as well as personally. Her nose looked even pointier from this angle. 'Can you imagine Mother trying to lose at anything, let alone bridge? Just play your best game and don't tell any prison stories.'

'Hmph. You are no use.'

I took her left hand and stroked it. One of her friends in prison had given her a mega henna tattoo on her last night inside. It was meant kindly, but the woman wasn't an expert. Like Mina's permanent chill, it was fading in the Spanish sunshine.

Mum and Dad had cooked on our first night here and made her very welcome, in the manner of a guest. After the second bottle of wine, Mum had asked what it was *really* like in a women's prison. Mina had let her long hair fall over her face, like she does when she's embarrassed, or scared. Or both.

I'd given her thigh a squeeze under the table, and she took a deep breath. She'd brushed back her hair and said, 'There weren't as many lesbians as I'd expected. Disappointing, really.'

Dad choked on his Rioja, and Mum coughed into her napkin before they both burst out laughing. Later, when we were clearing up, Mum had said to Mina, 'Pass the plates, dear.'

I'd let out a huge unconscious breath, one I'd been holding since they'd first found out about my new, criminal girlfriend. Pass the plates *dear*. It meant that Mina was part of the family now, and therefore entitled to all the Clarke family benefits, including the sharp edge of Mother's tongue, as Mina had discovered during her first bridge lesson the next day.

Mina pulled her wrist out of my hand and slapped my exposed thigh. Hard. 'You know what this means, don't you?'

I gave some thought. 'It means Dad and I get to smoke cigars while you play bridge.'

I got another slap for my pains. 'It means I need to get my nails done before the meal, and I need to find something to wear. See you inside.' She headed for the house, and I watched her go.

Antonella, the maid, would soon go round closing the windows, lowering the shutters and saying goodbye. Her last act before locking the front door behind her would be to turn on the aircon, the signal for the Clarke family siesta to begin.

Right on cue, I heard the bang of a window and the rattle of shutters from upstairs. I lit a cigarette just as the house phone rang. Dad uses the landline for his business, and usually lets it go to the answering machine, but today he took the call.

I drained my beer and got ready to go in, only for Dad to appear, holding the phone. 'For you,' he said.

'Who is it?'

Dad shrugged and passed me the phone. 'Put it back on the cradle when you've finished.'

I took the handset. 'Hello?'

'Is that Conrad Clarke?' said an Anglo-Indian-American voice.

The sun carried on beating down, but I felt a cloud move over my life. Our lives.

'Who's calling?' I said, knowing it could only be one person.

'Arun Desai. Mina's brother. I know she's with you.'

'Not at the moment, she's not. Why don't you call her?'

'I have. Many times. And messaged. She said she was going with you. To Spain. To *your* parents.' We both heard the accusation in his voice, and Arun made an effort to moderate himself. 'She said that she was switching off her phone, but I'm afraid that I need to speak to her. I think she's blocking my calls and messages.'

Mina's phone has not been switched off. That's a fact, and I know that she and Arun have had words on a few occasions since she started getting weekend release from prison. I know that because I've heard the raised voices and seen the pain in her eyes afterwards.

This was the first time I'd spoken to him personally, and he sounded more desperate than angry. Antonella had moved downstairs, and I'd be locked out soon. 'Perhaps she needs some space,' I said. 'It's been very hard for her to adjust.'

'Which is why I waited until she was released fully and not just on weekend leave,' snapped Arun. 'You must tell her to call me.' He hesitated. 'Our mother is sick. Dying. Cancer. The hospital in Bombay has sent her home.'

The words came out in a rush. Poor bloke. Instinctively, I glanced up to the shuttered windows of the master bedroom, where my bonkers but healthy mother would be doing the crossword before her siesta. I shivered, and toyed with the idea of leaving the bad news until we got back to England. No. That's no way to start a relationship.

'Where are you?' I asked. 'For the time zones, I mean.' Arun lives north of Cambridge, Massachusetts, but could easily be in India.

'At work, but she can call me any time. I'm flying to Bombay on Friday and on unpaid leave from next week.'

Antonella appeared at the patio doors. I picked up my glass and waved to say that I was coming in.

'I'll go and tell her now,' I said to Arun.

'Thank you, Mr Clarke. Tell her … tell her that I have her Indian passport. I will courier it to wherever she wants. She won't get in to India on her British passport. Not now she has a criminal record.'

The Villa Verde nestles in the hills, just above a little town to the north of Valencia. The town is far enough from the coast to avoid tourists but still be attractive to ex-pats, like Mum and Dad. They've lived here for a few years now, and love it.

The walk down to town is long enough to appreciate the view but not too long to tire you out before dinner. Dad does enough business with the local taxi drivers that it's always easy to get a lift home afterwards. It was way too long for heels, though, and I was swinging Mina's shoes in my left hand while my right hand held hers. The human population of the town was waking up from siesta, and so were the flowers.

In these last days of May, I reckon that the town is at its best, stuffed with blossoms, and the natural scents joined with the odours from a hundred cooks' open windows. Jasmine, garlic, paprika and nicotiana, all blended together as we wove our way through the streets. It was another corner of Paradise, and Mina did her best to treat it as such.

We hadn't got much sleep after I'd broken the news from Arun, not because she wanted to talk, but because she wanted to avoid talking. To him or me.

In the end, I'd hugged her to sleep, and the break in consciousness had been enough for her to pretend that it hadn't happened. For now.

We were an hour ahead of the parents tonight so that I could escort Mina to her appointment at the beauty salon to get her nails done. We arrived just as the owner unlocked the door. I handed over her shoes, we kissed, and I retreated across the road to give her a couple of minutes to get settled in. After that, I was off for a beer.

I lit a cigarette and let the warmth of baked brick seep through my shirt. The letters of the salon's name – Bellegente – sparkled in the last flush of sunshine, and I let my mind wander.

In my shoes, your mind might wander to your problems, perhaps, or what you're having for dinner. My mind wandered home, to Clerkswell in Gloucestershire, and I wondered what the angle of sunset would be at that latitude, and how much later it would happen. Sorry. It's just the way I am: navigational puzzles fascinate me.

And then I jerked off the wall as if I'd been scalded.

I turned and stared at the stucco. That wall faced north. It had never seen the sun, so unless the building were on fire, why was it warm? There could only be one answer.

Magick.

This was my first trip to Spain since I'd been catapulted into the world of magick. Mostly I'd forgotten about it while I was here – the craft part, anyway. It's hard to forget about the murderous ambush parts. They stick in the mind. After all, magick doesn't play the same part in my day-to-day life as it does in Vicky's or Hannah's. This wall, however, I couldn't ignore.

My magickal partner, Vicky Robson, senses Lux (the raw power of magick) with her eyes. I don't know how, but she does. I imagine it's a bit like bees being able to see further into the ultraviolet than humans can: to Vicky (and bees) it's just natural. How it is. For me, sensing magick is a bit like heat. Imagine you're standing in the snow in Iceland, next to one of those thermal springs. You can feel the currents of hot air. Or walking into a cold room where the central heating has just come on: you know where the radiator is without having to look. This wall was a bit like standing outside the boiler room of the Titanic. I stepped back to get a proper look.

The buildings opposite the salon, of which this wall formed a part, were all residential, a mixture of apartments and townhouses in pinks and yellows, with one exception: the one I'd chosen to lean against. It was a very old, single story white farmhouse set back from that white wall. There was a traditional wooden gate to the left with a spy grille, and next to it a brass plate. I took a closer look.

Mercedes del Convento
Lectuas de Tarot
Con Descreción

I was juggling the translation in my head when a loud buzz was followed by a click, and the gate sprang off the catch. Did I want a discreet tarot reading by Mercedes the Nun? Was there a line missing on the brass plate that said *Trampa* – Trap?

1 — *Padres, Patrons and the End of Paradise*

A young woman in her late teens or early twenties pulled back the gate and stepped over the threshold on to the pavement. She was dressed casually, in a sleeveless top and jeans, and she'd been cooking, I reckoned. The pulled back hair, lack of makeup, rolled up sleeves and large knife were all clues, so call me Sherlock. She looked at me and arched her eyebrows. She had a long, domed forehead and round eyes. Her mouth was on the verge of a smile most of the time, and not in a sultry way: her default expression was happy.

The only foreign country where I can blend into the background is Germany, and then only with practice. Everywhere else I might as well wear a Union Jack waistcoat. It was no surprise she spoke in English.

'Señor? Can I help? Mother is here today.'

Someone inside had sensed my own magick, of that I had no doubt. It would have been downright suspicious, to say nothing of rude, if I'd just walked off. I smiled and stepped through the gate into an exquisite courtyard garden that overloaded the senses with flowers, herbs and the ripe odour of an enormous marijuana bush. How had I not copped that smell outside?

Now that I could see the house properly, it looked even older, with lots of exposed aged wood and small, shuttered windows. The door was down a narrow side alley, and I could see a field sloping down to the river over the young woman's shoulders as she led me inside.

The smell of onions hit me from a kitchen down to the left. She pointed right and said, 'Please wait. One minute.'

I had to duck to get through the arch, and I blinked at the sudden darkness and warm glow. There was a lot of magick in here.

Shapes and walls came into focus. The room was smaller than I expected, about three metres square, with most of the floor taken up by a circular table and four chairs. The table was covered with a black cloth, and more black was draped to hide the contents of shelves and bookcases. The brightest thing in the room was a set of crystal glasses on top of a dark oak sideboard that looked vaguely familiar. Even the most rigid sceptic from the mundane (non-magickal) world would be creeped out in here.

I made my way round the table and leaned on the wall between the windows. Women's voices, muted by distance and magick, sounded from down the farmhouse passage. Talking of magick, I felt a weight on my hip that I normally ignore.

I've been wearing the Hammer, my magickally enhanced SIG pistol most of the time, yes, even on holiday. A key piece of magickal evidence had come into my possession, a piece that needed analysis. A lot of innocent people had died on the way, and until word had reached all corners of the magickal world, we'd still be at risk.

The Hammer sits in an occluded holster, for obvious reasons, and even powerful Mages don't normally see it. But there was so much Lux in here that it would be obvious to the householder, and Señora Mercedes is some sort of Sorcerer. Seeing is what they do best.

Taking it off was also a risk (I still knew nothing about these people), but I eased the holster off my belt and put it on top of a nearby table. Handy, but not too handy.

Sandals slapped on the terracotta tiles, and Mercedes herself came through the archway. I doubt she greets her regular clients in jeans, but that's how she was tonight. Jeans and a smart, red silk blouse (sleeves down and makeup on). She was exactly what you'd expect her daughter to look like in twenty-five years' time: fuller in the body and creased round the eyes, but what eyes. Unlike the daughter's, they were dark and deep set, and they swirled with mystery and glimpses of other worlds, fragments of sunlight and darkness. Scary, and it wasn't even a deliberate illusion, it was just a side-effect of her Sight.

Her eyes cleared, and she focused on the gun. I held my hands up and smiled.

'*Bienvenido, Señor*,' she said, rather stiffly.

I inclined my head and fished out a business card. I put it on the black tablecloth for her to take it or leave it.

'Speak Spanish?' she asked.

I shook my head. '*Solo en restaurante.*'

She smiled briefly and shouted down the passage. '*Mijita! Te necesito!*' She gestured to the table. 'Please sit.'

I pulled out a chair and sat down. Mercedes went to the sideboard and lit two candles. They burnt like torches, not candles. More magick. Behind the crystalware was a selection of dark bottles. She picked one up and said, 'Manzanilla?'

I know that word. Manzanilla is a beautifully crisp yet floral and salty sherry. Perfect for this time of day. '*Gracias.*'

She filled two glasses and put them on the table. Wonder of wonders, she also brought out an ashtray. She lifted a glass and said, '*En Paz*. In peace.'

It was the magickal offering that would bind us as host and guest, to come and go in peace. It could be broken, but even the most devious and powerful magickal creatures abide by the rules of hospitality; the consequences of breaking them can be frightening. Truly frightening. I lifted my glass. '*En Paz*. *Gracias.*' It was a very good sherry, and I made a mental note of the brand.

Her daughter appeared. As well as leaving the knife behind, she'd brushed out her hair and added eye shadow and lipstick. She'd also swapped the sleeveless top for a loose, long-sleeved blouse. All of these changes made her look smarter, yes, and also younger. I revised her age down to about nineteen. She took a stool near the archway and her mother asked her (I think) if she wanted a drink. She shook her head. Mercedes turned to me and smiled. 'Sofía,' she said. 'My little girl.'

Sofía rolled her eyes. 'Daughter, not little girl.'

Mercedes ignored her and lit a cigarette. I decided to wait. She spoke rapidly in Spanish and Sofía frowned. She said something back, and Mercedes pointed to the Hammer.

'Dio!' said Sofía. She drew a breath and said, 'Why is an English Magus standing outside our home, and why is he carrying a gun?'

I looked over my shoulder, towards the street. '*Mia novia. En Bellegente.* I was waiting for her.' I looked at my watch. 'One more hour.'

That threw them. I pointed to the business card. 'Mi Padre es Alfred Clarke. Mia Madre es Mary. Villa Verde.'

Sofía's eyes lit up in recognition and she smiled her open, trusting smile. Her mother buried her nose in her sherry and lowered her eyes.

Sofía pointed to the sideboard. 'Señor Clarke find this for us, also the table. Mother needed one of the right size. It fits.'

That sounded exactly like Dad, and if I'm not mistaken, that sideboard had once sat in the Villa Verde. Mother is not keen on dark oak.

Mercedes drew on her cigarette and crushed it out. She reached over the table and took my card. She held it at arms length and muttered something, then reached under the black crepe cloth and pulled out a small fabric purse. She carefully extracted an elaborately ornamented pair of gold pince-nez and squeezed them on to her nose.

'Special glasses for the clients,' said Sofía. 'They match my mother's *Gitano* costume.'

Gitano … Romany. Gypsy. That figured. Everything here was set up for your average New Age / Old World fortune telling gig (with cannabis on the side, if the ashtray was anything to go by). And yet there was so much magick, it had to be more than that.

Mercedes finally got my card in focus and jerked back. '*Madre de Dios!* You are *Inquisidor.*' She was appalled, and frightened, probably for good reason.

I serve the King's Watch of Great Britain, and we've been keeping the King's Peace in the world of magick since 1618. Before the Reformation, the same job was done by the Inquisition of St Michael. It still is in most Roman Catholic Countries (except France).

Mages can earn mundane money in all sorts of ways, but gaining benefit from magickal action is a big no-no, as is Divination – magickal fortune telling. It's okay to charge other Mages, but not the mundane public.

I held up my hands. 'I am on holiday with my girlfriend. I am visiting my parents. I have drunk your wine. I am here in peace.'

Mercedes understood me, but Sofía translated anyway. I'd come to the conclusion that the daughter had no magick, or so little that she'd never be donning Mercedes' gypsy sandals to follow in her mother's footsteps.

Mercedes forced a smile. She spoke, and Sofía said, 'Then please, a reading, so that we understand each other.'

Sofía looked a little worried as she relayed the words, and crossed her legs defensively. Mercedes spoke again. 'Mother never uses the magick unless the client is magick also.' Sofía and Mercedes both nodded to reinforce the message. I'll tell you for free that they are not very good liars.

I meant them no harm, so I smiled back. 'Of course. It would be an honour, but my time is limited.'

Mercedes nodded. 'Three cards only. The past, the present and the future.'

It was time for a cigarette.

Mercedes reached under the table and pulled out a domed chest that fizzed with magick. The wood was almost black with age, and the brass fittings had rustic engravings that generations of polishing had worn to bare outlines. There was no clasp or keyhole.

She placed the treasure chest on the table and worked the magickal lock. She lifted the lid towards me, so that I couldn't see inside when she rummaged for something. She pulled out a packet wrapped in royal blue silk. 'For the English. Mijita?'

Sofía got up to move the chest, closing but not locking the lid, and placing it on the sideboard. While she was there, she poured herself a drink.

Mercedes unwound the cloth, opened it out and spread it out on the table, leaving the tarot cards in the middle. She took the deck and fanned it out, face up towards me. 'You know these cards?'

'No. I have never had a tarot reading. Ever. I have only been a Mage – Magus – for six months.'

She shook her head. 'No matter.' She swept up the deck. 'First I clear the cards.'

While she shuffled, Sofía went to the archway and unhooked a curtain that cut off all the light from the passage. Sofía returned to the sideboard and, with a lot of effort, toned down the enchanted candles. So she did have *some* magick. Job done, Sofía returned to her stool and watched closely.

Mercedes placed the cards back on the blue cloth. 'Please. Pick up the cards, close your eyes and think of where you are now in your life, then shuffle them well.'

Now there's a challenge.

I took the deck and held it for a moment. The cards were warm in my hands with the pulse of Lux, and I closed my eyes. Where to start? Mina, of course. I pictured her happy smile, the one she'd thrown over her shoulder when she entered the salon, red scarf glinting against her white tunic.

I thought about the Villa Verde and my parents, then my mind drifted back, over the Pyrenees and across the English Channel to London, to Merlyn's Tower, home of the King's Watch. We've got a lot on our plates at the moment. I felt something like sparks coming off the cards, little jabs of heat that tingled rather than hurt, and I let them take me where they wanted. I saw the flash of a Dragon exploding, the darkness of Dwarven Halls, and then the lawns of my home, Elvenham House. Great birds, gods in the form of Ravens circled over head while I shook hands with my ancestor. He'd just given me a message, a message that there was old and dangerous magick in circulation. That magick was in a book called the Codex Defanatus, and its owner was the one who'd been trying to kill me. Probably.

I stopped shuffling and opened my eyes. Mercedes gestured for me to spread the cards in a big fan, face down, from right to left. When I'd done what she asked, Sofía spoke. 'Close your eyes again and imagine a mirror. Look in it and move your hand across the cards. When the image is in focus, take a card.'

I only look in the mirror when I'm shaving or on parade, so the image I got was my RAF uniform. To my alarm, the mirror shimmered and took on a life of its own: the *me* in the mirror pinned a new medal on its breast, the MC I'd picked up last week. It brushed its hand down the sleeve and looked at me. I jabbed my hand down on to a card and opened my eyes.

'Turn it over.'

A rather dashing chap in armour, plunging ahead on a horse greeted me. *Knight of Swords*, it said. In his right hand, he wielded a big sword.

Mercedes laughed and spoke in Spanish. Sofía laughed, too, before translating. 'What else would the heroic pilot see in the mirror? The card is what it seems: the Knight rushes in to save the day. But that does not mean it is false. You are a confident man, Señor. Not everyone is a hero in their own mirror.'

'My mother would have something to say about that.'

A flinch of pain flashed across Mercedes' closely guarded face. She understood well enough without waiting for a translation and motioned for her daughter to move on.

'Close your eyes again,' said Sofía, 'and draw three cards towards you, face down.' I did as I was bid, and Mercedes gathered the remainder together before putting them aside. 'The mirror in your mind clears the cards,' she said. 'Now we see more clearly into the past, the present and the future.'

I nodded to show that I'd understood, and she turned over the first card.

Two small children, boy and girl, staggered through the snow, the boy on crutches, just like I'd been after the helicopter crash. Behind them, a church window was lit by five golden pentacles.

'I need say nothing?' said Mercedes.

'No,' I replied. I pointed to the girl, her head covered by a shawl. *'Mia novia.* Mina.'

When we'd met, I'd been on crutches, and we'd been desperate, yes, but we'd made it. I pointed to the church window. 'Is this world of magick?'

'Si,' said Mercedes, then amplified her answer in Spanish.

'Your entrance to magick has clouded the cards to what came before in your life. You have found a new home.'

Mercedes turned the second card and the Devil stared back at me, sitting on a big pillar to which he'd chained a naked young couple, a pair of junior demons, judging by their tails. They also looked a bit like Adam and Eve to me.

Sofía was primed to say something, but Mercedes stilled her with a gesture. The older woman frowned at the card and shook her head. She cast a glance at the ceiling and muttered something to herself. She shook her head again and looked at me. 'This card, it is not Satan. This is all of the gods and Spirits and Dæmons of the world.'

She switched back to Spanish and Sofía listened carefully. 'The elevated ones have hidden the cards from us. They have drawn a veil that I – Mother – cannot see through. Perhaps we can see where your road goes next.'

Mercedes turned the last card.

'Nine of Wands,' she pronounced.

On the card, a rather bruised looking chap with a bandage on his head clutched a wooden staff. He was casting a wary eye over a thicket of eight more staves behind him.

'This is yet to come,' said Mercedes. 'Sofía?'

Without prompting, Sofía said, 'You will face many battles, many struggles. Perhaps there will be a … betrayal? You will need to stay strong. Very strong. No matter how bad things get, you must keep going.' She looked at her mother. 'Si?'

'Si. Gracias, Mijita.' Mercedes ran her fingers across the cards. 'You have not much magick, Señor Conrad.'

It was a statement, not a question. She's not the first to say it, and I'll no doubt hear it again before next week's out. She paused, then spoke slowly and deliberately in Spanish.

'You are in the shadow of the gods. That shadow hides much. You should come here again. Perhaps I can help more if we have more time. You should go now. She will be waiting.'

I looked at Sofía, who didn't look happy. Something in that translation had bothered her.

'Would it be right to offer your mother payment?' I asked.

'Not in coin.'

I stood up and retrieved the Hammer. 'Gracias, Señora, Señorita. I shall tell mi Padre you like his table.'

Mercedes looked down and put the four cards I'd chosen into a neat pile. 'I do not think he will remember us. *Via con Dios, Señor.*'

Sofía pulled back the curtain, and I blinked in the light. She escorted me to the street gate, and I shook hands before turning round to find Mina watching me from the payment counter in the salon.

'Who was that girl?' she asked when I'd finished admiring her blood red gel-coated nails. 'She had nice eyes, like you.'

'Mine are blue.'

'No. The shape, not the colour. Open. Friendly. I thought you were going to a bar to watch the cricket, not make friends with the local women.'

'So did I. I was not expecting a house of magick.'

She stopped and looked back down the street. 'Here? In that house?'

'I'll tell you over a drink. We should have time before the mayor turns up. He's always late.'

I finished my story as my parents were greeting the owner of the restaurant. I drained my beer and said, 'There's at least one mystery here.'

'Only one?'

'How did Mercedes know that I was a pilot? I gave her my Watch Captain card. It says nothing about the RAF on it.'

The dinner was a great success. Every so often, I caught Mina staring into space, and I knew her thoughts were in India.

When the cards were brought, I couldn't help a little shiver of flashback to Mercedes' reading room. Dad and I left the combatants to their bridge and adjourned to the terrace for cigars. I took out a fifty Euro note and put it on the table. 'I met some old clients of yours, Dad. They did me a favour, and I wondered if you could get them something. Anything but flowers. They've got enough of those.'

Dad took the note with wide-eyed curiosity. 'Who on earth is that, and how come they did you a favour?'

'Mercedes and Sofía. I don't know their last name.'

He blinked. 'Don't remember them.'

'They live…'

'Doesn't matter,' he interrupted. 'I'll look them up when I get home. Now, tell me about that phone call from the Indian bloke. Mina's not looked right since.'

The sun was beating down again, just as brightly as it had yesterday but dulled by the tinted glass into something bearable. Around the railway carriage, phones and laptops were being abandoned as travellers gave up the struggle and began to take as much of a siesta as the ultra high-speed train from Valencia to Madrid would let them.

Mina did not look sleepy. Tired, drawn and hurt, yes; sleepy, not at all.

She was hefting her iPhone in her hands, staring at the blank screen and touching the button occasionally to wake it up, but not unlocking it. It's a Plus-sized iPhone. She needs two hands to hold it comfortably, and her new red nails stood out against the black glass. I love looking at her hands. So nimble and delicate compared to mine.

Her eyes were still on the dead screen when she finally spoke. 'I still don't know, Conrad.'

'Know what, love? Whether to call him or whether to go to India?'

'Either. Both.' She looked up and blinked. The whites of her eyes shone out from the shadows of her face. She'd rubbed the makeup off her nose, and that was shiny, too. Her lip trembled. 'It doesn't matter how ill she is. She will try to marry me off to one of the Guptas. Probably the gay one with the ludicrous moustache.'

Mina's life is both simple and very complicated. Her parents were pioneers, the first from their families to leave India for England, and I know that Mina visited a lot when she was younger.

Then her eldest brother was shot dead, and her father died shortly after his child, while he was locked up in prison, on remand for drug smuggling. In the same attack, Mina's face had been beaten to a pulp with the butt of a handgun. I've seen a picture, and believe me, you don't want to.

While she was in hospital, her mother had fled to Mumbai and hidden her shame behind the shutters of her family's estate. Not her late husband's family. Her own. Arun, the other brother, had already emigrated to America by then.

With her face still in bits, it was no wonder that Mina had clung to the only man who had any time for her: an Englishman called Miles Finch. He loved her. He loved every broken bone of her. I know that because I knew him, and I know that Mina didn't love him quite as much, and that made her guilt even worse when he was murdered by the same scumbag who'd killed her brother and smashed her face in. Sometimes, when I can't sleep in the early hours, I hold her tight and I wonder if she's clinging to me like she clung to Miles, and that she'll see that for herself and leave me.

That's why her life is simple: no ties.

It's very complicated because she drank in the importance of family with her baby milk. It's in her bones, and they ache every time she looks round and sees only English faces.

I leaned forwards until her face had gone out of focus. 'You know what I'm going to say, don't you?'

'Yes. Say it anyway.'

'Go. For my sake.'

She leaned back. Her delicately shaped eyebrows plunged into a frown. 'For your sake? Why?'

'Because you'll regret not going so much that it will me hurt me.'

She put her phone down and wrapped her hands round mine. Even in the heat of Spain, they always felt cold to me. She fiddled with my Troth ring, the one that Odin had given me. I felt it pulse lightly with magick.

'I will talk to Arun,' she said. She rose from the seat and hitched up her jeans. Collecting her phone, she gave me a smile. 'This is a conversation for the corridor, not the carriage. You'll still be here when I get back, won't you?'

'Always.'

I watched her sway up the carriage and push the button for the doors.

Madrid was sticky-hot and dirty after the Villa Verde and the air-conditioning of the train. We could have gone straight home from Valencia, but we'd travelled via Madrid for a reason.

We'd left the UK with an important parcel to be delivered to the Israeli Embassy, containing an enchanted diamond. That diamond carried the magickal fingerprint of its creator, and it was our only definite clue in the hunt for the Codex Defanatus, that compendium of Works which was wreaking havoc across the magickal world.

We'd dropped off the parcel on our way to the Villa Verde, and now, on our way home, we had the results. To our shock, they'd been returned by Hannah's brother, Daniel Beckman.

My boss, the Peculier Constable of the King's Watch, is Hannah Rothman. She's 100% North London Jewish, though Reform, not Orthodox. Her brother had been, shared tapas with us, and gone, leaving Mina and I somewhat bemused.

'How is it,' she said, 'that Hannah keeps kosher and won't break Shabbos but won't set foot in Israel, yet her brother asks for extra pork sausage and is a committed Zionist?'

'You tell me, love. Families are strange things. At least we have the report.'

'Couldn't he email it to the Watch?'

'No. The Parchment inside this envelope is enchanted. They could have sent it by courier, though. I think Daniel just wanted to see us – me – in the flesh.' I pushed a cigarette packet towards Mina. Daniel had casually left it on the table. 'And to return this. Have a look.'

Mina opened the packet and slipped out the now mundane diamond. Her eyes bulged. 'This is worth a fortune.'

'I thought it might look good in a ring. On your finger. One day.'

She pushed the packet back to me. 'One day. You've been very patient, Conrad. You haven't asked me what Arun had to say.'

I stowed the diamond safely away and lit a cigarette. When I didn't answer straight away, Mina waved at the waiter and pointed to our drinks. He nodded and went back inside the hotel.

'Your mother is a very odd person,' she said. 'I suppose you know that.'

'Mmm,' was the only safe reply.

'I like her. I do not like my own mother very much. I don't think she ever liked me.'

That was harsh, but never having met her mother, I couldn't argue. She waited until fresh drinks had arrived before she continued. 'Arun says that she is not at death's door, but there is no way back. Breast cancer. She didn't go for a check-up until it was too late. It had spread all over.'

She left a silence for me to fill in my head: Mrs Desai had been too proud, too embarrassed, too stubborn and too fearful to go for a scan.

'I will go,' said Mina. 'Soon. There are things to do first, though. While you were in the shower, I had a message from Stacey. You remember her?'

'I do. We both owe her a debt. Is she okay?'

Stacey had been a friend to Mina in prison. Without Stacey's help, Mina wouldn't be sitting with me in Madrid.

'Stacey's good. She's coming out on Tuesday, and I want to give her some cash, obviously, but I want to be there, too. If her … ex-partner shows up, I want to help her get away from him. She won't stand a chance, otherwise, and he'll have his hands on her money before they get to Preston.'

'Of course. I've got to go up north as well, to sort out that business with the inquest. I can do that on Tuesday.'

'Good,' said Mina. She raised her glass. 'To freedom.'

'To freedom.'

2 — All Along the Watch Tower

'Wow,' said Mina. 'I had no idea that it was so big.'

'And I had no idea that you've never been before. How can you have lived in London all your life and never have gone to the Tower?'

She put her arm through mine. 'Because my primary school did not think that symbols of hegemonic oppression were suitable places for children to visit.'

'And they told you that, did they?'

'No, but they did tell it to Papaji when he asked why we were going to the climate change event for the third year running.' She paused. 'And we never went as a family, because most summers we were in Bombay or with Papaji's family.'

I got a bit confused. 'Were they not from Bombay?'

She shook her head. 'From Gujarat. Up country, as they used to say. My father grew up in a falling-down mansion. His family were very high caste, and they used a great chunk of mother's dowry on refurbishing it. I think he came to England while there was still some left for him. Come on, give me the tour.'

We were on our way to Merlyn's Tower, and we could have gone straight there via the staff entrance, but when I found out that she'd never been to the Tower of London at all, it seemed right for her to get the overall feel of the place first. I even bought her a ticket.

We couldn't do the whole thing, obviously, but we did make a circuit and go to the Waterloo Barracks to see the Crown Jewels. As Mina said herself, 'You can't take an Indian girl to the world epicentre of bling and not show her the money.'

Quite.

I also wanted to show her the ravens, and we were watching one of them hop about when two Yeoman Warders came up. One of them, the senior one, nodded to me out of respect for my RAF uniform, and his apprentice was doing the same until he did a double-take and snapped a smart salute.

'Mr Clarke, sir,' he said.

I disengaged my arm from Mina and returned the salute. His was a very familiar face, one I'd seen many times in a set of RAF overalls, usually emerging from a Chinook helicopter and pronouncing it fit to fly.

'Warrant Officer Keith Bradburn,' I replied. 'Bit of a change for you.'

'Yes sir. I've only been here a week, sir.' He glanced at the senior Warder. 'They're keeping me on a tight leash.'

I smiled. 'Good to hear it.'

He took another look at my uniform. 'I'd heard you were in a bad way, sir. I thought you'd left the service.'

'They couldn't do without me. Or I missed them. One or the other.'

The senior Warder spoke up. 'Mr Clarke works in that tower I was telling you about. He often comes this way.'

'I had no idea you'd noticed,' I said.

'We notice all the staff at your tower, sir, and you're the only one who always says hello and always means it. We've been waiting for you to ask to feed the ravens. They come closer to you than any other visitor. Closer than most of the Warders, too.'

I was impressed. Very impressed. To cover my surprise, I quickly introduced Mina, and after handshakes, I said that we had to be going.

I led Mina towards the Water Gate. 'How does that work?' she asked. 'Those guys live here, don't they? So how do they cope with a magickal tower?'

'They do live here. All thirty-seven of them and their families. They're all very loyal former Warrant Officers, remember, and they just don't talk about Merlyn's Tower directly, or look at it.' She shook her head and shrugged.

I took my cap off and waved some air over my head. The RAF uniform was designed to keep you warm on a winter's day at an exposed East Anglian airfield, not keep you cool on a hot spring day in London. It's a bit of a sweat box, but today was a special day for the King's Watch, so it was parade orders.

Mina looked at me. 'Are you 100% certain I won't have to dress up like you if I get the job?'

This was the third time (at least) that she'd asked me the same question. 'Yes. I'm sure. You could wear a uniform at home if you feel left out.'

'The only woman who doesn't look awful in that black get-up is Annelise, and she would look good in a bin liner. I think that Hannah should change the rules for her own sake, if no one else's. She doesn't have the hips to wear a skirt that tight, and Vicky looks like a checkout supervisor who's won employee of the month.'

'Steady on, love. Vicky died to get that Military Cross.'

She grinned. 'It was her who said it, not me, but don't repeat it. Secrets of the ladies' room and all that.'

I took her hand again when we were through the Water Gate. That way, she'd see Merlyn's Tower as it really is and not as it appears to the rest of the world. I stopped and said, 'There you go.'

She wrinkled her nose. 'Is that it?'

'What were you expecting.'

'It's all squat and boring. I was expecting something bigger. With turrets and mini-towers. Heads on spikes. Bats. That sort of thing.'

You can't please some people. 'The magick is on the inside.'

25

The big wooden door is only locked a few times a year, mainly because there are only two keys and there's enough magickal protection on the Tower to keep out an entire horde of Orcs, if some mad Mage decided to create one. I pushed the door back and Mina stepped nervously over the threshold.

By the time I'd closed the door behind us, she was reading a note taped to the Clerk's office. 'They're in the Watch Room,' she announced. 'I'm still not feeling the magick. Why are there no paintings, no impressive coats of arms?'

She had a point. The stairwells of Merlyn's Tower are completely unadorned and rather grim. Maybe that's the point. We climbed the curved stairs to the first floor, and I let us in to the Watch Room.

It was packed and close to chaos in there, because today's special event was the Induction of our newest recruit. Detective Sergeant Helen Davies was laying aside her police warrant card to take the Queen's commission and become Watch Captain for Wales. A lot of my fellow officers had come to welcome her and take a nosey at only the second woman to become a Watch Captain.

The Watch Clerk, Maxine Lambert, was directing operations as everyone moved tables, stacked chairs and unpacked the refreshments. The only one taking it easy was Maxine's deputy, Cleo. She was drinking tea and resting one hand on her now very prominent bump, and that bump was one of the reasons that Mina had come with me.

Maxine needs a deputy, and the Watch was recruiting for its first ever maternity cover. Mina was here to have a good look round, talk to Cleo and let Maxine run the ruler over her properly. They've met before, but only briefly.

Maxine welcomed us and introduced Mina to Cleo before checking her watch. 'We've got ten minutes before you're due upstairs. Let's get out, quick.' Maxine is the only other smoker in the Watch, and led the way through a little door to the back staircase and then up to the roof.

We lit up and spent a moment taking in the view of the Thames. 'Good news and bad news,' she said. 'The good news is that the panel for Cleo's job will be the Vicar of London Stone, the Boss and me. The official announcement was yesterday, and I've got a copy of the application form for Mina.'

'Thanks. What's the bad news?'

'The reason she's not on the panel is that a friend of hers from church is going to apply for it. Just to spite me and put a spy in the camp.'

If that sentence left you at a loss, I'll explain. When Maxine says *she*, it's not the Boss she's talking about, it's the Boss's PA, Tennille Haynes. Maxine and Tennille do not get on, and I've no idea why. I'm also too scared to ask, as is Hannah. I think.

'Mina wouldn't have it any other way,' I said, lying through my teeth. Mina will be devastated. There has been a thaw between Hannah and Mina. No doubt. But when Hannah had said that Mina's application would come second to anyone without a criminal record, she wasn't joking. That was a bridge I'd have to cross later.

We headed back to the Watch room, and I said goodbye to Mina. The other reason she'd come today was to collect a secure laptop from Li Cheng, the Royal Occulter, and that's what she was doing. We agreed to meet at a coffee shop after the ceremony, because only Watch members would be attending. Even Helen's husband would have to wait for her outside with the ravens and tourists.

I made my way up the formal staircase to the top floor, home of the Peculier Constable and of Maxine's nemesis, Tennille, who fixed me with a hard stare the moment I emerged into her domain.

'Watch Captain Clarke,' was what she said. Her tone supplied the subtext: *Watch Captain Clarke, in whose footsteps the Devil walks.* And when Tennille talks about the Devil, she really does mean Satan.

I don't know why Tennille hates Maxine, but at least I know why she dislikes me: her daughter, Desirée, was seriously injured in my command.

'How is Desi?' I asked.

'You'll see for yourself in a moment. And you'll see why I ain't happy. Go through. She's waiting.'

When Tennille says *she*, it's always the Constable she means.

I went through the impressive oak doors into Hannah's impressive office. As per standing orders, I saluted, and while Hannah made a half-hearted return, I checked out who else was there.

Vicky, of course, gave me a big grin, as did the Senior Watch Captain, Rick James. My eyes popped out when I saw Desirée and what she was wearing. Since last week, she'd got a uniform of her own, and that explained the latest reason her mother was upset with me. Tennille would prefer her daughter to be studying for her doctorate with the Invisible College in Salomon's House, not acting as a Reserve Watch Officer. Rather than blame Desi herself or Hannah, she takes it out on me.

I had expected a full contingent from Salomon's House, but there was only one – Francesca Somerton, Keeper of the Library. The others were all on holiday, apparently. Typical academics.

We'd all seen each other a week ago, but it seemed a lot longer. I was about to ask how everyone was until Hannah said, 'Grab yourself a coffee and sit down, Conrad. Have you got something for us?'

The coffee in Merlyn's Tower is generally very good and excellent in Hannah's office. I took a cup and slipped a folded envelope from my inside pocket.

'Give it to Vicky,' said Hannah. 'She's the expert.'

Vicky took the compliment in her stride. Her confidence is definitely growing. She slipped the Parchment out of the envelope and ran her finger over it. The paper looked blank to me. Completely blank.

Her fingers traced complex invisible patterns in more and more detail. I sipped my coffee and leaned right to whisper to Desirée, 'You look a lot better.'

'Getting there. I still need a stick to walk, but I'm getting there, thanks.'

Rick leaned over, too, and said, 'Good work in Spain, Bro. I got to spend half term with the kids. They're doing the big Tower right now with their Gran.'

Vicky let out a groan of frustration, then realised that we could hear her and put her hand over her mouth. 'Sorry, ma'am.'

'What?' said Hannah with a real edge. 'Is there a fault with the analysis?'

'Oh no. It's top notch, this. It's the diamond. Creating that fake Rockseed must have been so hard that whichever Fae created it, they used Quicksilver magick exclusively. There's no trace of their human side in this record.'

I'd better explain. The Fae are a different species. They are half-human, yes, but the human part is mostly biology. Most of their magick is in their other half, and that half uses mercury, known to alchemists as quicksilver, and Quicksilver magick is as alien to humans as the element mercury is toxic. If that was a record of human magick on the Parchment, Vicky could tell who it was just by looking at them. The Fae keep their Quicksilver selves completely hidden.

'Is there a way round this?' I asked.

Hannah gave a humourless grin. 'The Watch used to torture people. In the basement of the Develin Tower. If you put a Fae to the Question, you can see their Quicksilver Imprint. The equipment is still there, but sadly we had to give up the practice.'

'Not without a fight,' said the Keeper. Hannah had made a joke of it, but Francesca wasn't laughing. 'There is another way, isn't there, Vicky?'

'Aye,' said Vic, somewhat dubiously. 'If I can compare this Parchment to any other Artefact created exclusively with Quicksilver magick, I can rule them in or out. It's dangerous, though.'

'And it's not as if we have an elimination database,' said Hannah, ever the ex-copper.

'Yes we do,' said Francesca. 'We have that list of all the Fae nobles from 1689 who are still alive, so we track down Artefacts made by them, starting in the Library, and starting now. Here.'

She passed Vicky a cigar sized silver cylinder – an Egyptian Tube, concealing something powerfully magick.

Vicky rubbed a blank spot in the engraved surface with her finger. 'The Queen of the Heath?' she exclaimed. 'You're joking, aren't you?'

Even Hannah had flinched, and Desi looked most disturbed.

'Who…?' I said.

'The Queen of the Heath is one of the three Fae Queens in London,' said Vicky. 'That's Hampstead Heath, by the way.'

'And my prime suspect,' said Francesca. 'Go on, Victoria, open it.'

Hannah nodded her approval, and Vicky unscrewed the cylinder. She took out a piece of Parchment and carefully unrolled it.

'That's beautiful,' I said. The Parchment was about A5 size and had a poem on it. I couldn't read the flowing, extravagantly curled writing, but I marvelled at the miniature illuminations – and the way they moved with the text. In one verse, a hedgehog stumbled over the words, each one a little hill; in another, a butterfly flitted across the page, pausing to sip at the taller letters, which became flowers when it approached.

Vicky dropped the Parchment and rubbed her hands on her uniform skirt. 'Beautiful, aye, and deadly.' She turned to me. 'It's a Binding Charm. The ultimate love letter, if you're into emotional slavery.' She looked back at Francesca. 'Where did this come from?'

'It was sent to a past Warden of Salomon's House. He proved immune and lodged it in the Library.'

'Well?' said Hannah impatiently. 'Is it her?'

Vicky looked alarmed. 'I can't tell, ma'am. I'd rather not do the analysis here, and not without preparation.'

Hannah sighed. 'Fair enough. As soon as you can, Vicky. This is as far as we're going to get for now. If it's not the Queen of the Heath, can you keep looking for Artefacts, Keeper? Desirée?'

'We will,' said Francesca.

Hannah checked her watch. 'Thanks everyone. We'd all hoped for a breakthrough with that analysis, I know, but we'll get there. Soon. Rick, Desi, can you give us a minute?'

Rick moved quickly to get Desirée's stick and helped her up, holding open the door and waiting. He's a smooth operator, is our Rick, but I can't see a committed Christian like Desi falling for him.

Francesca got her things together and put them on the table. 'I'll be seeing you on Monday, Conrad. Vicky will explain. Have a nice weekend.'

'And you, Keeper.'

What was all that about? When she'd gone, Hannah went to get more coffee. Vicky half turned to me with a smile, and I was expecting an explanation about Monday. Instead, she planted a vicious kick on my bad leg.

'Are you okay, Conrad?' said Hannah.

I was not OK. I was bent double and gripping my leg, and coughing like I was dying to stop me screaming with pain. Parade shoes pack one hell of a punch.

When I'd stopped coughing, Vicky (who didn't look at all guilty) turned back to face the Boss. 'I was just saying to Conrad how thrilled I was that he nominated me to be a Watch Captain.'

'It's what you wanted, Vic,' I said, with rather more of a squeak in my voice than is good for my image.

'Aye, it was, until I heard about the psychological evaluation and conditions attached. Ma'am, I don't recall Conrad having to go through those. Or Helen Davies, come to that.'

Hannah waved a hand. 'Health and safety. Those two had come from the services. You haven't. Just routine.'

Vicky turned back to me. 'I have to take Jiu-Jitsu classes, and whose idea could that be, I wonder?'

It was mine, of course. 'You're looking well on it, Vic.'

'I haven't flaming started yet, so watch out when I do.' She softened a bit. 'I'm not so bad. I've been looking after Desi, and she made me go to the gym with her. Three times. How about you?'

'Later, children,' said Hannah. 'Helen will be here in a minute.' She searched for a piece of paper. 'This is where we are. Conrad will give a seminar on Dragons at Newton's House on Monday afternoon. It's open to all teaching staff from the Invisible College, all the Fellows, and especially the Candidates for Fellowship. You and I would call them final year students, Conrad.'

That was rather alarming. 'That's a lot of Mages. I'm not sure I can hold up the image of the Watch with an audience like that.'

'You can and you will. You don't need to make a speech, just a few words then take questions. After that, I'll be making a speech to the Candidates. If you two are going to work separately, we need to recruit at least two more Watch Officers, so don't scare them off.'

'No, ma'am. Not that I'm scary.'

She stared at me. 'You're not, but I don't want them thinking that the job is more dangerous than it actually is. Got that?'

'Yes, ma'am.'

'Good. After that, you're going on a road trip. I've read both your emails, and it's in everyone's interests for you two, with Francesca and Mina, to go to Cairndale.'

That was a turn up. Before I could say anything, Tennille stuck her head in to announce Helen Davies.

'Go and talk to her, Vicky. I need two minutes with Conrad.'

Vicky jumped up and collected her cap. Helen's calm head in a crisis had saved Vicky's life, and Vic was keen to say thank you again.

Hannah coughed. 'Good to have you back, Conrad. How was Spain?'

'Hot. Relaxing. Daniel sends his love.'

'No he doesn't, but thanks for pretending.' That was a bit harsh. He hadn't said the words, but Daniel Beckman cared deeply about his little sister. He wouldn't have risked his life going to Madrid for her if he didn't, but Hannah wasn't interested in hearing that. She ploughed on. 'Do you remember tricking me into agreeing for you to get your RAF wings back at my expense?'

My bad leg twitched. It was shattered in Afghanistan, and it got me invalided out of the RAF. As part of joining the Watch, I'd resumed my commission, kept my rank and my service record, but not my wings. I was no longer qualified to fly, and that hurt.

'It wasn't a trick, Hannah, I just...'

'...Never mind that. How important is it to you?'

I blew out my cheeks. 'Back then, very important. Not so much any more.' And it wasn't. I wasn't going to say out loud that I found magick to be even more addictively satisfying than flying choppers, though. I think Hannah got the message anyway.

She nodded. 'I'm glad to hear you say that, because the news is mixed. Long story, but the RAF won't put you through the full training programme unless you're available for active duty, and I can't have that.'

I can't say that I was surprised. Any form of pilot training is long and expensive, and I'd been out for over two years, so the backlog of flying hours and theory would be huge. Hannah doesn't need a pilot, she needs a Watch Captain. Ah well, it was only vanity.

'Cheer up,' she said. 'There's good news.'

'Oh?'

'I've called in a few favours, made a few promises and got a few rules bent. If you report to RAF Shawbury on Thursday, they'll put you through a two week conversion course and rubber stamp your ...' She checked her notes. The rules for the licensing of pilots are a complete soup of letters, and they keep changing. 'Aah. Here it is. They'll rubber stamp your CPL(H). How's that?'

'Probably illegal, Hannah, but very generous.'

She passed me a folder. 'I can't say you haven't earned it. Go and get Helen, would you, but give me a minute before you present her.'

I collected my bits and went for the door. 'Hannah, can I take a guest to Newton's House?'

'Mina? Of course you can. Banqueting Chamber, 1400.'

Vicky was fighting tears outside Hannah's office. Seeing Helen Davies had brought back the day she'd died – her heart had stopped for eight minutes. She turned away when I appeared.

Helen looked nervous, and she had every right to be. In a short while, she'd be descending the back stairs to Nimue's Well, signing her name in blood and meeting the legendary (and slightly deranged) water nymph Nimue, the oldest magickal creature of Albion.

'Vicky says I have to salute you,' said Helen, and she followed through. When I'd returned the salute, she came forward to give me a hug. 'I keep thinking I've made a huge mistake. How can someone like me fight Dragons?'

Helen has even less magick than I do. 'Don't fight them,' I said. 'Run as fast as you can and call me. Got that?'

'Yes sir.'

'Good. How's the family?'

We chatted for a minute until Hannah was ready. I presented her formally to the Boss and whispered my parting shot. 'If she offers you a glass of Dawn's Blessing, take it.'

When the doors closed behind them, Vicky and I walked slowly down to the Watch Room. 'What's with the road trip?' I asked.

'Doctor Somerton needs to see Theresa, and she needs an escort to Lunar Hall. That would be me, and I'll do me damnedest to find out about Madeleine while I'm there.'

'Excellent.'

'Did you bring me owt from your hols, Uncle Conrad?' said Vicky as we arrived at the Watch Room.

'Not after you kicked me like that. I'm giving it to Annelise.'

Vicky opened the door and we got ready for lunch, during which I have a special job: keeping the Constable away from the strawberry tartlets. They're both kosher and delicious, and have more calories than rocket fuel. So far, I haven't let her down.

3 — *Homecomings*

'Are you sure that you can get me to Heathrow by eleven o'clock?' said Mina.

Her finger was hovering over the Enter key on her new, enhanced, magickally and digitally secure laptop. It swayed slightly because we were on the train to Cheltenham. Whether or not I said yes, Mina was going to India on Wednesday. She was booking a return ticket with the return date left open.

I nodded, and she pressed the key. 'Done.' She closed the lid and shuffled in her seat. 'Now let's focus on more important matters. How are we getting home?'

I nearly said *taxi* before it hit me. 'Is that how you see Elvenham? Home?'

She tilted her head to one side. 'I quite liked Cell Nine in Charlotte House, but they kicked me out, so until I get a better offer, yes, Elvenham is my home.'

What was I expecting? A flowery declaration that she'd found true love and happiness? Part of me was, I suppose. I'll learn.

'There might be a surprise waiting for you,' I said.

'Is it an "Ooh, how nice" surprise, or a "You bastard" surprise?'

'Both, probably. It'll make packing for Bombay easier and harder.'

'Then I shall wait patiently to find out. Also, I will not talk to you.'

She opened her computer again and kept her promise for at least five minutes. 'Which ones are the Dwarves?' she asked. 'You've met two of them, haven't you.'

'Yes. Why?'

'It's hard to tell the Dwarves from the Gnomes in this database.'

Now that's a sentence I never expected to hear.

Mina was (briefly) a qualified accountant. As one of her convictions is for money-laundering, they won't be having her back any time soon. Whether or not she gets Cleo's maternity cover, she's been hired to look into an issue in the magickal economy. We're calling it Project Midas.

The magickal economy is suffering from something close to hyperinflation. I know, I know – not riveting, is it? I'll skip the details and focus on the main players, all of whom have given us data and trusted us – the King's Watch – to find out what's going on. That trust was hard won, partly by me.

Dwarves are found all over the world. Some are hairy and some have three legs, but they all live underground and make the best magickal Artefacts, usually from gold. Dwarves have an alien biology which partly involves silicon and they turn to stone if exposed to daylight. Oh yes, they're also very, very greedy.

'Hledjolf is the Dwarf in London,' I said. Mina nodded. 'He's the one who looks like R2D2. He gives me the creeps.'

'But he answers his emails. In fact he's the only Dwarf with email, but never mind. Who was the other one?'

'Niði. He lives near Dudley Zoo in the West Midlands. There's no data for him.'

'That's right. He was locked in to his Hall for thirty years.' She smiled. 'Until my hero freed him. Yes.'

'With help, but yes. The other two are Haugstari and Ginnar. Haugstari is the Old Man of Coniston.'

'The Lake District.'

'And Ginnar lives in Cornwall. For those two, the data was passed on by Gnomes.'

'Of course. Now I understand.'

Dwarves usually look male. They're not. In fact, as a species, they're asexual, but looking male made it easier to do business in the past. Gnomes don't just look male, they are *very* male, even though they're aren't fully human.

Gnomes are native to northern Europe, but like north European humans, they're now found all over the world. They are short, hairy and are very good miners, engineers and merchants. They do make Artefacts, but they're very much second to Dwarves in all things except steel. I have a Gnomish sword, and a beautiful thing it is. I've had dealings with three Gnome clans so far, and they can be tricky if you're not on your guard.

Mina looked up again. 'Why have only two groups of humans responded? And get me some tea before you answer.'

I was glad of the walk, to be honest. My bad leg does not like planes or trains.

'No cake?' said Mina when I got back.

'Myfanwy is baking. Save yourself for the good stuff.'

'If I must. Now, answer the question.'

'The Invisible College has to trust the Watch. We're both part of the magickal state. The reason we only got one other group's data is that no one else trusts us. We only got the Daughters of the Goddess because Rick James's ex-wife is one of their Guardians, and because they've suffered the most. They're on the verge of bankruptcy because they hold so many deposits from affiliated covens.'

'Good. Thank you.'

And that was that. She stared out of the window a lot, sent some texts and did a lot of typing, but not once did she speak to me until the taxi dropped us in the drive at Elvenham House in the village of Clerkswell, Gloucestershire.

There is a stone dragon over the door of my family home, and you have to say hello when you come back from outside the village. Mina made namaste while I was helping the taxi driver with the cases.

When I bowed to the dragon, Mina put her arm round my waist and said, 'You have made me happier than I have been since Papaji died. Of course this is my home.'

We were enjoying a long kiss when I heard a crunch of gravel. I looked up and caught a flash of pain in Myfanwy's eyes as she saw us.

Elvenham is her home, too, but only because she's under a Seclusion order for her part in the Dragon conspiracy and can't leave the parish for three years, and it looked like there was more going wrong than that. By the time Mina noticed her, the Welsh smile was back in place.

The women embraced, and Mina said, 'How much weight have you lost? Is it magick?'

'I dunno. Have you two had a good break?'

Mina started leading Myfanwy towards the kitchen. 'You know we have, because I sent you pictures. Now, tell me what's been going on. Conrad promised cake...'

I moved the cases on to the front steps. They're a bugger to wheel over the gravel, and the front door is closer to the main staircase. I'd have taken them straight in, but the doors only open from the inside. The guy who built Elvenham (James Clarke) had four live-in servants to answer the door for him. I have Myfanwy.

I was in the hall and unbolting the doors when Mina appeared from the kitchen. 'There you are. Myvvy has fallen out with Ben. You must do something.'

Mina has given up trying to pronounce *Myfanwy* and calls her Myvvy. Ben Thewlis is an old friend and captain of the cricket team.

'What happened? And why me?'

'Ben won't believe her story about why she can't leave the village. Typical man. He thinks it's all about him.'

'Why? What did she say?'

Myfanwy's cover story for being in the village and for being my housekeeper is a biodiversity study.

'She said that not leaving the village is a condition of her research grant.'

'No wonder he didn't believe her. That's lame.'

Mina glanced at me. 'She's even talking of giving up the cricket. She's only going tonight because I said that I needed moral support.'

Ben had suggested a women's cricket team, and Myfanwy has been the prime mover in getting it off the ground. In the absence of a female coach, Ben and I have been doing our best to get them good enough to arrange matches. They may not have a coach, but they do have a chair – Juliet Bloxham from the Big House, and it was Juliet who discovered Mina's criminal record before broadcasting it round the village. The Bloxhams and the Clarkes do not get on.

'I'll see what I can do,' I said. I pulled open the doors and light flooded in.

'What are these?' said Mina, pointing to half a dozen packing cases in the corner.

'The surprise I promised. Your stuff from London. Plus an extra case from the police. I got it all delivered here.'

When Mina was arrested, she spent a long time on bail before going to prison, time she used to get major surgery on her jaw. She also used the time to empty the house she'd shared with Miles. What little that was left had gone into storage.

She was rooted to the spot. 'Oh. I don't know what to say.' She stared at the boxes, not going close enough to read the labels. 'Later. Tea, cake and cricket practice first. You know, this is the first day I've been here that it's been warm enough to go outside. First of many, I hope.'

She walked off, giving the boxes a wide berth.

The home of cricket in our village is named after another of my ancestors (the whole village is called Clerkswell because of the Clerk's Well), and rejoices in the title of Mrs Clarke's Folly. It's a short walk from Elvenham, even with kit bags.

We walked through the gates and saw a whole host of women. Five or six times more than at any previous practice. Ben was being assailed, and jogged over as soon as he saw me. Myvvy and Mina went to get ready.

'Where have this lot come from?' I said.

'All over, and I'm very glad you're back. Most of the village mums are away on half term, and this lot is a mixture of students come home from university and cast-offs from other villages who'd heard that we were recruiting. I've already heard mutterings.'

This was not the time to sort out Myfanwy's love-life.

'Any wicket keepers?' I said.

'Yes. Two. Your Mina's going to have to prove herself.'

'And the Bloxhams?'

'At their apartment in Tenerife, thank God, so you're playing for the boys tomorrow. Let's get this show on the road.'

It was chaos at first. One group of women left as soon as they realised that we hadn't registered the team with County yet. Another group said I wasn't a qualified coach. I'm not, and I told them they were welcome to take over if they could do any better. One mother asked if Ben and I had been vetted and what our child protection policies were. 'No children allowed,' said Ben. 'That's our child protection policy.'

Eventually, we got a semblance of order after two of the men's team had been dragged from the pub to take names and keep notes. Sadly, one of the men was Stephen Bloxham's lawyer, so a report of tonight's shambles would be heading to Tenerife later. Oh well.

A couple of hours later, Ben emerged from the Inkwell pub carrying two pints of bitter and gripping a folder under his arm.

'Cheers, Conrad, I reckon we've earned this.'

We were sitting outside so that I could smoke and because we had things to talk about, starting with a progress report on the Clerkswell Ladies.

At the end of our pint, we'd decided that the team desperately needed to formalise things and become official. For one thing, they wouldn't get insurance if their only legal status was as a Facebook Group.

'Trouble is,' said Ben, 'Stephen Bloxham's offered to underwrite them for a year. He'll pay the start-up costs and buy the uniforms. It's a lot of money up front, and hard to say no to.'

'And no doubt they'll have Bloxham Developments on their shirts and Jules will be confirmed as chair.'

'No doubt. And if Mina's not back from India before they arrange their first match, that lass from Bishop's Cleeve will be wicket keeper.'

'She'll cope. At least I get to play tomorrow.'

Ben drained his glass. 'Our best bowler is on holiday, so you'd better not be rusty from lounging around in Spain. We're second bottom of the league, you know.'

'I know. I also know that it's my round.'

'Cheers.'

Ben was staring over the fields when I got back. Staring at the chimneys of Elvenham House. He picked up his pint and carried on staring. 'Myfanwy asked me to help her with online banking, you know. And she's paying you. She's paying you £500 a month to be your housekeeper. How does that work? And then there's this rubbish about not leaving the parish.'

He carried on staring. He was giving me the chance to change the subject if I wanted to.

There's a problem here. Myfanwy and I have both given an undertaking to the magickal Cloister Court not to entangle anyone on her behalf. *Entanglement* means deliberately bringing a mundane citizen into the world of magick for some reason. Mina is about as entangled as you can get.

That undertaking made my job very difficult, and I was chewing it over when Ben turned around. 'And there's something else,' he said. 'She let slip that you and Vicky were being presented with the Military Cross last week. Congratulations to both of you and all that, but it has to be connected. So does the fact that Myfanwy doesn't exist online. There is no Myfanwy Lewis on the internet except a one month old Facebook page.'

'So what's your worst case scenario, Ben? Seriously, what's your worst nightmare?'

'Terrorism. She's turned Queen's Evidence and is here to be de-radicalised under your watchful eye.' He managed a smile. 'When you're here. Presumably you've subcontracted some of it to me while you're away saving the world.'

That was far too close to the truth for comfort. Ben isn't the most demonstrative of men, but that doesn't mean he's blind.

I lit a cigarette and said, 'What do you think of her? As a person?'

'Bright. Daft as a brush. Gorgeous. Genuinely loves nature. Very generous.'

'Do you think she could hurt someone?'

'No way.'

'And you're right. She is a good person, Ben, and I reckon you're good for each other. Let her just be herself and accept that you'll not be going on holiday for a while. Oh, and Myfanwy Lewis is her real name. I can tell you that much.'

'What about the payments to you?'

'Office politics and income tax. It's a way for the Home Office to pay for her upkeep and keep it out of my boss's budget. That's all.'

He nodded and finished his pint. 'Why did she and Mina dash off after practice?'

'Long story. Let's go. Take her home to your place tonight and do us all a favour.'

'Thanks, Conrad.'

It's only a five minute walk from the Inkwell to Elvenham, and we spent it talking about tomorrow's game. It's an away match, so Myfanwy won't be going, and neither will Mina. They're going to work together on Mina's application for the Merlyn's Tower job.

We found them in the hall, surrounded by boxes. Some were labelled "Bin" and others "Charity Shop". In the middle, the girls were sitting next to one marked "Metropolitan Police". There was also an empty bottle of wine. That was quick work.

Mina was cradling the most gorgeous bolt of emerald green silk and weeping. I could see a couple of splashes on the fabric already.

'Come on, Myfanwy, let's leave them to it,' said Ben.

He walked over to Myfanwy and held out his hand. She let him pull her up, then patted Mina's shoulder and said, 'See you tomorrow, eh, Dwt?'

Mina nodded, and they left us in peace. I sat next to her and put my arm round her shoulders. I can fit all of her in one arm. 'What's up, love?'

She wiped her eyes with her sleeve and sniffed. 'This. When the poilce rounded up the Moorgate gang, they emptied all of the lockers at the garage. This is the contents of Miles's locker.'

'Oh. Your lawyer said that it was personal effects, so I had him send it to the storage company. I thought they were your effects, not Miles's.'

She put the green silk carefully down. As it moved under the light, it rippled and shimmered like a living thing. When she took her hands from underneath the cloth, it settled as if it were making itself comfortable. She showed me a rumpled piece of paper. It was a shipping note from Maharani Silks of Surat in Gujarat. 'Look at the date and the product description.'

It was dated two weeks before Miles was killed, and the colour was *Bridal Green*.

'The symbol of new life,' she said. 'Most brides get married in red, for the purity of fire. We got married in a registry office and I wore a red dress from Coast. Miles always said that I deserved an "Indian" wedding one day.'

I put the document down and held her closer while she cried some more.

When she'd sniffed herself to a stop, she sat up straight. 'Take this silk and hide it somewhere in the house. Now.'

By the time I got back to the hall, she'd gone to bed. I joined her upstairs and held her again.

4 — Dragon's Den

'Why is the ceiling blank?' said Mina, giving herself a crick in the neck to no avail.

'It isn't blank, you just can't see the frescoes. I must admit that I can't see them either.'

She grinned. 'You killed the Dragon, but you can't see the painted ceiling? What sort of Mage are you?'

Vicky stepped in to save my blushes. 'It's masked. There are rather too many naked bottoms for sober people. It was never intended that women would see them. Other than servants, of course.'

'I like the pillars,' said Mina.

There was a lot to like in the Banqueting Hall of Newton's House, even without the frescoes. You can find one of the entrances to Newton's House quite easily – it's just off Whitehall Place in London, which puts it in the West End.

Away to the east, the home of the Invisible College is Salomon's House in the old City of London, and they built this place near the Houses of Parliament for two reasons. First, it's closer to the seat of mundane power. Second, there's nowhere inside Salomon's House that's big enough to hold everyone at once.

The architect of Newton's House took his inspiration from ecclesiastical tradition. The Banqueting Hall is underground, and is shaped like a square cross with a lot of blue and gold columns to hold up the buildings above it. The centre has a grand dome, allegedly covered with enchanted frescoes, and one arm of the cross has a dais to hold the top table for banquets or, like today, to become a stage for presentations.

'Will you sit next to me?' said Mina to Vicky.

'I really wish I could, but I've got to be on stage.' She grinned. 'Tell you what, Mina, I'll do a swap, then you can sit next to Conrad.'

Mina gave her a dark look. 'And deprive you of the undivided attention of hundreds of Mages? That would be cruel.'

'It's not hundreds, but it's bad enough. Actually, you'll be over there. I'll show you.'

Mina leaned up to kiss me, then followed Vicky. I made my way to the stage. There was a table covered in a blue cloth with golden sunbursts, the colours and insignia of the Invisible College. On top of it were glasses, water jugs and four large name cards, one of which was mine.

Mages were drifting in from the street entrance in ones and twos, then the first group arrived from the door to the Old Network of tunnels under

London. Desirée was back in her wheelchair, which was odd enough; odder still was that Hannah was pushing and that the Dean of the Invisible College, Cora Hardisty, was walking alongside.

They paused in the shadows, well hidden by pillars, and I got a flicker of magick, and only because I was focusing on them. It happened as Desi got out of the chair and Hannah was passing in front of her. Aah. An illusion: it had been Cora in the wheelchair all along.

Dean Cora had been speared in the abdomen recently. She should be at home, but this was her comeback gig. She walked stiffly up to the stage, and I moved to meet her. I jumped down the steps and gave her an extravagant kiss. 'Take my arm on the steps,' I whispered.

'Thank you.'

I stood close enough to the Dean to make Mina jealous, and got her up the steps.

'I'm good from here,' she said at the top. I put myself between her and the gathering audience until she was seated. Hannah followed behind. Out in the hall, I could see Desi, Vicky and Mina talking.

I sat on Cora's right and said, 'That illusion was neatly done, but was it wise to come here at all?'

'No choice,' she said. 'Pour me some water, will you?' I poured, and she took some pills. 'I'm trying to do without the addictive ones. By the Goddess, it hurts. I suppose you'd know all about that.'

'One reason I started smoking again was to help with opiate withdrawal.'

She grunted. 'It's the late Warden's cremation on Friday. After the ceremony's over, Oldcastle is going to call a Board meeting. Choosing a new Warden is the only item on the agenda.'

Cora is Dean of the Invisible College and responsible for magickal education. An important job, yes, but she's only been in post for two years. The Warden's job is bigger than just the College: the Warden of Salomon's House is the de facto senior Mage in Britain.

'That's a bit quick, isn't it?' I said.

She took another drink and grimaced. 'They don't choose at the first meeting. They'll just declare the vacancy open.'

'Then what?'

'Any Mage of good standing can apply. Even you.'

'A bit early for me. Don't you have to be a Fellow at least?'

She shook her head. 'No. You have to be a Mage, yes, but that's not what puts people off. The Elder from the Daughters of the Goddess is a more powerful Mage than I'll ever be, but she won't take the Oath of Allegiance. The Occult Council have tried to make the Warden's office exempt from the Oath, but it's not their decision.'

'You're putting your hat into the ring, I presume.'

'Yes. Then, at the next meeting of the Board, all applicants get five minutes to make their case. There's a secret vote for every candidate, and all those with a positive score go on the ballot for election by the Fellows. I can't afford to be out of circulation.'

'Don't overdo it, Cora. You've already had one relapse. I tried to do too much after the crash and nearly died of sepsis. I think it was Mina's prayers to Ganesh that saved me.'

She looked out into the hall. 'Is that her, over there?'

'With Desi Haynes, yes.'

'She's … erm …'

'Tiny. Yes, she is, next to Desirée, most women are.'

'And even tinier next to you. Francesca says she's been through a lot.'

'She has, and yet she chose to get together with me.'

There was a burst of noise, and Hannah spoke up. 'Here they come.'

The main procession from Salomon's House began to file in from the Old Network. This was an informal meeting, so there were no gowns or strict precedence, but the senior academics led the way, and it was a very impressive turnout.

I went to the edge of the stage to say hello to Chris Kelly and accept a dinner invitation for a month's time. 'If Mina's back from India,' I added.

He looked alarmed. 'Is everything okay?'

'Fine, but I'll need to be flexible.'

'Good luck.'

Vicky reluctantly made her way to the stage and the Dean got out some notes. There were now about a hundred Mages in the hall, forty of whom were final year undergrads, or Candidates in the Salomon's House terminology. Over two thirds were women.

Cora leaned over and said, 'I'll introduce you. After your bit, I'll ask the first question, and I've primed Selena to ask the second. After that, you're on your own.'

I nodded, and she tapped her glass twice. With a deep breath, she levered herself upright and smiled.

'Welcome to this joint Salomon's House-Merlyn's Tower seminar. The Constable will be speaking to the Candidates later, and I'm glad to welcome Watch Officer Robson, whom many of you know. Her part in recent events isn't as well known as it should be, and that's something that the Constable will address.'

She took a deep breath. 'Our principal speaker today has a unique title, one that hasn't been held for centuries, and one that he prefers not to use himself – Dragonslayer. Instead, could you please welcome Squadron Leader Conrad Clarke, Watch Captain at Large and Swordbearer to Clan Flint.'

There was a gratifying amount of genuine applause from the hall as I stood up. I laid out a sheet of paper that Hannah had given me with things that I couldn't say. Across the top, in red pen, was this instruction: NO JOKES.

Spoilsport.

'Thank you, Dean, and thank you all for coming. I'm not sure what interests you most in all this, so I'm going to keep it short and give you more time for questions.'

The story of what happened with the Dragon Welshfire and the Druids of MADOC is one I've told elsewhere. I gave the company of Salomon's House an edited version that was heavy on magick and light on criminal conspiracies, except for one detail. This is how I finished:

'Four Mages died in Wales, including one of our own, Watch Captain Price. Watch Officer Robson was seriously injured. However, one of the Druids fled, and if you ever hear of the Bard Adaryn ap Owain, also known as Imogen Jones, then please contact the Constable. Thank you.'

I got more applause, and Cora said, 'Thank you. Perhaps you could describe Welshfire in more detail?'

I did. The Dragon I fought was a cross between a crocodile, a T Rex and an ostrich. And an orbital rocket, of course. Crocodiles are scary, but they don't breathe fire.

Cora threw it open to the floor, and chose the aristocratic Selena Bannister for the first question.

'Watch Captain, I ask this in a spirit of open enquiry and not as a personal slight. Are you sure it was a Dragon?'

That was a jaw dropper. All I could manage was, 'Erm…'

'Let me explain. All the images and records of Draco Albinensis, from magickal and mundane sources, are agreed that it has four legs and wings. The creature – the deadly creature – that you fought had only two legs and wings.'

I felt a twinge in my leg, and I remembered the vicious assault that Vicky had inflicted on Friday. It was time for payback. 'I think that Officer Robson is better qualified than me to answer that question.' I sat down quickly, before she could bottle it, and if looks could kill, I'd be deader than the Dragon.

She got up slowly and cleared her throat. I was very conscious that these were her peers and her teachers. This was her crowd, not mine, and talking about Welshfire could only bring back the trauma of her near-death experience.

'As you know,' she began, 'I'm an Imprimatist.' She coughed again and reached for her water.

I desperately wanted her to get this, but if I spoke out, it would only undermine her, so I whispered, 'Shove it up 'em, Vic. Give it large or I'll make a joke about your tattoo.'

'You wouldn't.'

I pushed down on the arms of my chair and rose an inch out of my seat.

43

'Yes!' she shouted. 'Ahem. Sorry. Yes, it was a Dragon. I examined the altar at the Caerleon Grove and the temporary nest in Bardsholm, and compared the residual imprints. It was definitely a Dragon.'

'So…' said Selena.

'It was very immature. Either Dragons create their own Glamours when they mature – which is very possible – or it grows front legs after the hunt. Sadly, Welshfire wasn't just killed, she was vapourised, so I didn't get to examine her in detail.'

Vicky sat down abruptly, and I said, 'Well done.'

'I hate you.'

The next question was one I could answer on my own (it was about the Lions of Carthage who guard the Dragon nests), and on we went. I deflected several questions about the Druids, emphasising how we'd only succeeded in the end because their leader had backed the King's Watch rather than the members of his own Order who'd hatched the Dragon.

The next question that really threw me came from one of the Candidates.

'Saffron Hawkins,' she said, when the Dean called her. 'Are you sure about the Dragon's diet? Is it true that they only attack humans because they've been trained to eat them?'

Vicky had found the confidence to answer several questions quite happily by this point. I looked at her, and she shrugged.

I pulled my lip and gave it some thought. 'I know that the final sacrifice – the human sacrifice – was crucial. I know that because they tried to sacrifice Officer Robson, and when she stopped them, one of the Druids sacrificed herself instead. I also know that Welshfire only said one thing to me: "Where's the girl?" She was annoyed that she hadn't had her promised meal.'

Saffron politely put her hand up again, and I signalled for her to go ahead. She brushed back a mane of blond hair and said, 'So it may be possible to have a Dragon that isn't a humanophage?'

Vicky and I both shrugged at that one.

Before the next question, I noticed the Custodian, Heidi Marston, grabbing her neighbour's hand to stop him speaking. What was that all about?

Finally came the question we'd prepared for most.

'Where did the egg come from, and are there any more of them?' said a woman whose name I didn't catch.

I know exactly where the egg came from: a tunnel connected to the Old Network.

'I have no idea where it came from,' I lied. 'There may well be more, and all that I can say is this: I bloody well hope not.'

'You and me both,' added Vicky in a stage whisper that got a few laughs.

Cora drew the seminar to a close and we got another, even bigger round of applause. 'And now,' she continued, 'the Constable will address the Candidates. I should remind you that this is a timetabled event, so yes, you do have to stay. We'll take a ten minute break, first.' She sat down and said to me, 'If you go into the Old Network, you can smoke.'

And so I did.

The academic staff drifted away, most pausing to say how interesting they'd found it. A number shook my hand, too. The last one was the guy who'd been restrained by Heidi Marston: the Provost of Salomon's House, Gregory Parrish. He's not a fan of the King's Watch, and didn't bother with the niceties.

'Those bloody Druids must have had access to powerful magick. Old magick. Where did they get it from?'

'That's why we want to talk to Adaryn. We'd very much like to know.'

We did know, in a way. They'd got it from the damned Codex Defanatus, but we're not sharing that information widely. Heidi knows there's old magick on the loose, but no more. Her intervention saved me having to lie twice in public.

Parrish blinked. 'Was there no evidence in the Caerleon Nest?'

'I'm sure there is. If you'd like to distract the Lions of Carthage for me, I'll have a look.'

'Why don't you just shoot them? That seems to be your first response to most things.'

'Only when lives are at stake. The Lions are safe underground, and no threat to anyone except Mages trying to hatch Dragon Eggs. The Romans put them there for good reason.'

'Hmm. Thanks for the talk, Mr Clarke. What you didn't say was most illuminating.'

I smiled and went back into the hall. Only the panel got refreshments, and I was parched. Cora had stayed on the stage to avoid the steps, and she'd been joined by Mina. To my surprise, Mina was having an earnest conversation with both Cora and Hannah. Vicky handed me a cup of tea and said, 'I believe you took five wickets on Saturday. Congratulations.'

'Thanks. What are they talking about?'

'Project Midas. It all goes way over my head.'

'Mine, too.'

'How's Myfanwy?'

I filled her in on our tame Druid's love life and grabbed more tea. Cora called the gathering to order, and Mina looked like Cinderella when the clock strikes midnight. She lifted her kurta (a gorgeous light blue over black leggings, if you're interested) and hopped off the stage in a scuttle. She didn't leave a glass slipper behind, but I know where to find her.

Vic and I took our places, and when the student body was settled, one of their number got up and raised his hand.

'Yes, Matthew,' said Cora wearily.

The young man was nattily turned out in a three piece suit that was fine down here but must have been a sweatbox in the London heat above ground. He bowed to the stage and said, 'Thank you, Dean. I found Mr Clarke's seminar fascinating, as did everyone I spoke to at the break, and I for one would come to hear the Constable without being told to. However, we wonder why this event has been timetabled, and why the Proctor is the only member of staff still here. No body other than the Watch has this privilege, and we question why they have been singled out for favour.'

That's the thing about Mages. Most go to private schools where the magickal curriculum can be hidden from prying inspectors, and Mages are very polite – except when they're trying to kill you. The mask usually slips at that point.

'Thank you, Matthew,' said Cora. 'Your point deserves an answer, and that answer has to come from the Inner Council. I shall make sure that you get to ask them at the next meeting.'

He bobbed up again and said, 'Thank you, Dean.'

Cora remained seated to introduce Hannah, and when the Boss got up to speak, she moved round to lean on the table and get closer to her audience.

Hannah shouldn't have to make this speech. The Watch has been recruiting Watch Captains from the College for two hundred and fifty years. There should be a Guardian at Salomon's House teaching offensive and defensive magick, and preparing those with an interest in the Watch to take a commission. There should be a Guardian, but there isn't, and the College isn't in a hurry to find one. And that's why we're here recruiting Watch Officers.

The idea is that they are teamed with an experienced Captain for field work. Poor Vicky. She got me.

Hannah's speech was a well-judged blend of duty and opportunity, and it came from the heart. She didn't ignore me exactly, but my invitation to join the Watch was hand delivered by Odin, which is not something you can legislate for. What she did do was big up Vicky's achievements, and boy did my partner blush.

Hannah finished, and Cora managed to get to her feet. Just. She put her hand on my shoulder to steady herself and said, 'As Matthew pointed out, we've kept you long enough, so rather than take questions from the floor, the Watch will be staying to see you individually. If you are interested in applying, and I personally hope that you are, then you can apply privately, via my office. Thank you for coming.'

There was polite applause for a second, until the Proctor (student police) got up and left. Most of the Candidates did likewise.

Cora sank down with a groan.

'What's changed?' I said. 'Not long ago you looked down your nose at Vicky for taking a commission, now you're actually promoting it.'

She sighed. 'That was a fit of pique on my part. Vicky was my student, and I wanted her to do a doctorate. When she preferred the money and the chance to see the whole world of magick, I took it a little bit too personally. What's really changed is that I saw the Warden go up in smoke at the same time as I was speared by a piece of flying metal. The Codex Defanatus has to be found, and found quickly. Hannah, you and the Watch are the only ones who can do it.' She tried to smile. 'It shows maturity to change your mind, doesn't it?'

Hannah and Vicky were down in the hall talking to a dozen or so Candidates, including the impeccably proper Matthew and the impossibly blond Saffron Hawkins. I got up to go, and Cora grabbed my arm. 'Let them handle it. If we're talking up here, I don't have to move.'

'Of course.'

She smiled the forced smile of the invalid. 'Mina's a whirlwind, isn't she?'

'Makes up for my sloth.'

'She knows more about the magickal finances of Salomon's House than I do. Then again, it's not part of my remit.'

'Yet.'

'Don't. Right now, I'd swap my heels for fluffy slippers. Ambition is a cruel mistress.'

That was rather alarming. The Dean must be tired. Either that or it's a play for modesty; it's hard to tell with Cora.

She changed the subject. 'Mina says you're all off to Lancashire via Little Marlow after this finishes. What's Francesca doing up there?'

Aah. Oh dear.

'Mina is a whirlwind, Cora, but she hasn't read the chapter on need-to-know yet.'

This time, Cora's grin was real. 'Go on. Tell me.'

'I can tell you we're all staying in Hartsford Hall tonight.'

'Isn't Carl Christie the chef there?'

'He is. We have a table for four booked at eight o'clock.'

'Lucky you.'

We passed a few minutes in small talk until the last Candidate had gone. When the door to the Old Network closed behind him, Desirée appeared from the shadows with the wheelchair. 'Can you help?' said Cora.

I took most of her weight down the steps, and she collapsed into the wheelchair. She looked around the group. 'Wherever it is you're off to, good luck. And thanks. Today was a big day, and you've all helped me more than you know.' Desi wove a Glamour around them. Hannah got ready to push, and they disappeared into the Old Network.

'I'll get me bags,' said Vicky.

Mina gave one last look at the blank dome and took my arm. 'You were very good today. I hope the audience is a lot smaller when I've finished Project Midas. If I ever finish.'

We started to walk to the stairs. 'Is there a problem? Do you need to talk to any Mages?'

'Yes, but I don't know the right questions. The problem is in the data. I shall pray to Ganesh tonight and give him the hand made Hartsford Hall chocolates as an offering.'

'Lucky Ganesh.'

'No, lucky me. And you. You more, I think.'

I wasn't going to argue with that.

5 — *Reunions*

Cairndale, on the Lancashire-Westmorland border, is a funny little town. On the north side of the river, it's all railway and red brick terraces, while the south side is all Georgian and grey stone. Except for the old mill. That's a bit of both.

The Market Square is on the south side, a brave outpost of independent shops and cafés. There was no market today, so we got a parking space outside our favourite café and waited to shuffle our deck of cards. That image, of course, brought back Mercedes and her tarot.

Last night's dinner had been a strictly social affair, with magick very much off the menu. Vicky is a Sorcerer, and Francesca has read all the important books in her library, so I told them what had happened in Spain. Francesca looked at Vicky, who shook her head in puzzlement before saying, 'Tarot isn't very popular in Salomon's House, Conrad.'

'Why not?'

'It doesn't sit well with Quantum Magick, that's why. You've never seen tarot cards before, right?'

'Correct.'

'So how can your shuffle make sense? How can you know which cards to pick out, no matter how much you open yourself up to the Sympathetic Echo?'

'I thought the cards did that. I thought the magick in them…'

Francesca jerked in her seat. 'She used an enchanted deck?'

'Even I could feel the magick in them, Keeper.'

They looked at each other meaningfully. Meaningfully to them. I was lost. Francesca broke the silence. 'You drew four cards in total, yes?' I nodded. 'What did she do with the rest?'

'Put them to one side.'

'Without shuffling again?'

'I'd laid them in a fan. She carefully scooped them up and put them to one side.'

'Then she was asking a question of her own, for reasons of her own. It sounds like you had a little divine intervention there, Conrad.'

'I didn't feel any presence.'

'That Troth Ring of yours is more than you think. Hence the Devil card.'

'Aye,' said Vicky. 'I don't know much about tarot, but I do know that the Devil is a warning sign – Danger, gods at work. The Allfather must have shaded the Sympathetic Echo and disrupted the answer to her private question. I bet she cursed when you'd left.'

'And the Nine of Wands?'

'That's real, right enough. Things are gonna get a lot worse before they get better.'

Mina had been listening intently to this. 'Would it be worthwhile going to another … what do you call them? Diviner?'

'No!' chorused Francesca and Vicky.

They were saved an explanation by the arrival of a modest silver hatchback. 'That's your lift,' I said. 'I'll get your stuff.'

Francesca is the younger sister of the late Warden, Sir Roland 'Roly' Quinn, the Mage whose job Cora would like. Roly was a legend in magick and will be a tough act to follow, especially as he's still around somewhere.

His cremation on Friday will be a modest affair, because although his body is gone, his Spirit lives on. Literally. When the Warden saved our lives in the bombing, he projected himself into the Spirit Realm and is now doing Spirit things. I'm vague on that point.

Vicky and Francesca were being collected by Susan, a mundane helper at Lunar Hall, home of the Lunar Sisters and scene of my first magickal victory. When Roly passed on, he left unfinished personal business with one of the Witches at Lunar Hall, Sister Theresa, and that was why Francesca had taken leave to find out what the old Witch wanted. I have a bone to pick with Theresa, too, but I'm barred from the Hall, so that's Vicky's mission.

Susan is a lovely woman. Brave, too, and a great cook. She gave me a hug and said, 'Mother Julia sends her blessings. How are you?'

'Good. Can I introduce you to … Oh.'

I turned round, and Mina had disappeared. The prison bus had arrived, and I saw Mina quickly escorting a young woman into the coffee shop just as a boy racer's car pulled into Market Square with bass pumping out of the open windows.

'Sorry,' I said to Susan. 'Vicky will explain.'

I locked my car and took up a defensive position outside the café.

The aggressive music died, and a man got out of the car. A big man, about thirty, wearing a sleeveless vest to show off his ink and his biceps. I looked at his legs. Thin, and his face was way too spotty for a man of his age. Steroids.

I retreated inside the coffee shop and got myself a cappuccino. Mina and Stacey were already closeted in a corner. One of the reasons I like this café is the generous provision of outdoor tables for smokers, so I took my coffee and took up watch.

Steroid Boy spoke to a fruit and veg seller. The prison bus is a familiar sight in Cairndale, and Stacey's ex soon found out he'd missed it. He looked around, scanning the shop fronts for a clue. His eyes lingered for a second on the coffee shop, and I tensed myself for action, then he caught sight of the sign pointing over the river to the railway station. The old bridge through town is now pedestrians only, and he thought about running to look for Stacey, but why would he run when he has a car?

The music boomed and he left the square. I had a feeling he'd be back, so I finished my coffee, collected the girls and drove us out of there.

Stacey didn't have the money yet, but she did have a phone. Mina had given her a new one, with a new number, and Stacey spent the next part of the journey glued to it.

I couldn't work out Stacey's age, even after I got a closer look. Her face was drawn, thin and lined and paler than white bread, unlike her hair, which was the shiny shade of jet black favoured by the prison hairdressers. Her clothes hung off her, except for a tight red top that I recognised – I'd taken it to Mina on a previous visit.

Our first job was to drive into Cairndale police station, much to Stacey's horror. 'Just need to sign some papers,' I said. There was a bit more to it than that, but I wasn't long, and I drove out with the Driscoll case as firmly buried as Diarmuid Driscoll himself.

We headed to Ribblegate Farm on the Fylde Peninsula and I heard Mina trying to persuade Stacey to stay at the farm with the Kirkhams.

'Just for a week. Kelly is a good person. She needs help. You can clear your head.'

'Is it like a real farm?' said Stacey, dubiously.

'Oh yes. With lots of cows. I'll give Kelly some money to cover your keep.'

'Extra money?'

'Oh, yes.'

I hadn't mentioned the appearance of the ex-boyfriend. For a couple of days at least, it would be good if Stacey thought that he hadn't turned up. It would give her some time to bond with the Kirkhams, and talking of bonding, I had some of my own to do.

I left Mina and a very nervous Stacey to get a tour of the refurbished farmhouse while I went to an old shed to meet a new friend.

At the back of the shed, a very sleek border collie bitch was taking it easy while her pups got to grips with the outside world. The pups were all playing, running and bounding as much as their little legs would let them. Falls were frequent and mum was keeping a watchful eye. All the pups were cute, bright and lively, but one stood out.

The Spirit of Roly Quinn is keeping a low profile, and I wish him luck. According to Vicky, he'll need it, because the Spirit world is very much one of dog-eat-dog, as my new friend knows only too well. The smallest of the pups made a beeline to me while all the others gave the strange human a wide berth.

'Hello, Scout,' I said. 'Pleased to see me?'

Spirits need Lux or they dissipate. One poor Spirit of unknown origin decided that I was good for food and merged itself with a new-born pup on a previous visit to become my Familiar Spirit. It's an honour to have a Familiar, but I have no idea what to expect.

He wasn't the smallest when he became my Familiar, but I've been away a lot, and lack of Lux stunts your growth. The little mite ambled up to me and blinked. It's not that rare for border collies to have one brown eye and one blue one, but when Scout blinked, the brown eye turned green, and I felt the drain of Lux when I scratched his ear. My arm went dead with pins and needles, and I had to kneel down.

'Easy, boy. Don't be greedy.'

His little tongue stuck out and he rolled on his back for me to tickle his tummy.

'Oh alright. Just this once.'

I felt the drain slow to a trickle, and he shook himself round. The green eye faded to brown, and he licked my hand.

'I thought I'd find you here,' said Joe, younger of the Kirkham boys. 'He's not grown like the others. Are you sure you still want him?'

'How soon can I take him? I'm on an RAF base for a couple of weeks, unfortunately.'

'Still a bit soon, especially if you're going to treat him like a working dog.'

By that, he meant *make him sleep outside*. 'Probably.'

'Then the more he gets used to it here, the easier it'll be. They're getting their first vaccinations on Thursday, so about four weeks' time do you?'

'Brilliant.'

'Good. Let's get some tea.'

Stacey was sitting as far from the table as she could. The poor woman looked terrified. Mina and Kelly get on very well, and were swapping stories about having to adapt to life with an Aga. Neither had been born into Aga households, and they might as well have been talking Hindi for all that Stacey could make of it.

We couldn't linger: it's a long way from the Fylde to Heathrow. Kelly had been running her eye over Stacey, in much the same way that Joe would look at a heifer in the auction mart. She nodded her agreement to Mina, and I collected Stacey's meagre belongings from the car. There were hugs all round and we left them to it.

'You never told me what Stacey was convicted of,' I said when we were back on the motorway.

'You never asked.'

'Because you told me not to ask that question about your … colleagues. In jail.'

'So why are you asking now?'

'Because you've never dumped one on a friend before.'

'I didn't dump her,' said Mina. I said nothing. 'Maybe. A bit. Stacey got a year for theft, handling stolen goods and fraud. She used to receive stolen credit cards and use them to buy things. Groceries, usually, or things she could sell on for cash.'

'And Kelly knows this?'

'It would have been wrong not to tell her. I think she'll be good, though.'

'Why?'

'Because I gave Kelly half of the thousand pounds to hold as a deposit on a flat when Stacey leaves the farm. She won't give it to her otherwise, and will only pass it on to the landlord. It's a good incentive for Stacey to grow up.'

'I thought she was older than you.'

'She's twenty-three.'

Mina is nearly twenty-eight. Poor Stacey.

Mina squared herself in the car seat. 'What Stacey needs is a good reason not to go home for a long time. I hope that Kelly gives her one. There are very few happy endings for ex-cons who don't have rich boyfriends like you. And don't say you're not rich; next to Stacey, you might as well be Bill Gates.'

We'd barely been alone since getting back from Spain, what with Myfanwy, the seminar and the road trip, and we spent most of the journey to Heathrow discussing practicalities. Arun messaged her to say that he was in India and would collect her from Mumbai airport. It's funny, Mina only ever says *Mumbai* when talking about the airport. The city is and always will be *Bombay* to her.

Arun will take Mina to a cousin's house in the city, and she was looking forward to seeing the cousin's wife, Radha Bhabi again. She wouldn't be going out to her mother's family estate until Friday at the earliest.

She didn't open up until we were on the M25, just a few junctions from the hotel and the airport. 'You know what I'm most scared of?' she said. 'That I won't care. That she will die and that it won't bother me.'

'You can't plan feelings,' was all I had to offer. True, though.

'I wish I wasn't going and I'm excited to go. It was you who said that feeling two opposites is normal. I wish your god had not blocked that tarot reading. Something is changing, Conrad, and we need all the inside information we can get.'

'The Allfather is not my god. We have an understanding, that's all.'

'Not from where I'm sitting. Where are we eating tonight? Wherever it is, it won't be as good as Hartsford Hall.'

'It won't, but it doesn't have to be. It just has to be good enough for today.'

'You should be a priest because you're so full of shit sometimes. It's a good job I love you.'

6 — Spare Part

Saying goodbye the next morning was terrible. I watched her go through security not knowing when – or if – she'd come back. All I could do was make sure that I was still alive to greet her, and be there for her on the other end of the phone she'd just given me.

Of course I had a phone already, just not a smartphone. I hate them. Mina had given me a £70 budget model and said, 'For me. Please. Everyone in India uses WhatsApp. The roaming charges are terrible. If you go on a mission, just let me know and leave it behind. Just until I get back.'

I spent fifteen minutes locking down every privacy setting I could find, then sent her a WhatsApp.

I love you too XXXXX came straight back.

I shoved the phone in my pocket and went to collect the car.

I got to RAF Shawbury, Shropshire, while the Stores was still open and went to collect my kit. Officers have to provide their own dress uniforms, but all the day-to-day gear comes from Stores.

'Well, well, well,' said a disembodied but familiar voice. 'If it's not the bad penny himself. I thought we'd seen the back of you, sir. Won't be long.'

The owner of that voice and its deep Yorkshire accent has been dispensing RAF Stores since I was an officer cadet. He'd delivered his welcome message from behind a closed grille, and I looked around. Why have they fitted CCTV since I was last here, I wonder?

The grille went up and the Stores Sergeant gave me a big grin. 'You've lost even more hair. Sir.' He took a closer look, and the smile disappeared. 'Sorry, sir. I couldn't see the scarring from down here.' He is not the tallest airman in the service.

'Acid,' I said.

'Nasty. How's your leg, sir?'

'Good enough to get me back here.'

'I couldn't believe it when I saw your name on the chitty. Have a look at this.'

He put a bundle of clothing on the counter and pointed to a hand-written note on the label:

SIZE: CONRAD BLOODY CLARKE SIZE

'You're a Stores legend, sir. Welcome back.'

It was the first time I'd smiled since breakfast.

The second WhatsApp came in while I was finding my way round the new accommodation blocks. Very smart they are, too. I got a shock when I saw that the message had gone to Myfanwy and Vicky as well.

Mina: *Arrived. No problems. First monsoon due tomorrow.*
Myvvy: *Wow! So exotic! Take care. Xxx.*
Me: *What's exotic?*
Myvvy: *The picture*
Me: *What picture?*
Mina: *Change your settings.*

Vicky didn't join in because she was presumably doing something at Lunar Hall. I logged on to the public WiFi, changed the settings and a picture of bright lights and heavy traffic appeared, just as a new message arrived. This one was for me alone.

I hope that you are missing me as much as I am missing you. Don't tell me if you're not. Just take care and don't crash any helicopters. You might not be so lucky next time. India is a very big country and I feel very small without you. Sleep well. Xxxxxxxxxxxxxxxx.

You don't need to know my reply.

I was expecting to fast-forward the story at this point. Being a pilot is all about practice, practice and more practice, and I'm afraid that flying practice is very boring. Unless you're the pilot, of course. I was looking forward to the training, yes, but I was looking forward to the scene at Heathrow Arrivals even more. As I went to bed that night, I imagined Mina's splash of colour behind a trolley full of cases coming through that gate and into my arms. Fate had other ideas.

'If you'd like to wait over there, sir, someone will be with you shortly.'

Feel free to substitute *madam* for *sir* in that sentence, and I'll bet you've heard it a lot in your lifetime. In the services, it's ten times worse, and not usually so polite. Welcome to the Defence Helicopter Training School.

My path to certification began with a Class I medical, and that began with my eye test.

'Read the chart, sir, starting at the top.'

'H for Hotel, C for Charlie, Tango, Alpha...' I carried on until I'd finished.

'Very funny, sir. Did we take a peek on the way in?'

There is no sarcasm quite like that from a sergeant to an officer. I'm used to it, but I had no idea what he was on about, so I smiled. Safer that way.

He tapped his computer, and the letters on the screen at the other end of the room shuffled randomly. Except for the huge H at the top. 'Again, sir.'

'Hotel, Tango, Mike ...'

This time he said nothing, and just made me sit in front of a fearsome, desk-mounted ophthalmoscope. Two minutes later, he switched off the light and sat back while I blinked away the tears.

'You're not wearing contacts,' he said.

'Why would I?'

'Have you had surgery, sir?'

'On my eyes?'

'Yes, sir. The leg surgery is in your notes. Good luck with the musculo-skeletal test later, by the way.'

'Thanks, and no, no eye surgery.'

He double-checked his computer. 'Then how can you explain this, squadron leader, sir? Your eyes are better now than when you applied for your commission twenty years' ago.'

That's a stumper. I could guess, and the answer would be magick. Mages age in strange ways. I wasn't going to tell the sergeant that.

'Good genes and a hangover, I expect. I remember having a skinful on the night before my first medical, so I must have under-performed then.'

He wanted to fail me. He really did, but he couldn't. He stamped a form, put it in my records, and then showed me the door. 'If you'd like to wait over there, sir, someone will be with you shortly.'

See? I'm not exaggerating. It happened eight more times before I got my medical certificate.

The rest of Thursday and all day Friday was spent in one-to-one theory classes or reading on my own. Thankfully, it's only a two hour drive from Shawbury to Clerkswell, and at least Myfanwy was pleased to see me.

'I've found us an ally,' she said after putting a slice of cake in front of me, placing the plate on top of the first invoice from the landscape gardeners. She's been supervising a makeover of the grounds. I started with the cake.

'Mmm. Delicious. Who's the ally?'

'It's a surprise. She's coming for tea tonight. I mean supper. You're all so middle class round here, I thought supper was cheese, crackers and hot chocolate. Why can't you call it *tea* like everyone else? How's Mina?'

'You know how she is. We're all in the same WhattsApp group.'

'Yes, but she was due to see her mother today, wasn't she?'

'I had a phone call from her on the way down. Her mum wasn't well today. Or, as Mina put it, her mother wants to wait until Saturday, when she can organise a reception committee to intimidate her own daughter. She's going tomorrow.'

'Poor Mina. I can't imagine what she's going through. Now, what about that Dragon seminar? You didn't tell them anything about me, did you?'

'No. You'd have a queue of Mages down to the Inkwell if they knew. You might even be at risk.'

'Of what, for goodness sake?'

'Some Mages would happily kill you if they thought they could get their hands on a viable Dragon egg.'

'Oh. I hadn't thought of that.'

'How's Ben?'

Her smile switched back on. 'All good, thanks to you. I think.'

'No ladies practice tonight?'

'No. I didn't want to bother you, Conrad, but it's all kicked off here. We're having a constitutional meeting next week to put the women's team on an official footing. That's why we need an ally.'

'We?'

'Team Elvenham. The other side are Team Bloxham. Tell me, Conrad, I know that Jules Bloxham said some horrible things about Mina, but you and Stephen have hated each other for years. Why?'

'It's not just us. Our fathers didn't get on, either. The Bloxhams are just jealous, that's all. They own the biggest, oldest house in the village, and they're much richer than the Clarkes, but we're the oldest family. So long as we're around, they'll never have that.'

I smiled, and Myfanwy took me at my word. What I said was all true, but there's a lot more. It would do her no good to know the real reason the Clarkes are in a stand-off with the Bloxhams.

'Anyway,' she said, 'Carole's down for the weekend, and they're looking at wedding venues, so no practice tonight, and no Ben either.'

Carole is Ben's sister. She's engaged to a Mage of some sort. A Mage who walked out of the pub when he saw Myvvy, Vicky and I sitting in the corner.

Talking of Vicky. 'Did you get a strange message from Vic last night?' I asked.

'No. I knew she had no plans to come down here, so I wasn't expecting to hear from her.'

I pulled my lip. I didn't want to worry her unnecessarily, but they are close. 'You know she went to Lunar Hall?'

'Yeah.'

'I thought she'd be gone a couple of nights, max, but she said something had come up and not to expect her back in circulation for a while.'

'That's not like her.'

I shrugged. 'She's getting promoted. Perhaps this is a trial run. She made a point of saying that she's still with Dr Somerton.'

'She's a card, is Francesca. Vicky will be okay with her.'

Myfanwy may be the first person in decades to describe the Keeper of the Queen's Esoteric Library as *a card*, but she was right: Francesca would keep an eye on my soon to be ex-partner.

Myvvy got up to cook. She waited until her back was to me before saying, 'It's a shame. All the wedding venues are out of the village, so I can't go.'

I murmured something and went to get changed.

It was another warm evening. Very warm in the kitchen. Agas do that. Myfanwy had insisted we and our mysterious guest eat in the morning room, so I spent half an hour setting up and laying a table. The dining room seats twenty, and I would have used it, but Myvvy feels it's a bit OTT. Perhaps it is.

'Here she is,' said Myfanwy from her vantage point in the kitchen. I went to get the door.

'Hello, Conrad,' said the sweet old lady on the doorstep.

I fought with every sinew not to retreat down the passage, and managed to mumble, 'Miss Parkes. I haven't seen you in years.'

'That's because you avoid me. Aren't you going to ask me in?'

I stepped back. 'Sorry.'

Miss Parkes ruled the village school with a rod of iron for nearly forty years. She carried on well after her sixtieth birthday, and only retired when she lost a long battle against arthritis. Her last triumph had been making sure that my sister won a scholarship to an intensely academic girls' boarding school.

I pulled myself together. 'Come through. How's things? How did you meet Myfanwy?'

I settled her in an upright chair in the drawing room and poured two glasses of Manzanilla from the bottle I'd brought back last week. It really is good stuff on a hot day.

'Thank you, Conrad. I found Miss Lewis on my doorstep offering to help with my garden.' She looked down her nose. 'I think she went to most of the old biddies, but I was the first to take her seriously. That garden was running away from me.'

Miss Parkes could afford servants if she wanted them. Time hasn't softened her Scottish accent, but it has taken its toll on the rest of her. No wonder she was glad of help.

Myfanwy breezed in and gave our guest a kiss. I tried not to stare. No one had ever kissed Miss Parkes in my presence.

'Hi, June,' said Myvvy. 'Won't be long.'

Who's June???? No one had ever called her by her first name, either. She's never been tall. She didn't need to be. She was still straight-backed and her hair was still in military waves, but her hands gripped the sherry glass with difficulty.

She saw me looking. 'This is a good day,' she said. 'Warm weather suits me. I'd join your parents in Spain if I were a bit younger. Missed my chance there.'

I did a lot of fetching and carrying that night. Anything to avoid being told off. Myfanwy found it highly amusing. The crucial moment came when they discussed tactics for the ladies cricket committee.

Myfanwy would nominate Miss Parkes for President, and they'd let Jules Bloxham become Chair. The key battleground would be the post of secretary.

'I suggest Nell Heath from the village shop,' said Miss Parkes.

'That would be lush,' said Myfanwy, 'but I've already tried. She told me she can't take on no more in the village.'

I'd been keeping quiet up to now. 'You need to make a sacrifice,' I suggested.

'You what?'

'Tell Nell you'll work Sundays in the shop during the cricket season. Ben might not be keen, but Nell will be your friend for life.'

'A very good suggestion, Conrad,' said Miss Parkes.

I couldn't help it. 'Do I get a gold star?'

'Not for that, but your father always kept an excellent brandy. I can't imagine he took it all to Spain. One of those might be worthy of reward.'

On my way to the cellar, I wondered how she knew about Dad's brandy.

I found Ben leaning on the big roller at Mrs Clarke's Folly the next morning. He was filling in the team sheet for today's men's game.

'Hi, Conrad. You're first on the team sheet today. I wasn't going to drop the Man of the Match was I?'

I lit a cigarette. 'Yes, you are. Team orders.'

'Eh? What team?'

'Team Elvenham. Do you know who Myfanwy's recruited? Miss Parkes.'

'No! Not Highland Parkes! Team Bloxham don't stand a chance now. Are you saying that Highland Parkes wants me to drop you? What for?'

'She said that I'd be rubbish today, and she's right. My head's in India, Ben, and if you rotate Stephen Bloxham into the team, you can rotate him out without an argument.'

'If you're sure?'

'I am.'

He tore up the team sheet and started again. 'You know, something weird happened the other day.'

'Sounds like my life. Go on.'

'Myfanwy poked me in the face. Hard. She drew blood.'

'What you two get up to behind closed doors is your business.'

'Ha ha. No, seriously. She came round and I said, "How's my little Welsh dragon?" and she stabbed me with a fingernail and says, "Don't call me that ever again." Then she burst into tears. What's that all about?'

Oh dear. Poor Ben. 'No idea. Maybe she misheard and thought you were calling her fat? How's Carole?'

'In a state. Her bloody fiancé is a piece of work, I'll tell you. He flat out refuses to have the ceremony in St Michael's, and that's why they're off to Ellenborough Park today. It's a beautiful place, and all that, and he's more than paying his wack for it, but Carole's had her heart set on walking down the aisle of St Michael's since she was old enough to raid Mum's wardrobe.'

He looked over the pitch towards his parents' house. 'Got me to be her groom whenever she caught me doing something wrong. Threatened to tell Dad unless I married her.'

'Rachael was the same, but I was too old to be the groom. I had to give her away, and she usually married her teddy bear.'

I got the call from Mina at half past five, 23:00 in India. We were batting (badly) and no one noticed me scuttle behind the pavilion. No one except Myfanwy.

'How is she?' I said. The line was terrible. Those Indian call centres who keep pestering people must have special equipment.

'She is Maamajee. She can be what she wants, and she wants most of all is to be a martyr.'

'Is it bad?'

'You have no idea. I don't think she'll let me leave India unless I take a husband home with me or she dies first. In fact, if I don't marry, it may send her to an early grave.'

'So it is bad.'

'I miss you, Conrad.'

'I miss you, too. Is she ill?'

'Yes, but she won't admit it. She was only out of bed for a couple of hours before she needed to rest. She's coming downstairs again soon. Conrad, I…'

'Yes?'

The line was dead. She WhatsApped later to say the nearest phone mast was broken. So was our batting: we were thrashed. It's a good job you can't be relegated from Division Two.

I spent Sunday with Myfanwy because we both needed it. Ben was off with his family, and all of her other village friends were with theirs. Even Miss Parkes was being entertained by the vicar.

'Let's do some nets,' I said. 'We'll have Mrs Clarke's Folly to ourselves.'

It was good fun. I'm a bowler and Myfanwy bats. She's good. We both worked up a sweat in the sun, then took a break, leaning on the big roller.

The other side of the ground is bounded by the paddock belonging to Clerkswell Manor, home of the Bloxhams. Their boy, who's about nine, was being pulled through the field by a young golden retriever. He was far too young to be exercising a dog that energetic on his own.

Myfanwy took a bottle of water from the cooler and drained half of it before looking around. 'There are worse prisons,' she said.

'On a day like this, I wouldn't be anywhere else.'

'Would you go to India if you could? Right now?'

The dog was definitely winning the tug of war. I hoped that someone was watching the lad.

'Today? No. She needs this time on her own. If there's a next time, I'll be there if it's the right thing.'

'What time are you going back to base tonight?'

'Late. There's no rush.'

'What's on your programme for tomorrow?'

'Simulators. They've bought a whole new fleet of training helicopters since I was last certified, so it's back to square one for me. So long as I don't fail any assessments, another two weeks should do it.'

We fell quiet, enjoying the sun on our backs. In the paddock, the retriever broke away from its master and made a bid for freedom.

Myfanwy bit into an apple and said, 'I hope that dog doesn't know about the hole in the fence.'

It did.

'Are we going to do something?' she asked, leaving it wide open whether or not we just stood there and had fun at the Bloxhams' expense.

'It's not the dog's fault,' I sighed. 'Nor the lad's. I'll go left, you go right.'

'Nah. I've got this.'

There are a couple of flower troughs by the pavilion, bursting with poppies, nasturtiums, violas and lots I couldn't name. Myfanwy jogged over and collected half a dozen blooms that were going to seed. I felt a tiny pulse of magick as she brushed the flowers. This was going to be interesting.

Behind her, the dog was racing round the pitch like it had never been let off the lead before. The boy was running up and down the fence in a blind panic. He was clearly too big or too scared to follow the dog through the hole.

'Don't let it get on the square,' I said. 'If it tries to dig that up, I'll have to shoot it.'

'Give over, Conrad, it's too nice a day for guns. Get yourself ready.'

'What for?'

'You'll see.'

She rubbed one flower on the roller, then crushed the others under her right trainer. She jogged towards the square, about half way across the pitch, then turned round and ran back to the roller. She whipped off her trainers and ran out again, barefoot.

She ran in a loop, avoiding her previous track and mystifying the dog, who'd seen her and wanted to play this new game. She circled round and drove the dog gently towards her trail. When the dog stopped to sniff, she stopped, too.

The animal wagged its tail furiously and started following the scent. Its nose barely left the ground until it got to the roller, and it – she – only looked up when I grabbed her lead.

'Easy, girl, easy.' She was a lovely dog. I let her lick my hand, and we were soon friends. I picked up Myvvy's trainers and we rendezvoused by the

61

paddock gate. The gate was locked, so I had to lift the dog over it to return her to young Bloxham. Myvvy leaned on the gate to put her trainers back on.

'Th…thank you,' stammered the boy. 'Are you going to tell my mum?'

'She's a great dog, but she's too strong for you, isn't she?'

He looked at his shoes. 'Mum says I have to take responsibility for her. Dad usually comes, but he's not back yet.'

'If you promise not to walk her on your own until you're big enough, we won't tell, will we, Myfanwy?'

'No, we won't. I'd take her in, now.'

'Thank you, Mr Clarke. C'mon, Floss.'

We turned back towards the nets. 'What did you do to those flowers? That was good.'

She blushed. 'That's nothing. Dognip, I call it. You just alter the scent of something that's already aromatic to make it smell irresistible to dogs.'

'I'm still impressed. Let's have a few more overs before lunch. I've reserved a table at the Inkwell.'

'People will talk.'

'They'd talk if we stayed in at Elvenham.'

She started to strap on her pads. 'It's a bit like Paradise here, isn't it? It'd be a lot better with Ben and Mina, obviously, but I'll take it for now. For today.'

She picked up her bat. 'Six overs. If I get six sixes, I get to choose from the wine list and you're paying.'

'And if I get you out six times, you're paying.'

'Deal.'

Neither of us won, and we headed back to Elvenham to get changed. 'Same again next weekend?' she said.

'Haven't you seen the forecast? The Jet Stream's moved south. Expect rain by Thursday. Summer's over for now, I'm afraid.'

'You can be a gloomy sod sometimes, Conrad.'

'I know. The Nine of Wands has been biding its time. It's going to rear its head soon enough.'

7 — *Speed Dating*

The Nine of Wands first made itself felt on the day that Roberta 'Woody' Woodhouse walked into our mess at Shawbury and whisked me off to Yorkshire. That's a day and a story that deserves to be told properly, so you can read about the many ghosts of Draxholt elsewhere. I've called it *Wings over Water* for reasons that will become clear. I learnt a lot about Necromancy and about other planes of existence on that mission; I learnt some more about Nimue and Madeleine, and I even learnt something about myself. Knowledge, however, always comes with a price. I did what the Nine of Wands advised and kept going.

Over in India, Mina's mother had gone into hospital for a procedure that might – or might not – improve her quality of life as she slipped towards the end. She didn't want Mina to visit her, so Mina headed up to Gujarat with a cousin on her father's side to see the other half of her family.

I was concerned, but not frantic, when the cousin messaged me on Mina's phone a few days' later to say that Mina was going on retreat and that she had left her phone behind.

I asked (politely) why Mina hasn't told me herself. *Because she didn't want you to talk her out of it*, said the message back from the cousin. There was an addendum a few seconds later. *She loves you. Of course.*

Of course. That didn't stop me worrying, though. Worrying that something would happen to her, and worrying that she'd never come back home, a point I made to Myfanwy one night, just before the end of my time in Shawbury. I would have talked it over with Vicky, but she was emotionally drained from trying not to go mad identifying Fae Artefacts and setting magickal tests for the Candidates who wanted to join the Watch.

'It's a bugger, isn't it,' said Myfanwy.

'It is, but I was hoping for more sympathy.'

'Aah. Bless. What happened to your stiff upper lip?'

'I'll ring Ben, shall I? I'll get more sympathy from him.'

'Give over, man. Just remember: she had to sit in jail while you went off chasing women, now it's your turn to wait.'

'I didn't chase women!'

'I know that, but look at it from her point of view. I know Ben isn't chasing women, but when he goes to see young farmers on business, that doesn't stop me worrying, does it?'

I sighed. 'Yeah. You're right.'

'I know I am, and I've got good news, too: I got the job at the shop. I start on Sunday, if Nell gets voted in as secretary. And the gardens are coming along. They should finish the hard landscaping this week. I can't wait to start planting.'

'Excellent.'

'I've been thinking, Conrad. You should invite your family for the weekend when I've finished. I'd love to meet them.'

'It's mutual. That's a great idea. There's something else, while I remember. Vicky told you about the Phantom Stag and the Arden Foresters, didn't she?'

'Well of course.'

'One of the Witches messaged me, and she wants to come down to Clerkswell. She fancies the cricket, and meeting a Druid. Her name's Erin Slater. She's an Enscriber. Can I give her your number?'

'Ooh. Yes please. And don't worry, I know to keep my mouth shut about Watch business.'

Warning: the next paragraph contains a lot of capital letters.

It took slightly more than two weeks, but on Tuesday 23rd of June, I got my papers stamped and a handshake from the Base CO. All I had to do was send the paperwork to the Civil Aviation Authority and I'd get my Commercial Pilot's Licence (Helicopter).

I stowed my luggage in the car and took a moment leaning on the roof with a cigarette to enjoy the sunshine. If you'll forgive the metaphor, I'd got through my flying hours on emotional autopilot. There had been no word from Mina at all. Nothing. And there was no one I could contact to check on her. Even Kai Ben's occasional messages said little more than that Mina's phone still worked and that, no, they hadn't heard from her.

I had to go back to work, now, back to the day job with the Watch. At least I'd see Vicky tonight, and catch up, and tomorrow should be good fun. It would be a lot more fun if Mina were there. I was going to give it until the weekend, then I was going to ring Arun.

I was done with training at Shawbury, but I wasn't done with Stores. The sergeant raised his eyebrows when he saw me again. He raised them even further when I showed him an email printout. He checked the reference number on his system and stared in disbelief. 'Let me get this straight, sir. A colonel in the Royal Military Police, who I've never heard of, has sent an RAF squadron leader to collect some combat uniforms.'

'That's about the size of it, and talking of sizes, here they are.'

'Eight combat uniforms? We haven't got these, and definitely not in those women's sizes.'

'Have you checked all your deliveries from today?'

He opened his mouth and closed it again. 'Just wait over there, sir, I'll be with you in a minute.'

Yes! One last time!

I waited. He reappeared, and plonked the plastic packets on the counter. 'I see that one of them is your size, sir. I didn't have you down as roughing it in the mud.'

I grinned. 'It's the job of the RAF to show the others how to do things properly.'

'Right enough, sir, but as to why you want seven RMP cap badges…'

I tapped my finger on my nose. 'Let's just say there's going to be some revenge exacted.'

He grinned and shook my hand. 'Good luck.'

Technically, I'm in 7 Squadron of the RAF. It's always been my unit, and we're best known for flying those enormous Chinook helicopters. What most people don't know is that 7 Squadron also does the flying for special forces. When you hear that the SAS are doing something in some far flung land, it will have been one of us who flew them there. I should know, I've done it often enough.

The SAS mostly keep themselves to themselves, but I did get to know one of them quite well, and when he left the service, he didn't become a consultant (or write books), he bought a farm in the Trough of Bowland, Lancashire, and built himself a boot camp. I'll be taking the uniforms there tomorrow, but that's tomorrow.

We could have stayed at Hartsford Hall again. I was very tempted, but said no for two reasons. First, it's a long drive through the Forest of Bowland to get to the farm, and second, I'd have to pay for everyone. I'm not that rich.

Vicky was waiting for me in the bar of the Waddington Arms (thoroughly recommended), where we were staying. The Candidates were in various B&Bs around the area and had been told to leave us alone.

I gave Vic a long hug. There was a pint of IPA waiting for me on the bar, and she'd bagged a table outside in the evening sunshine. It was very good to see her again.

'How are you bearing up without Mina?' she said.

'I'm bearing up.'

'You must be worried about her, though.'

'Yes.' I think she was expecting more, but I had nothing. There comes a point in any worry when going over it doesn't actually help. Just being with someone who understands is enough.

She nodded slowly and raised her glass. 'To Mina. May she come back quickly.'

'To Mina. Now, are you finally going to tell me what happened when you went to Lunar Hall?'

She grinned. 'No.'

'Seriously?'

'Well, aye. I literally have no idea what happened between Francesca and Theresa, because it all happened in private. I can tell you that there was no physical violence, and that they kissed at the end. Francesca said nothing to me, so there's no point trying to get me drunk or bribe me, 'cos I don't know.'

'Did you find out anything about Madeleine?'

'Less than you did. I read *Wings over Water*, and you found out that she'd given herself to Nimue. All Theresa said was that the Memorial willow was already there when she joined the coven, and that it was unique.' She shrugged. 'Perhaps next time. Theresa did say that there isn't really an imminent threat to Maddy's offspring.'

'Let's hope she's right. How was the mission overall?'

'It was … different. Working with Francesca had its own challenges.'

'So did working with Woody.'

She gave me a grin over her glass of wine. 'You know what that makes you, doesn't it?'

There was a cheap shot coming. I said nothing.

'Buzz Lightyear. Good job for you that the file's restricted, or everyone will be at it.'

Vicky and I have shared a lot. I know her pretty well, and I know when she's not happy underneath. 'What's up, Vic?'

She looked guilty for a second. Guilty that she hadn't hidden it well enough. She stopped trying to put on a brave face and looked thoroughly depressed. 'Get us another large merlot and I'll tell you.'

'Coming up.'

I went to the bar and got the drinks. She twirled the fresh glass in her hands for a moment before looking up. 'We've got a big problem. There's a spy in Salomon's House. At a high level.'

'I know.'

She jerked back. 'Eh? How?'

'The bombing. Only someone at a senior level could have planned that.'

'Why haven't you said?'

'Because Hannah wouldn't believe me, and because I wanted to catch them red-handed. I thought we'd get them at Niði's Hall. What's happened?'

'When Francesca was at Merlyn's Tower showing us that poem, on the day of Helen's Induction, someone was in the Library taking all the Quicksilver Artefacts. You don't have to worry about Hannah believing you now. She went ballistic.'

'What's been done? About the theft?'

'Not theft. Unauthorised access, and that's the problem. If we make it official, Francesca will carry the can. She'll be suspended and forced out. Hannah thinks she's the only one we can trust.'

I drained my pint and started on the second. I was inclined to agree with Hannah about the Keeper. There is no way that Francesca would be party to a bombing when her brother was going to be there. 'Tell me, Vicky. You held Cora's hand when she'd been speared by that piece of flying table. Was she really not wearing her Ancile?'

Cora had claimed that it was vanity that had made her go to the first ceremony without her magickal shield.

'No. She wasn't wearing it.'

'Then we can trust her. Up to a point. Have you been able to eliminate *any* of the Fae nobles?'

'Only three. The Queen of the Heath, the Princess of Ynys Môn and the Queen of Wye all check out. In other bad news, it's been pointed out that the Prince of Galway is also in the frame. He made a lot of visits to Britain during the period, and he still has interests here.'

A young lad carrying menus appeared and said that our table was ready. We didn't get back to business until we'd adjourned to my room for privacy.

Tomorrow, we were putting some Candidates through mental and physical tests. That was my department; Vicky had already put them through their magickal paces.

'How many applied?' I asked.

'Eleven put in a formal application. I've whittled them down to six.'

'How did you choose?'

'Simple. I said, "Do they have the right magick to stop Uncle Conrad getting stuck up shit creek without a paddle?"'

'I can't argue with that.'

'Shall we take a look?'

I shook my head. 'I'd prefer to do it anonymously. We'll give them a random numbered bib tomorrow then compare notes at the end.'

'If you're sure.'

'I am. And here's your combat uniform. I've put the captain's flap on for you. And the hat.'

The Royal Military Police are known as the Redcaps because … yes, you guessed. I handed her a uniform and the bright red beret. The RMP have another nickname, but we won't go into that here.

She stared at the beret. 'I am not wearing that.'

'Tough.'

'Seriously?'

'You're an officer.'

She stood up. 'Fine, but under protest, OK?'

'Noted. How's the Jiu-Jitsu going?'

'It's bloody hard. She's a psycho. Another year and I might last ten seconds before I get dumped on me arse. G'night, Conrad.'

'This feels really weird,' said Vicky when we arrived at Lester Howarth's farm/boot camp.

'Did I get you the wrong sized uniform?'

'Not the combats – or the stupid hat – I mean this. The assessment. It feels like I'm going dating with you watching me chat blokes up. And me watching you.'

'I wouldn't have put it like that, but I know what you mean. I don't want to two-time you, either. Look sharp, here they come, and there's Lester.'

A minibus pulled into the farmyard as former SAS sergeant Lester Howarth emerged from the barn. He wasn't smiling. He was saving that for later.

He came across and shook our hands. 'Morning, sir. Good to meet you, Ma'am. Everything's ready.'

'Then carry on, Sergeant.'

I put my hand gently on Vic's arm to hold her back as Lester got the Candidates into the barn and handed out the numbered bibs. We followed behind, and I got my first good look at them. The anonymity thing wasn't going to work for one of the Candidates – I recognised Saffron Hawkins straight away. The other five were new to me, and we had a total of four women and two men. They were all individuals, all with different things to offer, especially in magick. Putting numbers on their chest didn't make them less of an individual. In some ways, it helped. All I had to go on was what they did today.

They were all between twenty-one and twenty-three years old. All were at the end of a four year course with the Invisible College. All had read my briefing note specifying hard physical activity, and all had dressed appropriately. That's where the similarity ended.

Number 1, a woman, was the shortest of the six. She had a lot of strength in those shoulders and a lot of strength in that chin. She'd been the first to grab a bib when Lester was handing them out.

Number 2 was the tallest of the women and rather on the ethereal side. She had wide blue eyes and tended to hold her head as if listening to some unheard music.

Number 3 was average. Average height (for the women), average build, average… you get the picture.

Number 4, the first of the men, was the tallest overall. I had some sympathy with him, because unless I'm mistaken, his hairline is already receding. We're probably both related to royalty.

Number 5 was Saffron Hawkins, and I could see why she'd cultivated the big blond hair. Today it was tied firmly back, and without the distraction, her face was thinner, sharper and longer than I'd thought before.

Number 6, the other male, was the second shortest of the whole group. He may even have some Gnomish blood in him. He was definitely mixed race, and had his hair cropped almost to his skull, a look that didn't go with his earnest level of concentration.

I've seen a lot of candidates – small "c" – over the years, and one thing I've learnt is that you can't judge much from the first line-up. I fixed their size and shape in my mind for future reference and took a look round the room.

The barn was divided into sections, and we were starting in a briefing room complete with maps on the walls and wipe-clean boards. We waited to one side as Lester got them standing in a line. Four of the Candidates were taller than him, and the other two only a fraction shorter, but they were all being wary, keeping him in sight at all times. I don't blame them, and part of the effect came from his not having said a word yet: he'd just handed them a bib and pointed to a line on the floor.

He stood in front of them for a good thirty seconds before he spoke. That's a long time. A very long time when you're already nervous. They were watching him so closely that when he drew breath to speak, they did the same and stood up straighter.

'Good morning and welcome to Whitewater Farm Boot Camp,' he said. He made it sound like a threat or sentence for bad conduct. 'Normally, you lot would be a bunch of social workers from Preston or a sales team from Manchester, and I'd lay into you and shout a lot for effect. Not today.' They were now very, very nervous. 'I have no idea what division of the funny brigade you're joining, but your lives could soon be at stake. And so could your comrades'.'

He pulled two red berets from his pocket and twirled them around, one on each hand. 'At the end of today, two of you will go home with these. Possibly. If Squadron Leader Clarke thinks you're good enough.' He stopped twirling and put the berets away. 'From the moment I say "Go" until the moment I say "Stop", you will be assessed. Some of it will be obvious. Some won't. Some I have no idea about. If you want to leave at any time, just go. Put your uniform in that bin there and knock on the farmhouse door. My wife will run you back to Waddington. Is that clear?'

They nodded.

'The first exercise is the Advanced assault course. Listen carefully. In the changing room are six uniforms and six lockers. Get changed. Put your spare kit and all electronic devices in your locker. Find your way to the start of the Advanced course and line up. Go!'

He turned and walked out before they'd even reacted. They looked around, bewildered, for some sort of clue. One of the lads, Number 4, pointed to a door and said, 'Changing room!' as if he'd found the Holy Grail. Five seconds later, we were alone.

'Does he scare you as much as he scares me?' said Vicky.

'More. I've seen him in action.'

We set off and took a path away from the buildings, towards the woods. 'Lester's over there,' said Vicky, pointing right.

'And the Advanced course is over there,' I replied, heading left. 'As you'd know if you'd checked the map, like I did yesterday afternoon when I dropped off the uniforms.'

'Is it going to be like this all day?'

'No. It's going to get worse. For them.'

Four of the Candidates appeared together, still fastening their combats. They saw Lester and jogged over to him. The last two Candidates came out and came over to us, casting nervous glances at their comrades. Their faces broke into big grins when they heard Lester shouting at the others.

When all six were together, Lester gave them the instructions for the assault course. 'Your first pass will be timed,' he said. They looked at each other. They're not stupid. They'd all heard *first*. He didn't give them a chance for questions, he lined them up and said, 'On my mark, with a twenty second gap. Ready. Go!' Number 1 went. We split up and took positions at various points to keep an eye on them.

The course had beams, nets, monkey bars, hurdles and tunnels. We lost our first Candidate at the water tunnel.

She was catching up with Number 2 when she saw the sign for the tunnel:

Length 10m

Height 1m

Depth of Water 75cm

She pulled up. 'I can't do that.'

It was me on duty. 'Never mind, Number 3,' I said. 'You can find your own way down, can't you?'

'Is that it?'

'I'm afraid so.'

Number 4, one of the men, caught up with her and dived into the tunnel. He was followed by Saffron Hawkins, who stopped and said, 'Bea? What's up?'

'I can't go through there.'

Saffron looked at the tunnel, at Bea and at me. I was looking at my stop watch. She patted Bea on the shoulder and said, 'It's shit, isn't it?' before following Number 4 into the tunnel. I gave Saffron a bonus mark for that.

Bea took off her goggles and slumped back down the hill.

'And again,' said Lester as Number 2, now in the lead, finished her third circuit. Her eyes widened, but she started off at a slow jog. They'd got the message about not being timed.

'Why?' said Vicky. 'And how many more times?'

'Six in total,' said Lester. 'As to why, it's to test their willpower. They have to keep going, even though they don't know when they'll be allowed to stop.'

Vicky shook her head and walked back to her station at the scramble net.

'Stop!' said Lester to Number 6 as he finished his last circuit. He collapsed into a heap with the others. Lester continued, 'You now have a break. The kitchen is at the back of the barn. Mine is tea with two sugars. The officers take it without sugar because they're sweet enough already. Weak or cold tea will be heavily penalised. Go!'

Vicky burst out laughing when they were out of earshot. 'This is beyond cruel, Conrad. I didn't have to do any of this.'

'Yes you did. You had to prove yourself in Wales, and look what happened. You died.'

'Aye. Fair point. You're still enjoying it far too much, though.' Lester and I grinned at each other.

When the tea arrived, on a tray, with biscuits, Vicky grinned. 'On second thoughts, I could get used to this.'

Lester took his tea and headed to the armoury.

'What's next?' said Vicky.

'Hard core paintballing,' I said. The tea was very good.

'Is that a metaphor, or are there rocks in the paint?'

'It's like a normal paintballing game, but they don't have guns.'

'How does that work?'

'It's to simulate a situation where they don't have Anciles, but we do.'

'Go on.'

'Lester doesn't know magick, and I'd rather keep it that way. He's going to brief them on their mission, then take up a position out of sight with a radio. I'm going to listen to their planning and follow them through the woods. You're going to be in the woods next to a flag, armed with a paintball gun. You shoot anything that comes for you.'

'That sounds like fun. Why does Lester need a radio?'

'This exercise has strict casualty rules. If you hit anyone, they have to fall down immediately and the others have to radio for advice. He may order them to bind up someone's leg or retreat and re-group.'

'So how are they gonna succeed?'

'They're allowed to use magick. So are you. And I will definitely be using my Ancile, because I know that you will be tempted to shoot me.'

'Spoilsport. Give us a hand up.'

The door to the briefing room closed with a soft click as Lester left us to it. He'd explained their objective, and his parting words had been, 'Squadron Leader Clarke will give you the rules on weapons.'

The five remaining Candidates, all wet and in various stages of exhaustion, turned their eyes to me.

'Captain Robson will be defending the flag. She has two paintball guns. You will have none. You may use magick. Any magick that will not hurt her. I will be here to listen to your planning and then to observe in the woods. From this point onwards, I'd like to remind you of what the Constable said in Newton's House. She wants the Watch to be part of the solution, not part of the problem. Any questions?'

Number 4, put his hand up. 'Will Captain Vicky be using magick?'

I gave him a death stare. Number 6, the other lad, elbowed him in the ribs. 'It's Captain *Robson*. And say *sir*.'

I made a mark on my clipboard. A plus for Number 6. He'd had very few points either way so far. 'Captain Robson will use any magick she sees fit. Anything else? No? You have ninety minutes. Your time starts now. Go!'

'Right,' said Number 1, 'Andy, you get the map…'

Their biggest problem, which Number 6 soon realised, was lack of time. He got several plus points for that. I wasn't assessing their plan, as such, for a good reason. These Candidates are all intelligent young people with powers over the universe not granted to the mundane world. That is no preparation for a live mission. Their plan was rubbish.

What I was looking for was whether they had any idea of risk factors, and if they did, whether they spoke up when someone said something patently stupid.

Number 1 was not doing very well on that score. She seemed to think that leadership was about getting her own way. It may be in certain circles, but we'd made it as clear to them as we could that lives were at stake here.

When they'd agreed their plan, they took themselves up to the "drop zone". This was a circle, out of sight of the woods, from which they had to begin their mission. Essentially, they'd been told that the big red rose flag of Lancashire in the woods was a hostage, and their mission was to retrieve it in one piece. Lester had told them that the printouts in the briefing room were an "intelligence report". No one thought to ask how reliable it was. It wasn't. The map showed the location of a white rose, Yorkshire flag. Their only advantage was that Vicky didn't know their map was rubbish, either.

I had no idea what Vic would do. A big dirty grin had come on her face when Lester showed her how to use paintball gun. The Candidates could be in for a hard time.

Before leaving the drop zone, they all tried to adopt magickal camouflage. Killing sound waves is not that difficult, and even I can manage a Silence. Visuals are harder, and a complete Glamour of invisibility is nigh-on impossible for even the most powerful specialists.

Number 1 and Number 4 could do a very good chameleon, as I soon discovered. They could stand very still and fade into the background way past the point of detection, unless you were looking very hard, or were a gifted Sorcerer like Vicky. Number 2 opted for a kaleidoscope, where three slightly fuzzy versions of herself appeared. That was tricky. Number 6 turned himself into a version of me. It was very good, too. I wondered if Vicky would notice he was limping with the wrong leg. That left Number 5, aka Saffron Hawkins.

I don't think that Glamours are her strength, judging from some of her comments in the planning session, and I was impressed how she used her limited abilities. When the group spread out, she was last. When no one was looking, she turned herself into Lester's wife, and ambled along as if she was going for a walk. She was the right height, similar build and same sex. It would make Vicky think twice, especially as she stuck to the obvious path, just like Mrs Howarth would do. I gave her a head start and followed. There are a lot of brambles in those woods: another reason to stick to the path.

They were about half way to the (wrong) target when I heard a *thwack thwack* from the left. We all had earpieces, and mine burst into life. 'Man down, man down,' said Number 4.

'Control to team. Identify yourself. Over.'

'Number 4 to Control. Number 1 has been hit on the leg. Over.'

'Above or below the knee? Over.'

'That's above the knee. Over.'

'Control to Number 1. You are seriously injured and cannot move. Control to Number 4. You have a twenty minute first aid time out. You must protect Number 1. Control to all team. You must make sure Number 1 gets out at the end. She cannot move on her own. Control out.'

We'd allowed the Candidates one advantage. Vicky had no radio at all, and they had their own channel for communications that neither Lester nor I could hear. We had told them it would be taped, though, and that a review of the recording would form part of our assessment. The crackle from my earpiece told me that they were talking to each other. I pulled it out and listened. Idiots. Number 2 had forgotten to modify her Silence, and I could hear her loud and clear. So could Vicky. *Thwack thwack…*

Ahead of me, Saffron carried on her walk up the path as if nothing were going on. Chaos broke out over the public channel as it was soon realised that Number 2 had a chest shot. She was declared dead. Saffron reached the Yorkshire flag and had one hand on the flagpole when she realised her mistake. She patted the flagpole and turned round to head back to the farm. When she got to the trees, she stopped and pretended to receive a call on her mobile. Over the public channel, she said, 'Number 5 to team. That's the wrong flag. It's a white rose. I checked for Glamour, and it's genuine. We've been given the wrong location. Over.'

'Number 4 to team. We retreat and re-group. Over.'

'Number 6 to team. There's no time. Over.'

I decided to put them out of their misery. 'Base to team. Updated Intelligence report. Hostage location has been confirmed as four hundred metres south south west of original location. Over and out.'

'Saffron, switch to the private channel,' said Number 6, earning him a minus point for breaking radio protocol and a plus point for realising they were making idiots of themselves.

About a minute later, Saffron abandoned her disguise as Mrs Howarth and legged it past me and back to the first flag. She'd seen there was a path from there running in the right direction, and she ran down it. I jogged along to keep her in view

When she sighted the red rose, she summoned her reserves of energy and broke into a sprint. Vicky shot her in the chest. Twice. They had two minutes left, and got nowhere fast. Lester broke the news over the radio and told them to report to the barn kitchen, where lunch would be waiting. Vicky and I ate in the farmhouse, and the Howarths left us alone to compare notes.

'I was gutted,' said Vicky when we met up. 'I'd put me beret on a stick and put a Glamour on it to look like me, and I was hoping one of them would fall for it. What do you reckon to them, then?'

'Number 1 is a liability. She's not going to make it. It's too close to call between the others. One more test.'

'This soup is gorgeous. And the bread. What test?'

'It's your turn to be shot at. Possibly.'

She looked worried. 'Do I have to take my Ancile off?'

'No. That's the point. You're going to wait in the changing room. Lester's going to give them all paintball guns and put them in the briefing room. I'm going to call them into the office, one by one, and tell them that you're a traitor, and they have to shoot you. When they come in, pretend that I've got your Ancile and react accordingly. It's a moral test.'

Vicky looked alarmed. And worried. 'Was this your idea?'

'Yes. Let's see how they get on.

As part of the test, I showed them an Artefact and said that it was Captain Robson's Ancile, so they'd think she was defenceless. We weren't planning to put Number 1 through this test, and started with Number 4.

'You what?' he said.

'I'm afraid so.'

He peeled his bib off and said, 'No way. I'm done. I'm not joining an organisation with a shoot to kill policy.'

'Good. You've just passed. Well done. Put your bib back on and go through that door to the kitchen. Wait there and don't talk to the others.'

He looked bemused, but put his bib back on and left.

Number 2 went into the changing room and shot at Vicky. Oh dear.

Both Numbers 5 and 6 took a different approach. Instead of shooting Vicky, they tied her up at gun point and got their phones out to call the Constable. Full marks to both of them.

'We won't mess around,' I announced to the group a few minutes later. A minibus had arrived and was waiting in the yard. All their combat uniforms were in the laundry bin and we'd let them sit down.

Numbers 1 and 2 were already in the bus. Number 2 had been full of apologies and said that it, 'wasn't like me. I'm not a violent person. I must be exhausted.' Number 1 had sniffed and said that she had no intention of taking up the post anyway. I just smiled.

That left us with Numbers 4, 5 and 6, or Andy, Saffron and Xavier, as I'd learnt to call them before the moral test. They all looked utterly shattered. 'If you're no longer interested in joining the Watch, please leave now, with my thanks for your time and effort. A glowing reference will appear on your file. Are you still up for it?'

'I am,' said Saffron.

'Me too,' said Andy.

Xavier nodded. 'Yes, sir.'

'Then you've all passed. You're all eligible. Andy, you're going on the reserve list. Saffron, Xavier, on behalf of the Constable and the Duke of Albion, I would like to offer you commissions in the King's Watch as Watch Officers, starting at the rank of lieutenant.'

The emotion got the better of them. As it should. They'd all given everything today. We let them hug it out before holding a brief ceremony. Vicky gave her beret to Andy as a souvenir, to show he'd made the grade, and then I presented Saffron and Xavier with their own RMP headgear. Xavier saluted, and the others joined in.

'The good news,' I said, 'is that you only have to salute and call me *sir* when we're in uniform. The bad news is that your duties start today. You two have to take that bin of filthy uniforms with you on the train and wash them. Take the spares, neatly pressed, to Merlyn's Tower when you're summoned for Induction. That will be soon, and will come from the Constable's office. Until then, you're dismissed and have my permission to celebrate in whatever way you like.'

Lester made one final appearance, and there were final handshakes before Vicky and I headed into the afternoon sunshine. 'Could you drive the first section?' I said. 'My leg's playing up.'

'No problem,' said Vicky, and we climbed into my trusty Volvo.

'Set course for Merlyn's Tower?' she asked.

'Ribblegate Farm first. I need to make sure Scout's Lux levels are topped up. We also need somewhere to get changed. It's against regs to appear at motorway service stations in uniform.'

8 — Welcome Home

'So who gets to choose?' I said. 'Who decides which one of the new recruits gets landed with me?'

'The Boss,' said Vicky firmly. 'She was quite clear that she would make the allocations, but it's fairly clear that Saffron will be stuck with you. Poor lass.'

'Why?'

'She's the better Mage. It's as simple as that. Xavi – Xavier Metcalfe – studied for one year with the last Guardian and was highly rated. Since the Guardian left, he's switched to studying with the Oracle, with focus on Necromancy with a sideline in Occulting. And we were pronouncing his name wrong. He finally had the courage to tell me it's *Zavvy* not *Havvy*. He's not bad, but Saffron has real promise.'

'She seems very driven. Did you know her when you were at Salomon's House?'

'A bit. She's more of Desi's friend than mine. Have you come across the Hawkins family before?'

I pulled my lip and sifted through some of the background reading. 'There was a Hawkins who was Constable in the Edwardian period. And there's one on the Occult Council. Is she related?'

'Aye. Hawkins is one of the older Mage families, and one of the first to adopt Prima Materna for their name.'

It's been known for a long time that aptitude for magick passes through the female line. When women were first admitted to the Invisible College, one of the more forward thinking Mages suggested that magickal families should take their surname from the *Prima Materna* – the first mother of the line. There are complications, though, as I was about to discover.

'You should know that she's also related to the Custodian.'

'Oh.' The Custodian of the Great Work is Heidi Marston, the larger than life senior Artificer at Salomon's House. 'Is Saffron one of Heidi's Gang?'

'Only by default. She's tried to get ahead on her own merits. Sometimes she tries too hard. She's a very good Artificer, though.'

Heidi knows that old magick is on the loose, but she hasn't been directly involved in our campaign to track it down. 'How closely are they related?' I asked.

'Not that close. Heidi's mother had no gift to speak of, and she took her husband's name. Heidi has the right to call herself Hawkins.'

'But Heidi likes to stand out.'

'That she does.'

I shifted in my seat. I really wanted to stretch my leg out, but even the Volvo won't quite let me do that unless I put the seat right down. 'You've seen her a lot more than I have, Vic. Is there anything I should know?'

We were stationary at some traffic lights. We'd be at Ribblegate Farm in ten minutes or so. Vicky drummed her fingers on the steering wheel. 'I don't know. They all asked a lot about you. What you were like to work with. Stuff they had every right to know.'

She paused, and I was dying to ask what she'd told them. Somehow, I resisted.

After some thought, Vicky said, 'She's good, but she's not always as good as she thinks she is. Watch out for that.'

'Thanks, Vic. That's good to know.'

She looked at me sideways. 'Saffron asked if you had a girlfriend. When I said yes, she said, "Thank goodness." You can make of that what you will. Oh, and I asked all of them if they played cricket or supported Sunderland. No on all counts.'

I did of course have another reason to visit Ribblegate Farm. I hadn't forgotten about Stacey while I was in Shawbury, and after Mina dropped off the grid, I'd asked for regular updates. It had been three weeks since we'd left Stacey with the Kirkhams; she'd lasted two weeks before Steroid Boy turned up in the farmyard to take her away. Kelly had said she'd fill me in when we met up.

I got changed and went to see Scout. He had grown a lot, and I'm sure I saw a glint in his eye. That dog is going to be trouble. He's still gorgeous though. Vicky took a lot longer to get changed (I'm just stating a fact), and Kelly came over to see me in the yard.

'I hate to say this,' said Kelly, 'but it really was down to social media. She just couldn't stay off it. Mina helped her create new identities and all that, but she gave too much away, and the next thing you know, he's tracked her down.'

'How was she?'

It was cooler in the shade of the barn, and Kelly wrapped her oversized cardigan round her. 'Stronger, I think. She really wanted to get a job, you know, but all the ones she fancied needed a criminal record check. She wouldn't even apply.'

'What happened?'

Kelly snorted. 'He messaged her, and she called him. We sat up late over a bottle of wine, and I tried talking her out of going with him, but she's convinced that he's changed. How many times have we heard that?' She looked at the farmhouse. 'Perhaps, if she's stronger, he might not try it on quite so much. Perhaps she'll walk away this time. You know what he did?'

'No.'

'The next day, after he took her away, he was back. Wanted the five hundred quid I'd held on to. The one good thing I did was get her a bank account of her own. I transferred it to her. She must have told him I'd hung on to it.'

'Was he violent?'

'Joseph saw him coming.' That's Kelly's father in law. 'When the useless lump came into the kitchen, Joseph was cleaning his shotgun at the table. I said I'd transferred the money back to Mina to stop him getting his hands on it, and he didn't argue.'

'Shame. Thank you so much for everything you did.'

'Conrad, what do you think…'

She was going to ask about Mina, and then she saw the look on my face and turned round. Vicky, now resplendent in skinny jeans and a black top, was walking barefoot over the farmyard. Not even I would do that. She was also holding her phone and looking ill. I gave Scout one last tickle and hurried over to meet her, Kelly right behind me.

'It's Mina,' said Vicky. 'She's on her way back. We need to get a move on.'

'I'll get your stuff,' said Kelly.

'What's happened?' I asked. The question I really wanted to ask was *how come you heard this first?*

'The Boss has been on the phone. It's complicated. Mina's been hurt, somehow. It's not serious or nothing, but she's been in trouble.'

'Trouble?'

'Aye.' She drew a deep breath. 'We have to get to Heathrow. There's enough time before the flight lands. The Boss got a call from the Foreign Office when Mina's plane left India.'

'Eh?'

'I know. What's the GoI?'

I wanted to scream *get on with it.* 'The GoI is the Government of India. The federal government, if you like.'

'Right. The GoI called the Foreign Office to say that Mina was being stripped of her Indian citizenship and deported. They said that the GoI agent accompanying her on the flight would only hand her over to the Constable.'

'What in Nimue's name is that all about? That can only mean that she's been in magickal trouble.'

Kelly appeared with Vicky's uniform over her arm and her trainers in her hand. In the other hand, I was pleased to see a flask. I lit a cigarette while Vicky hopped about putting her shoes on. It was a good job it hadn't rained recently.

Kelly pressed the flask into my hand, along with a packet of Jaffa Cakes. 'Let me know, yeah? When you get a chance.'

'Of course. I'll be back soon for Scout anyway, but I'll tell you what I can when I can.'

'Thanks, Conrad.'

'Was there nothing else?' I asked when we drove out, thinking that Vicky might have something to tell me that was not for mundane ears.

'No. Air India, Terminal 2, 21:35. That's all they said. The accompanying agent has her phone, too. And that's it. I'm so sorry, Conrad.'

'But she's alive and not seriously injured.'

'That's what they said. You know Hannah, she wasn't gonna take that for an answer. She said she pushed and pushed but the Foreign Office didn't have anything else.'

I calculated the flight time in my head. 'She must have heard a few hours ago.'

'She did. She's been trying to work her contacts in Whitehall and India, but no one knows anything. She was on the verge of calling you when I buzzed her to say the assessment was done. She says, and I quote, "I know he'll be mad I told you first, Vicky, but I don't want him driving off and leaving you." I told her you wouldn't have done that.'

'I wouldn't.'

She tried a smile. 'Do you know what she said next? "I know that, but he might well charge into the ladies' toilets and drag you kicking and screaming out of the cubicle." I think she has a point.'

'I think she does.'

Getting to where we wanted to be at Heathrow Airport was a little like being talked down to a strange landing strip by air traffic control. Ruth Kaplan, Hannah's twin sister, was on the phone, guiding me through a series of vehicle check points until we passed the last one and I saw her standing outside a low building in her police inspector's uniform. Handy. She'd already said that Hannah was waiting inside.

A sign on the building said UK Border Force. It wasn't a police station, but it felt very much like one as Ruth got us issued with Visitor badges and taken through security. It was starting to wind down at the end of a long day, and I saw sweaty Border Force employees hanging up their uniforms and getting ready to go home. The British government is not generous when it comes to air conditioning, and it was like a sauna in here.

Ruth had been trusted with a magnetic key, and ushered us into a room marked *Interview Room Six Viewing Gallery. High Security.* I immediately looked for the two-way mirror. It must be behind the closed blinds. There were unlit monitors and silent recording equipment on a desk built against the same wall. And four chairs. None of us made a move to sit down.

'I'm so sorry,' said Ruth. 'I really am, but Hannah gave me this. These.'

She handed over two pieces of paper. One was an email printout and the other was a handwritten note from the Boss. *Give Ruth your case. Don't argue. Leave this to me.*

The case contained the Hammer and its mundane twin. I had spent all day trying to select new Watch Officers who would be part of the solution, and it would be hypocritical of me to disobey a direct order. I passed Ruth the case. She looked very relieved and disappeared out of the door.

'Keep it together, Uncle C,' said Vicky. 'Not long now. She'll be over London, I reckon.'

'This must be the only part of the airport without information screens. Did I see one in the foyer?'

'I'll go one better,' she replied, and got out her phone.

While she was searching for the information, I glanced at the printout. The header information had been cropped off, leaving just the message.

Our agent will hand over the prisoner only to the Constable of the United Kingdom. This must be done in a secure room with no one else present and with an exit to the return flight that must remain open and unlocked at all times.

I put the paper down. I was so tempted to go in search of the plane that I nearly walked out. The only thing that stopped me was that Niði's labyrinth is easier to navigate than the airside of an international airport. Mina would be in that room before I even found the way to the gates.

'Wheels down in ten minutes,' said Vicky.

'Thanks.'

The door opened, and Ruth backed in, carrying a tray. I went to help her and came face to face with Cora Hardisty.

'Dean? What…?'

Vicky took the tray and we all moved away from the door. Cora was looking as dishevelled as the Border Force guards: her linen suit probably looked great first thing this morning. At least she was walking rather than being pushed round in a wheelchair.

She had tears forming in her eyes. She leaned forwards and picked up my hands. Her fingers were hot and slippery against mine. 'I am so sorry, Conrad. So sorry. This is my fault.'

'How???'

'Sit down. Both of you,' said Ruth. She pushed a chair into Cora's legs and she collapsed gratefully. I took a seat next to her. She did not want to let go of my hand. Vicky and Ruth gave us some space. A tiny part of me was glad that Vicky looked as puzzled as I felt.

'Do you remember the Dragon seminar?' said Cora. I nodded. 'When you went for a fag break, Mina wasn't talking about Project Midas. She was pumping me for information about magick in India.'

Vicky drew a sharp breath. I gripped Cora's hands even harder. 'And you told her? And you didn't tell me?'

She shook her head. 'You don't own her, Conrad, and she made me promise. That's the point. She's scared of losing you.'

'I…'

I didn't know what to think. Somewhere inside my head was a man scrabbling to get hold of a cliff edge before he slipped down to the crashing waves and the needle rocks below him. I couldn't get any purchase on this idea at all, until I thought of Miles. Of course.

My shoulders slumped. 'You know. About her husband.'

'Husband?' said Cora.

I let go of one of Cora's hands to wipe my eyes.

I heard Vicky whispering over my head. 'He died. Violently.'

'No, no, no,' said Cora. 'That's not what she meant. She worries about you being in danger, obviously, but that's not why she wanted the information.'

I turned to look at Vicky. Before I could protest my innocence, Vicky said, 'And she doesn't mean losing you to other women, either. Tell him properly, Cora.'

It was Cora's turn to grip my hand. Her wrists aren't as strong as mine, but her nails are a damn sight sharper. 'Listen, Conrad. Mina has been in the presence of the Morrigan. Something I've never done. And she's met the Allfather. She's received the blessing of the Goddess, apparently. She's scared of losing you to magick. She's scared that a mundane partner will never be enough.'

I recoiled from that, physically and emotionally. *Lose me to magick?* How could that be? Cora pulled me back.

'She wanted a way in. Something to put her in the magickal world as more than a bystander.'

'I thought the gods were very sparing on who they enhanced. I now know that the Allfather only chose me because of my link to the Codex.'

'There was more to it than that, Conrad. Mina didn't want power over Lux. She just wanted something. Anything. And I thought she could handle it.'

She finally released my hand. Confession over. Except it wasn't. Not quite.

Vicky, being Vicky, wanted to help. 'And she's survived, hasn't she? She'll be here soon.'

I gave her a smile, to show I'd heard and appreciated what she'd said and that I knew she'd be there for me, but I wasn't done with the Dean yet.

'What was your price?' I said.

Vicky took a step back. Ruth started unwrapping sandwiches. Cora looked at the floor.

It was Vicky who blinked first. 'Tell him, Dean. You owe him that much. Don't worry, everything you've said stays in this room, doesn't it, Ruth?'

'If it's not criminal, Cora, then it's none of my business. It's between you, Mina and Conrad.'

'It's not criminal,' said Cora. She glanced at Ruth. 'But it is a little underhand. We did mention Project Midas. Briefly. I asked Mina to cast her eyes over the accounts for Salomon's House. I thought it might be useful in the election.'

I sat back and took a deep breath. If Mina had paid a high price for the information, I don't think I could have let Cora get away with it. This, I could cope with. 'I can't blame you for that, Cora. I've done worse. A lot worse. Let's focus on the future, shall we? Or the present. I wasn't hungry until you came back with that tray, Ruth.'

She passed me a plate. 'You might think twice when you've tasted it. I think these places have a special magickal Ward that doesn't permit fresh food to enter. I've got tea, too.'

She was right about the sandwich. 'Where's Hannah got to?' I asked.

'She wanted to meet the plane herself. I have to stay in here, and there was no one else she trusted available. Hang on.'

She checked her phone. 'It's at the gate now. I'll get things set up.'

Ruth put down her plate and lifted the blinds. The only surprising thing about Interview Room 6 was the fresh, powder blue paint job. Everything else, from the concrete floor to the bolted down chair was as you'd expect. There were two doors, one to the right and one straight ahead. The one to the right led to the same corridor as our room, the other one was marked *To Gates*. Ruth flicked a couple of switches and the viewing gallery went dark. A crackle from the ceiling told me that the audio feed was now live. 'Press that button and speak into that microphone if you want to be heard in there.'

We dumped half-eaten sandwiches on the tray, and I grabbed a piece of flapjack. I was finishing my tea when the left hand door opened.

I stood up and leaned forward as Hannah came in. She wedged the door open with a piece of folded paper, then moved behind the table. An enormous, stocky Indian man came into the room, trailing Mina behind him. She was attached to his left wrist by a pair of handcuffs. He was at least six foot tall, and must weigh fourteen stone, perhaps more underneath the swirling white robes. He blocked my view of her completely, and he wasn't in a hurry to come any further. He scanned every inch of the room carefully, and judging by the hand gestures, he was using magick to help him.

'My god,' said Vicky. 'I would not want to share an aeroplane toilet with him.'

Ruth coughed. I didn't mind. I'd rather think about the absurdities than the reality. 'Got to give him credit for the moustache though,' I added.

'You're not wrong, Uncle C. That's epic, that 'tache.'

It was. It went round his face like a Red Arrow doing an airshow display.

'Did you just call the Dragonslayer "Uncle Conrad"?' said Cora.

We all burst out laughing at that point. And stopped when the man came further into the room.

Mina's head was up, her hair was held back and her nose was pointing defiantly at any curious bystanders. Fury was the main emotion in her eyes.

And breathe. My Mina was back.

I took a proper look at her, and tried to work out why she looked a funny shape. She was wearing white, too, and she sort of looked like a reverse hunchback – there was a strange lump around her left collar bone. And the outfit didn't look like her clothes. The shalwar trousers were way too long, for one thing, and her Indian wardrobe doesn't have much white in it because...

'They've come here straight from a funeral,' I said. 'That's why they're in white.'

'Poor bairn,' said Vicky. 'Not her mother, surely?'

Mina looked round and spotted the mirror straight away. She didn't take her eyes off it. She lifted her left arm, but it wouldn't rise all the way, and she bent forward to blow a kiss at the mirror. At me.

Her captor hadn't spoken yet. His first action inside the room was to sweep his arm around in an imperious gesture, more like a stage magician than the Mages I'm used to. It worked, though, and when he started speaking, I couldn't hear a word. He'd placed the three of them under a Silence, and everything else unfolded in dumb show.

Hannah was side-on to us, so I could tell when she was speaking. She turned to face Mina and said something. Mina replied, adding a nod, then a shake of the head to the next question. I could guess what Hannah had asked: *Are you okay? Have they mistreated you?*

The Indian Mage had been carrying a large briefcase in his left hand, the handle disappearing into his meaty fist. He gently lifted it, tugging Mina's arm along, and placed the case on the table. He popped the catch and took out a piece of paper. He spoke. Hannah picked up the paper and read it. Carefully. She asked Mina another question, and Mina pointed to the briefcase. Hannah shook her head in disgust and took out a pen. She signed the paper with a flourish and slid it back to the man.

He nodded, and touched the handcuffs with his right hand. They unlocked. It was funny, but my brain added the *click* noise that my eyes said should be there. Or I'd just experienced telepathy. One or the other. Mina extracted her hand and rubbed her wrist, carrying it over to her left side because her arm wasn't keen on bending. Oh dear.

The Indian Mage reached into his briefcase and took out Mina's laptop, phone and purse. He placed them on the table and gave her a paper to sign. Don't you love bureaucracy? She signed.

He snapped shut the case and swirled his hand again.

His voice was cultured, even and deep. 'I have dreamt many years of coming to England and meeting the Constable of Merlyn's Tower. It is such a sadness to me that it should be on an occasion like this.'

Hannah couldn't bring herself to play along, and simply said, 'I hope you have a safe journey.'

They nodded to each other, and the Mage headed off to his plane. He pulled the folded paper out from under the door and closed it behind him.

'Who else is with you, Conrad?'

It was so good to hear her voice again that I just stared at the glass. Mina's eyes dilated in panic, and Ruth pressed the button. 'This is Ruth Kaplan. I'm with Conrad, Vicky and Cora. He's a bit overcome, but he'll be with you in a second.'

'Could you all come?' said Mina. 'There's something you all need to see.'

I jerked out of my paralysis and pressed the button. 'We're on our way, love.'

Ruth led the procession out of the viewing gallery, down the corridor and round to the interview room. Her magnetic key let us in, and she held the door for me to go first.

Mina held up her hand as I approached. 'Just a kiss,' she said, turning her left shoulder away from me. With an audience like that, we weren't going to go for the full *Gone with the Wind*, but I did let her know how much I'd missed her. It was mutual.

When we'd disengaged, Mina turned to Hannah. 'Thank you for coming. I am so sorry to inconvenience you.'

Hannah snorted. 'That depends on how good your story is. I have never had anything like this happen before, but you're not okay, are you Mina? Why do you need an audience?'

'Because you all need to see this, and I don't want to do it more than once.' She looked at Vicky. 'Can you help me get this kameez off? Thank goodness it's too big for me.'

What on earth was going on? The baggy white kameez tunic, long sleeved, covers everything you'd want covered in public. Mina froze for a second. 'We're not being recorded, are we?'

'No,' said Ruth. 'Definitely not.'

With Vicky's help, Mina eased the kameez over her head, pulling her left arm out last. My jaw clenched until my teeth hurt when I saw her. There were deep scratches along her right abdomen, but they were healing. She wasn't wearing a bra, and that was shocking enough, but not as shocking as the big dressing above her left breast and the matching one on her left bicep.

Behind me, Cora moaned softly and sat down on one of the chairs.

'Oy vey,' said Hannah.

'Hashem preserve us,' said Ruth.

'Bugger me,' said Vicky.

Mina gave a grim smile. 'It gets worse. Conrad, can you peel off the dressing. It's overkill. The wound has nearly healed, but the prison doctor wouldn't let me travel without it. Same with my arm, but you need to see my chest first.'

There was a lot of padding, held on by a criss-cross of medical tape. I got my fingernail under three or four of the strips and peeled them back. 'I'm going all in with the rest. Ready?' She nodded, and I ripped it off.

Underneath the dressing, about four inches wide, was a burn. A burn that was healing into a blue colour. Magick pulsed faintly from it, but it was the shape that made me gasp. I stood back and let everyone else see. Burned and carved into my poor love's chest, just above her breast, was this image:

Hannah and Ruth were stunned into silence. Cora had covered her eyes, and it was Vicky who spoke first. 'Ohmygod! Mina! Whoever did this is truly evil.'

'They are evil, but the image is not. Hannah, Ruth, I am so sorry to show you this, because I know what it means to you and every other Jew in the world. Forgive me. It was not meant to be like this.'

Hannah pulled herself upright. 'And I know what it means in India. Good luck and prosperity, isn't it?'

'Yes.'

Hannah half raised her hand towards the mark. 'It's an Ancile. A living Ancile burned into your flesh. How? Why?'

'You should always be careful what you wish for,' said Mina quietly. 'I wished for magick, and this is what I got. My arm got burnt, too, when I tried to stop them. It is almost completely healed, under the dressing. I think we've seen enough. Vicky?'

'Right.'

She shook her head when I offered to put the dressing back on. 'It doesn't hurt much, but the medic didn't want any awkward questions.' Vic helped her get the kameez back on, and Mina put on a brave smile. 'Myfanwy must know, but no one else, please?'

'Of course,' said Hannah. 'Let's get out of here.'

'Not yet,' said Mina. 'There's something else, and it's best if I say it now, while you're all here. It concerns the Watch.'

'It's a bit crowded in here,' said Cora. 'I'll wait outside if it's Watch business.'

'And me,' said Ruth. 'Would you like me to get you anything? Tea? Food?'

'Tea would be very welcome,' said Mina. 'The food in business class is very good. I am not hungry, thank you.'

Vicky blurted out, 'I've gotta ask, Mina, were you handcuffed to Mr Moustache the whole time?'

She laughed. A proper laugh. 'That would have been the worst torture of all. No. He undid the handcuffs when we were in the air. He was a perfect gentleman.'

Ruth opened the door to leave, and Cora got up, too.

'Please stay, Dean,' said Mina. 'You must sit down. You need to rest more than I do.'

Cora sank back. 'I thought my contact was just an academic. I'm so sorry, Mina.'

'What happened is not your fault. Please. I am grateful for your help.'

I got one of the movable chairs and insisted that Mina sit down. I couldn't wait any longer. 'What happened, love? How did it come to this?'

'Stand behind me, Conrad. You are too tall, and I want to hold your hand.'

I did. I stood behind her and she reached up to take my hand.

'I have been in one of those cells with no magick for nearly a week. It didn't affect me at all, and they looked after me. Hannah, could you read the charge on that sheet?'

Hannah took the paper and scanned it. 'Sacrilege and destruction of religious property. Really?'

'That is what I pleaded guilty to. How I got there is complicated.'

Ruth reappeared with a cup of tea and took up as discreet a position as she could.

'Thank you,' said Mina. 'Before the Sword of Brahman took my laptop away, I did a lot of work on Project Midas.'

Vicky had had one brief chat with Hannah on the journey down from Ribblegate Farm. Hannah had told her that the Sword of Brahman is India's answer to the Watch. Their chief had not been returning Hannah's calls. I'm guessing he would know that Mina has been handed over.

'This can wait,' said Hannah.

'I'd rather not. I want to do something positive.'

'If you're sure?'

'I'm sure. We had several monsoons while I was there. During the second one, I had a flash of inspiration.' She allowed herself a smile. 'I wondered why the data seemed familiar, and then it came to me: I was looking at a massive case of money laundering. Feel free to disapprove, Constable.'

Hannah shook her head. 'Repentance is always in fashion at Merlyn's Tower. I wouldn't have let Conrad in otherwise.' Without thinking, she took off her headscarf to re-tie it.

It was the first time that Mina had seen the damage to Hannah's skull. She stared, then quickly looked away. When the scarf was back in place, Mina continued. 'Conrad, how much do you trust that Gnome, Lloyd Flint, and the rest of his clan?'

Hannah's eyes narrowed with interest, and Cora looked up, too.

I pulled my lip with my free hand. 'Lloyd, I trust with my life. Absolutely. The others, not at all. Lloyd doesn't trust them much, either.'

'It is as I thought,' said Mina. 'I need to see that Dwarf, Niði. He is the only innocent one. And Lloyd needs to take me there so that you can look him in the eye, Conrad. If the Dwarf confirms what I've thought, there is a lot of laundered gold sitting with the Clan Flint.'

Hannah was struggling with this. She didn't want Mina in any further danger, but this was too good a lead to ignore. She looked at me over Mina's head. The message was clear: it's up to you.

I had no problem with Mina getting involved. Well, I did, but as Cora pointed out, I don't own her. If she went with me, I could keep an eye on her. My problem was Vicky. I don't think a prolonged underground adventure is what Vicky needs at the moment.

I cleared my throat. 'If I might suggest, ma'am, it would be good if Hawkins or Metcalfe became involved. Coming with us could be their first field assignment.'

Hannah nodded her head. 'Good idea. When?'

'Monday would be good,' said Mina. 'This could all change if we leave it too long. If it hasn't already.'

'Right,' said Hannah. 'Vicky, you're coming back to London with me. We can do Saffron and Xavi's inductions on Friday. And your promotion to Watch Captain. Conrad, you're going to take Mina home, and don't even think of coming up to town. Clear?'

'Ma'am.'

'We'll head off,' said Ruth. The room was a lot bigger without them.

Vicky moved next. 'Give us your car keys, Conrad. I'll get me stuff.'

Mina let go of my hand, and I moved away. Vicky bent down to whisper something to Mina, who replied, 'That would be very good. Thank you.'

'Wait here a minute, Conrad,' said Vicky.

'Let's wait outside,' said Hannah. 'I've seen enough interview rooms in my life.'

'You're not the only one,' said Mina.

I picked up the bits and pieces, and we gathered in the corridor. Being a good Airman, I even got the tray from the viewing gallery. When I returned from finding a rubbish bin, Vicky was leading Mina away, leaving Hannah and I alone.

'Thank you, Hannah.' I said. 'I owe you big time for this. I can't imagine what you must have felt seeing that … sign. And to see it like that, and then carry on. Thank you.'

Hannah shrugged. A very Jewish shrug that said *we have all seen worse and lived.* 'Don't worry, Conrad, I'll make sure you do extra assignments to pay me back.'

The girls emerged from the ladies toilet. Mina was dressed in some of Vicky's clothes. She looked almost normal, and judging from the fit of the sleeves, she'd taken the dressing off her arm. She bowed to Hannah, and we walked out of the Border Force building hand in hand. It was dark outside, but my sunshine was back.

Mina had her priorities straight. 'Do you have a charger in the car, Conrad? My phone battery is flat.'

9 — Don't mind me

There was a charger in the car. Mina fiddled with her phone while I set the satnav and drove out of the Border Force compound. We'd be home in two hours. I accelerated on to the motorway and turned to face her for a second. 'Your mother?'

'She died on Saturday, while I was under arrest. I agreed not to fight the deportation if they let me attend the funeral. Ha! I have now brought more disgrace on the Guptas than even Maamajee thought possible. Turning up to the funeral handcuffed to a police officer was a master stroke.'

'I am so sorry, love.'

'I know. And I am so sorry. I could see it on all their faces, you know.'

'Whose faces?'

'Hannah. Cora. Ruth, even, and above all, Vicky. They were all as worried about you as they were about me.' She held up a hand. 'Don't deny it, Conrad. It's good. Accept it. I do. I am so sorry I couldn't tell you what was happening, but the Sword of Brahman are like you. They follow their own laws. They would let me contact no one.'

'I was on the verge of coming to look for you.'

'I guessed. That was another reason to get out. There are two good things to come out of this.'

'Are you counting the controversial burn mark as one of them?'

'Yes, but it's not a burn. I was tattooed with boiling ink. It was as bad as it sounds.'

I couldn't get my head round that. She patted my thigh. 'It was over quickly. They made the four dots first, then gave me anaesthetic. Do you want to know the other good thing?'

'I want to know everything.'

'You will. The other good thing is that Papaji's family have taken me in. Metaphorically speaking. I will tell you everything, after we have called Myvvy and you have told me how Stacey is getting on.'

She cried more about Stacey than she did when telling me some of the terrible things that she'd been through. I listened all the way back to Elvenham, and after. Myfanwy had left food out and was spending the night with Ben, to give us some space. I still can't believe some of it, especially that her real offence was entering a temple of magick whilst menstruating. Mina had put together some complicated deal involving her late father's family, a priest, a divorce and a dowry. Mina's slice of the action was supposed to be an Ancile.

She was taken into a temple-within-a-temple, and things went from bad to worse. Just before they'd boiled the ink to tattoo her, the chief priest had said, 'You have defiled the temple, and we shall defile you.' On the way out, back in the public area, she had picked up a brass statue, smashed it into her escort and then run amok destroying some of the images. I don't blame her.

At the end of the story, I'd asked her how she felt about Ganesh after what she'd been through.

She pointed to the troth ring on my right hand. 'Some of those who claim to worship Odin are white supremacists. Some Christians, and many Muslims, are homophobic bigots. Some Hindus are patriarchal misogynists. The gods do not police their flocks in this life.'

I have never been tattooed with boiling ink. I don't know if I'd be quite as philosophical as Mina.

She'd been forced to leave everything in India except the borrowed funeral clothes and her laptop. A cousin was going to send some of her stuff on. In the morning, she came down for tea and toast, then went back upstairs for a long bath. It was another hot day, and I went into the garden for the first time in weeks to see how the landscape gardeners had got on. I was not expecting to be greeted by a familiar voice.

'Is that you, Conrad? It must be.'

I turned round to find Erin Slater standing by the house. She's that Witch from the Arden Foresters who Vicky and I met in the adventure of the Phantom Stag, the one who'd wanted to meet Myfanwy. She was carrying a battered, Victorian looking carpet bag. For that to have survived this long, it must be enchanted. I walked over. 'Was Myfanwy expecting you?' There was an edge in my voice. I couldn't help it.

She looked embarrassed. 'She said you wouldn't mind. I've been here every day this week.'

'Didn't she get in touch last night?'

'There was a missed call, but she didn't leave a message. Is there a problem?'

'She's at Ben's. Do you know the way?'

'Yeah. Can I leave my car here? The parking by his cottage is terrible. I'll walk round and get out of your way.'

'Sorry, Erin. Of course you can. We'll catch up later, I'm sure. Myfanwy will explain.'

Ten minutes later, Myvvy sent me the most apologetic text message I've ever received. Apparently, her old school friend Erica was wondering why she shouldn't come round when she had no idea where Myfanwy lived. Myfanwy had sent last night's message to the wrong person.

Erica - Erin. Easy mistake to make. I made Mina a fresh cup of tea and took it up to the family bathroom.

The mark on her arm was a neat line of blue ink and scar tissue. 'It's magick, too,' said Mina, 'but no one knows what will happen. It might just throb when I go to temple.'

'Do you want to go away? We could check into a spa hotel until Monday.'

She shook her head. 'When I get out of this bath, I want to be normal. I want to go to the Inkwell tonight and drink wine. I want to go to ladies cricket tomorrow and kick those interlopers' arses back to Allington. Hah! Our greatest enemy will not put cuckoos in our nest.'

'Steady on, love. You've never been to Allington, never mind developed a life-long hatred of their cricket team.'

'But you have. It's the one thing that Jules Bloxham and I agree on.'

'What else do you want to do?' I asked.

'Put down roots. Like a tree. Here.'

'In the bath?'

'Shut up and get my special shampoo. You can wash my hair.'

Myfanwy came round the next morning, still full of apologies, and spent a long time in the garden with Mina. I served them lemonade and caught up with three weeks of domestic housekeeping. You know the sort of thing.

One of the calls I had to return was to one of the extended team of Merlyn's Tower Irregulars – people who have helped me out above and beyond the call of money. The Kirkhams were founder members, as was Alain Dupont, a French postgrad student in London. Alain can hold his nerve in very difficult circumstances and is an eloquent shrugger, both qualities I admire highly. I've tried to set him up with Vicky in the past. No luck so far.

'Good news,' he said. 'I 'ave an interview with your sister's company next week.'

The world of wealth management is a bit like the world of magick: small and interconnected. My sister, Rachael, doesn't have a Military Cross or the title *Dragonslayer*, but she's an even bigger name in her world than I am in mine. I promised Alain that I'd get him an interview for a placement with Rachael's firm, and I had. That left me with a debt to Rachael. I'm working on it.

Erin reappeared in the afternoon and joined us for tea before women's cricket practice. According to Myfanwy, Erin was a bit of a lost soul, and had been more or less evicted from her workshop in Stratford, where she practised the art of magickal Enscribing. Erin, too, was full of apologies when she arrived. I waved them away and sat her down in the kitchen.

'Are things not too good in the Foresters?' I asked.

'I'm from Bristol, and I only went up to Henley in Arden to get away from the Daughters of the Goddess. I thought a mixed circle might be more fun. After Ioan died, it's become so cliquey that I don't fit in any more. I'm a bit of an outsider there. I'm still going to gatherings, but the guy who leased me space in his Scriptorium is a Materianist and he wanted shot of me.'

'Serves you right for waving a shotgun at Aaron.'

'Says the man who carries an automatic everywhere.'

'Fair point. I tend not to make accusations without evidence, though.'

She grinned. 'Touché. You have a lovely house, Conrad, and Myfanwy's great company.' She shrugged. 'I've been working here all week. Don't worry, I haven't been in your study. We've actually set up a place in one of the stables, given that you haven't got any horses in them. I was going to offer to pay, if you'll have me.'

I'd spent a lot of money renovating the old stables recently. I'd hoped to have a horse in them, but I hadn't got round to getting my paddock back from the farmer who rents it off me.

'It's not really designed for human habitation, and definitely not when the winter comes, but you can have it for nothing until the end of June, if Mina doesn't mind, and we'll see.'

'Mina doesn't mind,' said Mina, appearing from the hall. 'You must be Erin. Of course you can work here. More importantly, can you play cricket?'

She could play cricket. Wonder of wonders, she was actually an excellent slip fielder. Since my last appearance, Clerkswell Ladies Cricket Club had become a legal entity and acquired its own kit. In two weeks' time, they were going to play a friendly match against one of the teams from Cheltenham. One week after that, it would be very *un*friendly.

Clerkswell Men play in Division Two of the East Gloucestershire league. Every year, we also play one game against Allington, for the Clarke-Briggs cup. It's been held annually for over a hundred and twenty years. If we're in the same division as them, it's presented after one of the regular league games, but for the last five years, they've been in Division One, and a special game has been arranged. We haven't won it for ten years. That's a long time.

When Clerkswell host Allington in the special cup match this year, it will be preceded by a twenty over women's game. I've already messaged Hannah and told her that only an imminent zombie invasion will keep me away. After tonight's practice, the committee will be deciding who to appoint as captain. It's a two horse race.

I would gladly step down as bowling coach, if they could find anyone who could do the job half as well. They can't, so I put them through their paces until it was time for a pint in the Inkwell while the committee met in the pavilion. Mina was more determined than ever to find out about magick, and dragged poor Erin into a corner to pump her for information while Ben and I made ourselves comfortable outside.

'Who's ended up on the committee?' I asked after we'd compared notes on tonight's practice.

'Jules Bloxham is chair and Miss Parkes is honorary president, but she still gets a vote. Putting Nell forward for secretary was a cunning plan, too. Nell nominated Myfanwy to the committee on the grounds that the team was Myfanwy's idea. No one could object to that. Jules got her friend to be treasurer.'

The two other members of the committee were the vicar and a woman I'd never heard of. The two candidates for captain were, of course, Myfanwy and Juliet Bloxham herself.

'How do you think it'll go?'

Ben made a sour face. 'Myfanwy is going to refuse the nomination. She'd love to do it, but as she can't leave the village, it would be a nonsense. She's also going to 'fess up and say that she has an anxiety disorder that means she can't travel. They'll think she's bonkers, of course, but you can't argue with that, can you?'

'She is bonkers.'

'I know. I wouldn't have her any other way. Cheers.' We drank to Mad Myvvy and Ben asked if I wanted to be rotated into the team for tomorrow's game. It was a home match, against difficult opponents.

'Yes please. How are the wedding plans coming along?'

'Don't. Do you know what the prick did last weekend? He actually booked rooms at the Ellenborough for mum and dad, as well as him and Carole. They didn't set foot in the village all weekend, and I had to go over there for Sunday lunch. At least with Myfanwy starting work in the shop she had a good excuse for not going down there. I pushed Isaac again to have the ceremony in St Michael's, but he was adamant. The hotel have had a cancellation, and they've booked it for Saturday the twentieth of September.'

'This year? That's a bit quick, isn't it. I thought weddings took at least eighteen months to organise.'

He gave me a dark look. 'Carole jumped at it. She said they've been getting on so well that she'd rather do it now.'

I could not afford Isaac Fisher on my to-do list. If he were avoiding me – or Vicky, or Myvvy – for a good reason, it would come out sooner or later. I let it go with a grunt.

'Sorry to hear about Mina's mother,' said Ben. 'Myfanwy sometimes thinks I'm a carved ornament, you know.'

Where had that come from? To my knowledge, Ben had never used an image like that before. 'What d'you mean?'

He put his pint down. 'Mina disappears to India for weeks and goes off the grid. She comes back with no notice, and Myfanwy spends all day talking to her about it. Yet when I ask her what happened in India, Myfanwy gives me a load of rubbish about Bollywood films.' He picked up his drink and finished it. 'Another?'

'Please. You have the patience of a saint, Ben. I'm not sure I could put up with it.'

'It's worth it. She's worth it.'

I turned to look away from the pub. The light was fading, casting its last shadows across the pub garden. The Inkwell borders a meadow, with a post-and-wire fence separating them. The wooden posts cast long shadows over the grass. Nine of them. You could almost say they were nine wands.

Ben came back with Mina and Erin, as well as more drinks. Myfanwy wasn't far behind. She said the committee had named her senior vice-captain, and we drank to that. Sometimes life's pleasures really are that simple.

The question of the day was this: *What do you wear to meet a Dwarf?*

The answer of the day was NOT this: *Well, I'd wear linen jacket and…*

Mina had not been happy with my first answer, so I'd pointed out that:

a) England was in the middle of a heatwave and

b) Dwarves work with white hot metal and have forges to heat it and

c) the canal tunnels are cold, damp and draughty.

Apparently, that was no help, so I shut up.

Mina had opted for white trainers, black leggings and a loose red top with elbow-length sleeves. The mark on her arm didn't hurt much, but she wasn't quite ready for it to be seen in public. In a few moments, we'd find out what Saffron was wearing when the 10:32 from London arrived at New Street Station in Birmingham.

'You must be used to this,' said Mina.

'What? Hanging around railway stations waiting for strange women?'

'Give me strength! No. I meant having to work with someone new at a moment's notice.'

'Pretty much. In the RAF, I could be sure they've had the same training as me. Not this time.'

'Is that her? With the hair? By Ganesh's tusk, she looks so young. Or I am suddenly old?'

'If you're old, I'm ancient.'

'You are.'

It was Saffron. She had opted for a sportier but otherwise identical version of Mina's outfit. She also had a backpack, a handbag and a large suitcase.

'Has she packed for the apocalypse?' said Mina.

'Probably. I did say that there might be a few overnights.'

I didn't need to wave. Saffron headed over and I made the introductions before leading the way to the local train.

'You were at the Dragon seminar, weren't you, Mina?' said Saffron. I mentally gave her a plus for observational skills, then remembered that she'd passed the assessment. Still good, though.

'I was,' said Mina. 'Just keeping an eye on him.'

'Does he need an eye keeping on him?' said Saffron. There was a mixture of banter and concern in her voice. She was wondering what Vicky hadn't told her.

'Oh yes,' said Mina gravely. 'And that will be your job soon. Good luck.'

'You're scaring her, Mina.'

'Oh no,' said Saffron. 'I'll keep him in line.'

The clapped out bone-shaker of a train that would take us to the heart of the Black Country was already spewing diesel fumes on to the platform. We climbed into the carriage along with night shift workers, students and a collection of pensioners suddenly eligible for their free travel. Mina grabbed a corner pair of facing seats, and Saffron built an intimidating wall of luggage.

'How did your induction go?' I asked.

'Scary. I could feel the power in that well. I kept looking over my shoulder in case she appeared.'

Saffron is a Watch Officer. She has a Badge of Office, and to get it she had to go down to the basement of Merlyn's Tower and sign the Annex of Westphalia. In the centre of the basement is a well, and that well is one of the homes of Nimue. Watch Captains, like me, have to drink from her hand. She is very scary.

'And you have an Ancile?' I asked that question because when I first met Vicky, neither of us had one. It nearly cost us both our lives.

Saffron nodded, a gesture that went awry when the train jumped over a set of points. 'Yeah. Auntie Heidi made me one when I was eighteen.'

'Is that what you call her?' said Mina, whose observational skills are second to none. She'd clocked Heidi Marston at Newton's house.

Saffron adjusted her hair. It was something she must do a lot. 'Only to wind her up. At college, I have to refer to her as Custodian or I get in deep shit.' She looked at Mina again. I'm sure she could sense the Ancile on her, and also that Mina is not magickal. She half formed a question in her head, then abandoned it and turned to me. 'What's the briefing for this mission? Just so I don't put my foot in it.'

All I'd said was that we were meeting a Dwarf, and I was reluctant to bring her any further in just yet. 'Escort duty, mostly. Mina needs some information for a bigger operation. Depending on Niði's answers, we may need to look elsewhere or we may have some business with the Gnomes. I trust Lloyd Flint, but we'll be playing our cards close. OK?'

'Gotcha. Right.'

We arrived at the first stop. There were five more before we got to our destination, Coseley. A couple of students got on and sat behind us, so conversation turned away from magick. Mina did ask a lot of questions about Saffron's background, and the poor kid got more and more embarrassed as Mina forensically dissected a childhood of privilege, private school and a fast track to the top table at Salomon's House.

95

When we got off the train, Saffron insisted on struggling alone with her bags up the ramp and over the bridge to the car park. We walked in front, and Mina whispered to me, 'What on earth is she doing slumming it with the King's Watch? No offence, but she's either a spy or she has issues.'

'Slumming it?'

'Would I be working for the parish council if I could get a job with Price Waterhouse?'

'If you didn't have a conviction for fraud, dear, I'm sure you'd be running Price Waterhouse by now.'

Mina turned her nose up and maintained a dignified silence until a maroon people carrier pulled in to the car park and Lloyd got out of the passenger side. He still wasn't driving, then, but he'd added a short prosthetic to his left arm. He was wearing a sweatshirt, and a metal prong stuck out of the sleeve, a bit like a giant tuning fork.

Lloyd is a Gnome of Clan Flint. Not just that, he's the Clan Second and he co-opted me to be the Clan's Swordbearer during our last encounter. He also cut off his own left arm at the elbow. Gnomes are master Artificers, and I'm sure magick will furnish something more impressive than the prong one day.

Gnomes are long lived and will get through a lot of wives. Lloyd was still on his first, Anna, and he trusted her more than any of his clan. I'd met her, briefly, and she got out of the car with a scowl.

'He didn't say who you was last time,' she pronounced. 'If I'd known it was you, I'd've give you a piece of my mind.'

Anna is a good head taller than Lloyd. A striking woman in many ways, and possessed of a fine Black Country accent. Saffron was already frowning as she tried to understand her.

Anna wasn't finished yet. 'Last time you took Lloyd down the mine, he come back with only one arm. Try not to let it happen again.'

'I won't. I will. Of course.'

'And if he does get summat lopped off, mek sure it's his head, then I can examine it, 'cos he needs his head examined.'

Mina bowed and brought her hands together. 'Namaste.'

Anna sniffed and turned away from me. 'Pleased to meet you. I'm Anna.'

'I'm Mina. Would it be possible for you to take a couple of bags? Just until we're done.'

'Of course, duck. I'll load 'em up.'

'We can't use the front entrance,' said Lloyd when Saffron's luggage was stowed and Anna had driven off. 'I'm sure that Irina or the Clan have put cameras on the tunnel to Niði's Hall, but they don't know about his new door. It didn't take him long to get online and buy a phone, you know. It's not far to walk. Five minutes, max.'

Niði the Dwarf has been out of circulation for thirty years, trapped in his own Hall. During that time, a Persian Mage called Irina had infiltrated Clan

Flint, and was our prime suspect for the money laundering. Irina had also sprayed my head with acid, so you could say we all had a score to settle.

As we walked along, Lloyd wasn't entirely happy that Mina wouldn't share her findings yet. I gave him a look and said, 'Lloyd, she hasn't shared them with me or the Constable either. She's a perfectionist when it comes to data.'

He turned his attention to Saffron. 'Are you one of the Hawkins clan?'

She looked a little nervous, but held her own. This was the first time she'd met a Gnome, and they can be intimidating. Especially to women. 'We're a family, not a clan. And we're not mafia, either. Some of us happen to be Mages, that's all.'

'Your mother is the top Occulter working in private practice. Your first cousin once removed is the Custodian of the Great Work at Salomon's House. And that's just the headlines. I'd say you were pretty connected.'

That was too much for Saffron. She looked down and blushed. Mina wasn't having that. 'Give her a break, Mr Flint. It's bad enough for her that she has to work with Conrad, never mind you having a go, too.'

'I'm used to it,' said Saffron, 'but thanks anyway.'

'How's the clan?' I said.

'Difficult,' said Lloyd. 'Wesley has doubled down and refused to admit he did anything wrong. There's nothing I can do unless I call him out over it. My brother is all for taking him on. It doesn't help that Niði has locked himself in again and won't take sides or give testimony. It's a good job he bought that phone, or I'm not sure how we'd have got to see him.' He turned back to Mina. 'Do you really need to see Niði and only Niði? Can't Hledjolf help?'

'No,' said Mina. She added a smile to soften it a little.

It felt weird to be talking to a Gnome about a Dwarf while we walked along an everyday footpath in the bright sunshine. We climbed a slight rise and a wisp of wind brought a waft of decomposing waste.

'Urgh,' said Saffron. 'What's that smell?'

Lloyd grinned. 'Money. And our destination. Over that bridge, see?'

He pointed to a small footbridge over a canal. On the other side was a great pile of rotting rubbish, and behind it a slew of metal clad buildings, one of which had the tall chimney of an incinerator.

'This is one of ours,' said Lloyd. 'It saves waste from going to landfill and generates green electricity. Makes a tidy profit, too.'

'Not what I'd call green,' said Saffron.

We crossed the footbridge and the smell got worse. Swarms of flies descended on us, just to make our lives complete.

'You take me to the most romantic places,' said Mina.

'Wait until you see Niði's Hall.'

Across the footbridge, a path led round to the right, circling the waste site and disappearing. Lloyd turned left, where there was just a narrow ledge of iron grating between the canal and the solid concrete wall.

'It has to be strong to stop leakage,' said Lloyd, patting the wall. 'Just another ten metres.' He looked at Mina. 'You can't go last. There's Wards and you'll fall in the cut if you hit them.'

'The cut?'

'The canal. Conrad and – Saffron, was it? – will form a magickal bridge.'

He turned to the side and shuffled along the ledge. It had not been designed with my size in mind, and I let my back hug the wall. Mina followed.

About four metres along, the wall tingled against my back, pushing me away from it. It wasn't a strong Ward, just enough to deter adventurous children. I pushed back, physically and mentally, until I was past the Ward and onto a larger ledge, formed where the retaining wall veered away from the canal. I held out my left hand and guided Mina over the dangerous zone.

'I felt that,' she said. 'On my arm. It itched like crazy.'

'Interesting.'

Saffron had passed the Ward, too, and made straight for an unremarkable section of concrete wall. 'Wow,' she said. 'That is beautiful work.'

Mina grinned. 'Looks like you've got a live one here, Conrad.'

I stared at the wall, trying to open my Sight. Nothing. I closed my eyes and did the same. A light flared on my retina, and I opened my eyes in reflex. There, instead of concrete, was an ornate pair of stone doors surrounded by blocks of stone covered in runes. I kept my focus on the door and reached out my hand to Mina.

She grasped it and sucked in her breath. 'Amazing. Finally, a door my height.'

Lloyd took out an Artefact and presented it to the doors. With a shouted command in Old High North Germanic, the doors parted. I had to bend nearly double. Even Lloyd had to duck.

Beyond the doors, stairs led straight down in a vicious drop. As with most Dwarven places, it was lit by glowing stones in the vaulted ceiling rather than lightsticks. No one spoke as we focused on the slimy steps and uneven walls.

We emerged on to an underground dock next to an underground canal. I stroked the wall and said, 'We've bypassed the boat lift, haven't we? This is the same level as Niði's new Hall.'

'You're right,' said Lloyd. He pointed right, to the north east. 'Niði won't let us use that entrance. Cycling the boat lift costs too much Lux at the minute. This is only the second time he's let me in since we were last here.'

'What's wrong?'

Lloyd put his fingers in his mouth and made a piercing whistle. 'The boat'll be here soon.' He looked down the left tunnel. 'Niði has had a lot of catching up to do. He needs to rebuild his strength and repair his Hall. He's very vulnerable, right now. Vulnerable for a Dwarf, that is.'

The boat dock wasn't very big. Just large enough to make a platform to access the stairs we'd come down, and the canal itself was barely wider than a standard narrowboat. After all, the only traffic was internal, so it didn't need to be any bigger. Mina shivered at the sudden change in temperature, and Saffron joined in.

The left tunnel lit up suddenly, and we could see a flat-bottomed plastic boat moving towards us, soundlessly and without any obvious motor.

Saffron wrapped her arms round herself. 'Is it just me, or does that look a lot like transport to Hades?'

It wasn't just her: I'd been thinking exactly the same.

Lloyd leaned down and grabbed the boat with one hand. He pushed up his left sleeve and used his prosthetic prong to grip the boat and keep it steady. Gnomes have enormous upper body strength. 'In you get.'

The little boat was cosy, but stable. Lloyd got in last. I'd say he got in at the stern, but this craft was blunt at both ends. It was only the stern because we were going left. He touched the flat back of the boat and murmured something. With a jolt that nearly threw him in the water, the giant punt moved forwards. I'd been gripping the sides for balance, and let go when one of them came dangerously close to the wall. Mina grabbed the nearest steady object: me. Saffron looked like she'd been punting all her life, and stared at the rough hewn tunnel in awe.

'You have brought an offering, haven't you?' said Lloyd.

'Saffron?' I said.

'Yeah. I picked it up from Vicky at the station this morning.'

We lapsed into silence after that.

Brighter lights ahead signalled our arrival at Niði's Hall. The canal split to form two basins either side of a central dock, and Lloyd headed to starboard. The boat drifted into the dock, close to some steps, and he grabbed a bollard. We climbed out, and I gave him a hand up. I'd been here before, and knew the way to go, so Lloyd said, 'Over to you, Watch Captain. My work is done until it's time to go back.' Lloyd stood aside to let us go first, and tagged along behind as we left the dock.

The last time I'd been here, the lower Hall had been a work in progress, with half-finished arches and very little decoration. It was hard to believe the transformation.

Instead of leading to a rough tunnel, the dock now led to a colonnade of Gothic arches. If you peeked through them into the unlit spaces beyond, you could see piles of stone waiting to be taken away. There were a couple of new side-tunnels now, barely illuminated. Dwarves have a very low tolerance for light, and in their private spaces it's barely above pitch black. They usually put on a show for visitors, and that's what Niði had done in his receiving room.

It wasn't quite as tall or as big as a cathedral. Think well-appointed parish church, as constructed for a horror film. It had more of the soaring, elegant arches and light came from where clerestory windows would be if we were above ground. Not being a church, there was no altar or stained glass in the east end, and the arches there were a continuation of the sides. What those arches did have was the beginnings of decoration and carving. From what I can see, Dwarves prefer to build first, then carve. Humans wouldn't do that because we'd mess it up. Dwarves are nothing if not confident.

Niði obviously hadn't finished his workshops, because there was a forge to one side, glowing with magickal and mundane heat. No one was shivering now. Niði was standing at the forge, working something in the hot coals and taking it out to give it the occasional bash with a hammer.

'Master!' I said.

The Dwarf looked up. Up being the operative word.

'He really is shorter than me,' said Mina. 'I don't believe it.'

Niði took out his work and put it in a cooler part of the forge. He took off his leather apron and dropped it on top of a nearby bench. If you want to know where Dwarves, who rarely venture above ground, get hold of leather aprons, it's best not to ask. Apparently.

He came over to us, and we bowed low. Mina added namaste.

'We come in peace and seek knowledge,' I said. 'Please, accept this gift.'

Saffron stepped forwards and unzipped her backpack. She took out a small box and offered it gingerly to the Dwarf.

Niði is what you'd expect a Dwarf to look like: short, bearded, dark and possessed of glimmering eyes. Albion's premier Dwarf, Hledjolf, looks like R2D2. Personally, I find Hledjolf a lot creepier but Saffron was clearly not a fan of Niði. Perhaps she just doesn't like beards.

The Dwarf took the box and opened it. A thick gold ring glinted on bed of velvet.

Well, what else would you give a Dwarf? They got their reputation for a love of rings for a good reason. This one wasn't magickal, as such, but would be a good starting point if you wanted to make an Artefact. Niði evaluated it carefully, taking it out and weighing it in his soot-blackened fist. He offered the box back to Saffron, and slipped the ring into a pocket. 'The Constable has been generous. Welcome in peace. Please, sit.'

Stone benches were arranged at a stone table, and Niði had covered them with furs to protect human and Gnomish backsides. There were already tankards on the table. Oh goody. I was looking forward to this.

The Hall of a Dwarf isn't just a home, it's part of them. Imagine having your lungs, heart and sexual organs outside your body, if you can. It's gross, but that's what the Hall does. It soaks up Lux, and the Dwarf draws Lux from his Hall like we breathe the air. Deep in one of the caverns is the spawning rock, and I'd seen a mini-Niði emerging from the rock on my last visit, so it wasn't a surprise when a second Dwarf came in carrying a jug.

This second Niði looked similar to the first, in the way that brothers are similar, but they're not just similar, they're the same, or part of the same. The cosmetic differences are only for show. Dwarves share consciousness in ways

I have no hope of understanding. The second Dwarf was swathed in rough cloth, and I reckon that it was still forming itself underneath the hessian and hair. It – he – put the jug down and left.

Niði filled the tankards and we drank the three toasts. Dwarven Ale is legendary, and great on a hot day. Mina raised her eyebrows in pleasure and Saffron looked like she was taking medicine. Takes all sorts.

'What does the King's Watch want with Niði?' he asked.

Mina pushed her hair right back and turned to face the Dwarf, crossing her legs over the bench. 'Thank you for your hospitality, Master. You are very kind.' Niði nodded an acknowledgement, and Mina continued. 'I would know more of Alchemical Gold, if you can help me.'

Niði looked blankly back at her. 'You are a human,' he said. 'You can have no knowledge of this.'

'You are the Master. Who else would I ask?' Niði blinked. Flattery works on Dwarves, too. I'd told her that, and also told her that Niði has vision, but little imagination, if you see what I mean. Some of his artwork is beautiful, but it's very … concrete. She took a breath. 'A natural Dwarf is possible, is it not? One born of a rockseed with no parent?'

'Such a thing has been known. Not since humans were trying to build those pyramids, I grant you, but it has been known.'

'Suppose one turned up in your Hall. What would you need to teach him before he could make Alchemical Gold?'

Niði rubbed and pulled at his beard. He took a long draught of ale. 'Why do you want to know? You are not even a Mage.'

'All the more reason for you to explain it to me, Master.'

Niði scratched his nose. I think that may be a Dwarven shrug. Maybe. 'You take Mother's gold to start with.'

'That would be ordinary gold,' said Lloyd. 'As it comes from our Mother Earth.'

'And that would be mansplaining,' muttered Saffron.

Mina ignored them. 'And then what, Master?'

'You Reduce it with silver. Without silver, the Lux will flow in and out, like a tankard with no bottom. The silver traps the Lux inside the gold. It circulates endlessly. You humans do the same with electricity and call it a *superconductor*.'

This much we knew. Well, this much Vicky and Myfanwy knew. It was the next questions that Mina wanted the answers to.

'What is *Reducing*, Master?'

He pulled his beard. 'It is the oldest principle in Alchemy. You change the nature of one thing with another. Reducing the gold makes it alchemical gold. You must know of Lydian Electrum.'

Mina nodded enthusiastically. 'It is a naturally occurring blend of gold and silver, from Lydia in Greece. Lux is measured by how much can be stored in one Troy ounce of Lydian Electrum, but Alchemical Gold can store so much more.'

'It can. And only Dwarves can Reduce Mother's gold to make Alchemical Gold.'

'Why?' said Mina.

Niði's black brows contracted. 'Do you insult me?'

'How can a human insult Mother's favourites? You are great, I am nothing. Is the Reduction something in you, or in your great skill that no human could ever master?'

Niði thumped down his tankard. 'No creature can match us in gold. Our skill is supreme.'

Mina turned to me. The Dwarf hadn't claimed magickal exclusivity for his race, only superiority. 'I thought so,' she said. She turned back to Niði. 'And then?'

'The Alchemical Gold is placed in a golden lattice at the centre of a Collector. When it is charged with Lux, you have the finished article.'

Mina put her hands flat on the table. Saffron and I eased back a little. It was our signal to be ready. Mina was about to upset the Dwarf.

'Great Master,' she said. 'You spoke of the pyramids. Have you ever seen them by moonlight.'

'Yes, I have. Once.'

'Could I turn one upside down and balance it on its point?'

Dwarves are greedy. Very greedy. When it comes to treasure, they are blind with greed. But they are not stupid. 'That would be impossible,' said Niði. He was answering Mina's question, and his tone said that he'd heard the subtext: *Why can't a human make Alchemical Gold?*

'Why is it impossible?' said Mina.

'Because you don't live long enough. You would be dead before you could turn a pyramid upside down. Or make Alchemical Gold.'

Mina nodded. 'Thank you, Master. If I find some, should I bring it to you?'

'Where would you find it?'

'There are over half a million Troy ounces sitting in the First Mine of Clan Flint.'

Lloyd choked on his ale. 'What the fuck are you on about?'

It was Niði's reaction that shocked me most. He pulled a great chunk of hair out of his beard. 'By the Mother, you lie!'

Saffron, sitting on the other side of the table, shot back and nearly fell off the bench.

Mina re-crossed her legs in the opposite direction. 'I may be wrong, Master, but I would not lie to you. There is, or was, Alchemical Gold on deposit with Clan Flint that could only have been created by humans.'

'Gnome!' said Niði. 'What do you know of this?'

'Nothing, Master,' spluttered Lloyd. 'I swear by the Mother that this is the first that I have heard of it.' He turned to me. 'What is this? What in the Mother's name are you on about?'

'I once said to you, "What if I come to the First Mine with a warrant?"'

Lloyd looked sick. 'And I said, "As Swordbearer, you wouldn't need one." Is there no other way?'

I shook my head. 'I brought you down here so that you'd see how serious we are, and how seriously we're taking this. You're innocent, Lloyd. I believe that.'

'This could tear the clan apart.'

'If Irina's already moved the gold, we'll follow it and say nothing about the clan. But if it's still there…'

'Let's go.' He turned to the Dwarf. 'Thank you, Master.'

The Dwarf nodded to Lloyd, Saffron and me. To Mina, he said, 'If I never hear from you again, I know that you lied. If you tell the truth, you will come back and Niði will make amends. Go well, mortal.'

We were back on the boat before anyone spoke.

'I don't know about you lot, but I need summat to eat,' said Lloyd.

It was the first thing we'd all agreed on.

10 — A Miner Scale

And it was just about the last thing we agreed on. Lloyd is a modern Gnome, but he's still a Gnome. He was very reluctant to allow Mina or Saffron to enter the First Mine, but he couldn't bring himself to say *because they're women.*

When Mina suggested they be classed as guests of the Swordbearer, Saffron mutinied. She was no one's guest, and wanted to be there by right. When she knows Mina better, she'll understand that Mina fully agrees with her. After all, it was Mina's stance on women in temples that had got her tattooed with boiling ink.

Things nearly fell apart when Mina took Saffron away from Lloyd and said to her, 'Saffy, this is not our Locus Lucis…'

'My name is Saffron, alright? I am not a character from *Absolutely Fabulous.* Are we clear?'

I will never get to meet Mina's parents, but just for a moment, I got a glimpse of her mother. Mina put her left hand on her left hip, jutted her right hip out and pointed a finger in Saffron's face. 'No, you are not from *Ab Fab,* because then you would be funny, and I am not laughing. What do you think Conrad is going to do next?'

I was agog. I had no idea what I was going to do next.

Saffron squared up to Mina. 'He's going to stand up for the rights of the King's Watch. I hope.'

Mina shook her head. 'He is going to accomplish his mission. For that he needs both you and me inside the Mine with him. He has found a way to achieve that. Don't make him order you.'

Saffron moved some of her hair around and gave Mina a big smile. 'Let's go, shall we?'

Anna had collected us from Coseley Station in the people carrier, then dropped us at a pub in the middle of nowhere to eat and make plans. This was one of Lloyd's safe places, and we left in a smaller vehicle with me at the wheel. The one thing Clan Flint's First Mine did not have was a back door, and we had to approach the front as discreetly as possible.

'Why would this Irina woman put CCTV on Niði's Hall but not your First Mine?' said Mina. That question was worrying me, too.

'Because the Clan Second is the custodian of the mine. When Conrad called me, I went over every inch of the entrance with magickal and mundane detectors. It's clean.'

That was reassuring. Less reassuring was the question of accomplices. 'Irina never had access to the mine on her own, did she?'

Lloyd looked out of the window. 'Turn left here. No, she didn't.'

'Then she must have had at least one Gnome working for her.'

'You don't need to tell me that. Park by the fence.'

The Black Country is covered by hundreds of small housing estates, workshops, industrial sites and pockets of history. We were above that, on a slight hill to the west. To our left was a golf course and ahead were some scraggy fields. Just beyond them, I could see the tanks and rotating arms of a sewage works. I really did take Mina to the most romantic places.

Lloyd got out and when he'd locked the car, he pointed down the slope. 'The main entrance is off the access road to the sewage works. We just have to cross a couple of fields.'

Mina looked at her trainers. 'It's a good job we haven't had rain, or you'd be carrying me,' she said.

'Which part of "First Mine" made you think it would be clean down there?'

'The part where you said it was a centre of Gnomish faith and heritage. No one has mud in their temple. What do they grow here?'

'Grass. It's a meadow. They'll be making the first cut soon.'

We stuck to the edge of the field, because the grass really was too long to walk through comfortably. Lloyd stopped at another gate. 'Let me check this out. It's just down there.'

We hung back as he moved quickly, ducking to keep his head below the hedge. When he turned a corner, he stopped and stayed still for nearly a minute, then waved us down. This hedge was much older and thicker than most of them, and bursting with life. Lloyd was squatting by a slight gap which had a wooden panel in it, nearly swallowed by the hedge on either side.

'Give us a hand, Conrad. It should lift out.'

With a bit of tugging and shaking, we lifted the panel out, and I got to see what was on the other side. A sheer drop was the answer. 'You two, follow that track down and wait for us.'

Mina and Saffron wobbled down the barest of tracks to the side of the drop while we re-fitted the panel. By the time we'd caught up with them, Saffron was already casting her Sight over the entrance to the First Mine of Clan Flint.

No one said it, but we all thought the same: *is this it?* Lloyd knew exactly what we were thinking, and a big grin spread over his face.

The only sign that this was a site of major magickal importance was the road. They'd done their best to camouflage it using the natural lie of the land, but a well-made road of tarmac ran up from the side of the waste water treatment works. I'm sure it's well Warded, but any naturally gifted human who walked up that track would find only a pair of steel plates set into the hill.

No locks, no warning notices, no visible hinges, nothing on which to let the mind take a grip and imagine going inside. I found myself already looking at the sewage plant as being more interesting, and that's how Occulting works: the magickal art of hiding things. Sometimes you bend light, if you want your object to be invisible on Google Earth, but usually a mis-direction Work will do the job. Look away now. Nothing to see here.

'What did you expect?' said Lloyd. 'The west front of St Paul's Cathedral? This is for Gnomes, not humans. Take out your sword, Conrad.'

I'm not just called the Swordbearer, I have an actual sword to go with the job. Its name is *the Anvil*. I took it off my back and drew the sword from the sheath. Most of the magick in the Anvil simply doesn't work for me, because I'm not a Gnome, but I'd never brought it here before. Lines of power crawled up and down the blade, like eels in a bucket. Sometimes they made shapes – a flash of lightning, a wild boar – and sometimes they lined up geometrically, but this sword knew where it was.

'Is it just me?' I said.

'Or are those doors glowing red?' said Mina.

'You can open up,' said Lloyd.

It was a test. Could I find the key to the mine within the sword. Or within myself. I walked up to the doors and closed my eyes.

I felt the heat of Lux radiate from the door and from the Anvil. It was like holding a burning brand in front of my face. I let the heat wash over me, like emerging into the midday sun after being inside. I tried to feel for patterns, for differences in the temperature. There. Just there, on my right hip, the Lux was moving slowly in a circle. I followed the movement across my body and found counter-currents moving up my chest and down my left arm. But not my right arm.

A different pattern was playing out, starting at the wrist holding the Anvil. This was more fleeting, like eddies in a fast-moving stream. Great. Now what?

It was the movement that gave me a clue. A physical key does not change. It always fits the lock, and if it breaks, it is no longer the key. This key was dynamic, as was the lock. They both changed continuously, never quite fitting together. Now, was I supposed to wait for them to align, or was I supposed to do something? A key must be turned…

I felt a spiral of Lux forming over my chest, a clear enough shape, and I willed a circle of heat on my arm to grow, to spawn and to break, to form its own mini-spiral. The shape changed slowly, almost too slowly to catch up with the one on my chest, and I thought I was going to fail, until the little spiral wormed its way up my arm and merged with the big one. Like a coiled spring, the combined spirals unravelled and blew away. Two satisfying *clunks* echoed from the steel plates.

'Welcome, Swordbearer,' said Lloyd. 'You are now bonded to the First Mine.'

'Does that mean he's going to turn into a Gnome?' said Mina, with real worry.

'Wrong way round, love. The mine is now a little bit human.'

Saffron was well away from Lloyd, but closer to me. I heard her mutter, 'Mina is not your *love*, Mr Gnome.'

I opened my eyes, and saw that two great gilded handles had appeared on the steel plates, along with twin engravings of the clan coat of arms. Across the top of the arms was the clan name *Flint* and underneath were crossed double-headed axes. Lloyd has an axe just like that. The centre of the arms was the traditional Gnomish blacksmith's brazier. Instead of floating on the shield, it stood on firm ground, and that was echoed in the motto: *Vom Felsen.* German, *From the Rock.*

'Not bad, for a human,' said Lloyd. The look on Saffron's face said differently. She thought I'd made the magickal equivalent of unzipping my flies look like winning a marathon. Mina was more impressed.

Lloyd grabbed the right handle in his hand and stuck the prong of his prosthetic on the other one. With a surge of Lux, I realised that it wasn't just a prong – it was magnetic, and he was creating the magnetic field. He used his arm and his magick to pull back the doors. 'After you,' he said. 'I need to close them in such a way that the mine looks unoccupied. That might be beyond Conrad for today.'

There was plenty of headroom for me, and plenty of light from the lightsticks mounted in iron sconces on the walls. I looked down, partly out of curiosity, partly to see if Mina was going to be asking for a piggyback. Marble. The Gnomes had imported marble to floor their mine. Beyond the short entrance, the floor sloped steeply down, and marble gave way to finished sandstone. The daylight behind me faded and the doors clunked again.

I have been doing some research into Gnomes, as much as I can without actually going to the Esoteric Library. I know that every clan has a First Mine, and that they dig them in magickally rather than minerally favourable locations. Gnomes are laid to rest here, and their family covers the body with rocks. One at a time, over generations and generations, on the anniversary of the death. And not just any rock, they have to chip it from the First Mine as part of extending the space. The First Mine is also where they make offerings to Mother Earth. And keep their treasure. The last bit is the one that most people care about.

We descended quickly and were soon well under the hill. The Chamber of the Mother would be next, and I prepared myself for glory. This time it really was a case of *Is this it?*

The Chamber was like the inside of a circus tent, with a shallow ceiling on top of plain walls only three metres high. It wasn't all open space: in the centre of the Chamber, a pillar rose to the top of the conical ceiling. I looked closer and realised that the pillar wasn't a structural feature, it was a solid piece of cast iron, about a metre in diameter, and a conductor of Lux. Like the biggest magnet you've ever seen.

'*Mutters Nadel*,' said Lloyd. *Mother's Needle*. Their symbol of Mother Earth wasn't female, or about crops and fertility, it was a tribute to the molten, magnetic core of the planet. Iron. 'It would be an honour if you would join me. All of you. We make a ring around the needle and take a moment. Don't worry, there won't be dancing today.'

Someone had to hold Lloyd's prosthetic. Mina was nearest, and did so with a smile. I held her hand, and Saffron moved slowly to complete the circle. We all felt the Lux, in our own ways. I closed my eyes and it throbbed against me like waves. Mina jerked my hand down, reflexively, and I opened my eyes to look. She was staring at the spot under her blouse where the tattoo was. It had obviously sprung into life when we joined hands.

Lloyd said a short prayer in Old High North Germanic. I made out the words *Mother* and *Death*. Sounds about right.

He let go of Saffron, and we all stepped back. 'What do you reckon?' he said.

The plain walls of the Chamber had sprouted doorways, or we'd acquired the power to see them. The largest and most ornate was opposite the entrance, with the doors themselves a good eight or nine feet high and made of iron, with gold and silver carvings repeating the clan crest in the centre and other illustrations surrounding it.

Other than this one, I counted eight doorways, four on each side, and all different. All had some sort of pillars, pediments and other architectural features around a single, deep set door. Some of the pillars were Gnomish figures holding up the lintels, others were simple and classical, one pair even had trees. All were ornate except one, close to the entrance, and all but that one had the clan crest – with a difference. Instead of the central brazier, there were two, three, four… up to eight smaller braziers under the crossed axes.

As Lloyd spoke, the words of the travellers tale I'd read echoed in my head. Word for word, they were the same: 'Eight dug the First Mine, and One was chosen for the Mother, and here he lies.' Lloyd pointed to the double doors.

'Really?' said Mina. 'They murdered him?'

'A self-sacrifice,' said Lloyd. 'Every Gnome of Clan Flint is descended from one of the other seven.' He nodded at the doorway with five braziers and the trees for columns. 'I am of the fifth house, and all my ancestors lie down there. I will, too.'

Saffron pointed to the lesser door, the one with no crest. 'What's that?'

'Storage and utility room. We don't leave the chairs and tables out normally, and there's even water and a bathroom in there. That's the only door you can open, because it's not locked. Even I can't open any door but first and fifth. Conrad can open first.'

The look on Saffron's face said she disagreed, and that it was time and energy not blood that made the difference. I am agnostic on questions like that.

He moved to the biggest door and placed his hand and his prosthetic on the braziers. Another reason for the prongs: he couldn't have reached the centre of the carvings with only one arm. The doors swung back soundlessly. 'It gets a bit more complicated after here.' He grinned. 'Don't go wandering, unless you're with me or you're a Navigator.'

'Yeah. Like there's a Navigator here,' said Saffron.

'Didn't Victoria tell you?' said Mina. She pointed to me. 'Him. He's one. I don't know how good he is, though.'

'Oh. No. She said you did a bit of Geomancy, that's all.'

I shrugged. 'Let's go, shall we?'

The tunnels beyond the first door (or should that be First Door?) were short, branched a lot and often re-connected with themselves, as well as sloping up and down. They were not laid out to a grid pattern. 'We have a lot of stuff in the fifth house,' said Lloyd, 'but everything which belongs to the whole clan is kept in the first house. The most important site, to us, is the first cairn. That's where the first was laid to rest. Most human visitors are more interested in the treasury.'

'Should the Swordbearer add to the first cairn?' I said, so as not to offend.

'If you're around on the twenty-third of October, then yes, that would be good. And join the party afterwards of course.'

Saffron had been fingering the rather rough-hewn walls. 'I've also heard there are workshops here.'

'There were, in the early days. It's hard to organise ventilation on a big scale. Some still come down to do small jobs. See?' He led us down a short tunnel that ended in an iron door. He pulled it open and showed us an arch-shaped long space, way too low for me to work in. On one side, there was a bench formed from the native rock that had stains and depressions. It was otherwise empty. 'My grandfather made rings in there, but there's nothing left. We clean up after ourselves.'

We came to a longer, straighter tunnel. I was sure that Lloyd had deliberately taken us on a slightly roundabout route, whether that was to test me or confuse Saffron, I don't know. Along the left hand wall of the tunnel was a series of doors. These were all plain, adorned only with single wrought iron braziers.

'The first is not always at the beginning,' said Lloyd. 'That's an old Gnomish saying. The main door to the treasury is the fourth along. It's not locked.'

'Why not?' said Mina, a note of scandal in her voice.

'Only those who are bonded to the mine can open the first door, and the treasury is common property, so there's no point in a second lock.'

And there was one of the biggest differences between Gnomes and humans. There is no human treasury on earth that is kept in common for long. Sooner or later, it's robbed or someone puts a lock on it.

'Be very, very careful in here,' said Lloyd. 'I'm not joking, neither. Most of the Alchemical Gold is in stasis, but some of it is in a Collector lattice.' He was looking at Saffron when he spoke. I think she got the message, but whether she'd heed it is another matter.

These doors stood proud of their doorways, and moved on runners. It opened with no more sound than the air being disturbed. Lloyd walked through the opening and I motioned for Saffron to follow. Mina took my hand. 'I can feel it from here,' she said.

'So can I.'

The treasury room was wide, deep and low. I could touch the ceiling easily. There were pillars scattered around for roof support, and this was one of the most claustrophobic underground spaces I've ever been in. That was partly the oppressive roof, and partly the skin-crawling feel of magick.

It was in the air, on my clothes and up my nose. I hadn't taken three steps inside when sweat started to trickle down my back.

'The gold is this way,' said Lloyd.

All around the treasury were pallets. Ordinary warehouse pallets. On each one was something individual. Some had neatly stacked steel bars, some copper, some other metals. Other pallets held one box, one trunk, one case. The smallest boxes were on trays to stop them falling through the slats. We passed a couple of electric pallet trucks, and somewhere outside must be a forklift. We were a long way from the surface.

Mina gripped my hand. 'Even my Ancile is throbbing now. It hurts, and it feels like I've got something alive under my skin, and that is not nice.'

Sweat had broken out in my armpits, on my forehead and all over my chest. Where the Anvil touched my back, it felt like hot stones had been strapped to my skin.

Lloyd stopped in front of a wall formed from uncut rock. It was about seven metres long, and the treasury continued well beyond the ends of the wall. It looked like a shield to me.

'Conrad, can you raise a deflector?'

'Never heard of one. Can you show me?'

'Probably not worth it. I've got some here.'

He picked up two thin gold chains, formed into a single loop. He placed one around Mina's neck first, then me. The heat dropped, but only by a fraction. He ignored Saffron, so presumably deflectors are part of the curriculum for Artificers.

Lloyd had his serious face on. 'If you feel burning on the soles of your feet, like walking on a beach in Greece with no shoes, then get out, quick. Clear?'

'Clear.'

He walked round the end of the wall and into a bath of light and heat.

If I could have taken a photograph, you'd have been disappointed. There was a lot of gold, yes, but not *that* much, and it was spread around on more pallets, these ones made of steel. It wasn't the quantity, or the fact that the gold was shaped into doughnuts, it was their presence. They felt alive.

If you walk blindfolded into a room, you just *know* if it's full of people. I just *knew* that those gold rings were alive in some way.

'Here you are,' said Lloyd. 'Now what?'

Mina reached into her bag and pulled out a magnifying glass. 'How close can I go to them?'

Lloyd looked like she'd suggested hand-feeding hungry tigers. 'Singly, they're safe enough, but you'll have to take off your Ancile. It might burn out.'

'That is not possible,' said Mina.

'Why?' said Lloyd.

Mina turned so that her back was to Saffron, and lifted up her left sleeve. The ink in her tattoo was *moving*. That really was gross.

'Fuck me,' said Lloyd. 'I have never … Sorry.' He shook his head.

Mina lowered her sleeve and handed me the magnifying glass. 'You can play Sherlock.'

I took off the sword, and my jacket. My shirt was so sodden and so stuck to me, that I had to take that off, too, to get at the chain of Artefacts round my neck and remove them. For good measure, I took off my gun holsters. 'What am I looking for?'

'Makers' marks,' said Mina.

Lloyd bent down to rub at a spot on the metal pallet. 'This one was created by Niði. Been around a while.'

Mina shook her head. 'It will be on the gold itself. Perhaps there will be a discrepancy. I take it you don't often get up close and personal with the goods.'

The heat of Lux got exponentially higher the closer I got to the golden doughnut. It was about an inch and a half thick and eight inches in diameter. Much hotter and I'd need to take my trousers off, too. I backed away and crawled round the pallet, just looking for an irregularity. Nothing. I sighed. 'I think we might need to turn it over.'

'I'll get you some tongs,' said Lloyd. He disappeared from the gold store and I moved right away from the treasure.

Saffron coughed. 'Excuse me, sir, but did you get all those scars with the King's Watch?'

I am a long way from letting Saffron into my past, but she deserved an answer. 'No. Only the lion bite and the one on my hand. Oh, and that one.'

'Here you go,' said Lloyd. He handed me a pair of fabric gloves with silver thread running through them and a hefty pair of blacksmiths tongs.

I put the gloves on and bent down. At arm's length, I couldn't move the gold, it was too damn heavy. I shuffled closer and got a good grip with both hands. With a dull clang, the doughnut flipped over. 'Aah. There, see?'

'No,' said Lloyd. Mina and Saffron peered from a safe distance and shook their heads.

I could see *something* on the bottom. With great reluctance, I took the magnifying glass and peered closer. 'There are runes. Hang on.' I committed the runes to memory and stood up. 'Pen and paper?'

Mina shrugged, and it was Saffron who obliged. She handed me a lovely little leather notebook and folded open the second page. She'd obviously bought it or been given it to start her career in the Watch. I did exactly the same on my first day at Cranwell. I jotted down the runes and showed them to her first.

'Niði', she said. 'In the Dwarfish variant of the Elder Futhark.'

'Can you jot down *Hledjolf, Haugstari* and *Ginnar*?'

She obliged, and I tried another doughnut. Hledjolf this time. On the third, there was something different. 'Niði again, and then a small triangle.'

'Eh?' said Lloyd. He double-checked the invisible inscription on the pallet. 'This says Niði, all right. A triangle?'

'Yes. Let me compare it to the first one.'

My knees were hurting by now, and my bad leg was playing up something rotten. The titanium tibia was really, really hot inside me, to the point where it had to be acting as a magickal antenna of some sort. With gritted teeth, I got as close as I could. 'All the others were inscribed with a stylus,' I said. 'That one over there, the one with the triangle, was stamped.'

Mina lifted her eyes to the roof. 'Thank you Ganesh.' She looked at Lloyd. 'There is the proof. That Alchemical Gold was not made by a Dwarf but by a human.'

'How do you know? And how did you know that it was here?'

'Can I put my shirt back on?'

'No,' said Mina to me. To Lloyd, she said, 'In the end, it was the only thing that made sense. There is no magickal Bank of England to regulate the money supply, so the inflation in prices for magickal goods could only make sense in terms of a sudden influx of currency. The same thing happened after the Spanish looted Central America and brought shiploads of silver back to Europe. I assumed that England was being used as a tax haven – that Mages and Creatures from elsewhere were sending deposits here.'

'Some do,' said Lloyd.

'But not enough. And that isn't all. Alchemical Gold is a physical currency. For this to make sense, actual physical deposits must be made. Again, with no clearing bank, this could happen. All I had to do was work out how and where.'

Lloyd looked suspicious. 'Does this involve double entry accounting?'

'Oh yes,' said Mina with a happy grin. If I didn't love her, I would be convinced that lawyers and accountants were two of the Four Horsemen of the Apocalypse. If you are one of those, don't take it personally.

Mina patted my arm. 'Don't worry. I shall keep it simple. If some Mage turned up with a truck full of gold, what would happen?'

'Even Gnomes would ask awkward questions about that,' said Lloyd.

'Precisely. The magic figure – no pun intended – seems to be 200 Oz Troy.'

Lloyd rubbed his chin. 'Sounds about right. No one would ask questions about that.'

'And that was another reason for me to see Niði this morning,' said Mina. 'It is not easy to pull the wool over the eyes of a Dwarf, but Conrad tells me that anyone can walk into the offices of Flint Holdings and make a deposit.'

Lloyd looked embarrassed. 'Up to a point.'

Mina *tsked*. 'Well beyond that point. Hundreds of accounts for fake Mages were opened around the country with every Gnome and Dwarf and Human who takes notes of deposit. The physical gold was deposited here, in small amounts in their names. At least one of your cashiers must be in on this. The gold is transferred to accounts elsewhere, but only on paper. It then gets shuffled around the country until the deposit is credited, here, to one of four fictitious accounts.'

'Eh?' said Lloyd. 'The data was anonymous. How do you know they're fictitious?'

'Mr Flint, you have four account holders with over 200,000 Oz each, none of whom has ever made a withdrawal, and all of their deposits were laundered.'

It made sense. With no single authority to regulate things, it would be exactly as Mina described it. She was the first person ever to have had access to all the data. Brilliant. 'You are a genius,' I said. 'Well done. Now please don't tell me I have to check every single doughnut.'

'Torus,' said Lloyd. 'That shape is a torus. I've got an idea. Let me get the scale. Please put your shirt back on, mate.'

I buttoned up while he fetched a little trolley with a special scale on it. There was a gibbet-shaped structure on the platform, about a metre high and made of cast iron. From the arm dangled a hook with a canvas sling.

Lloyd took off the sling and opened it out. 'This is a two man job.' He looked at Saffron. 'Or two person.'

It wasn't just me who was getting hot. Saffron was now positively red in the face, so you couldn't tell whether she was hot, embarrassed or angry. Probably all three. 'I think Conrad's done enough,' she said, and stretched out her hand for the other end of the sling.

Lloyd took his end and stood to one side of the torus with the triangle stamp. 'We slide it underneath and lift. As this one's upside down, can you flip it over, Conrad? Then we put the sling on the scale. Right?'

'Right.'

They got in position, I flipped the golden torus and with a grunt, Saffron hoisted her end and they moved round to the scale.

'What do you hope to discover?' said Mina.

Lloyd waited until the sling was safely attached to the hook. 'Whoever made this thing used a mould, and poured from a distance. It's the same size exactly as Dwarven work, but I'm betting it's a different weight. They'll have used slightly different materials, and by Archimedes' principle, this will weigh different. This scale only weighs one thing: a torus of gold. Have a look at the red needle, Mina. Where is it?'

Mina peered at the neck of the scale. 'It is stuck to the left of the red zone. Nowhere near the green.'

Lloyd checked for himself, then stared at the scale. This was a huge fraud, and it had been perpetrated on his clan. It was going to take a lot of digesting. He shook himself awake and said, 'Conrad, you and Mina can make some tea. There's a kettle in the store room of the Chamber of the Mother, and you can smoke in the little room at the end. Saffron, can you give me a hand to weigh some more?'

She couldn't really refuse, could she?

We both breathed deeply when we walked out of the treasury room. That felt very good. So good that I took Mina in my arms, and we enjoyed a big kiss. 'Congratulations, love,' I said. 'That was immense.'

'I know. I've a feeling I'll never get the same chance again, once word gets round. They were far too generous with their data. Especially Lloyd.'

'It wasn't Lloyd, it was his uncle Wesley, the Clan Chief, which tells me that Wesley had no idea what Irina was up to.'

Mina turned right, the way we'd come.

'Let's try this way,' I said, going left. 'I'm sure there's a more direct route.' There was. The treasury was down two levels from the Chamber, but Lloyd had brought us up one and down three. It was at least two minutes quicker. 'Don't tell Lloyd about this,' I said when we got to the Chamber.

The store cupboard was more of a suite, with lots of tables, benches, boxes of tankards and other party goods in one section. There were hot-plates in a small kitchen and a long urinal in a separate room. It took Mina a couple of minutes to find the two tiny cubicles for women. I let her make the tea while I found the smoking room.

I had idly wondered about ventilation before, because there was no obvious source of fresh air. The smoking room had its own extractor, and wasn't far from the surface, but the mine as a whole? There must be some very well disguised vents on the hill somewhere.

As well as speculating about ventilation, I was trying to put together a plan. It was wonderful to find evidence of money laundering, but we hadn't arrested anyone. There was so much weight in gold down there that they'd obviously left it. We had to shake the tree, somehow, and in a way that led to Irina and her accomplices turning up to the mine. By the time we'd carried the tea back to the treasury room, I had a plan.

Saffron was on the verge of passing out. I wondered if Lloyd was pushing her for the fun of it or assuming that she could cope until she said differently. Or until she dropped to the floor.

'How've you got on?' I said, passing Saffron a mug of tea. She drank half of it without taking her lips from the rim.

'We've found six, all close to the front, but not in the front row. Easy to get at, but not the first to be moved if you need a pallet.' He pointed to the electric pallet truck. 'Should I move them?'

'Doesn't matter. We're going to ambush them in here, tomorrow afternoon.'

'I like the sound of that. What are you gonna do? Give them a call and make an appointment?'

'You need to get Wesley out of Flint House tomorrow morning, but make sure he's back in the afternoon. And you need to be there in the morning, but gone in the afternoon. We also need Vicky, her new partner, and also one of the Merlyn's Tower Irregulars.'

'Mmm?' said Saffron. 'Why have I never heard of them?'

I passed her an Irregulars badge. 'I give these to people I think might be on our side. One of them is an Enscriber, and she's at Elvenham, which is where we're heading now.'

'Elvenham? Your home?'

'Yes. There's plenty of room.'

'Is there a hot shower and cold beer?'

'Yes to both.'

'Then I don't care how much room there is.'

11 — Chain of Command

'You need to give him your gun,' said Lloyd.

'Eh?'

'What?'

'You're joking, aren't you?'

We were gathered in the function room of the pub we'd been to yesterday, ready for part two of my plan.

Part one had gone smoothly this morning, when Vicky and I had turned up at Flint House in Earlsbury and kicked up a fuss. We'd demanded to see the Clan Chief (whom Lloyd had sent on a wild goose chase) and demanded an audit of the clan gold deposits. We'd done it visibly and loudly to ensure that as many Gnomes and human employees as possible knew why we were there.

I'd left a packet for Lloyd, and in that packet was a forged document knocked up by Erin last night. She'd had great fun producing a fake warrant from the Cloister Court for Lloyd. It would be very wrong for Vicky and I to serve a fake warrant, but Lloyd...

After we had gone, Lloyd had waved the warrant around and left it where it could be read by anyone. That same anyone would also know that we were due back at two o'clock to see the Chief. And when I say *we*, I mean that loosely. Vicky had done all the talking this morning, and would do the same again this afternoon. Her silent partner, however, would not be me but Xavier Metcalfe.

That illusion of me he'd done during the selection process had given me an idea. He was very good, and once he'd practised my limp last night, he was pretty much spot on. Except for the gun, apparently.

'Once you're inside Flint House,' said Lloyd, 'that gun and all its magick stick out like a sore thumb. With your gun, no one will suspect that he's using a Glamour. Without the gun, everyone will look twice.'

'You can't go down the mine without the Hammer,' said Vicky. 'You won't even have an Ancile. Way too risky.'

'You've got the Anvil,' said Lloyd. 'Inside the Mine, you should be able to activate it. I'll show you.'

'Too risky,' said Vicky.

I pulled my lip. 'It's a risk, yes. If I can't activate the Ancile, the operation is aborted.'

'Do you promise?' said Vicky.

That wasn't her right. More than anyone except Mina, Vicky knows that I can't break a promise. She shouldn't be asking that. I put it down to her worry about the mine and what happened at Niði's Hall. 'Just this once,' I said. 'I promise.'

I took off the holster and passed it to Xavi. 'Whatever you do, don't try to fire it. Now get going.'

They left, and we got our equipment ready. Mina stuck her head into the room and announced that our transport was ready.

'What do you mean?' said Lloyd. 'We're using my car.'

'No,' said Mina. 'There is too much to carry over the hill. I have called an Uber. He can drop us right outside the mine.'

And when she said *we*, she meant it literally. There had been a full-on row at Elvenham last night when Mina announced that she was going down the mine with us.

'Just this once,' she'd said, after a lot of raised voices. 'I found that gold, and I will see it through. Don't worry, I will hide in the corner when they come.'

I'd thought it through for a minute, then I'd said, 'What about next time?'

'What next time?'

'If I stop you this time, you'll never forgive me. What about next time, though? Next time might be a lot more dangerous. Lloyd won't be there next time, for certain, and we won't have home advantage.'

'Then I promise. It's not just Clarkes who keep their word.'

I had one last thing to say, 'What about Saffron? What if your presence puts her at risk?'

Mina had clearly thought of that. 'She is under your command. I am not. Her safety comes first. You do nothing to save me if she is at risk.'

'Do you know how hard that is, when I love you so much?'

'If you truly love me, you will be the officer I want you to be.'

At that point, I had kissed her, and she'd known she was going to get her own way. Once Hannah finds out, and she will, it is possible she may fire me, but Mina had been engaged by the Watch to complete Project Midas, so you could argue she was part of my command. That's what I'll tell Hannah, anyway.

Activating the Ancile built into the Anvil was easier said than done. We'd been inside the First Mine for nearly half an hour before I got the hang of it, and even then it was hard to keep up whilst doing anything else. And practising was making my head hurt, a sure sign that it was draining more Lux than I could spare.

'Try it inside the treasury,' said Lloyd.

Reluctantly, I moved back into the claustrophobic sauna of the treasury room and brought up the Ancile. That was much easier, but trying to accomplish an ambush in a wide open space was going to be hard, and Saffron had already stripped down to an athletic vest. If we spent too long near the gold, we'd all die of magickal heatstroke before Irina and friends showed up.

Lloyd had assured me he could sense the doors opening, so we waited outside the treasury room. And we waited. Vicky and Xavi could only keep up their act for so long, so the enemy's window was limited. It was about half an hour's drive from Flint House to the First Mine, and I'd told Vicky to make her excuses at three thirty. If no one had shown up by four o'clock, the operation was off.

Mina had picked her hiding place inside the treasury room – a wooden shipping crate as tall as her and away in a corner. Lloyd had said that there was an enchanted rock drill inside (who knew such things existed), and that from a distance, it would mask her Ancile.

As well as my row with Mina last night, there had been a lot of activity at Elvenham. Saffron Hawkins won an imaginary award for being the first magickal visitor to say the house was 'charming'.

'That means she grew up somewhere even bigger,' Myfanwy had whispered.

'From what I hear, *bigger* isn't the half of it,' added Vicky.

Saffron got on much better with Erin than she did with anyone else, including Xavi; Vicky said that they hadn't mixed much at Salomon's House when they were students. Xavi was earnest, had a noticeable Yorkshire accent and also had mundane parents. He'd grown up in a very different world to Saffron.

At 14:45, Mina stopped making funny faces and said that she couldn't hold it any longer, and that she was off to the bathroom. She left via the official route, and had been gone for about five minutes when I heard a whisper in the distance.

I looked up, but Lloyd was already on his feet. 'The doors. They're here.'

'You felt something,' said Saffron. 'I saw it in your face.'

That was interesting, but not important. We had about two minutes to get into position, and Mina was out there. On her own.

I don't pray to Odin. If something goes well, I give thanks, but I don't pray in advance. If Mina managed to dodge the invaders, I would owe the Allfather big time. We entered the treasury, and Lloyd closed the doors from the inside.

'Could it be someone else?' I asked as we retreated behind the shield covering the gold storage area.

'Unlikely,' said Lloyd. 'It's no one's anniversary today, and visits to the mine are normally made in the evenings. Unless it's business.'

We took up positions behind the wall, Saffron and I to the left, Lloyd to the right. And then we waited again.

'Where are they?' whispered Saffron. 'Shouldn't they be in a hurry?'

'They'll be here when they're ready.'

They weren't ready for another three slow, agonising minutes. Saffron kept fidgeting, moving her ponytail, wiping her hands on her leggings, shuffling her feet. It was really irritating. I was on the point of telling her to stand still when there was a slight change of pressure in the air. I held up my hand and braced myself.

The whole treasury room had a slight hum, and the air was so heavy that ordinary footsteps were hard to hear, but there was no mistaking the voices.

'Slater, you get the pallet truck, I'll get the tongs.' The voice was male and local. It could only be a Gnome.

Lloyd let out a low moan. Right up till this moment, he'd hoped that Irina would turn up alone, despite all the evidence that at least one Gnome was up to his neck in this.

I counted to three and dropped my hand. We moved round the edge of the shield and took stock.

'You bastard,' said Lloyd

The three Gnomes stopped dead in their tracks and backed away. Irina, on guard by the door, moved into the room.

Lloyd was staring at the Gnome in the centre. 'Our father will be weeping in the cairn,' said Lloyd. He lifted the great two-headed axe of the Clan Second and pointed at the Gnome. 'This is my brother. Jackson.'

Saffron had moved beyond me, to my left, to get a clear run at Irina. One of the other Gnomes moved to block her, and then we all stopped.

We'd worked out a negotiating strategy of sorts. None of the Gnomes had attacked anyone that we knew of. Their crimes could be sorted out by the clan, but Irina was heading to the magickal prison at Blackfriars Undercroft.

'Put down your weapons,' I said. 'Surrender yourselves to the clan and to the Watch.'

'And leave half a million in gold to rot?' said Jackson Flint. 'I don't think so. Why don't you humans move aside and we'll be quick about it. And you, Lloyd. We'll take nothing that belongs to the clan, so there's no harm, no foul, eh?'

'It's not yours to take,' said Lloyd. 'It may not belong to the clan, but it's in our trust. What are you going to do with it, anyway? You'll be cast out of the clan for what you've done.'

'We'll go abroad,' said Jackson. 'Dig our own First Mine. New mine, new clan.' He turned to Saffron and me. 'No one has to die, least of all you two. This isn't your fight.'

'That's what Irina said to Lloyd,' I responded. 'He stood by me, and I stand by him. Besides, I'm not leaving without Irina.'

She was in a vulnerable position. She was trapped down here (assuming the Gnomes had closed the doors behind them), and if her allies turned against her...

And then I saw something that gripped my heart in my chest. I choked for half a second. I had to do something, and do it now. I drew the Anvil from its sheath and levelled the point at Irina. I tried gathering Lux from around me and projecting it off the tip of the sword towards Irina. I struggled down a breath and put on my parade ground voice. 'You attacked me. You assaulted an officer of the King's Watch. You will face justice.'

It sounded awful to me. Cheesier than a Dwarf's feet. Saffron fidgeted in my peripheral vision. She must have thought I'd gone mad. It worked though.

Irina screamed and collapsed as Mina whacked her from behind with a heavy pewter candlestick, right on the side of her knee joint

Mina was wearing black from head to toe, and I'd seen her creeping up on Irina, hence the cheesy dialogue and the pathetic efforts at magick, just enough to stop Irina feeling Mina's Ancile.

Jackson and his two friends turned round to look, and do you know what? Not one of them jumped to Irina's rescue.

Irina was down, but she wasn't out. She wouldn't stand on that leg again without surgery, but Mina was in her personal space and Irina could attack with magick. She rolled on to her back and I sensed the prickle of Lux from here.

Mina dropped the candlestick and stamped her foot on Irina's bad knee. Irina screamed, lost concentration, and Mina pulled an automatic out of her leggings. It was my mundane SIG P226. Well, I wasn't going to leave her completely defenceless, was I?

She pressed her foot down again on Irina's leg. That would hurt, but it would guarantee that a shot from the SIG would not be deflected. She levelled the gun at Irina's chest using a perfect two-handed grip, and Irina got the message.

'I will shoot.' Mina barked out the words. 'I will shoot on three if you do not remove your Artefacts and turn over. One … two …'

'I surrender,' said Irina. She lifted her hands, then scrabbled at her neck. She pulled out two chains of Artefacts and used a tiny flare of magick to open the clasps.

Mina lowered her left hand. 'Place them in my palm.' She collected the Artefacts and stuffed them into the pocket of her hoodie. She backed off and said, 'Roll over.'

All this had taken place in seconds, before either party could formulate or execute a plan. I hadn't taken my eyes off Mina, and I'd been trusting that Saffron and Lloyd would be watching the Gnomes. When Mina went to tie up Irina, I turned my attention back to my opponent.

'I've got what I wanted,' I said. 'You can surrender to the clan now, confident that Irina won't stab you in the back. I have no quarrel with you.'

Jackson shrugged. 'Slater, you deal with the *Weißbrut* then help Dixie finish off the *Hexe Hure*.'

There was still a fair distance between the two sides. The Gnomes stepped back and rearranged themselves. The guy who'd faced me looked very nervous, and had barely taken his eyes off the Anvil. He now faced off against Saffron.

'What did he call us?' she said while they moved.

'He called me a snack. Whitebread. He called you a Witch Whore.'

'Thought so,' said Saffron. We'd picked spots with enough room for our weapons and a clear line of retreat. I didn't want to break formation until we had them on the run, but Saffron started to move towards Dixie.

'Hawkins! Hold!' I shouted.

She was too close to the Gnome to look at me without exposing her flank, and I saw her go rigid for a second, then she stepped back. At this point, Jackson had got round to face Lloyd. He reached into his pocket and pulled something out with his fist. He raised his sword, threw some pebbles at Lloyd and charged with a scream. Slater and Dixie did the same, but without the pebbles.

The pebbles were missiles, of course, so Lloyd's Ancile deflected them. When they hit the ground, or the crates, they exploded like fireworks. At that point I had to focus on Slater.

He was armed with a sword. The Anvil is a longish, straight, cavalry sabre. Slater's was a modern version of an infantry rapier, shorter and lighter than the Anvil. It also had magick.

The Gnome's sword flashed and flared, light and flame. I braced myself, and something inside the Anvil answered the attack. Where Slater's sword flared red, mine sent out a blue tongue of light, and the two cancelled each other. His sword flared deep purple; mine went green. He stopped trying and started sweating.

I was taller than him, and with the Anvil's length, I hugely outreached him. It was just a question of whether he was any good. He wasn't bad, but he was no master, as he quickly discovered.

In his shoes, I'd have forced me to keep my sword up. His shoulders were twice my size, and his blade half as heavy. In a stand-off, I couldn't keep my weapon en garde nearly as long as him, so it was down to me to attack, and he let me.

I feinted twice and parried his counter. I feinted again, and he had to retreat. His foot caught the corner of a pallet and he stumbled. He attacked twice, forcing me back, but I knew what was behind me. The next time I attacked, he looked behind him. Fatal.

He put his blade up to guard his body and left his flank exposed. I took half a step and slashed him. The Anvil has an Eversharp blade. It bit deep, and Slater collapsed in a heap of blood, trying to hold his guts in. I kicked his blade away and turned to look at the others.

Lloyd had his back to the wall shielding the gold. Those explosions had blinded him and he'd backpedaled away. A large axe is not a weapon you can use easily when your back's to the wall, and he was forced to take big swings to keep his brother at bay. Jackson was feinting and probing. Unlike Slater, Jackson had the patience to wait until his opponent tired. I turned to Saffron.

I hadn't believed it last night when she showed me her weapon of choice: it was a two metre long steel chain with spiked balls at each end. On its own, not a problem, but with her magick and skill, it was a formidable threat.

Dixie was bleeding from deep wounds in his left leg, and had no idea what to do. He was scrabbling around, trying to find cover and keep Saffron at arm's length. Lloyd could hold his end up for a while, and I started circling to outflank Dixie. They'd moved a long way from their starting point.

I *think* the Gnome was about to surrender. He'd seen me and tried to take cover behind a large crate. He certainly wouldn't beat Saffron in a foot race if he tried to flee, and Saffron didn't let him. She vaulted on to the crate and swung her chain. Bad mistake.

The Gnome dropped his weapon and lunged forward. He grabbed her ankle and pulled. She didn't stand a chance, and crashed on to the crate. Dixie twisted her ankle so hard that she had to roll with it or have it wrenched off. Gnomes really are that strong.

I was running to help, but Dixie dived on top of her, reaching for her neck.

Saffron had enough chain free to cast a loop, and the air shimmered as she used magick to direct the loop over his head. He caught her throat in those great hands. She pulled on the chain.

There was an audible crack from Dixie's neck and smoke rose from between their bodies. Half a second later, I caught the whiff of burning flesh. I hauled Dixie's body off Saffron and she started coughing. She was lucky the Gnome hadn't broken her neck, but she'd have her first scar.

Mages can draw on Lux stored in Alchemical Gold if it's been prepared into a suitable Artefact. It's normal to have a few round your neck. Even I have a couple. Saffron had used so much Lux to move the chain that she'd caused the doodad to heat up enough to melt her vest and burn her skin.

'Mina! Is Irina secure?'

'Yes.'

'Get the water. Saffron needs it.'

Saffron was still struggling for breath and there was panic in her eyes. I ran my fingers under her hair and down her cervical vertebrae. All present and correctly in line. 'Help's coming,' I said.

I headed for Lloyd. I could see that he was tiring, and that Jackson would soon have the advantage. Lloyd saw me coming and grinned. He let his guard slip on his left, and Jackson swung at him.

Lloyd put his prosthetic up and it hit his brother's sword with a clang of metal and magick. Lloyd had magnetised his tuning fork prosthetic and for half a second it gripped Jackson's sword, long enough for Lloyd to force it down and move his right foot forward. That gave him enough room behind to put all his strength into an upward swing and take his brother's head off in one blow.

12 — From the Other Side

Lloyd slumped back against the wall and let his axe slip to the ground. He was neither smiling nor triumphant, and before I got to him, he was already wiping tears from his eyes. I put my hand on his shoulder and he stood up straight to put his good arm round me. 'Stupid git. He always thought he was cleverer than me. And he was.' He broke away and wiped his face with his sleeve. 'Better check that Witch.' He sniffed and looked left. 'What happened to Saffron?'

'Mageburn. Mina's attending, I'll check Irina.'

Irina had been watching proceedings as best as she could, with a shattered knee and her hands cable-tied behind her back. She flinched away when I towered over her and lifted my sword. I let it hover in front of her face for just a second before I put it back in the sheath. I was careful of her leg while I checked her bindings and patted her down. I took a phone out of her back pocket and found nothing else. Mina had already moved her bag well out of reach.

Saffron was up on her feet and leaning on Mina, with Lloyd in attendance.

'Arms up,' he said. She lifted her arms and he pulled her vest over her head with one hand. He took a small knife out his pocket and, using the prosthetic to generate magick, he did something with the tip of the knife. Saffron bit her lip so hard that it bled and she swayed on her feet. Mina gripped her tighter, and a disk of gold flipped off her chest and landed on the floor with a thud.

'How's that?' said Lloyd.

'Better,' said Saffron. 'By the Goddess, that hurts. Oh that hurts.'

Lloyd nodded to her and backed off. He turned and went looking for Slater who had been alive when I last saw him.

Mina gently let go of her. 'Do you want me to get you a coat?'

'Nah, you're all right,' said Saffron in a very good impersonation of Vicky. 'Painkillers would be good, though.'

Mina nodded and went to get the Oxycontin.

Saffron grimaced and started walking over. She wanted to put as much distance between her and the dead Gnome as possible, and I don't blame her.

'That was … I …' she said. 'I thought I'd feel differently.'

'You nearly died, Saffron,' I said. 'And you've just taken another life. It doesn't get any easier, and it shouldn't. You did well enough, but it was close.'

'I know, I know. I was cocky. Stupid, stupid girl.'

I left it there. She knew what she'd done wrong, and that was the most important thing for now.

Lloyd shouted across the room. 'He's gone. Slater's gone.'

Mina arrived with the painkillers. She gave Saffron two pills and a fresh bottle of water.

I waited until Saffron had taken her medicine and turned to Irina. 'I'm going to lift you and prop you against the wall.' She wasn't heavy and I moved quickly. She grunted with pain when her leg dragged across the floor. I could see the swelling pressing against her trousers already.

Lloyd appeared with four camp chairs, and we all collapsed into them, making a ring around Irina. 'I am very much going to enjoy locking you in a Limbo Chamber,' I said. 'I hope you'll bear that in mind when we start asking questions.'

'I will answer your questions,' she replied, 'but there will be no Limbo Chamber for me. I am pregnant.'

'So what?' said Saffron.

A Limbo Chamber prevents the flow of Lux. I've been in one, and it's bad. The more magick you have, the worse its effect. The jailers at the Undercroft have a saying: *taking the short route.* It means suicide, and a lot of Mages take it. However, it has been known for centuries that putting a pregnant Mage in a Limbo Chamber can have terrible effects on mother and child. It was finally stopped by George III, in one of the rare instances of direct royal interference with the world of magick.

'She's exempt,' I said to Saffron. 'No pregnant women or nursing mothers. The court might order her child to be taken away at birth, but that depends on what we charge her with, and whether she co-operates.'

'She might be lying,' said Saffron.

'I'll get Vicky to have a look at her. She's a better pregnancy test than any blue stick.'

'Really?' said Mina.

'Yes. Saffron, are you sure you don't want a coat?'

'Don't tell me you've never seen a half-naked woman before.'

I glared at her. That was a crass thing to say, and she should know better. If our prisoner wasn't sitting there, I'd have called her out. She got the message and picked up her coat, drawing the sides loosely in front of her. She even got out her notebook.

'Right. We'll start with you full legal name, Irina.'

'Irina Ispahbudhan. My family are from Persia. You will see that I grew up in Paris when you put me through your system.'

Saffron was writing everything down. 'Thank you,' I said. 'Were any other Gnomes or humans involved in Earlsbury?'

'No other Gnome was involved. They would have been here if they were. Dixie was going to take his wife with him. She works at Flint House. Slater and Jackson were going to leave their wives behind.'

Saffron shook her head but didn't say anything.

'Where did you get the Gold?' I asked.

'We are the Golden Triangle,' she announced.

'As in the stamp on the torus ingots?'

'And fire.'

Saffron looked up. 'The triangle is the Alchemical symbol of fire. I should have twigged.'

'Who are the other two members of your triangle?' I said.

'The Golden Triangle was forged by the Master. He created it,' said Irina. She turned to Saffron. 'Do you know of Eilidh Haigh?' She pronounced the first name as *Ayley*.

Saffron couldn't believe it. 'No! I've met her. She's from a really big family of Scottish Mages. She moved down to London a few years ago and did a bit of teaching at the College. She's an Artificer.'

'When did you last see her?' I asked.

'About a year ago. Auntie Heidi mentioned that she'd got a better offer.'

'That's one way of putting it,' I said.

'You've met her, too,' said Irina to me. 'She was on the dock at Niði's Hall.'

Ah, yes. Lloyd and I had been ambushed outside Niði's front door, not the back one we'd used yesterday. Irina had pretended to be Hannah, and when I saw through her, she'd sprayed me with acid. The back-up crew had been led by a Mage, and that must have been Eilidh. When Lloyd and I fought them to a standstill, Eilidh had retreated, killing one of her mundane bodyguards along the way to stop him talking to us.

Irina spoke again. 'I would never have killed anyone like she did. We had to get that diamond back.'

'You tried to kill me,' I said.

'I sprayed your head, not your eyes, Watch Captain.'

I didn't believe her, but I couldn't get too personal about it. That diamond was our only link to the Fae who'd bought the Codex Defanatus, and the magick they'd used to make the Gold had definitely come from the Codex. This could be a big breakthrough.

'Why did you need the diamond, Irina?'

'The Master ordered us to. He threatened us all, and said he'd kill us if we didn't get it for him.'

Damn. This don't sound promising. 'Is the Master one of the Fae, Irina?'

She shook her head. 'He is human. Completely human, but he used a mask whenever we met. He found the lost Works that allowed us to Reduce the gold, and he set up the forge. Eilidh ran the forge, he took the reduced metal to a Collector to enrich it, and I picked it up from a safe place in the Old Network.'

'Where is the forge?'

'I do not know.'

'Then how do you know Eilidh?'

'We would meet occasionally, and after you turned up at Flint House, I had to contact them urgently. I had been told that if anyone ever started asking about Niði, especially the Watch, I had to crash out and call an emergency number. Eilidh picked me up and we were based at a hotel until we tried to snatch the diamond.' She coughed. 'Could I have some water? And I think I deserve some non-opioid painkillers.'

'Yes,' I said. Mina was already out of her seat.

We were done for now, and we all knew it. I could see that Irina was using her magick to block some of the pain (a nice trick if you can manage it), but she did need medical attention. There was nothing we could do immediately, and it was time to clean up and re-group. Mina returned with the ibuprofen, and I stood up.

'Is there a stretcher down here?' I said to Lloyd.

'Close enough. We can put her on a pallet and use the pallet truck.'

'You will not,' said Irina.

'It's smoother than being carried out on a plank, believe me,' said Lloyd. 'This is gonna take a while. Any chance of a cuppa?'

Mina said, 'I will go, if I'm not needed to keep watch on the prisoner.'

'Arrest her, Saffron.'

She perked up. 'What? Me?'

'I haven't got my Badge of Office, remember? I'm sure you've got the words written down somewhere.'

She had. They were in the back of that notebook of hers, and she took great delight in placing Irina under magickal arrest. Lloyd beckoned me over to his brother. He'd placed the severed head next to the body. It was gross as it sounds. Try not to picture it.

I am not immune to these things; I've just had more practice at looking away.

'Have you ever seen *Antigone*?' said Lloyd.

'No. Greek, isn't it?'

'That's right. Sophocles. Propaganda, through and through.'

'Sorry?'

'In the play, the king of Thebes, Creon, gets in trouble for not allowing this lass to bury her brother. He orders her to be bricked into a cave, alive, and she tops herself. His son dies, too.'

'Sounds about right. Not keen on happy endings, those Greeks.'

'It's a travesty. There was a Gnome called Crane, of Clan Marten. The first and only clan to venture south until the Roman Empire came along. It's a long story, but he was betrayed and attacked. He left all the dead Greeks to be eaten by the wolves and the birds, as he should. Sophocles called him *Creon* and changed the story.'

That was interesting, but there wasn't much to say. It clearly had a bearing on the current situation, so I waited for Lloyd to say his piece.

'Jackson, Slater and Dixie will not lie in the First Mine. They will be minced up and fed to the pigs. I'm only telling you that because you have a right to know, as Swordbearer. If you want to resign, that's up to you. If you don't resign, then it stays within the clan. Fair enough?'

'If Slater hadn't died, what would the clan have done?'

'Patched him up and kicked him out.'

Lloyd had saved my life. He had killed his own brother rather than let him walk away with the treasure. There was only ever going to be one answer. 'I accept your decision,' I said. 'But under protest, and I want the clan to debate it at some point. If Mina asks me a straight question, I won't lie to her.'

'Fair enough. Can we move them out of here?'

We stashed the bodies in a nearby empty room, and Mina returned with the tea. Lloyd started work on fixing up a pallet for Irina. Before we left, he had one more surprise.

He took two small boxes from a pallet in the far corner. He gave one each to Mina and Saffron and said, 'You two defended the First Mine for no other reason than it was the right thing to do. Clan Flint is grateful. Thank you.'

The boxes were made of cardboard. Highly decorated cardboard, but cardboard nonetheless. Mina and Saffron looked at each other, and opened them together. Inside the boxes were shiny, green velvet pouches, and inside each pouch was a small metal hammer and a piece of rock. The girls looked at each other again, then looked at Lloyd.

'Fire kits,' he said. 'The rock is flint, the metal hammer is enchanted. They'll light just about anything, but I'd save them for special fires. Shall we go?'

Irina demanded a demonstration of the pallet truck before we lifted her carefully on to it. Lloyd took great care, and I walked ahead with Mina. I took her hand and said, 'What happened?'

She squeezed my hand. 'I opened the store room door to come back, and there they were, leaving the Chamber of the Mother. I just picked up the first heavy object I could find and followed them. I wasn't going to attack Irina until you started with the prophet of doom business.'

'What made you change your mind?'

'I was in darkness, yet you could see me. No one else could. I thought that was an omen from Ganesh. He had opened the door, and I had to step through.'

We arrived at the entrance. 'Talking of opening doors,' I said. 'We'll have to be careful. Vicky and Xavi will be waiting outside as backstop. We don't want them to think we're Gnomes.'

'No one would ever think you were a Gnome,' said Mina. 'And I wouldn't have it any other way.'

13 — *Auntie Heidi, Auntie Hannah*

The heatwave rolled on. London was baked and dried out like tanned parchment stretched across a frame. At home in Clerkswell, Myfanwy was rigging up a hosepipe to the well until I told her that water for the Inkwell took priority at all times. It was cool down here though.

Blackriars Undercroft, located in the cellar of the old monastery, is buried under the new Blackfriars railway station, and the temperature is always the same. The physical temperature, that is. The emotional temperature can vary a lot.

The Battle of the First Mine had taken place on Monday. It was now Friday the third of July, and we were wrapping up the last interview with Irina Ispahbudhan. Vicky, Xavi and Saffron had taken her from the Black Country to London where a surgeon had said he couldn't operate on her knee until the swelling had gone down.

Since then, she had been debriefed in teams, starting with Saffron (arresting officer) and Annelise van Kampen (Watch prosecutor). They had hammered out a confession to the crimes she would face in court. I hadn't taken part in that interview because aggravated assault on a Watch Officer was one of the crimes. Once she'd signed her confession, we'd begun the interrogation in earnest, and this was the last session.

Irina (and her unborn child) were propped up on a day-bed with a big brace around her knee. She wasn't suffering from total withdrawal of magick, but the Undercroft has very little free Lux, and without her Artefacts, she was struggling.

This was going to be a short, early morning session. Her breakfast things were still piled outside her cell, waiting for the deputy to remove them. I started the voice recorder and got the ball rolling. 'When you attacked us – Lloyd Flint and myself – on the dock, how did you know that I would be in possession of the diamond? And why were you interested in it? It has nothing to do with your money laundering operation.'

The guarded look came back to her face, the one that told us we were getting near things she wasn't happy to give away, presumably because she was still scared of the people behind all this. 'It was an obligation of the Master's. He was told that he had to retrieve it, and that's why he sent both Eilidh and me, plus her bodyguards, to intercept you.'

'And what about the Fae Squire?'

'He was sent to us to assist in the operation. You are not stupid, Mr Clarke. You can guess that it was a Fae noble who laid the obligation on the Master, and before you ask, I have absolutely no idea which one. The first and last time that I or Eilidh met the Squire was in the hotel the night before the operation.'

This bunch, the Golden Triangle, were a cut above some of the operations we'd come across before. Their internal security and implementation of a need-to-know protocol was worthy of the mafia. What she said had the ring of truth.

After that, I sat in the corner while Mina rattled off some final questions for clarification. When Mina had made a note of the last answer, she looked up. 'Thank you for your co-operation, Miss Ispahbudhan. Interview terminated.'

Mina stopped the voice recorder and stood up to pack away. 'One last thing,' she said. 'When I was pointing a gun at you, why didn't you call my bluff?'

Irina had been as good as her word. I didn't doubt any of the answers she'd given us, nor did I think she was holding anything significant back. There hadn't been much chit-chat, and nor was there now. 'Because we'd heard all about you.'

Mina stopped packing her bag. I stood up straighter. 'What had you heard?' said Mina.

'The Master told us. He said, "Watch out for a little Indian girl hanging round with Clarke. She's done time for shooting a man dead." It wasn't hard to guess that he meant you.'

Mina and I exchanged glances. Very few people in the world of magick even knew I had a girlfriend, let alone her ethnicity or criminal record. It is from such little threads that you can build up a tapestry. Mina fastened the strap on her bag and pulled it over her shoulder. I pressed the button for the deputy bailiff and we left Irina to her fate.

From the Millennium Pier at Blackfriars, you can get a River Bus direct to the Tower of London, if you get your timing right. It was pulling up to the pier when we jogged down to meet it, and we enjoyed the breeze on the river as it took us east.

We didn't go straight to Merlyn's Tower, because I had a duty to perform. I signed us in through the staff entrance to the Big Tower and we went looking for the ravens. The main area was already packed with tourists in large groups and small huddles. I found a quiet place and got a small packet out of my pocket.

There is a survival shop in London that sells curried giant worms as part of its Australian bush tucker range. They are very popular with all sorts of magickal creatures, and the staff at the shop think I am the ultimate mad Englishman, given the amount I've bought there. I opened the packet and put some on my palm. I tossed them up and down, and thought about it. Did I really want to ask a god to eat out of my hand? Probably not.

I put the withered, smelly worms on the low wall and stood back. I rubbed the Troth ring that the Allfather had given me and closed my eyes. *For Mina's survival, Allfather I give thanks.* When I looked again, two ravens were standing by the worms, giving me the big eye. They *cawed* loudly and bobbed their heads to eat. A promise made, a debt paid.

'Could you do that again, sir?' said Warder Bradburn.

'If I had to.'

'Had to?'

'Don't ask.'

He turned to Mina. 'Morning, Ma'am.'

'Namaste. You look rather warm in all that thick wool.'

'Don't get me started. Do you know it's hotter in here than Helmand at the moment?'

'But you're not regretting it?'

'No, ma'am. Second best decision I've ever made, after joining the RAF in the first place.'

'Are you flying solo, yet?' I asked.

'No, sir. The senior warder is keeping watch on me from over there, in the shade.'

'Wise man.'

'I won't keep you.'

We shook hands and made our way to Merlyn's Tower. I'd been in and out of the building a fair bit, because, wonder of wonders, Hannah had taken some leave and left me in charge of debriefing Irina. Her sister's youngest is still under school age and they'd left Ruth's husband, Moses, to sweat it out in London with the older girl while they went to the seaside for a week. Auntie Hannah. Until you've seen it, you wouldn't believe it. Today is Friday and Shabbos begins tonight: Ruth wanted to be home for Friday night dinner and Hannah had called a Project Talpa meeting.

Talpa is Latin for *mole*, and this whole journey had begun when I first encountered the late Lord Mayor of Moles. He'd been the first to sample the curried worms, too. After Saffron had interviewed Irina, I'd given my new partner a copy of the Project Talpa files. There was no doubt she'd proved her physical courage in the First Mine, and we couldn't keep her out of the loop any longer if she was going to be my partner.

The next day, I'd asked if she had any questions.

'Loads,' she'd said. 'I don't know where to start. I still can't believe you had the Morrigan in your garden and didn't tell me when I was staying with you.'

'You didn't need to know, then.'

She was struggling to accept this, and I hoped that she'd got the message about keeping *everything* about Project Talpa within the small group who were working on it.

'Tell me one thing,' she'd said. 'You gave hospitality to the Morrigan. She always gives a gift in return. What was it?'

'You're well informed,' I'd replied. 'No one else knew that.'

'So?'

'It was personal.'

It was actually a wedding cup, but no one else needs to know that.

'Oh. Fine.'

Mina and I skirted the wall and approached Merlyn's Tower just as Saffron herself came through the security gate. She was wearing a bright blue floral summer dress and leather sandals. I only mention this because she'd had the dress made for her. Vicky had told me that Saffron had been on the phone while they carted Irina down to London. She had called her dressmaker and asked for a high-necked summer dress to hide the Mageburn. It had been ready for her next morning. I can't wait to see where the Hawkins clan live.

We greeted each other and went up the stairs to Tennille's domain, then straight through the open door to Hannah's office.

Mina went first, then Saffron, and when all three of us were inside, Hannah stood up and led the rest of the room in a prolonged round of applause. I could get used to that.

Like the Undercroft, Hannah's office kept out the worst of the heat. Given the number of bodies in the room, that was a good thing. Tennille put cups of tea down at our places and closed the door behind her.

The usual suspects were there: Hannah, Francesca, Cora, Rick James, Vicky, Desi and Xavi. To Saffron's great embarrassment, they'd been joined by Auntie Heidi Marston herself. I wonder whose idea that had been?

Everyone was dressed for the heatwave, according to their age and religion. This ranged from Hannah's loose and modest linen suit to Rick's shorts. He's got the legs for it, according to Mina. I have one of the legs for shorts; no one needs to see the scars on the other one.

'Good morning, ma'am,' I said. 'How was the holiday?'

'Over. Mina, you start.' There's another reason Hannah doesn't live in Israel. She gets very grumpy in the heat.

Mina said her bit in the professional, forensic and eccentric style I love, then answered all the questions. With great reluctance, given the presence of Auntie Heidi, Saffron reported on the Battle of the First Mine.

The only way to describe Heidi Marston is *larger than life*. She is large, for one thing, and makes sure that everyone knows about her omnivorous sexual appetites. No one knows of a more skilled human Artificer than Heidi, which is why she's the Custodian of the Great Work at Salomon's House. Cora had text me last night to say that Heidi had put herself forward for Warden, which made her presence today even stranger.

The Custodian has a big following amongst the younger Chymists, all of them female. Vicky calls them Heidi's Gang. She is definitely not a member, but her best friend, Desirée, is a fully paid-up fan.

Saffron shifted in her seat and focused on Hannah. She peppered her report with lots of *ma'ams* and *Constables*, to the evident displeasure of Auntie Heidi. For a first time, Saffron did well. Much better than I would have done at her age. It was now my turn.

'What have we learnt from Miss Ispahbudhan?' said Hannah.

I straightened up in my chair. 'She is the closest suspect to the Codex to have co-operated with us. Not that we've learnt very much. I hope that the Custodian can tell us something more about Eilidh Haigh.'

'What!' boomed Heidi. 'Where did that come from?'

'She is one of the three sides of this criminal triangle.'

Heidi looked outraged, confused and disbelieving all at once. It was the first time I've seen her at a disadvantage. Now I know why she'd been invited.

'Are you sure?' she asked.

'Irina Ispahbudhan is terrified. She wants to be in the Undercroft because she's scared of her co-conspirators. It's in her interest for us to track them down as quickly as possible, and she named Eilidh Haigh. I believe her.'

Heidi put her hands on the table. She has blacksmith's hands. She drummed her fingers up and down in wave patterns and the table reverberated. 'And Eilidh was the one who attacked you at Niði's dock?'

'According to Irina.'

She took her hands off the table. 'You know she's one of the Haighs of Dumbarton?'

I looked around. Everyone else was nodding. It was news to me. 'The only Scottish Mage I know is Lady Kirsten, the rich one who throws epic parties.' I said.

Heidi snorted, and Vicky looked uncomfortable. She's been to one of the parties.

'You could say that,' said Heidi. She looked at Vicky. 'I couldn't possibly comment.' Vicky looked at the table, and Heidi continued, 'Lady Kirsten is of the Darrochs of Stirling. They may be richer and more powerful than the Haighs of Dumbarton, but the Haighs are older. Eilidh is from a junior branch. A bit like me.'

Saffron was busy making notes, and ignored her aunt.

'What is Eilidh Haigh doing down here?' said Francesca.

Heidi became serious again. 'She wouldn't say. I know she's not welcome north of the border because she told me so, one night when she was drunk. When she dropped out of sight, I thought she'd been forgiven and snuck back to Scotland with her tail between her legs. I should point out that the Hawkins family and the Haighs are not connected in any way.'

'Good to know,' said Hannah dryly. 'What's she like as a Mage?'

'What is she alleged to have done, Conrad?'

'Ran a forge Reducing gold.'

Heidi whistled. 'No … Seriously?'

'Someone's been doing it. I've seen the product.'

'She's good. With the right Work, definitely, but I can't imagine where she got it.'

'She got it from an unknown male,' I said. 'Irina calls him the Master, but I won't. Never glorify the enemy. I'll call him the Apex, as we're talking triangles. According to Irina, the Apex put the conspiracy together. He supplied the ancient knowledge and took the Reduced Gold away to enrich it somewhere. All Irina could tell us was that he wore a mask and that he's fully human, young and a prodigious talent. He's tall, thin and probably from South Africa. She doesn't even know whether he's of African or European descent, or something else entirely.'

Heidi and Saffron both frowned, and for the first time looked at each other.

'Ring any bells?' I said.

'Mmm,' said Saffron. 'There was a postgrad student at Salomon's House when I was in my first year. Willem van der Westhuesen. He was expelled, wasn't he, Custodian?'

Heidi nodded. 'Unauthorised biological experiments. Sent straight back to Johannesburg with no references.'

'Any other leads?' said Hannah.

'Do you have Eilidh's phone number?' I asked Heidi.

'Hah! I do. Surely she won't have kept it the same.'

'Only one way to find out. I also have the location of the drop-off point in the Old Network, and the key to open it. Irina's phone records, too.'

Rick James had been following everything closely. 'Who's the father of her child?' he asked.

'She says it's a cousin, but Mina doesn't believe her.'

'No,' said Mina. 'The Ispahbudhan clan are Zoroastrians and mostly mundane. That's why I could look into them. Cousin marriage is strictly against their faith. That's one of the things I think she is lying about.'

Hannah looked at Mina. She tipped her head to the side. 'What's the other.'

'The obvious one. She has a stash of Gold somewhere and wants to pick it up when she is released.' Mina looked around the group and shook her hair back. 'I should know. It's what I did, except that I spent the money on maxilo-facial surgery.'

Hannah coughed. 'Thank you. Any more questions?'

I asked a couple more about the Haigh family, and Heidi wanted us to go back to Irina with questions about the nature of the Alchemical Gold. Hannah said no.

When it had gone quiet, Hannah picked up her pen. 'This is what we're going to do. All mundane information, including Eilidh Haigh's phone number, can go to Ruth by email. She's the best person to pick that up. Vicky, can you explore the drop-off point next week? I need you and Desirée to carry on with your research and help out down here. I shall get in touch with my Scottish Depute and ask him to make discreet enquiries with the Haighs. Francesca, you've got a friend in South Africa, haven't you?'

'I have.'

'Ask her about van der Westhuesen. Conrad? I need you and Saffron to cover the Mercia Watch, for all sorts of reasons.'

I was disappointed not to be following up the other leads, but Hannah had done exactly what I'd have done in her situation. I turned to Saffron. 'Do you mind slumming it in Clerkswell?'

My jaw dropped when she said, 'Do I have to?'

'Not unless we're on a mission, no.'

'Then I'll stay with my family in Oxfordshire, if that's okay. It's near enough to the M40.'

'Fine. One less for Myfanwy to cater for.'

She tried a diplomatic smile. 'And I'm rubbish at cricket. It's all you lot seem to talk about. That and village gossip.'

Hannah shook her head. 'I don't know how they stand the pace of country life, Saffron. Good. I need to see Conrad and Mina, but all of you in the Watch can have the rest of the day off. Those at Salomon's house can go back to work.' She smiled. 'Ah Gutten Erev Shabbos, everyone.'

Saffron gave me a funny look when she was dismissed along with the others, especially when Vicky gave me a hug and said, 'See you soon, Uncle C.'

I said I'd call Saffron later, and when everyone else had gone, the three of us settled in the comfy chairs. Hannah brought over a stack of papers from her desk, and I recognised the one on top: it was Mina's application for the maternity cover downstairs. This did not look good.

'Another group reduced to a smouldering wreck,' said Hannah. 'First the Arden Foresters, now Clan Flint.' She said it with a rueful smile. 'They'll be on their best behaviour in Mercia with you around.'

'I hope so.'

'What happened to the clan after you left?' she asked.

'Wesley offered his neck.'

You might have realised that Gnomish politics can be brutal. You don't resign as clan chief, you offer your neck to the axe. It's up to the clan second whether the axe is used to cut off your chain of office or your neck.

'And?'

'Lloyd let him live. The clan will choose a new chief tomorrow. I'm not sure if Lloyd will stand or not.'

Hannah nodded. 'How's your wound, Mina?'

'In here, it is very itchy because there is so much magick. I am wearing jeans so that I can stick my hand in the pocket and stop me scratching it.'

'My head is the same in this weather. You did excellent work in Earlsbury, Mina, and we both know that the bloodletting has left an even bigger problem up there than who gets to be clan chief.'

'Yes. The Gold.'

Hannah picked up Mina's application form and held it out to her. 'You're overqualified for this job. I'd like to offer you a better one: Peculiar Auditor.'

Mina took the application form and placed it on the coffee table in front of her. 'I had no idea such a thing existed.'

'It didn't until this morning. The Cloister Court will have to decide who owns that Gold, and I know of no one better to advise the Court than you. It's a three year contract and you can work from wherever you want.'

Mina looked at me in disbelief. 'Conrad? Did you know about this?'

'No.'

'There is one condition,' said Hannah.

Mina tipped her head on one side. 'Only one, Constable?'

'Only one that matters. You have to stay out of my Watch Captain's combat operations unless I authorise it personally.'

Mina's skin colour (if you're interested) is a little towards the fairer end of the spectrum for Indian women and the lightest spot is the nape of her neck. That's where she blushes, and she was blushing now. 'All of them, or just Conrad's?'

'All of them. He wouldn't say no to you, but I have to. Sorry, but that's the condition.'

Mina moved her head around in a snakey sort of way. That meant she was about to lie. 'Good. I have no desire to witness any more decapitations. Once was too much.'

'Thank you,' said Hannah. 'You'll be paid by the Watch, and I'll be your line manager, but you'll be an officer of the Court. Both of you need to be in the judge's chambers at the Royal Courts of Justice at eleven o'clock.' She put on an innocent face. 'Have you been there before?'

Mina lifted her hair away from her neck. 'No, so that's another one I can tick off my list of courts. Does my status mean I don't have to wear a uniform? Shame.'

'Don't rub it in, Mina. I might get you to wear a deputy bailiff's uniform.'

'Why am I going to see the judge?' I asked. 'Not that I don't want to.'

Hannah stood up. 'You've been a naughty boy, that's why. Ah Gutten Erev Shabbos. Both of you.'

For the first time, Hannah embraced Mina. They both looked like they meant it.

14 — Oath of Allegiance

We caught the river bus back to Blackfriars and wandered up Farringdon Street, then along Fleet Street to the Royal Courts. We don't always hold hands when walking through London. Only when there are no clothes shops.

'What do you think of Saffron?' said Mina.

'You're not sure about her, are you?'

'Most people are complicated,' she said. 'Especially women. I don't understand everything about Vicky or Myvvy, still less Hannah, but I get them. I know where they're coming from. Saffron, not so much.'

'She's coming from incredible wealth, power and influence. What's not to get?'

'Oh yes. That much I get. So wealthy that Elvenham House is beneath her. So why is she in the Watch? I am not getting a strong sense of duty from her.'

I mulled it over. 'For the rush. For the badge. In one weekend, she acquired the power to arrest any Mage in the country, including her cousin. If she'd stayed at Salomon's House, she'd be Auntie Heidi's young apprentice.'

'Perhaps.'

'We'll see how she gets on next week. The life of a Watch Captain is not all sword fights and plunder. Here we are.'

We stood outside the impressive Victorian facade of the Royal Courts and looked around. Like the Old Bailey, you get a strong sense of immovable state power from buildings like this.

'I had hoped to see the Cloister Court itself,' said Mina. 'Myvvy says it's full-on creepy and ancient.'

'So I've heard. It's also very expensive, and doesn't sit that often.'

The Cloister Judge is also a judge in the mundane Court of Appeal. She uses her maiden name there, so I wouldn't bother trying to look her up.

We did security, we did directions, and we soon found ourselves high up at the back of the Courts being shown into the judge's rather cramped chambers. That's the price you pay for being a part-timer, I suppose.

The Honourable Mrs Justice Bracewell stood up to greet us. There is rather a lot of her, both in height and width. You could say that she is a solid presence. Her face was dominated by large framed glasses in a delicious red-blue combination that made it hard to tell her age, which could have been anywhere over fifty. Her brown hair was tied back, presumably ready to don the full wig that was resting on a stand nearby, next to the voluminous red robes. I say that her wig was *resting*. It definitely looked more like an exotic animal than a fashion statement.

There was no comfy seating area, so she waved us into two well-padded chairs in front of her desk and sat back down behind it. 'Thank you for coming, Miss Desai,' said the judge. She sat back and rested her hands in front of her. 'If I know the Constable, she will have offered you this post.'

Mina looked wary. 'Yes, my lady.'

I half expected the judge to say *call me Marcia*, but she clearly preferred to be formal. 'The Constable does not run the Cloister Court, even if she's the only one with the resources to hold investigations. The Peculier Auditor will be a sworn officer of the Cloister Court. Tell me, Miss Desai, why should I trust you?'

Mina gave the slow Indian nod that means she's thinking. 'You should trust me today because you trust the Constable. After that, you can judge for yourself, my lady.'

The judge didn't nod, she blinked. 'And there won't be a conflict of interest? Neither with the Constable nor with the Watch Captain at Large?'

I am the Watch Captain at Large. Mina allowed a smile to twitch the left corner of her mouth. 'With the Constable, no. With the other officer, all I can say is that I will do my best to keep him in line and make sure he doesn't slack off too often.'

The judge did her best to stifle a smile. 'Good luck with that.' She picked up a brief, loosely tied with purple tape. 'This is going to be monstrously difficult to sort out. The Gnomes want the gold, the Crown wants the gold … and no doubt more parties will crawl to the surface. The Constable tells me you cracked this using accountant's intuition. I didn't know there was such a thing.'

Mina lowered her head. 'Some of us even read poetry, my lady.'

'Hah. Well, you can't use intuition in evidence. I want it all tied down with names, dates, transaction details and paperwork. You'll need warrants for that, and I've got a bunch here for all the main players. Just remember, you don't work for Iain Drummond, still less Annelise van Kampen or the Gnomes. Got that?'

Mina nodded.

The Judge took a substantial parchment out of a drawer. 'This is a commission from the Court. You'll need to swear an oath.' She pressed an intercom and summoned her clerk. Mina took the Judicial Oath and the clerk left after signing the parchment as a witness. Mrs Bracewell placed the commission underneath the Golden Triangle papers and deftly re-tied the ribbon. 'Tennille Haynes will sort out your contract of employment. I expect weekly updates by email. We'll arrange face-to-face meetings as and when. Welcome to the Court.'

She shook Mina's hand and passed over the bundle. We sat down again, with Mina cradling the documents like a new pet.

'So …. Mr Clarke,' said the Judge. 'My husband wanted to meet the Dragonslayer. He would have loved your seminar last week, but he was out of town.'

'Your husband, my lady?'

'He's an esoteric antiquarian. A Mage of strictly limited talents, but I don't hold it against him. A bit like you, from what I hear.'

'I have a talent for survival, my lady. If Mr Bracewell has one, he should join the Watch, too.'

She actually laughed at that. 'I'll tell him to put in his application. He's survived thirty years with me, so anything's possible. Now, I'm sure you're wondering why you're here. It's because I haven't heard from you.'

'My lady?'

'Have you read the Seclusion order for Myfanwy Lewis?'

'Annelise explained it to me.'

She shook her head. 'I bet she explained enough to get you and Miss Lewis out of her hair and no more. You are Miss Lewis's supervising officer, and you have duties that go beyond providing lodgings and an entry into village society.'

This sounded ominous. It sounded like the judge knew something.

'You should read the order, Mr Clarke. Especially the section on providing reports to the Court on Miss Lewis's magickal activities.'

'To my knowledge, her magickal activities have been limited to a spot of gardening, my lady.'

The judge rapped her knuckles on the ancient desk. 'Precisely. She is a Herbalist. I have heard a rumour that she is planting a Herbal garden. Only a rumour, mind, because if it were true, I would expect her supervising officer to give the Court a full report. Am I making myself clear, Mr Clarke?'

'Crystal, my lady.'

'Good. You'll be pleased to know that there is no duty to report on her morals. I've heard rumours there, too.'

'Ben Thewlis is lucky to have her,' said Mina sharply.

'Of course. I'm sure.'

I frowned as the implications of this sank in. Only a Mage could have dobbed Myfanwy in with the judge. A Mage who'd been to Clerkswell, or had talked to one of our magickal house guests. The judge wouldn't reveal her source to me, so I didn't bother asking. Not yet. I tried a different tack. 'As you said, my lady, I have strictly limited talents. My knowledge of mundane gardening is very slight; my knowledge of Herbalism is zero.'

'Which is why Miss Lewis will write the report, you will submit it and an expert will review it. They may need to make a site visit.'

The clerk buzzed through with a time warning, and we got up to go. Mina had been looking around, and spotted something on the judge's shelves. Something that wasn't big, fat and legal in nature.

'Is that *Bid Better, Play Better* on the bottom shelf?' she said.

'Yes. Do you play?'

'I am a beginner only. Conrad's mother is the expert.'

The clerk was fussing with the judge's robes. 'You're not Mary Clarke's boy, are you?' said Mrs Bracewell.

'I am.'

'Then you have a very good teacher, Miss Desai. Good luck with the gold.'

We stayed quiet until we were walking down the steps and back into the sunshine. 'I wonder how she knows your mother,' said Mina.

'And I wonder how she knows about Myfanwy's garden. Clearly a well connected judge.'

'Yes. I hope Myvvy's not planning to poison the opposition with something from the garden.'

'Doesn't need to. Just serve that beef-free chili and the other team will capitulate.'

'No!' said Myfanwy. 'How much?'

Mina repeated the salary for Peculier Auditor.

'I don't believe you,' said Myfanwy. 'You left here the other day unemployed and now you're the biggest earner at Elvenham. Respect, Mina.'

'They're getting me cheap,' said Mina. 'There should be another "1" on the front of the figure.'

Myfanwy grinned. 'You won't be needing my board and lodging payments now, will you?'

Mina waved her hand airily, as if such things were beneath her. 'That's Conrad's department. I shall need to put all my salary towards a suitable wardrobe.' She looked down at her tunic dress. 'Seriously. I may need suits. The judge clearly thought this outfit was a little disrespectful. On the other hand, I am definitely buying Champagne at the Inkwell later.'

There was no women's practice tonight, because tomorrow was a special day. There was a blank in the men's fixtures, and the 4Cs (that's the Clerkswell Cricket Club Committee) had graciously allowed the ladies to practise on the main ground. Nets are all very well, but you can't practise outfielding in them, nor can you afford to play your first match on a wicket you've never used before. Not when you're the home team.

It was a party of four at the Inkwell. We'd invited Erin, but she had to go to a Foresters' meeting and would be coming down in the morning. Ben looked very pre-occupied, and I asked what was up when the girls went off to have a quick word with Nell.

'All sorts,' he said. 'This weather's awful. Too hot and dry after a cold spring. I've got crops all over with no depth of root.'

I know enough about cereal agronomy to nod sympathetically, and he knew enough not to go any further.

'And the wedding,' he added. 'Carole's gone into full Bridezilla mode. Mum's spent the week in London going dress shopping, and Dad's refusing to get involved because Isaac's paying for everything, so it's landed back with me. Do I look like a wedding planner?'

'No, mate, you do not. You look like a man who needs cheering up,' I said with sympathy. Reynold, the landlord, paraded towards us with an ice bucket and Champagne flutes. I pointed to him and said, 'He looks like one, though.' The landlord deposited the ice bucket and turned the label to face us.

'Reynold, can you take over organising Carole's wedding?'

'I am no one's gay best friend,' he responded. 'Nor do I have an obsession with interior design.'

'We can see that,' said Ben.

'If you had taste, I'd be offended by that remark. Enjoy the Champagne. What's the occasion, anyway? More wedding bells?'

Ben and I gave each other the *hunted male* look. It's instinctive. 'Mina's got a job,' I said.

'Then I hope she remembers to tip well.'

We didn't overdo it at the Inkwell, and we were at Mrs Clarke's Folly in good time. Ben and I had agreed that from today, we'd let Juliet and Myfanwy run the show. Jules had even enrolled on a coaching and leadership course. I may dislike the woman, but I wasn't going to question her commitment. Ben thinks she's doing it to prove to Stephen that she will make a better captain than he did. He only lasted a year in charge of the men's team.

'What's up?' said Ben. He pointed to the pavilion, where Jules was looking at her phone and talking to Myfanwy. After some arguing, they came over to us at our station by the large roller. Juliet looked upset and Myfanwy looked furious.

'Noticed anyone missing?' said Myfanwy. She didn't wait for a reply. 'That bitch from Allington, the wicket keeper, well she wasn't a wicket keeper, she was a snake in the grass, that's what she was. She's only been coming to spy on us, and she's poached Emily.'

Ben and I stood up straight. Emily Ventress, at fifteen years old, is the closest to a natural fast bowler I've seen in years, and the team's secret weapon. 'What do you mean?'

'I've had a text,' said Jules. 'A bloody text. Emily says that Allington have offered her regular games all summer, and she's going to register with them.'

'What are we going to do?' said Myfanwy.

'We're going to get on with it,' said Juliet. 'Your friend, Erin, said she'd like to try her hand at bowling, and Mina was my choice for wicket keeper anyway.' She frowned. 'What's up with her today? She's never had a problem with getting changed before, and now she's wearing that Under Armour top with the long sleeves.'

'Rash,' said Myfanwy. 'She's got a bad rash. Or sunburn. Something like that.'

'Sunburn? Whatever. Let's get going.'

She strode off and Ben followed. I caught Myfanwy's arm and whispered, 'Don't let Erin bowl.'

'Why ever not?'

'She's an Enscriber. She's got magick in her fingers, remember? She'll never be able to hold it back.'

She sighed. 'Fair point. I can have a go, I suppose.'

'You can, but you'd be far better inviting Miss Parkes to tea tonight. She taught Emily's mother, don't forget. Miss Parkes is your secret weapon, not Emily. Send her round chez Ventress after tea, and I'll bet Emily's mum will be so scared that she'll never sign a parental consent form for registration with Allington. Then you take Emily aside in the shop tomorrow and she'll soon see the error of her ways.'

'You are a devious sod, Conrad. I'll get on it.'

The Sunday morning farming forecast said that there were signs of the jet stream moving south again, and that the summer would be interrupted in a couple of weeks. There was no sign of that on a long, hot drive through the never-ending roadworks of the M6.

'Can't I use magick to hide it?' said Mina. She had unbuttoned the top of her dress and was staring down at her chest, at the swastika tattoo. There was a large lorry on our nearside, and I don't think Mina realised that the driver could look down and see it, too. If he chose.

'Vicky says not, love. I'm not sure why.'

'Then I'll have to pick my moment to go topless in the dressing room. I lost two pounds yesterday sweating in that thing.'

'I'd wait until the Allington match. Until you're losing. Peel it off at the crease and make sure the opposition get a look. That'll put them off their strokes.'

'Ha ha. We're moving.'

We were heading to Ribblegate Farm, partly to collect Scout and partly to help Stacey. Mina's former cell-mate had rung yesterday evening in something of a state, that was clear, but she hadn't wanted to talk on the phone. We had no idea what we were going to find when we got to Blackpool, or when Kelly and Mina got to Blackpool. According to Kelly, Stacey found me too scary, so I was banned.

We arrived in the farm after their Sunday dinner, and Kelly was all set to go. Unfortunately I had something very embarrassing to do first.

'Would you mind coming to the dog kennel?' I asked.

'What, me?' said Kelly.

'All of you. Including Natasha. The baby can stay asleep.'

'Why?'

'Clarke family tradition. Goes back generations. It won't take a minute. Please.' Kelly rolled her eyes and swapped her heels for wellingtons. She gathered the rest of the family, and I got the gift from the car.

Vicky had sent me a book from the Esoteric Library, with special permission from Francesca. It was called *The Ways of the Familiar Spirit*, and was very clear about what was necessary before we left Ribblegate Farm. I had bonded with Scout. Magickally bonded. If he'd been an adult dog, that would have been all that was necessary, but because he was a new-born puppy, he'd also bonded with the Kirkhams and his mother. Those bonds need to be unwoven, for his sake more than mine.

Joseph, Joe, Kelly and Natasha surrounded the dog kennel, and the mother dog looked at us suspiciously. Scout was jumping up and down and wagging his tail.

'Sit,' I said. 'And I mean it.' He sat. 'Good boy. Stay.' I turned to the humans. 'It would mean a lot to me if you all said, "Goodbye, Scout," and tickled his ears. Or his tummy.'

Natasha didn't hesitate. She picked him up and gave him a kiss. 'Goodbye Scouty. I'll miss you.'

'Tasha! I've told you not to do that,' said Kelly. She took the dog out of her daughter's arms and plonked him on the yard floor. 'Goodbye, Scout, you evil creature.' She was half-serious when she said that, and Scout barked loudly. Kelly did the business, though, and gave him a good scratch.

Joseph and Joe gave him a quick ruffle and said goodbye in their own way ('Alright, lad,' and 'Now then, Scout.' The book hadn't been specific about the words). That left the mother, and the biggest challenge.

I unwrapped the package and took out a joint of venison. Other meats had been ruled out on religious grounds (Mina) and tradition (you shouldn't feed raw pork or lamb to young dogs). I placed the meat in front of Scout and his tail went bananas. 'Take it to mother,' I said. He whined and sniffed the meat. 'Go on, boy, take it to mother.'

The book had been clear about this. If he ate the steak, I'd be going home with a pet, not a Familiar Spirit. He whined again and nibbled the meat with his little puppy teeth. I held my breath and realised that it had gone very quiet. Scout nibbled the meat again, and this time clamped it in his jaws. He dragged the steak over to his mother and put it in front of her nose with a bark.

'Good boy. Here.'

'What on earth is that you've got?' said Kelly.

'Curried worms.'

'Now I've seen everything,' said Joe. Scout took the worms from my hand and chewed them enthusiastically. 'That dog's not right in the head, Conrad, I'm telling you. He's bright, though, I'll give him that.'

'Can we go now?' said Kelly.

'Of course. Thank you all so much.'

I waved Mina and Kelly off in Kelly's car, then I showed Scout the back of my Volvo XC70, complete with dog bed. He was still too small to jump in, so I made him comfy and said, 'We're going for a drive, and you're going to meet something special.'

I spent the afternoon down the road at the Fylde Equine Research Centre, owned by an old acquaintance, Olivia Bentley. Given that the last time we'd met, she'd had to deal with a murdered farmer and fire in a stable full of horses, she was quite pleased to see me. Naturally, she fell in love with Scout.

'What are you doing here, Conrad?'

'Fancied a gallop. I'll pay, obviously.'

'No problem. Becka will sort you out.' She gave me a look. 'Where's Mina Finch? I'd like to meet her.'

'It's Mina Desai now. She's got business in Blackpool. She only let me come today because she saw on Twitter that Amelia's in London.'

Olivia gave me a knowing look. I once dated her sister, Amelia. We won't go there today. 'Enjoy the ride,' said Olivia.

We did enjoy it. Scout loved exploring the new environment and meeting horses for the first time. I told him to *stay* when I wanted to put the horse through its paces. He was still there when I got back. Asleep, yes, but still there. At that moment, Mina rang, and it wasn't good news.

Steroid Boy hadn't exactly been faithful while Stacey was doing time, and he'd done it with one of Stacey's "friends" from school. That was bad, but people have got over worse. He carried on carrying on with the friend after Stacey was released, to the point where several of Stacey's other friends had let her know about it. Shortly after, Steroid Boy had cleared out Stacey's bank account and cleared off with anything saleable from the flat. Stacey was now left with a tenancy she couldn't afford and everyone looking at her.

'What did you do?' I asked when we left Ribblegate Farm two hours later.

'No, Scout, get back,' said Mina. 'Is he always going to do this?'

I pulled in to the side of the road and turned round. 'Listen, Scout, you do what the mistress tells you. Understand? Basket. Now.'

He scrambled back over the seats and into the rear area.

'Is he going to live in the house?'

'No. He can sleep in the first stable for now. We'll review the situation in the autumn. About Stacey?' They'd brought the young woman back with them from Blackpool, and installed her at the farm.

'I paid the landlord a month's rent and told him to keep the deposit. He agreed to waive the rest of the tenancy. I will give Kelly more money at some point. Some men are very stupid. Very, very stupid.'

I wasn't going to argue with that.

Myfanwy was working in the garden when we got back. She peeled off her gloves and came to meet us, drawing a piece of paper from her pocket. 'I've got it,' she announced triumphantly. 'Emily and her mother have both signed. Ben's going to hand deliver it to the association secretary tomorrow.'

She and Mina high-fived while I opened the car.

I lifted Scout from the back and held him up. 'See that dragon, boy? You have to bark at him whenever we come home. Got that?'

I put him down and he looked up at the stone. He considered it for a second, and there was a flash of green in his brown eye. He barked. Loudly.

'Oh, he is so cute,' said Myfanwy.

Scout scampered across the gravel drive and climbed the front steps with some difficulty. When he got to the front door, he did his best to lift his leg and urinate on the door. Then he turned to us and opened his mouth in what can only be described as a grin.

'You bad boy,' said Myfanwy. 'If you do that in the house, I swear down I will have you at the vets and castrated faster than you can say *sausages*.'

'You know what?' I said. 'It's good to have another man around the house.'

'Be careful, Conrad,' said Mina, 'or you may end up with him in the stables.'

15 — All Quiet on the Mercian Front

'Watch Captain Clarke, may I present Saunders, the new Chief of Clan Flint,' said Lloyd.

He hadn't put himself forward. The new chief was anything but new in years, being much older than the disgraced Wesley. He was small, even by Gnomish standards, wizened and nearly bald. His beady eyes looked over me, then took an age to consider Mina. Saunders was clearly an old school Gnome.

'He's the Swordbearer,' said Saunders in a nearly impenetrable Black Country accent. 'He should kneel.'

I left that one for Lloyd.

'I presented him as Watch Captain, Chief. He's Watch first and clan second. The Watch only kneel for the King.'

'It should always be clan first. Can I sack him?'

'Not without killing him.'

'Not today then.' He looked at Mina again. 'Who are you?'

'Namaste, Chief,' said Mina with a deep bow. When she looked up, she put her finger on her cheek. 'How many Indian women do you think work at Merlyn's Tower? I'm sure you know exactly who I am, Chief. If you need help with the spelling, it's on this warrant to search and seize your records.'

'Give it to Lloyd, then clear out, the lot of you.'

As I said, an old school Gnome.

Lloyd escorted us downstairs. 'Will you ever be chief?' I asked.

'I hope so. One day. I didn't stand this time because I'd be vulnerable. I'm the last of the Fifth House, and I haven't had a son yet.'

Being the wife of a Gnome is not an easy job. Gnomes only father sons (i.e. other Gnomes) every eighth child. That's seven mundane, human daughters before they get a son, and not all of those daughters come to term. It's not considered polite to ask how many children any given wife has borne.

'Does Saunders have sons?'

'Two. They both died a long time ago. It's the Third House that bothers me.' He shook his head. 'If something happens to me, get out quick, Conrad. When they put me in the Mine, lay your sword on top and walk away. They can't touch you, then. If you don't, the new Second might put you to the test.'

'Let me guess: a fight to the death.'

'Got it in one. And you can't use the Anvil.'

'I'll bear that in mind.'

'I'll be in my office, downstairs,' he said to Mina. 'Chief Saunders has delegated this mess to me to sort out.'

146

'I'll see you shortly.'

Mina and I took a moment outside the Flint House compound to say goodbye. 'Will you be alright in there?' I said. 'I know you will, but I have to ask.'

'It depends. If they have written ledgers, it may take me a while, now go and play with your new friend.'

'I hope you don't mean Saffron.'

She blinked at me. 'Why would I say that? I meant Scout, of course. I'll call you.'

We had parked the car a good walk from Flint House, near Victoria Park. The car was empty when I got back to it, so I wandered into the park to look for Saffron and Scout. I found them, away by the fountain, and Scout was in trouble again.

You may be asking why I sent Saffron to look after the dog rather than meet the Gnomes. It was her suggestion, and it came to her about five seconds after she'd heard about Mina's new title. We'd picked Saffron up at Earlsbury Station on our way to Flint House, and we'd taken a moment standing round the car before we set off. I'd told Saffron on the phone that Mina had a new job, and when Mina had explained that she was now the Peculier Auditor, Saffron had pulled so hard at her blond mane that it needed rearranging. After doing it back up, she'd volunteered to take Scout to the park.

When I got closer to the fountain, I could see Saffron on one side and Scout on the other, with a park warden closing in on them, shouting, 'What are you doing? That dog needs to be on a lead!'

That dog had something in his mouth, too, and Saffron had been chasing him fruitlessly round the fountain.

'Scout! Sit!' I said. He sat, and put Saffron's now soggy and lightly chewed mobile phone on the ground. Luckily for her, it had a cover on both sides.

The three humans converged on the dog, and he wagged his tail. I bent down and scooped him up before the warden got any funny ideas. 'I'm so sorry,' I said. 'He must have slipped out of the car without his lead.'

'That's right,' said Saffron. 'Too quick for me.'

'I'll take him back now.'

The warden reached for his pocket. The jumped-up jobsworth was going to give us a ticket. Specifically, he was going to give Saffron a ticket. He got out his pen and opened the pad of fixed penalty notices.

Saffron reached and touched his pen. 'I'm so sorry,' she said. 'He's such a little scamp. It won't happen again.'

'No, it won't,' said the warden. When he tried to write, his pen wouldn't work. *Little scamp* indeed. I'm talking human here, not canine.

'Saffron, we're part of the solution, remember?' I said, as gently as I could.

She turned to me. 'What? You're not serious.'

The warden was looking dubiously at us, and took a step back. 'What's going on?' he said.

I put Scout down and gave him a treat. 'If there was a good reason for there not to be a paper trail showing us in this park, then yes, we could sabotage this gentleman's pen or give a false name. Today is not that day.'

The warden stared at his pen. 'You did that?'

I took out a business card. One with the full RAF titles and logos on it. 'This dog is going to be the new squadron mascot. I'm looking after him until he's old enough.'

The warden read the card. He stood straight and said, 'Earlsbury Council is proud to support our services. But even well-behaved dogs can scare children or run into the road if they're not on a lead.'

'I'm sorry.'

'We'll leave it there for now, if you and your daughter could take him straight out.'

'Ohmygod no,' said Saffron. 'I'm not his daughter.'

The warden raised his eyebrows.

'This is Lieutenant Hawkins, Royal Military Police,' I said.

The warden blushed and put his book away. 'Well, thank you sir, ma'am.'

I slipped him a fiver. 'For a new pen. C'mon Scout.' I picked up the little scamp along with as much dignity as I could muster and walked towards the gates, leaving Saffron to stare at her phone. When she joined me at the car, she was carrying it in a (clean) poop bag.

'Wait until I tell Erin about that,' said Saffron. 'Your daughter! It's the hat that does it, Conrad.'

'My head has been scorched by a Dragon and burnt with acid. It does not like the sun, and don't change the subject. I wasn't joking back there.'

'It's your bloody dog, not mine. You should have had the ticket.'

'What happened?'

'He wanted a bloody ice cream, that's what. And when I wouldn't buy him one, he jumped up and nicked my phone.'

'How on earth do you know he wanted an ice cream?'

'He stood by the van and howled. He also projected hunger strongly enough for every old lady in Earlsbury to take pity on him. I'm surprised it wasn't the RSPCA who turned up to arrest me for neglect.'

I had to laugh. Saffron didn't think it was funny until I held my hands up and said, 'Fair enough. We'll get him a lead for public places, and if he does it again, we'll put his name on the ticket.'

'Damn right we will.'

'And we'll say nothing about the fact that you sat on the bench with your phone and ignored him.'

It was her turn to blush. 'What? How did you know?'

'Because you will have been messaging every Hawkins in your contact book to tell them about the new Peculier Auditor. Did you tell them to hide all their ill-gotten gains under the bed?'

She grinned. 'It's a fair cop. I won't do it again, but Mina's job is public knowledge, right?'

'Correct.'

She brushed back her hair. 'Did it go okay with the Gnomes? And what next?'

'Mina can cope with our diminutive allies. As for what's next, you're going to read this folder while I go and get us some coffees.' I opened the back of the car. 'And you, Scout, are going to lie down and be a good boy.'

That folder was the best I could do for a handbook. England and Wales is divided into fourteen Watch Districts, and we had been given responsibility for District 5, also known as Mercia, covering the old counties of Staffordshire, Warwickshire and Worcestershire. That is a huge percentage of the mundane population, but it's actually the least important Watch, simply because there isn't much magickal activity there.

You know about Clan Flint, and if you've read Vicky's adventure of the Phantom Stag, you'll know about the Arden Foresters and the Fae Prince of Arden. Beyond them, there isn't a lot. A few isolated covens, a few Fae Nobles and a scattering of Mages. That's all I could find in my predecessor's records.

I got back with the coffees and passed one through the passenger window while I stood outside the car to have a smoke. 'What do you reckon?' I said.

'Thanks for the coffee. Who did this?'

'Me. I put it together from what records I had.'

'And who made them?'

'My predecessor, Mack McKeever, now of New England.'

'Oh, him. I'd forgotten about him. It's … pretty rubbish.'

I sighed. 'I'm not surprised. Mack had a flexible approach to his duties. He definitely took bribes from Clan Flint, and I'll bet he pocketed a lot of the summary fines he dished out.'

She looked at the file again. 'Is Malvern in Mercia?'

'Malvern is in Worcestershire, so yes, it's in Mercia.'

'That's where Bertie lives. Hang on.'

She reached over to the driver's seat. A discarded pair of latex gloves and her old phone case nestled in the folds of the poop bag. She picked up her phone and thumbed through to a contact. She pressed *dial* and swept back some hair to get the phone to her ear.

'Hi, Bertie, it's Saffron … thanks …' A long pause. 'Yes, that's right … Any chance of lunch? … Yes, of course I'm on duty … He's the Dragonslayer … One o'clock? … Great. See you soon.'

She looked up at me. 'We've got nothing else on, have we?'

'No. Lunch with Bertie sounds good. Who is he?'

'She. Alberta Hawkins. I've no idea how we're related, but we are. Everyone calls her Bertie, and no one can say no when she rings up. Once you get her going, you'll find out all you need to know about magick in Mercia.'

She should have asked first, but she'd just analysed the situation and come up with a plan. I wasn't going to knock that. 'Good idea, Saffron. You put the postcode in the satnav and I'll take Scout to find a lamp post. But not in the park.'

'I thought you were a Navigator. What do you need a satnav for?'

'Which has the worst traffic? The A449 or the M5 roadworks? If I could answer that, I'd ditch the thing. I also use autopilot when I'm flying. It has a longer attention span than I do.'

Scout did his business, I found a bin for the poop bag and the coffee cups, and we set off (A449 is the answer). This was the first time we'd been alone since Saffron was inducted into the Watch, and I wondered how she'd react. She sent a couple of messages while I was sorting out the dog, then put her phone away when I got in to drive.

I have been told that (for a man), I'm a good listener. For now, I was content to talk rather than pry. The first thing Saffron wanted to know was what I'd left out of the Dragon seminar, and when I'd given her the headlines, she wanted to know about my time in the RAF. In the backwash of chat, I did discover a few things about her. That she was the middle child of three, for example, and that her younger brother has no Gift. She avoided talking about her older sister, other than saying that she hadn't stayed on at Salomon's House after taking her Fellowship.

'I'd forgotten how nice it was round here,' said Saffron as we slowed down to approach the village of Colwall, up in the Malvern Hills.

'How long since you came?'

'I've only been once. When I was about nine. Nearly all the Hawkins are in the Thames Valley, but not Bertie. She comes to us. Turn right there, then right on to Mathon Lane. It's along there.'

'Is it occluded?'

'No. Warded and guarded, yes, but not occluded. It's about a quarter of a mile.'

'You must have a very good memory if you haven't been here since you were nine.'

'No. I texted my father for directions.'

'What's it called?'

'It's the most stupid tradition in our family, but all the houses are called "Something Roost", because we're hawks. This one is Mathon Roost. I told my family that the landlord wouldn't let me change the name of the flat, so in London I live at number 43.'

If I live long enough to retire and hand over Elvenham to the next generation, I don't want to follow my parents to Spain. I want to live in Mathon Roost. Mina may have other ideas, but we'll cross that bridge when we come to it. For now, I was going to sit back and admire.

The drive from the road twisted and turned, as magickal drives often do, as that makes it easier to put Wards and redirections in place. When we rounded the last bend, it was to find a beautiful, warm-brick cottage with a red tiled roof. Rooms slumbered behind curtains either side of the wisteria-framed door. The welcoming image of the front was completed by planted borders and hanging baskets, but that was only the start.

Like a declaration of intent, a Triumph motorcycle was parked in front of the door. A gaudy, red Triumph, with this year's number plates. Saffron leaned over and put her hand on the car horn for a good five seconds. Scout did not like that.

When I opened the tailgate to let him out, I pointed the finger and said, 'You are going to be so good it hurts.'

Saffron was arranging her hair (she'd had the window open). 'He doesn't understand you. If he was that clever, he wouldn't be a Familiar.'

Scout looked at her and barked. He understands exactly what he wants to understand, though I got the impression he had become a Spirit well before modern technology came on the scene.

The front door opened, and Bertie Hawkins held out her arms for Saffron to run into. You could see the family resemblance, especially in the eyes and the cheekbones. Lots of hair, too. Bertie's was a light brown and straight down her back. She had thicker hips and a bigger chest than Saffron, but somehow looked lighter on her feet, as if she had a harness running up her back. She was wearing jeans and a man's white shirt, which suited her perfectly, as did the red toenails showing from her sandals. It was only when you looked closely that you realised how old she was. You'd peg her mundane years at something around or over a well preserved sixty; in Mage years, that's probably about ninety.

'Saffy, darling! This is a surprise,' she said when the hug was over.

Saffron turned round. 'Bertie is one of three people who get to call me *Saffy*. Hmm. Bertie, this is Conrad.'

'How d'you do,' she said, matching her brisk words with a firm handshake. 'Ma'am.'

She hooted. 'Don't call me that, whatever you do! It's *Bertie*, or *Miss Hawkins* if you want to sound like a tradesman.'

I am a tradesman. Richer than most, yes, but a tradesman nonetheless. I just smiled. 'A pleasure. You have a beautiful house.'

'This isn't the house, this is just the front. The house is through and down. Come on, there's lemonade.'

She was about to move when she lifted her head and looked around, then down. 'Who's this gorgeous creature?' she said as Scout scampered round. 'Great heavens! Is that a bonded Familiar?' She bent down to let him sniff her hand. 'He is. I haven't seen one of these in simply ages. Where did you get him?'

'He got me. I was visiting friends on a farm in Lancashire when it happened.'

'Assuming your farmer friends aren't Mages, he won't have been there. Did you sense him before that?'

'I think so. He probably latched on to me somewhere in the Lakeland Particular.'

She considered Scout again. 'Stranger and stranger. You must have disturbed something when you were rushing about. The dog form was very young when you bonded, wasn't he?'

'His eyes were still closed.'

She nodded thoughtfully. 'In the dark days, when Witches were hanged, having a Familiar was a useful thing. Most Mages think they're too much bother, now.'

I bent down. 'You're not too much bother, lad.'

We followed Bertie down a long, dark passage leading through the cottage, with closed doors on either side. Instead of a kitchen, we came to the top of a staircase that only led down, not up. There was a top floor to the cottage, but goodness knows how you get there.

And then you saw the down-downstairs and forgot about the front.

The doorway emerged into the middle of an open space the size of two badminton courts, with a vaguely kitchen and eating area to the left and behind, then a series of modern couches scattered around to the right and behind. On the right hand wall was a baronial fireplace with a vase of fresh flowers in front of it. On the rear right hand wall was a *big* television. The space was large enough for some couches to face the TV, some the fireplace and one looked out, which was where your eye was drawn first.

The whole of the far wall was glass bi-fold doors. Only the central pair were open, the rest closed and shaded to keep out the sun and the heat. Bertie slowed down enough for us to appreciate the space, and Saffron stopped to say, 'Wow! I don't remember this.'

'I opened it out a couple of years after your last visit, dear.'

'It's stunning, Bertie.'

'And a bugger to keep clean. Come on.'

Through the doors was a spectacular view to the east and south, down over the hills to the Severn Valley and the city of Worcester beyond. You didn't notice the terraced gardens until you'd finished drinking in the view.

'I hope you have a gardener,' I said. 'If you don't, I am truly humbled.'

'I have two,' said Bertie. 'Doesn't make it much easier, but you're right. I couldn't manage without them. Have a seat.'

To the right, away from the windows, was a seating area covered by a large sunshade. I turned round and took a step back to look at the house. Above, and set back, I could see the blank back wall of the small cottage. The whole of the downstairs space had been engineered out of some original cellar, massively blown up and carved out of the slope. I was truly impressed.

We settled down, and Bertie made sure I got the best view, while Scout went off to explore the gardens. Her home-made lemonade was exactly what we needed after dealing with the M5, and Bertie did me the honour of welcoming me as the lead guest. In the weird code of magickal hospitality, I'd normally be an appendage to Saffron, who was family.

'How's Trixie?' said Saffron after the toast of welcome.

Bertie *hmmphed*. 'That's my daughter, Conrad. She's not called Trixie, obviously, but when she was younger, I made the mistake of saying that she could be *tricksy*. The name stuck, much to my embarrassment. She chose the Daughters in Glastonbury ahead of Salomon's House.' She turned back to Saffron. 'She's fine, and so are the twins. They're even tricksier, if that were possible. Now, Conrad, tell me all about that Dragon.'

You know that story, so I'll move on to lunch.

Bertie served us a light and fresh salad, back in the kitchen. There was a *lot* of marble in there. We ate at a small table, in the shadow of its much larger formal cousin. When she'd put some slices of quiche in front of us, she said, 'It's an honour to have you in my house, Conrad, but unless the Watch are a lot less busy than they pretend to be, I do wonder why you're here.'

Before I could answer, there was a terrible sound of screeching cat and barking dog from outside. I stood up to investigate, and Scout ran through the door, his tail firmly between his legs. 'What's up, boy?'

Bertie found it very amusing. 'He's discovering his limitations, that's what's up. A young border collie is no match for Marmalade. He's lucky she didn't take an eye out.'

Scout barked plaintively at me, then went over to a shady corner. He turned round on the flagstone floor, then moved over and started eyeing up some throws on the back of a settee. 'You can have the red one,' said Bertie.

Scout moved his head in confusion. 'Aah,' said Bertie. 'I did wonder. He has doggy-vision, see? He can't tell which throw is red. Here, boy.' She rubbed her hands together and did something I've not seen before. She formed a small ball of light in her palm and let it rest there, like a marble. She blew on the ball and it flew over, bursting on the red throw. Scout jumped up and grabbed the edge of the throw. With great gusto and wagging of tail, he pulled it down, dragged it to a corner and trampled it into a bed. In seconds, he was asleep. It's a dog's life, isn't it?

'Have a look at this, Bertie,' said Saffron, passing her my meagre folder of Mercian Mages.

She looked at the Post-it note on the cover first. 'Since when did that disgusting creature Saunders Flint become clan chief? I never thought he'd see the light of day again.'

'Since Saturday. Chief Wesley was collateral damage in an internal dispute,' I said. She'd find out the whole truth sooner or later, but that was a distraction I could do without today.

She scanned the rest of the document and passed it back. 'Look's like you've been sold a pup.' She glanced at Scout. 'Two pups.'

'We wondered if you could fill in some of the gaps?' said Saffron, in the sweet voice that only young female relatives can get away with. I used to cringe when Rachael did that to Grandma Enderby. Works every time, though.

Bertie sniffed and shook her head. 'Hmm. You've got the Worcester mob in there. I'll text you the rest of my local contacts, but your biggest gap is Staffordshire. The forgotten county of magick.'

'How so?' I asked. 'This quiche is delicious.'

'Thank you. Staffordshire is where Mages and other creatures went when they weren't welcome in the Marches, the Danelaw or the Palatinate.'

She'd named the three Watch districts to the north, west and east of Staffordshire. All covered by experienced Watch Captains. 'What does that mean?' I asked. 'In practical terms.'

'It means that the magickal world there is very clandestine. You need to know about the Brewers. That's a nickname, but they really are based in Burton on Trent. It's a collective of Artificers. You should see them. As for the rest, I'd start in Lichfield. Tetty Johnson's House.'

'Thank you. That's very generous.'

'Worth it to hear the Dragon story from the man himself, though it's a shame you didn't bring Vicky with you.'

'Perhaps next time.'

'That would be nice. Coffee? Outside, I think. The sun has gone round a bit. You go and smoke, while Saffron helps me clear up.'

There was a very large, very orange cat in the middle of the garden settee. 'You just wait, Marmalade,' I said. 'We'll be back.' In response, the cat licked herself.

Bertie brought the coffee and had developed a frown as dense as the heat. 'Saffron's just told me about the Peculier Auditor. She says you're "an item" with her, and that she's mundane. Sorry, what was her name again?'

'Mina Desai, and yes, you could say we are an item.'

'I wonder whose idea this was?' she said, more to herself than me. She passed me a cup of coffee and gave me her attention. 'It will be one of those three.' She looked agitated. Bertie Hawkins doesn't have a veneer of privilege:

she has a solid wooden core of privilege, so you couldn't say that it had slipped, it had just shown a different side to itself. She was going to explain who *those three* were, then stopped and turned to Saffron, then back to me. 'Please excuse me, Conrad, this may be impertinent. Have I got this right? Mina was your girlfriend before you joined the world of magick, and she's been dragged into this?'

'More or less. Her first encounter with magick was shortly after mine. Should I be worried?'

'Mina can handle herself,' said Saffron. 'She took down a Mage on her own. And she understands double entry book keeping.'

Bertie tried for a reassuring smile. 'Then I'm sure she'll be fine.'

I couldn't let it rest there. Not with Mina likely to do most of her work on her own. 'Who are *those three*?'

'Oh. Marcia, Cora and Hannah. They all have agendas about how magick should be governed in Albion. Please excuse me, Conrad. The Malvern Hills are a long way from London. The politics of the Occult Council are above my head.'

'And mine.' It was time to change the subject. 'What should I know about Saffron that isn't in her files?'

Saffron went suitably red, and Bertie leaned back to laugh. 'Don't get me started! I presume she hasn't told you about the London Zoo incident.'

'No!' said Saffron. 'You can't tell him that! I was only eight.'

'Perhaps not. She was in a band at school. You can still find videos of Starlight Hair on Youtube.'

'I shall look them up.'

Saffron, now a deep shade of crimson, put her cup down. 'When are you going to get your licence back, Bertie? It's a shame to see that bike lying idle.'

That was out of order, and clearly hurt Bertie deeply. I reached for my phone. 'Mina's had enough of the Gnomes,' I said, pretending to read a text. 'We'd better extract her. Could I…?'

'Of course. It's the door under the stairs.'

Scout was determined to climb the stairs on his own, despite the fact he could barely see over each riser, so I left him to it while I visited the bathroom. He was barking loudly when I emerged, and I jogged up the stairs to see if he needed rescuing from Marmalade.

The little mite was barking at a door. A door that hadn't been there before and was right where you'd expect a staircase going up to be. I scooped him up and went out the front. Saffron looked like she'd been apologising. Good.

I stowed Scout and went to shake hands. 'Forgive me for not bringing a guest gift,' I said. 'I didn't think that Hinkley Services would have anything you'd welcome, or that you'd do me the honour of making me your guest.'

'Your story was gift enough,' said Bertie.

'Thank you, Miss Hawkins.'

Saffron didn't notice what I'd said, and hugged her relative. Bertie was eyeing me over Saffron's shoulder. She'd got the message: I was a tradesman who wasn't pretending otherwise.

'Hinkley Services,' said Saffron when we'd driven off. 'They all have these phone accessory shops, don't they?'

'There's only one way to find out.'

16 — Backhand

She waited until I was on the road down from the Malvern Hills before speaking again. 'They're not all like that. Honest.'

She thought she could brush it away. I wasn't going to let her get off so easily. 'Who's not like what?'

She *hmmphed*. 'My family. They don't all think they own the world.'

'On a sample of two – Bertie and Heidi – it's not looking good.'

'What about me?'

'You took the oath. You're not family any more.'

'What! All I bloody heard when I was in Clerkswell was *Clarke this* and *Clarke that*. They've even named the cricket ground after your family. I don't see you renouncing that in a hurry.'

'In the unlikely event that my sister develops magickal powers, I'll be the first to lock her in the Undercroft. Until then, it's not a problem.'

'Oh. So where does that leave me? Do I move out of my flat and block all their contacts in my phone?'

I was tempted to tell her to grow up. I resisted. 'Just do what I do: don't talk about the Watch. Don't discuss your cases. Pretend your family are mundane. Until you need their help, of course. Then it's okay to ask questions.'

'Oh. I never thought of it like that.'

'Why would you? My mother worked all her life for GCHQ. I know that she was a cryptanalyst, and I know what they served in the canteen. The bridge club used to meet at our house, and I played cricket for and against them a few times. That's it. Thirty-five years of nothing. I don't know whether she told Dad any more than that. I grew up with it. You didn't.'

'So who did she talk to? What about her mental health?'

'You have me to talk to, Saffron. That's what partners are for. And friends. Up to a point. Mina knows a lot, and that will change now she's in the loop. Myfanwy knows some of it. You killed someone last week. That's definitely something that's worth talking about.'

'It was … self defence.'

Oh dear. I'm sure she was going to say *it was only a Gnome*. That could be a problem. I'd pushed her as far as I could today.

'And taking me to see Bertie was an astute move,' I said. 'You were spot on with that. Good lunch, good contacts, lovely lemonade. Unless there's an emergency, I know what we're doing tomorrow.'

She accepted the change of subject gratefully. I'd given her a lot to chew on. I honestly don't know whether she'll spit or swallow, if you'll pardon the image, but I have faith in her. She really will think about it.

'What are we up to tomorrow, then?' she asked.

'Lichfield. Your homework is to find Tetty Johnson's House.'

'I've never heard of her.'

'Neither have I, but I assume she was Samuel Johnson's wife.'

'Who?'

'Really?'

'Yes. He wasn't a Mage, so…'

'That's two lots of homework for you, then. I shall test your spellings as well.'

'Yes, teacher. What's your homework?'

'I shall consult with the Royal Occulter.'

I did feel slightly guilty when I picked Mina up from Earlsbury, and I was wondering how to tell her what I'd been up to when she lessened the guilt level by telling me that she hadn't had to spend *all* day with Gnomes.

'Anna took me out for lunch. She said she was feeling sorry for me, but I think she wanted to know what really happened in the First Mine.' She gave me a sidelong smile. 'She didn't believe that two women and two cripples had taken out three Gnomes and a Mage.'

'No man is a hero to his friend's wife. *Cripple* is a bit harsh, though I suppose I was limping a lot when we went to see Niði. You should have told her that one of the women was a Hawkins. That would have impressed her.'

'Really? I've not seen much to be impressed about.'

'Scout ate her phone today. And nearly got her a ticket from a park warden.'

She turned round. 'You are a very good dog. You should keep this up. Understand?'

Thankfully, Scout was fast asleep. I dread to think what would happen if he took her literally.

'How did the data gathering go? Judging by the weight of that case, you've hit the mother lode.'

'Put it this way: I will be working from home tomorrow and for the foreseeable future. Anna was nice, once you got past the protective attitude.'

'Protective of Lloyd?'

'Yes, but it's more that he represents her daughters' future. She has three. If Lloyd goes the same way as his brother before they're eighteen, the clan will abandon them.'

I was about to tell her what I'd been up to, when my phone rang and the handsfree display showed an ominous name: *Sister Bigbucks*. Rachael. And yes, she really is richer than me.

'Hi sis,' I said. 'You're on speaker and I'm with Mina.'

'Oh. Hi.'

'Hi, Rachael,' said Mina.

Rachael paused for half a second. 'Good news or bad news, Conrad?'

It was an old family game. Dad used to say that, and when we asked for *good news*, he'd always say, "The good news is that things could be worse." The important thing, today, was not the news itself, but that Rachael was referring to our shared past. A sort of sibling olive branch.

'I'll take what I can get,' I said.

'The good news is that your French friend got the job. He was a little peeved when I told him that I was off to Frankfurt soon, but there you go.'

'Excellent. Thanks for giving him a chance, Raitch. I owe you one.'

'You do. How's that coming along?'

Rachael and I had made a complex bargain about my past and its impact on the future. A journalist was pestering Rachael for an interview, and the only way I could get her off Rachael's back was to get Mina a job with the magickal establishment. That way, the security services (without knowing why) would tell the journalist to go away. There was more to it than that, including me giving said journalist an off the record briefing and Rachael giving Alain Dupont an interview. It looked like this was going to work out.

'All over bar the whispering,' I said. 'I'll give my contact a call tonight.' I paused. 'None of this sounds like bad news, Raitch. Why am I fearing the worst?'

'Because Carole has asked me to be chief bridesmaid, that's why. One of her friends is going on her own honeymoon in September, and another one is going to the Alaskan oilfields and can't get out of the contract. I may be third choice, but at least I know the area.'

Mina was giving me severely raised eyebrows. 'Does this mean what I think it means?'

'If you think it means I want a bed over the weekend, then yes it does.' She drew breath and tried to be light-hearted. 'How many people have you got staying there now?'

We'd fallen out big time when she accused me of filling her childhood home with strange women. Technically, this is true, but it's a question of attitude.

'There's always room for you, Raitch,' I said, dodging the question.

'Do you play cricket?' said Mina hopefully. She knows full well that Rachael hates cricket.

'I prefer tennis, and I'd love a game, but someone dug up the court and replaced it with a herb garden for some reason. My backhand will never improve now.'

'Such a shame,' said Mina. 'You could have joined us for practice on Friday night and watched our first game on Saturday morning.'

'Does the women's practice end in the same place as the men's?'

'If you mean *in the pub*, most definitely. About eight thirty.'

'I'll see you there. Unfortunately, Carole is dragging me away on Saturday, so I'll have to miss the game. Ciao, Conrad. Nice talking to you Mina. Bye.'

'What was all that about?' said Mina as soon as the display had confirmed that the call was truly ended.

'Which bit?'

'The cloak and dagger part.'

'It was about you, mostly. Do you remember me telling you about Juliet Porterhouse of the *Sunday Examiner*?'

Mina wasn't happy at the thought of having to pick at old scars, but she couldn't find a better solution to the problem. That was one item ticked off the to-do list. Unfortunately, I don't think the Nine of Wands was finished with me yet. I don't even think it's really started.

'I am not wearing a wig.'

'Not yet, Saffron, but you soon will be. There's a very good shop just outside the station.'

She didn't budge. She folded her arms and remained fixed to the concourse of Birmingham New Street station like a well-placed pedestrian obstruction. The last minute commuters paid her as much attention as does water flowing around a stone.

'Why?' she said.

'Advice from the Royal Occulter.'

'I can't believe that you rang him and that he suggested *wearing a wig*. Either you're winding me up, or he was winding you up.'

'Shall we discuss this outside, before Scout goes mental and bites someone?'

My Familiar did not like being put on a lead. He *really* didn't like it. He understands a lot, but railway by-laws are beyond him. Myfanwy and I had only convinced him when she borrowed a cat travel carrier from Miss Parkes and threatened him with going in that as an alternative. He took one sniff and lay down with his head on his paws.

I picked him up and carried him out of the station with Saffron a long way behind. I found a quiet corner and gave Scout a treat. Saffron finally came up and gave me a filthy look.

'It's like this,' I said. 'I want to do a sting on them, and I want you to do it. And record it on video, so I asked Li Cheng the best way to stop covert filming being blocked by magick, and he said the best person for that was yet another of your cousins in Oxford. *GG*? Something like that.'

'The Great Geek. Heidi's daughter.'

I rubbed my forehead. I was already getting a sun headache. 'Heidi has a daughter?'

'Yes, but they don't speak. It was Heidi who gave her the nickname, and that's one of the reasons they don't speak. GG's good, if a bit odd.'

'Of course she's odd. She's a Hawkins. We haven't got the time or budget to see her, so I asked for an alternative. He said "go clear." He also said you'd know what that means. Then he said, and I quote, "She looks like a Hawkins and sounds like a Hawkins. She needs a disguise." That's why I asked you to pack something you wouldn't be seen dead in.'

She looked appalled. 'I didn't think you were being serious. I packed my outdoor gear because I thought we might be getting dirty.' She shoved her finger into her hair. 'How do you expect me to get a wig over this lot?'

'No idea. That's why we're going to the experts. We'll walk in, I'll say that I'm a TV producer, you'll say that you're an investigative reporter and we'll let them sort it.'

She considered this for a second, and pulled her hair back from her face. 'Who should I be?' She struck a few theatrical poses and looked around for a mirror. Sadly, the outside of Birmingham station was not designed with narcissists in mind. It was yet another 180 degree rotation in attitude; not a concern in itself, but something to watch.

'You need to think like a junior Mage who needs the money and is willing to take bribes,' I said, in an effort to clarify things.

She looked uncertain. 'How do you know that's what they'll try.'

'Why is there no reference to them in Mack's notes? Got to be worth a try.'

'Okay.' She shook herself down and hunched her shoulders. 'Hiya, I'm the new Watch Captain…'

Ouch. It was quite a good Geordie accent, but she clearly thought of Vicky as being someone who needed the money. She does, but Vicky would never take a bribe. 'Whoah, Saffron. Captain Robson is far too well known. Try someone else.'

She opened her mouth to deny it, then closed it and closed her eyes. 'Alright? I'm takin' over from McKeever. Same deal.'

'Much better. The wig shop's round this corner, and then you can go mad and get yourself a new outfit.'

'Please tell me you're not coming shopping.'

'You're not Mina, so no. I'll spin them a yarn at the wig shop then leave you to it. There's a train to Lichfield at 11:03.'

'You know you'll have to stay in or near the station in Lichfield.' She waved her hand as a sort of advance apology. 'No offence, but you're packing so many aggressive magickal items that a half decent sorcerer will know there's heat in town. If they look.'

'I thought my items were shielded.'

'As individual items, they are. It's just the general vibe, you know? A bit like seeing a tank coming down the street on CCTV. You don't know who's driving, but it makes you take an interest.'

That was good to know. 'C'mon Scout, we're off.'

We sat in different compartments on the train. 'Helps me get in character,' said Saffron. I'm telling you, this girl has a future as an actress if she loses her magick.

The wig was expensively cheap – it cost the King's Watch a packet for Saffron to look like she'd had platinum ombre shading put into naturally dark hair. I'd asked her what had inspired the overall look, and she'd said, 'I thought of the cleaners at the Cherwell Roost. They dress like this.'

I tried not to wince when she said that. Changing her attitude to people who do an honest day's work was above and beyond today's mission. And then another thing struck me: the Hawkins family cleaners also have a much larger cup size, it would seem. The only problem was that she didn't look like any Mage I've ever come across.

I'd asked her what *going clear* means, and she'd said it was when you bring your magick, internal and external, into a state of rest. It's how the more powerful Mages sleep at night, and how they play cricket without cheating. Unfortunately, it also means she won't be able to use her Sight. I weighed up the risk, and decided that Bertie wouldn't have pointed us in that direction if there was a real threat. I knew where Saffron had gone, and that it would take six minutes at a steady jog for me to get there, so I didn't start worrying until a quarter of an hour had passed.

Lichfield City station does not have a lot to entertain a Watch Captain, never mind the Watch Captain's hyperactive Familiar. Border collies (when not asleep) have a very low threshold for boredom and are very sensitive to moods. If I got stressed, Scout would go off the scale, so I looked around for something to entertain him. The forecourt was paved with standard 24" paving slabs, and some bizarre memory gave me an idea.

Believe me, a six foot tall man playing hopscotch with a large puppy gets a lot of attention. It was good fun though. If you're wondering, Scout had to play by jumping, not hopping, and every time he got one right, he got a treat. That dog is a fast learner.

I was almost disappointed when Saffron messaged me: Got it. Let's see if your hound can follow my scent. Saff.

I'd piled up our bags, including Saffron's clothes, and got her dress out for Scout to sniff. 'Find Saffron!' I said. 'Find her!'

I think he cheated at first and set off the way he'd seen her walking (with a big roll of her hips) rather than sniff her out. After a couple of minutes, he started dipping his nose to the pavement and weaving from side to side. He made a positive turn into the open air shopping mall, and right again when we were inside. After that, he seemed a little uncertain, and he sat down. *There.* His brown eye went green for a second, something that Myfanwy and I had discussed while Mina was playing with him in the garden. Could Scout use magick to track people, particularly Mages? It seems he can.

With a *woof* and a wag of the tail, he set off out of the mall, through some back streets and onto Tamworth Road. At the end, where I knew he'd need to turn right for Tetty Johnson's House, he got confused again, shaking his head and whining. I wonder...

I gave a tug on the lead. 'This way, boy.' He was reluctant at first, then got excited. Saffron must have doubled back on herself and re-crossed her own trail. Scout found her two minutes later, sitting outside a coffee shop and using her phone. She'd even bought me a cappuccino.

She eyed Scout carefully. 'Did you find me? Or was it daddy?'

'I am not that dog's father, and it was him who found you.'

'Well done, you manic mutt,' she said, and gave him half a chocolate brownie. Suddenly, he liked her a lot more.

There was a padded envelope on the downwind chair, next to my coffee. I lit a fag and peered in the envelope. Stuffed full of twenty pound notes. 'Excellent work, Saffron. Any problems?'

'No. They were expecting someone, and they just didn't know whether that person would be on the take.' She looked at me, concern written all over her face. 'Do you think this is endemic in the Watch?'

'I hope not, otherwise Hannah will have us carrying out sting operations all over the country. What does family legend have to say on the subject?'

She looked down. 'They're not very complimentary about the Watch, but I've never heard them say anything about them – us – being bent.' She looked up again. 'Do you want to know what my mother said when I broke the news about my commission?'

'I'm hoping she said, "What a brilliant opportunity to learn from that fine body of Mages." Go on. Disappoint me.'

'She said, "Why you want to join that bunch of musclebound knuckledraggers, half-wits and no-hopers is beyond me."'

That was a bit extreme. 'And why *did* you want to join? If you don't mind me asking.'

'A chance to see some action. A chance to sniff around magick that's normally well hidden. A chance to test out new Artefacts. And also, it'll be what you said.'

'Oh? What am I supposed to have said?'

'I'll bet you said, "She wants to rub her family's nose in it." There was some of that, yes.'

It was time to change the subject. 'Have you checked the covert video?'

'All present and correct. I've just backed it up to the cloud, too, in case they try to erase the hard drive on the camera. And I looked up Doctor

Johnson. Now I understand what you were on about with checking my spellings. Makes my cover name a bit embarrassing.'

'Go on.'

'I told them I was Sammy Johnson.'

I felt my mouth drop. 'You called yourself Samuel Johnson?'

'*Sammi*. With an "i". We had a cleaner called Sammi. The Johnson part must have popped out of my subconscious.'

I shook my head.

She looked at me accusingly. 'You said his name was Dr Johnson. I didn't know what his first name was, did I?'

I gave Scout a scratch. 'If you've only just looked him up now, how did you find Tetty Johnson's House?'

'It's known as Tetty's. I rang one of my uncles last night. He knows a Mage who knows a Mage who knows all the disreputable magick emporia.'

I put my coffee down. 'And it never struck you that his friend-of-a-friend might tip them off?'

'God, no. This uncle's not a Hawkins. He would die rather than admit any connection to the Watch.'

'I thought all the men took the Hawkins name.'

'He's my dad's sister's husband's brother. I think. He's young enough to have tried chatting me up without it being sleazy. That's how I got his number.'

'Do you want to get changed before we go back.'

She thought for a moment. 'No. That was fun, and if I stay in character, it'll keep them guessing.'

I stood up and shared some of the luggage.

'What's it like in there?'

She grinned. 'You really need to see it for yourself.'

'At least tell me who you dealt with.'

'There's someone mundane out front.' She shouldered her rucksack and we set off. 'She called out the owner when I triggered some of the Wards. One of them rang a really loud bell. You needn't have bothered staying at the station: that place is so shrouded in protection you could have a fleet of tanks outside and they wouldn't notice.'

'Squadron.'

'What?'

'Tanks come in squadrons, as do aircraft and horses. Only ships come in fleets.'

'Noooooo. Reeeally? I never knew that.' She was back in character. I shook my head and lengthened my stride.

Lichfield is a small cathedral city that most people only come across in pub quiz questions. It has a lovely historic centre, and that history is mostly Georgian. Even away from the main centre, most of the buildings are made of characteristic small bricks with elegant windows. I was about to ask where to go, when Scout ducked through the arch of an old coaching inn and barked loudly.

I looked up. A signboard over the arch told me that I was about to enter Red Lion Yard – Home of Boutique Shopping. Through the arch and into the old coach yard, and already my skin was tingling with the heat of Lux. I looked around, and all the shops were boarded up except one. *Tetty's Hats* said the cursive gold script on the blacked out window. They had got the signwriter to add images of improbable headgear, too. To make absolutely sure they got no unexpected customers, there was a large Closed sign on the door.

I bent down to unclip Scout's lead. 'Stay here,' I said, gesturing round the yard. He got that. He also ran up to one of the shuttered shops and started barking. 'Has he sensed something?'

'Smelt something, more like,' said Saffron.

'Eh?'

'That's his food bark. It's different to his magick bark or his *you sucker* bark.'

'Don't tell me you're a dog whisperer.'

'No. I'm young, that's all. I haven't spent years sitting next to helicopter engines.'

'I am not going deaf!'

'No need to shout. His food bark is slightly higher pitched, that's all.'

'Scout! Here.'

When he'd torn himself away from the alleged source of food, I went up and pushed on the door of Tetty's Hats. *Booong.* Saffron was right about the bell. I went inside and …

Found myself in a hat shop. Or millinery workshop, to be accurate. A few examples of the art were arranged on long poles near the front, and most of the room was taken up with benches, stackable crates and works in progress. It was mostly dark, with only a daylight task lamp illuminating the milliner herself. She didn't look up.

'Through there,' whispered Saffron.

There was a track from the front door to the right, avoiding the hat space and leading directly to another door. This one was emblazoned with a rampant red lion; not the old pub sign, but something painted especially. Yes, it was a lion, and yes it was red, but not like any heraldic red lion I've ever seen. Something tickled my memory, and I tried to mentally scratch it. No good. I shrugged and opened the door into the den.

'Very nice.'

We were now in some part of the old pub, as reimagined by a Scandinavian restauranteur, and that's what it was: a restaurant. Even I could smell cooking from here. No wonder Scout had gone bananas.

'Where is everyone?'

'They only open in the evenings. Here she comes.'

A very tall woman of African heritage in chef's whites emerged from a screen that hid the entrance to the kitchens. She did not look happy when she saw us. She strode through the restaurant, wiping her hands on a towel.

'What do you want now? And who's this?' she said. Her heritage was African, but she'd learnt her English down the road in Birmingham.

I touched the Badge of Office on my gun, and she recoiled with horror. 'Watch Captain Clarke. We need to talk about this.' I put the envelope on one of the tables. They were already laid out for tonight's service. 'I should point out that my colleague recorded you as well.'

'So? It's just a fee for you to keep my registration private.'

I placed my finger on the envelope. 'This is evidence. If I take it in, you'll be prosecuted for bribery. I don't think either of us want that, do we?' I slid it in her direction, disturbing the cutlery. 'On the other hand, if you take it back, I've got no evidence.'

She shoved the envelope on to a chair and seemed more concerned about rearranging the cutlery. 'What do you want?' she said.

'You can start by telling me about this place.'

'It's a restaurant.'

'I hope your food's better than your jokes.'

'I wasn't joking. It's a restaurant. That's it. We serve food to Mages who want to eat Nigerian fusion cuisine with other Mages, and who want to dine in peace. We're one of the few places outside London that don't have the Daughters of the Goddess or the King's Watch or some other bunch of jackboots breathing down our necks every five minutes.'

'There was twenty grand in that payoff. That's close to a year's income on the minimum wage. That buys more than silence.'

She took the towel out of her waistband and polished one of the wine glasses. 'He'd give me a name, sometimes. Ask if I'd seen them and who they were with. That's all.'

I nodded. I'd got enough for now. 'Do I need to book ahead?'

'You are not coming here during service. Ever. If anyone except Tetty knew you'd been here, I'd be bankrupt or dead in a day. Both, probably. Are we done?'

'I need your contact details.'

She frowned. 'Didn't Mack give them to you?'

'He buggered off to the States and left me with a crock of shit. I just guessed he was on the take and that you were paying him. Turns out I was right.'

Fury rippled across her face. I would not want to be her sous chef right now. 'My name is Fadesike. You can get my number from Elizabeth.' With that, she returned to the kitchen, her back rigid with anger.

'Elizabeth?' said Saffron.

'Tetty.'

Back in the hat shop, I coughed politely and the milliner looked up. 'Fadesike said you'd give us her number. Could I have your card as well? There may be a wedding in the offing.'

'Sure. Pass me a leaflet from over there.' She looked up Fadesike's number and wrote it on the leaflet.

'Thank you.'

Back in the coaching yard, I called Scout over and clipped on his lead.

'Wedding?' said Saffron, still in Sammi mode. 'Did you propose over the weekend? Can we expect a visit from an enraged snake woman?'

Under the archway, I noticed a mailbox unit with flaps for each of the businesses. Interesting.

'Don't worry, I'll let you know if I propose to Mina. You wouldn't be interested in the wedding. It's just village gossip.'

'I asked for that, didn't I?'

'You did.' We were well away from Red Lion Yard now. I turned and pointed back to it. 'What do you reckon, Sammi?'

Saffron had been rolling her shoulders as if they ached. 'I think it's time to put Sammi away for now. That wig woman pulled my hair so tight when she cornrowed it that my scalp aches. And these chicken fillets are chafing my nipples something rotten.' She grinned. 'Was that too much information?'

'I've heard much worse complaints about women's body armour. There's a pub near the cathedral with a beer garden where we can leave Scout while we eat.'

'Then let's go to the cathedral first. I need to find a decent sized toilet, and I'll have to put a Glamour on before we go in.'

And so it came to pass that an illusory Saffron Hawkins, to disguise the fake Sammi Johnson, went into the cathedral. The real Saffron Hawkins emerged a good while later.

17 — Accidental Damage

'This is a nice place,' said Saffron. 'And this is good food. I didn't think there'd be quite so many lunches at the taxpayer's expense in the King's Watch. Or train journeys.'

'Would you prefer to eat in the First Mine? No? Thought not. Something will happen soon. The Nine of Wands will see to that.'

'Nine of Wands?'

Damn. I'd forgotten that I hadn't told her about the tarot. I waved it off. 'Doesn't matter. Family legend. Now that Saffron and her hair are back, could she give me her take on this morning's events?'

She put down her fork. 'Is this a test?'

'No. The CO should always ask for thoughts before giving his own. Or hers.'

'There's something off about the Red Lion business. I can't put my finger on why, though.'

'Try.'

She racked her brains. 'Mages don't normally like Nigerian food. Except for Desirée, of course. And they must charge a fortune to make enough money to throw twenty grand around.'

'How are you at maths, Saffron?'

'Maths? Like most people: pretty rubbish. Why?'

'Did your maths teacher ever say, "Correct answer, but show your workings."?'

'Yeah. Didn't often get the correct answer, though. Unless I copied off Lucy and she wasn't in a bad mood. Sometimes she'd put the wrong answer down, just so's I'd copy it.'

'I used to do that.'

'Copy?'

'No. Put the wrong answer deliberately. I hated the lad next to me. Anyway, you're right about the Red Lion. Something is *very* off. Yes, you need to trust your instincts, Saffron. You also need to become more suspicious and improve your observational skills.'

'What do you mean?'

'Go back to the beginning. Bertie said we should go to Tetty Johnson's House. Why would she say that if it's called the Red Lion?'

'That could just be Bertie.'

'Possibly. Then add in the extreme levels of magickal obfuscation. All that to hide a restaurant? Why not just make it a private dining club?'

'So they don't get environmental health inspections?'

'True, but what about deliveries? A restaurant will have up to half a dozen deliveries a day. Where do they deliver? What does it say on the delivery note?'

'They must … I don't know.'

'Start with what you do know. The Cherwell Roost sounds like a major establishment. How does your family interact with the mundane world.'

She thought that was hilarious. She put her fork down again to laugh. 'You don't know the half of it. My uncle. My real uncle, Mum's brother, runs the place. Most of the house is open to the public five days a week. It even has a name: Cherwell Manor. It's only Cherwell Roost in Mage circles.' She paused to think it through. 'Most of the staff think it's completely mundane. Deliveries go to the café. Once the punters have gone, the housekeepers take over. There are four of them, all entangled.'

'And you'd rather stay in a tourist attraction than at Elvenham? One of us must have done something to upset you.'

She shook her head. 'I'd rather stay at my cottage in the grounds and eat in the main house, thank you very much. If it were a choice between Elvenham and the goldfish bowl – that's what I call it – then I'd be sharing gardening tips with Myfanwy in a heartbeat.'

That was strangely reassuring. 'Red Lion Yard. What else?'

Now she'd got the hang of it, she thought harder. 'The backhander. The bribe: she implied she was paying Mack for the privilege of being a grass. That doesn't make sense. Oh, the payment was supposed to cover three months, by the way. It's on the tape. What is she doing that she'd pay so much to hide it? None of it makes sense.'

'Good. Two more things. The heraldic lion on the restaurant door looked wrong.'

'Did it? I'll take your word for that.'

'And the letterboxes in the archway. There were five. One for Tetty's Hats, clearly in use. Three for obviously made up businesses that have never existed. They were locked closed. That leaves one. Tetty Johnson Holdings Ltd.'

She pushed her plate aside. 'Basically, I failed, didn't I? Sorry, Boss.' She looked upset. Not peeved or put out: upset.

'I'm not the Boss. That's Hannah. OK?' She nodded. 'And you didn't fail. Failure would mean someone in hospital or in the mortuary. We are in the pub having lunch, so no failures. And we haven't got to the magick yet. That's why you're partnered with me, remember?'

'Thanks. Thanks, Conrad. As for the magick, I keep expecting you to have more Sight than me because you come across as if you do.'

'Vicky and I worked on that. When it was my turn to lead, I always pretended to know what I was talking about, and she'd butt in to correct me. Go on. Tell me about the magick.'

'After all the Wards and sensors, I got nothing constructed. There's lots of Lux around, but nothing … structural. The First Mine was full of all sorts of things. Like walking into a magickal factory. This, not so much.'

'Good. That's just what I need you to tell me. Now why do you think Red Lion House is like that? I should warn you that I have no idea.'

'You should go and feed Scout and have a smoke while I think about it and get us some coffees.'

Ten minutes later, Saffron discovered us playing doggy hopscotch. I think I'll call it *hopscout*. She was appalled.

'Stop that now! You'll end up on Youtube if you're not careful. So will I, and that is so not going to happen.'

'Don't tempt me. If you can think of a less embarrassing game to play with him, go ahead.'

She put the coffees down. 'What did you think about the right hand side of the yard?'

'What right hand side?'

'Precisely. This is why I was so long getting the coffees. Have a look.'

She gave me her phone and her notebook. The phone had Google Streetview on it, showing the entrance to Red Lion Yard. The notebook had a plan of the yard, with Tetty's Hats, the restaurant and kitchen marked. They took up the left hand side and rear of the yard. There was a blank line down the right. A wall, I'd presumed.

I checked Streetview again. The arch was clearly in the *middle* of the old coaching inn. There was a whole eastern section missing from our memories.

I passed the notebook and phone back. 'Excellent, Saffron. Spatial awareness is normally my forte, and I'm happy to say that this is a spot on piece of work. I must have been distracted.' I looked at Scout. 'You are a big distraction, you know.' He wagged his tail.

Saffron beamed. 'What do we do now?'

'We go to our homes. When we get there, I do nothing. You, on the other hand, will write it all up and email it to me.'

'To check my spellings?'

'If necessary. Here's one of the unwritten rules: put in the report only what you're happy for every other Watch Captain to read. Everything else gets passed on to the Boss off the record. The only exception is when we have a fatality. In that case, we write three entirely different reports *and* give oral feedback. Before you start, I'd read a couple of the reports in Maxine's archives to get a flavour.'

She nodded enthusiastically. I used to think about reports that way once.

We loaded up our gear and headed for the station. 'And tomorrow?' she said.

'The Brewers, I think.'

'Shall I bring Sammi along?'

'I don't think so. We'll save her for special occasions.'

Visiting the Brewers of Burton upon Trent was nowhere near as interesting as our trip to Red Lion Yard, partly because word had got round that we were on the prowl. Not only were the Brewers expecting us, one of them held out a mug of tea and said, 'Can you accept this? I wouldn't want anyone to get the wrong idea.' Ha ha.

Saffron wasn't entirely happy with my critique of her report (including the spellings), and there was a certain amount of sulking on the train north. After that, she livened up and really enjoyed herself mooching around the Brewers' Loft. Not surprising, really: this was a collective of Artificers, and she's an Artificer. She enjoyed herself so much that Scout and I went to Newton Park and exhausted ourselves playing hide and fetch.

Saffron really does have too much time on her hands. She'd given me a tennis ball on the train this morning and told me that she'd enchanted it. If I rubbed it in a certain way, it would both stop smelling of anything and act as a temporary magickal beacon. When Scout wasn't looking, I hurled the ball deep into the trees, and he had to find it.

'It's not just good fun,' she'd said, 'It will help train him to find magick. Oh, and try to listen to his different barks, too.'

We met up again in mid-afternoon. I couldn't help noticing that this was the third similar dress she'd worn this week: different fabrics, all made from the same pattern and with a high neckline. 'Is that Mageburn still bothering you?'

'A bit.' She looked away. 'I tried to get it to heal without a scar. Not very successfully, I'm afraid. I may need cosmetic surgery.'

'Or live with it. You've seen the scar on Mina's arm. She's going to share it with the world on Saturday.'

'It's a mark of shame. Incompetence. Can't have that.'

I heard another voice in her reply: there was a distinct echo of her mother or grandmother there.

She turned back to me. 'Am I on report duty again tonight?'

'Of course. I'm not skiving, you know. Last night I had to help Mina, and tonight I've got to work through Myfanwy's submission to the Cloister Court.'

Our train to Birmingham was arriving. We'd have to stop talking magick in a second. 'Tomorrow?' she said.

'Depends on your report. Either we follow up some of your leads or check in with the Arden Foresters.'

We did neither of those things. In the early hours of Thursday morning, I was woken up by thunder. Distant thunder. I tried not to disturb Mina and slipped out of bed to see if I could find where the storm was breaking. I looked to the west, where we get most of our rain from (the Welsh are so generous in that respect), and if there was a storm out there, I couldn't see it. And then my phone burst into life with Monti's Czardas, my ringtone for Hannah. Mina groaned, and I grabbed the phone.

'Boss?'

I slipped out of our room before Mina woke up completely and headed downstairs.

'Are you awake?' she said.

'Are you?'

'I'd swap this situation for a nightmare any day. You need to get dressed and get to the John Radcliffe Hospital in Oxford.'

'Is it Saffron?'

'Is what Saffron? I assume she's asleep in your guest wing. This is a long story, Conrad, and I need to make more calls. Dom Richmond will be at the hospital in a minute. He can fill you in.'

'Saffron is at home. Cherwell Roost. Is there danger?'

'Not immediately. There's been a mundane casualty, and you need to be very careful who you talk to. You can fill me in later. Oh, and don't use the A44. It's closed.'

I filled the kettle and plonked it on the Aga.

'I'll make the tea,' said a sleepy Mina. 'You get dressed and I'll have it ready. I assume you're going out.'

'Oxford. No idea why yet. Thanks, love.'

I waited until I was in the car before I called Saffron and filled her in. 'You'll be there before me. Do you know Dom Richmond?'

'Met him once. He was at my induction ceremony.'

Dom Richmond is the Watch Captain for Sussex. In the King's Watch, Sussex stretches all the way to Oxford. Don't ask.

'I'd rather we approached this together. I'll meet you in the car park.'

'And I'll see if there's anything online about the A44.'

Mina had made a large flask of tea. I passed Saffron a mug when I found her battered Land Rover Discovery at the John Radcliffe. It was just after five in the morning.

'Did you stop to make this?'

'No. Mina did. She wants us both fully functioning. What have you found out?'

'Major incident on the A44 just north of Woodstock. Police are describing it as terrorist related and Thames Valley Counter-Terrorism are in charge. Road closed. At least one fatality. No mention of other casualties. Nice tea, by the way. Don't suppose she packed breakfast?'

'Myfanwy did that. Here.' I passed her a paper bag with the Clerkswell Village Shop logo. 'Myfanwy is also looking after Scout. A hospital is not a good place for a dog. He'll be fine so long as I'm back by noon. Anything else online?'

She shoved a sandwich in her mouth and shook her head. I did the same and looked at my phone. Vicky and Xavi were on their way up the M40, but wouldn't be here for a while. I sent a message to Dominic Richmond: *Here. In Car Park. Where are you?*

Answer: *A&E. Look for the armed coppers and tell them you're with me.*

I showed Saffron the screen and her eyebrows shot up. 'Wow. We really are in the eye of a shitstorm, aren't we?'

We were, and just how much of one became clear when we found Richmond in a side corridor. To be exact, Saffron found him. I've never met the bloke before.

He was lurking, close enough to keep an eye on the room with the armed men outside and far enough away to use his phone without anyone hearing. 'Ah, Clarke,' he said, shaking hands. 'Glad you could make it. Good to see you again, Ms Hawkins.'

He made it sound like we'd been invited to make up a four at golf, not the aftermath of a major incident. I waited to see what was next.

Richmond is one of the older Watch Captains, and according to gossip he had his nose put out of joint when Rick James was made Senior Watch Captain. Goodness knows what he thought when the Boss appointed me At Large, with direct access to her office; in most instances, Richmond has to answer to Rick.

To look at, he was pretty unremarkable: average height, early thirties, thinning hair. He did have a slightly bulbous nose, and that's about it. All three of us were wearing what had come to hand when our phones went off.

'Does the name Morris Chandler mean anything to you?' said Richmond.

Of course it did. It even meant something to Saffron, which showed that she'd read the reports and had a decent memory. When Eilidh Haigh ambushed Lloyd and me outside Niði's Hall, there had been eight of them: Eilidh herself, a young Fae, Irina Ispahbudhan and five others. One of those never left the boat, but the other four were mundane humans. They'd been tricked or press-ganged into Eilidh's service from a gym in Sandwell, and she'd armed them with Anciles, body armour and machetes. One was dead, and we got DNA and fingerprints from the rest. One of them was Morris Chandler. I knew that, Saffron knew that, and so did Richmond, so why was he asking?

'He's in there,' said Richmond, pointing to the single ward behind the screen of armed police.

'What? Where are the rest of them?'

'I was going to ask him that, but the Constable has insisted on your involvement.'

'Better bring me up to speed, then.'

He pulled a face. 'It's complicated. I need to stand guard, and I don't want to go through everything out here. There's a tactical van outside – you can use this fire door. Talk to the inspector.' He looked at Saffron. 'There's only room in the van for one more.'

I looked at Saffron, too. She gave me the barest of nods: she understood. 'Two Mages are better than one for guard duty,' I said. 'You take the other end of the corridor.'

'Sir.'

The fire door had been propped open with a rock, and the tactical van was as close to the building as it could get, with an armed copper standing behind it. I hopped outside and identified myself to the officer. He peered at my RAF badge and muttered into his radio. Someone inside the van opened the door and a plain clothed female officer waved me inside. Richmond was right: they really did only have room for one more.

Three officers were crowded into the van. The woman who'd opened the door made way for me to get inside, then closed the door behind. A male constable in uniform was working the communications, and the inspector was standing at the back with his arms folded. He did not look happy to be here.

'Squadron Leader Clarke,' I said, holding up my ID again.

'Are we at risk here?' he said. I liked him already.

'Yes. My colleagues and your officers should be enough to discourage an attack, but I can't be certain.'

'Who's the target?'

'The man you have in custody.'

'Not the hospital? Not the surrounding area?'

'No. This is a terrorist level threat, but they are not terrorists. This is effectively organised crime.'

'That's something, I suppose.' He considered me for a moment. 'What should we do to secure the situation?'

'I need a full report before we make any decisions. The sooner I know what's happened, the sooner we can proceed.'

'Fine. We're still trying to piece things together, and there's a hell of a mess on the road, but this is what I know. We started to get reports from the public at 03:30. Drivers along the A34 were calling 999 and describing an erratic pursuit, starting just north of Oxford. A Mercedes 4x4 was being chased along the northbound carriageway by a Land Rover Sport. At 03:35, both vehicles entered the Peartree Interchange. Do you know it?'

'The A40/A34/A44 interchange. I know it.'

'There was carnage. Three vehicles crashed taking evasive action. At that point, the control room dispatched a patrol car and activated the armed response vehicle. A very wise decision. Both target vehicles headed up the

A44, and the patrol car was less than a minute behind them. The ARV was about ten minutes behind that.'

The inspector took a breath. 'This is where it gets tricky. The Mercedes tried to go round the Woodstock roundabout and double back on to the southbound carriageway. It collided with a lorry, and two more vehicles smashed into them. The Land Rover went off the road to avoid the pile-up and, and that's why it was out of sight when our patrol car got there. The officer parked across the carriageway with blues on to stop oncoming traffic, then went to investigate the accident. He was approaching the four-vehicle RTC and there were shots fired. It was just getting light at this point, so he had a good view, once he'd taken cover and called it in.'

'Did they fire at him?'

'No. The Land Rover had gone round the roundabout and stopped at the entrance to the southbound carriageway. Vehicles were still coming round it, slowly, and we hadn't stopped the traffic at this point. One male and two females got out of the Land Rover and approached the accident. All were wearing balaclavas and black clothing. The shots were fired at them. The male and one of the females moved to attack, and some form of weapon was discharged. One of the southbound drivers panicked when he heard the shots and crashed into the roundabout. Another tried to reverse and was smashed from behind. The three suspects tried to get into the tangle of crashed vehicles, and that weapon was discharged again. It smashed into the tractor unit of a large lorry, destroying it and starting a fire.'

He took a swallow from a bottle of water. 'If this mess ever ends, I am going to recommend that patrol officer for every award going. He pulled the dashcam out of his vehicle and stood behind it, filming everything and shouting instructions. It may have made all the difference, because the suspects saw him filming them and started arguing. At that point the ARV was getting nearer. The ARV team knew the northbound carriageway was blocked, and they crossed over. When the suspects saw and heard it coming, they launched a number of incendiary devices into the crash zone and got back into their vehicle. They headed south and managed to dodge the ARV.'

'Any sign of them?'

'As you can imagine, every emergency protocol short of nuclear war had been activated by now. I was at home getting dressed and every vehicle in Thames Valley was on the alert. Nothing. That Land Rover never arrived at the Peartree Interchange, and on all CCTV, it has no index. That's no number plate to you.'

I let that pass.

'Back at the crash site, the original patrol officer and the ARV team approached the burning vehicles. They found a white male with a submachine gun and serious injuries trying to crawl out. As soon as he saw them, he threw the gun down and started shouting.' The inspector consulted the comms officer. 'Have we got that footage ready?'

'Sir.'

We turned to watch. In the background, burning vehicles flared out parts of the camera as it tried to adjust its light level. The officer who'd filmed it lowered the camera and it focused on a pitiful sight. Dressed in black, with blood coursing down his face, a man crawled forward with one shattered leg. My titanium tibia throbbed in sympathy. There were tears in his jacket and more wounds visible. He looked into the camera and said, 'Get the Constable! Get Conrad Clarke! My name is Morris Chandler and I surrender. Get the Constable. You'll all be killed if you don't get them.'

'We ran his name. And yours. His name came back as a dangerous wanted suspect. Your name came back with a note: contact Security Liaison. Now it's your turn. What the hell do we do?'

I pulled my lip and closed my eyes to get the image of Chandler's pain out of my vision. 'What are the casualties?'

'A van driver went through his windscreen and died before the fire brigade could get to him. There are two others seriously injured and several with minors.'

'Do you have a name for the van driver?'

'Preliminary.'

I could only see one way out of this unholy mess that would make the world a better place. I pointed to the video screen. 'Who's seen that? Where is it stored?'

'It's restricted to counter-terrorism. We took the original footage straight from the ARV.'

'I need to make a call. Get that footage off the system.' He bristled. 'I didn't say destroy it. This gang have the resources to hack almost any system: get it off your servers, and quickly. Lock the original in a safe at headquarters. I need to make a call, then we'll have a plan.'

I took the chance to light a cigarette when I was outside and waiting for my call to Hannah to connect. She answered on the first ring. 'Well?'

'We have one of Eilidh Haigh's gang, ma'am. Looks like he escaped and they pursued him. He surrendered to the police. I need authority to take urgent action. We need to protect his life and protect his information.'

'Granted. Do what you have to. Should I come up to Oxford.'

'No need at present, ma'am.'

'Get on with it, then. And may Hashem guide you.'

The armed officer let me back in to the van. 'That footage is off the system,' said the uniformed constable.

I nodded and asked the inspector what the name of the deceased was.

'Provisionally identified as Kristoff Varcik. Polish national.'

'Are the hospital itching to get Chandler into surgery?'

'Yes, and he won't consent until he's seen someone he recognises. He didn't believe that Captain Richmond was high enough up the food chain.'

'Here's what's going to happen. From this moment, until you hear otherwise from the top, Morris Chandler is the one in the morgue and Kristoff Varcik is the one in A&E. Otherwise, proceed exactly as normal. Stand down all but one armed officer, and station him or her inside the room. Wrap up this van and clear out.'

'You are joking. Sir.'

'In twenty-four hours, you can announce Varcik's death and blame it on forensic confusion. We can sort out what happens to Chandler after that. By now, London central command will have heard from my boss. Check it out.'

The plain clothes officer had been following every word we'd said, and at a nod from the inspector, she made a call. When she'd been connected, she said, 'Requesting clarification of operational command transfer.' She listened for twenty seconds and nodded to herself a few times. 'Right. Thank you.' She disconnected. 'Confirmed, sir. Transfer to Squadron Leader Clarke and only him. Until further notice. Came all the way from the Cabinet Office at 10 Downing Street.'

The Inspector nodded once. 'You heard what he said. Get on to it. Varcik is in surgery if anyone asks. Including his family. Start the procedures for declaring Morris Chandler deceased.'

'Thank you,' I said. 'I now need to go and put that into effect. I may pass on messages via one of my team. OK?'

'Understood.'

18 — Exercise

Richmond was staring at his phone rather than staring at the corridor. Down the other end I could see Saffron paying rather more attention to her duties.

'Hannah's put you in charge,' said Richmond disbelievingly. 'And she did it by text.'

'Report?'

'What?'

'What's the status?'

He pulled himself together. 'Chandler calmed down when I told him you were here, but he still won't talk to anyone except you.'

'Chandler's dead. The man in that room is Kristoff Varcik. Understood?'

'No.'

I leaned in to whisper. 'If Haigh thinks Chandler is dead, they won't attack the hospital. Now do you understand?'

'You could have said.'

'I didn't think I'd need to. Hawkins and I are going to talk to Varcik now. You're going to put that phone away and focus.'

'Why not me?'

I paused and took half a second to see it from his point of view. 'Because I'd rather have you outside on watch than Hawkins. You've got the experience. She hasn't.'

'Oh. Right.'

The armed police were listening to a message as I approached. While I waited for them to finish, I waved Saffron to me. I showed the officers my ID and we went into the room. Chandler was clearly in the VIP suite. Not only did he have the large room to himself, there was a separate area for medical staff, occupied by a doctor and a nurse. Another armed officer was in the opposite corner.

'Clarke! You're here!' said Chandler. 'You've got to protect me.'

I held up a hand to shush him and spoke to the medics. 'I need five minutes with my witness. After that, he'll consent to surgery.'

The doctor was young and nervous. She was also resolute. 'We can't leave our patient. He is not medically fit to be interviewed alone.'

'Sir?' said Saffron.

'Yes?'

She coughed. 'I think they've been watching *Line of Duty*. They think you're going to silence him as part of a giant conspiracy.'

I hadn't thought of that. The medics were looking at some notes and blushing. Saffron was right. 'One of you can stay,' I said in a loud enough voice for Chandler to hear. 'The other needs to go out and start changing all the records. There's been a mistake. This man's real name is Kristoff Varcik. Isn't that right, Mr Varcik?'

'Yes.'

The doctor made a quick decision: was her patient under threat? No, she decided. 'Mr Varcik? Are you going to let us treat you?'

'Yes.'

'Then I'll stay,' she said to the nurse. 'You go and sort out the paperwork. And tell the surgical team.' The nurse picked up some folders and left.

We moved over to Chandler's bed. In a model of efficiency, Saffron got out her notebook and pen.

'You've got to protect me,' said Chandler.

'We will.' I bent down to whisper. 'That's why you've changed your name. The poor sod in the morgue is Morris Chandler. His name will be released to the media. His wife will be informed.'

'No! That's why I escaped. I found out on Facebook that she's pregnant. And it's mine. It'll kill her.' He looked panicked and in pain. It was only adrenaline that was stopping him from going into shock.

'If you co-operate, we'll catch them. That's the only long-term solution. I'm sure the police can get Mrs Chandler to play along with the deception. When you're released from prison, you can forget all about it.'

He was already shaking his head. 'Not going to prison.'

I leaned even closer. Even super-sharp eared Saffron had to bend down. 'Do you remember the last time we met? You attacked a Gnome. A clan second, in fact.'

'And Eilidh killed one of us. I'm the victim here.'

I shook my head. 'We have a treaty with the Gnomes. Someone else attacked the clan second last week. You do not want to know what they did to him, and he was a Gnome. Humans get even worse punishments. We can protect you from Eilidh Haigh, and we will, but unless you co-operate, we can't protect you from the Gnomes.'

'Sir, look,' said Saffron.

The dressing around Chandler's leg was starting to leak blood. Chandler went even whiter when he saw it.

I stood up. 'Decision time, Mr Varcik.'

'All right, all right. They're holed up at a cottage near Newbury. Place called Stockcross.'

'Who? Who's there?'

'Eilidh Haigh and that other witch, Jane Jones she called herself, but that's not her name. They've been keeping us prisoner since … since the business with the tunnels.'

'Keeping who prisoner?'

'Me, Owen Holt and Marissa Leon and Eve Maguire.'

'Anyone else?'

'That Irina woman was with us for a bit. And the South African guy came a few times. Not for a while.'

'How did you escape?'

'Went shopping in Newbury yesterday. Jane Jones came with me and let me drive. I bought a set of realistic kiddy's keys. You know, the ones you give toddlers to stop them stealing yours. I put the fake keys in the bowl and no one looked. It was hot. They've been letting us have the windows open. I jumped out in the middle of the night and took the Mercedes.'

'What were they up to? It's been six weeks since Niði's Hall.'

'They was gonna attack them three Gnomes once they'd got the gold out of the mine, that's what we were training for. Then you lot stopped 'em and took Irina. I think they've bin trying to find a way to let us go without us being arrested.'

'Is there a forge at this place? Like a blacksmith's?'

He shook his head. 'They talked about it. I ...'

He slumped back. More blood was coming from the dressing.

I shook him and spoke up. 'Kristoff? Do you consent to surgery?'

'What? Yes. Yes.'

The doctor was coming over, and I had one more job to do. I reached under his shirt and found his chain of Artefacts. 'Saffron, can you remove this without cutting it.'

She answered by doing. In five seconds, she had it in her hands.

'All yours,' I said to the doctor.

I gathered everyone together outside the room and moved us away from the door. There was going to be a lot of medical activity round here in the next few minutes.

'Saffron, is there something like a personal beacon in those Artefacts?'

She looked at them carefully. I recognised the unblinking eye of an Ancile, and the twin masks of a Persona. There were two others I'd not seen before, one of them in the shape of an open triangle made of gold. She touched her finger to it. 'This one. It's faded a lot since I took it off Mr Varcik, but I could feel it in there all right.'

'You know what to do with those, don't you?'

'Sir.'

I addressed the three armed police officers. 'Get the inspector on the radio and tell him to come inside.'

It didn't take him long to appear, and I took him even further down the corridor. 'Mr Varcik's going into surgery shortly,' I told him.

'And the threat level?'

'I need an officer to take Lieutenant Hawkins to the mortuary and give her access to Mr Chandler's body. After that, you can all stand down, except for one plain clothes officer and one personal protection officer in the room with him. He'll need to be arrested for causing death by dangerous driving.'

The inspector's eyes stayed dark, but his mouth smiled. 'Is he going to be tried as Kristoff Varcik?'

'No. By the time he's out of surgery and the anaesthetic's worn off, you can arrest him as Morris Chandler. He won't argue, or if he does, just stick a garden gnome on the table.'

'A garden gnome.'

'Yes. He'll get the message.'

'What about the attempted murder?'

'Self defence. You'll need to inform Mrs Chandler and get her onside with this for a few hours. I want Morris Chandler's death announced all over the media as soon as you can get an FLO to her house. Say that he was pronounced dead on arrival at hospital.'

He nodded. 'Are you sure it's safe to pull everyone out of the hospital? I need to know that.'

'My team will protect the mortuary. If the gang think he's dead, they'll want to make certain. They won't actually open the drawer in the morgue, or if they do, they'll get a nasty surprise.'

'Fine. I'll oversee the pull-out, but everything else is above my pay grade. I can't announce things or brief family liaison.'

'Thanks. I'll make sure your governor knows how well you've done here. I'll organise everything else.'

We shook hands, and he turned to one of the armed officers. 'Dave, go with Lieutenant Hawkins. The rest of you report to the command vehicle.' He walked out of the fire door, talking rapidly into his radio as he went.

'And me?' said Dom Richmond.

'You're coming with me to have a conference call with the Boss.'

Saffron: *My phone is running out of charge. Can't we swap places?*
Me: *No. I'll send you in a spare.*

'I am not going into a mortuary until I have to,' said Mina. 'And that is that.'

'Do you think Scout would do it?' I suggested.

'I am sure he would. He would also eat the phone and be attacked by hospital staff. Why don't you give the poor girl a break? Five minutes won't hurt.'

'Five minutes might hurt a lot. I'll take it in myself.' I levered my tired body off the grassy bank and knocked the clippings off my trousers. 'Call me the second you see anything suspicious.'

If you approach the John Radcliffe Hospital in Oxford and follow the signs for *Deliveries*, you'll notice a grassy bank on your left with a windsock to tell the incoming air ambulance pilot what the ground conditions are like. That's where Mina and I had set up an observation post, and for once my RAF ID was the right thing to convince the anxious hospital security guards that I was there on official business. They didn't ask why I had a short Indian woman and a border collie with me to make an inspection of the helipad.

I shook my leg to get out the stiffness and ambled up the road, past the children's wing and on to the completely anonymous concrete building that stretches for over 100 metres on the edge of the hospital. Here you'll find the laundry, supply stores, maintenance workshops and the mortuary.

And in the mortuary was Saffron.

'Love the coat, Saff,' I said.

'I am freezing my tits off. Literally. When I started turning blue and shivering, the staff stopped trying to chat me up and got me some thermal protection. It's all right for you. I'll bet you're sitting in the sun having a picnic.'

'Not yet. We didn't want to start without you.'

'We? Who else is out there?'

'Mina and Scout.'

'Now I feel really depressed. Here I am, sitting next to a room full of dead people while you canoodle in the sunshine or play with your psychotic dog. The Constable didn't say anything about this when she recruited me.'

'Scout is not psychotic.'

'He's a border collie. They're all mad.'

'Fair point. Here's a phone. It's got my number in it. Have you had a hot drink?'

'Yes thanks. Three. And I need to pee all the time. Are you sure you can't do this?'

'I wish I could. Then again, if I could project power into that Artefact, I wouldn't be me, would I? You need to keep it broadcasting until they turn up.'

It was quiet in here, or it was until my phone burst out a Bollywood song. 'What's up?'

'A young woman radiating magick has just ridden past on a bicycle. She's heading your way slowly. You have about ninety seconds.'

'Shit. Thanks.' I ended the call. 'They're coming. One of them is. On a bicycle. Turn down the power and take cover. Quickly.'

The plan was bonkers, but it was the best we had: see if anyone turned up to verify that Morris Chandler was dead. Saffron had taken up position in the mortuary at nine o'clock, when Chandler's name had been released to the media. Mina had turned up shortly after with Scout and the picnic. Myfanwy does look after us.

I ran to the entrance and cracked the door. No sign of the cyclist. I legged it across the service road as fast as I could and into the blood transfusion centre. My job was to stay out of sight and observe. According to Saffron, if I put my magickal weapons in the car and she put a shield on them, I should be pretty much undetectable.

Several staff were either moving to intercept me or call security. I held up my badge, shouted, 'Major incident team!' and kept going until I was half way through the hospital. When the cyclist arrived at the mortuary, she'd extend her Sight well beyond its normal range. I needed to be outside that extended range, and Saffron needed to hide herself magickally.

It was a risk, yes. You have to take some risks, and my team live or die according to my judgement of those risks. If more than one Mage had turned up, then Saffron would have run: I'd made sure that the mortuary had a back door and that her car was waiting outside it.

I found a quiet corner and gripped my phone, waiting for messages. Two minutes later:

Saffron: *She's leaving.*

Mina: *She's gone past.*

Me: *Meet at the helipad. Picnic time.*

Saffron: *I am so not doing that again in a hurry.*

'It was crude,' said Saffron as she munched a sausage roll. 'The target just swept the area. All she would have seen is the Artefacts, a few living people and a lot of dead ones. That wasn't Eilidh Haigh.'

'What did she look like, Mina?'

'A woman on a bicycle. Attractive, I suppose, if you like sweaty women in Lycra. Some men do. She had long hair. She was white. There was a maple leaf on her top. With the helmet and the mirror shades, I couldn't see her face.'

'Maple leaf?' said Saffron. 'Rings a bell. Can't remember where, though.'

'Good work, everyone,' I said. I broke my sausage roll in half. 'Even you, boy.'

Mina rubbed his ears. 'Especially you.'

Saffron looked puzzled. 'How come?'

'How did you think I was going to spot incoming Mages?' I said.

'Look for anomalies. Something like that. After all, you've met them before.'

'And I'd have to get way too close. They'd see me long before I saw them. That's why I got Scout – and Mina – down here. With permission from Hannah. It was your idea. I've been training Scout to alert us when he spots magick, and his job was to sound the first alert. Then Mina goes to fetch him, and if her arm tingles, we fire the warning gun.'

'Sneaky.'

'It worked.'

'What now?' said Mina.

'Saffron and I are waiting for the Boss to decide. For you, it's back to the Gnomish ledgers or shopping in Oxford.'

'Much as I'd love to go shopping, Erin will want her car back. The Peculier Auditor should have her own vehicle, Conrad, and not be reduced to begging from the Arden Foresters.'

'Couldn't agree more. We'll have to … hang on. What's that?'

An ambulance came round the service road at speed and turned into the helipad access. A team of ground crew emerged from a nearby building, donning their visibility clothing. When the ambulance killed its engine, I could hear the distant roar of a helicopter.

'Incoming air ambulance. We'd better shift,' I said.

'You can take Scout, and I've left some clean clothes and your shaving gear in the Volvo,' said Mina. She grabbed the last Jaffa cake and gave me a kiss. With a wave to Saffron, she jogged off the mound towards the car park.

Saffron and I bundled everything away and cleared the area before the security guards arrived. We were loading up my Volvo when Hannah called. We dived into the front and I put the call on speaker.

'Is everything okay?' said Hannah.

'Yes, ma'am. I spoke to the police five minutes ago, and Chandler is still in surgery. He's alive, but there were complications during the operation. No suspicious activity anywhere else.'

'Good. I want you two to watch the hospital in shifts.'

Saffron and I looked at each other. She was thinking the same as me. 'What about Haigh's gang, ma'am?'

'Dom has identified the property they're using. With Vicky and Xavier to assist, he can manage. They're going to take a break, then start observations.'

Saffron's face went blank. Except for her bottom lip, which she chewed. She was still thinking the same as me.

'Ma'am, is that the best use of resources?'

'I know you too well, Conrad. You're not the only Watch Captain in England. In fact, there will be two of them on this job: Dom and Vicky. Don't worry, I've told him to be careful. Are you okay to take the first shift? Saffron can go home for a couple of hours if she wants to.'

Eating the picnic, and getting up before dawn, had made me think it was much later than it was. The dashboard clock was saying 12:00.

'We'll keep you posted, ma'am.'

'Don't worry, Conrad, I'll do the same. Well done, both of you. That was a good plan you came up with.'

'Don't forget Scout and Mina. It wouldn't have worked without them.'

She laughed. 'Are you going to put dog food on your expenses now?'

'I already have.'

'Go away and look after Morris Chandler. Goodbye.'

I pulled my lip and stared at the main building of the John Radcliffe. Ugly thing.

'You've got serious reservations, haven't you?' said Saffron.

'Have you?'

'Not my place to say, chief.'

'I am not your chief. You are not a Gnome.'

'What do I call you then? *Sir* is for emergencies, and you won't let me call you *Boss* or *chief*. Vicky has a monopoly on *Uncle Conrad*, so what does that leave?'

'I know you think I'm too old to use my first name, but give it a try, okay? And if you have genuine reservations, you should speak them. And the reasons.'

'Always show your working out?'

'Always. That way we can avoid prejudice.'

'Your report into the Niði's dock ambush. It said there was only one Mage: Eilidh. The bike girl must be that Jane Jones, and what if that South African Mage – presumably Willem van der Westhuesen – is there? That's three Mages and three bodyguards.' She opened her window. It was rather hot in the Volvo. 'In your report on the Dragon affair, you summoned every Watch Captain you could for reinforcements. You only attacked when Vicky was kidnapped.'

'You have an excellent memory, Saff.'

'You called me that in the mortuary. I was too cold to object. Do it again, and I will call you Connie.'

'That's what Helen of Troy called me. You are not in her league. Try *Conrad*. It won't hurt, I promise.'

'Fine. Stop avoiding the question. You wouldn't go in against three Mages and three bodyguards, would you?'

'That's not the real issue. The real issue is that I wouldn't send those three in, but Hannah just did. Then again, she knows Dom Richmond as a Mage, and I don't. We'll leave it there. Do you want to go home and crash out for a couple of hours?'

'Yes please. I'll look after Scout, too. You can't take him up to surgery.'

'Thanks.'

She wound up her window and opened the door. 'See you later, Conrad.'

'I hope you're on overtime,' I said to a very sleepy looking detective constable, the same one who'd been in the command van.

She yawned. 'Yes, sir. They've changed the personal protection officer, though. There's a strict limit on how long you can be on duty with a gun.'

She was sitting on one of those corridor chairs, looking like a concerned relative. The armed officer was on the other side of the sterile area, near the recovery room. There was no way through to Chandler without passing one or other of them. I plonked myself down next to her.

'Any news?' I said.

She looked at her notebook. 'During the operation to repair his leg, his system started to shut down. They had to rush him to the MRI room. Something in his abdomen had ruptured. They had to pull a specialist surgeon out of another theatre. It was quite dramatic. I ended up holding his drip because the nurse had to run off for more blood. If he survives this, he's going to be in a bad way.'

'Poor sod.'

'Didn't he try to kill someone? Several someones?'

'Yes. Doesn't stop me being sympathetic. I once delayed an evacuation to pick up some wounded Taliban.'

We fell silent for a moment. 'Do you like gardening?' she said.

'Why?'

'You're not going to talk about your job, are you?'

'No.'

'Neither am I, so it's gardening or something else.'

'Not gardening. How about cricket?'

She gave me a strange look. 'Do I look like a cricketer?'

'My girlfriend plays. So do most of her friends.'

'Holidays. What's your dream holiday?'

'Have you done a lot of observation duties?'

'It shows, doesn't it? Go on. Where would you take this girlfriend of yours? And don't say *to the next cricket world cup.*'

Three hours later, I knew all about her divorce, her lack of children, her opinions on the Great British Bake-Off and pretty much everything about her except her name. There was a moment of excitement when Chandler came out of surgery and into recovery, and that was it.

Saffron wafted in to give me a break wearing the yellow version of her new dress and looking radiant.

'I hate you,' said the detective. 'That dress is gorgeous. Where did you get it?'

Saffron deftly changed the subject to avoid saying that she had a dressmaker on speed-dial and handed me an envelope.

'GG has a basement she lets out to students, and it's empty at the moment. You can crash there. All the details are in the envelope.'

'Where's Scout?'

'In the car park. I told him to hide and wait for daddy.'

I shook hands with the detective. 'Nice to meet you. I hope you've gone when I get back.'

'If I'm still here when you get back, it's because they've admitted me as a patient. Good luck.'

Hannah rang at six thirty, dragging me out of a deep sleep half an hour before the alarm was due to go off.

'We've found them,' she said. 'Chandler was telling the truth. They're at a property rental in Stockcross, near Newbury. You can be there in an hour.'

'Just me?'

'I rang Saffron first so that she could get going. She's joining the others. You can provide support.'

I pulled my lip. If I said something, I'd regret it. If I said nothing, I'd probably regret it even more. 'Ma'am, is this the best use of resources?'

I heard her sigh down the phone. 'I knew you'd say that. I thought you'd be a lot ruder, so you must have mellowed. This has to be Dom Richmond's show. He's got Vicky, Xavi and Saffron to help him and you in support.'

I still wasn't happy, but she's the Constable. It's her job to make difficult decisions. 'Not just me, Hannah. He's got me and Scout.'

'I can't wait to meet that dog. Rendezvous with them at the Hare & Hounds in Speen. I'll text you the details.'

19 — Support

All the way down the A34, I had visions of Dom Richmond laying on a banquet at the inn before strolling up to Eilidh Haigh and saying, 'You're under arrest. Come quietly.' It wasn't quite that bad.

Dom and Saffron were already in the village; Vicky and Xavi were drinking mineral water and waiting in the bar. The first thing Vicky did was send Xavi to get me a large coffee. 'I got you this,' said Vicky, pointing to a carrier bag. 'I knew you'd be hungry.' She looked at Scout. 'By Nimue's well, he's grown. Is he hungry, too?'

'Always. Dog food keeps better than human food, so I've got a bag in the car. He gets better fed than I do. Ravenous mutt. Thanks, Vic. What's going on, and why was I the last to hear of it?'

She glanced at Xavi, who was still waiting to be served. He'd gone to the other end of the bar without being asked. 'You weren't going to be involved at all until Hannah insisted. She wanted another Mage on the op, and he would only take Saffron, not you. I think the Boss wanted you to run your eye over his plan first, but Dom's definition of support is different to Hannah's.'

'What do you mean?'

'Not for me to say. Here comes your coffee.'

Xavi walked carefully over with a large bowl of pick-me-up and put it in front of me. He bent down to say hello to Scout, offering his hand to be licked, then rubbing under Scout's chin. He frowned, as if he had something to say, then shook his head. Xavi is a Necromancer: maybe he could sense something of the Spirit that had become Scout. He sat up straight and looked at me. 'Has Vicky told you it was her who found them?' he said.

'Ruth found them, not me.'

'But it was your idea to use the police to contact all the property rental agencies.'

'Aye, well, it doesn't matter who found them. They're at Lilac Cottage. Here.'

She opened her laptop and showed me an aerial image of Stockcross village. She pointed to a lane on the edge of the village. 'Lilac Cottage is the only property on that side of the road. As you can see, there's a field behind it, then the churchyard.'

I studied the screen. 'What's the plan?'

'Dom and Saffron are in position at the church. They're going to cross the field when we approach from the front. Xavi's been practising his Occulting, and he can throw a total shield over us until we're on the driveway. That way, we can block their escape route. We go for the Mage or Mages and tell the mundane occupants to run for their lives.'

'And what's my part in this?'

'Stay this side of the A34 until we call you for prisoner transport. Dom says that Eilidh will be using extra magick to look out for any Mage coming into the village who hasn't got special protection. You don't have that.'

Xavi had been checking his phone constantly. He looked up. 'They're ready. I'll tell them we're leaving now.'

I took a Bluetooth earpiece out of my pocket, along with the spare phone I've been carrying. 'Call me and put this on the dashboard when you get to the village.'

She nodded and stuffed the phone in her pocket. 'See you soon, yeah?'

'Absolutely.'

There wasn't time to eat or do anything other than finish my coffee outside while I sent a text, and then get the Volvo ready for action. All that I could really do for that was turn it around to face the exit and have the engine running. I tried to work out the kinks in my back and settled down to wait.

Vicky didn't bother with pleasantries. I answered the phone and heard a clatter as she put it somewhere in her car.

'We're in position,' said Xavi.

I eased the Volvo out of the car park and on to the road, moving slowly so as not to get too close to the A34 junction. I couldn't jeopardise their mission by encroaching the target area, but there was no way that I was going to sit in the pub and wait to be summoned. As soon as they breached the boundaries, I was heading into Stockcross.

Xavi spoke again. 'Saffron says there's been some Occulting at the property. Can't make out who's in there. It'll make it much harder for them to see out.'

I took that as encouragement and increased my speed.

'Let's go,' said Xavi.

Vicky has an Audi TT convertible. I heard the engine roar into life.

'Entering Glebe Road. Go.'

That was Saffron and Richmond's cue, and I took it as mine, too. I put my foot down and tore across the roundabout on to the Stockcross road.

In my ear, I heard the clunk of car doors opening. I tried to picture what was happening as they approached the large cottage. Some owner had taken the name literally, and painted the render a delicate pinky-purple. Vicky and Xavi would be lining up to blast open the front door. You can put blast-protectors on inanimate objects, but that's serious magick, and you'd need one for each door and window.

I was on a straight road now, and I really put my foot down. So long as no one came out of the Vineyard Hotel…

Richmond and Saffron had to cross a 60m field to access the rear of the property. They'd be arriving about now.

I heard the muffled *thump* of a serious blast of magick let off under a Silence. Vicky must have shoved the phone in her pocket. The Silence was lifted, and I heard Xavi shouting *King's Watch*. More thumping. Then a *whoosh*.

'Vic, it's tear gas. Get …'

The sound of coughing filled my ear. Shit. Double shit.

I got to the built up part of the village and had to slow down. It was late evening, but still early enough for children to be out playing. At this speed, I'd stand no chance of avoiding them. I slalomed left into Church Road and put my foot down again.

'Howay Xavi! Come 'ere!' shouted Vicky. I could hear the shredding in her voice as the gas took hold. They'd be retreating now.

I had a choice: left into Glebe Road, or carry on to the church. Vicky and Xavi's car would be blocking the main entrance, so I carried on, praying for a gate into the field. There. I moved right, then swung left and smashed straight through the gate. The bars of the gate were stronger than the hinges and it flopped down. The car bounced over the wood, smashing it further, and I could see Lilac Cottage diagonally opposite me.

The cottage grounds stuck into the field like someone had taken a bite out of a piece of sliced green bread, and I could see smoke coming from the *back* as well as the front. The property was bounded by a six foot fence, and one of the panels was already down, presumably the work of Richmond. I gave thanks for the drought that had rendered the field firm and accelerated again.

Two figures ran out of the gap in the fence: Saffron and Richmond. Saffron's chain swung loose, and Richmond had his dagger by his side as they both tried to deal with the effects of gas. I blew hard on the horn to let them know I was coming, and headed for the gap. Saff turned to look, and grabbed Richmond's hand to pull him out of the way. With my right hand, I touched the Hammer and brought up my Ancile.

Two of the bodyguards, wearing respirators, emerged from the gap in the fence, then fell back when they saw me. I slammed on the brakes and pulled up with the nearside to the fence, loosening my seatbelt as I did so. 'Scout! With me!' I shouted. I pulled the door open and rolled out of the car, taking the Anvil from the passenger footwell.

Over the phone: 'I'm gan'in round the back.' Vicky.

'Saffron, clear the smoke. I can't see,' said Richmond.

I stood up, using the car as cover, and braced my gun on the roof. Richmond had not only levelled the fence, he'd blown down some small trees, and I could see into the garden. There was no one there, and the forced air from Saffron's blast was blowing the smoke back towards the cottage. 'Scout. Stay,' I said, then moved up to the fence.

I looked round the edge and saw the back of the building, with french windows standing open and no sign of life. I looked left and saw a gap leading round to the front. Vicky was coming that way, and she was now wildly outnumbered. I stuck to the fence rather than cross the open lawn and headed for the gap.

Which was mostly filled with the bulk of a Range Rover Sport. One of the big ones that you need two parking spaces for in the supermarket. Someone was chucking stuff into the open boot, and beyond the car, I could see Vicky facing off against two of the bodyguards.

The Range Rover's engine fired. It had been driven in, and was facing me. I hadn't noticed that there was a driver. The woman who'd been loading the boot threw two more tear gas grenades towards Vicky and opened both passenger doors. I moved forward, pointing my gun at where the driver would be sitting and again sticking to the fence.

The two bodyguards dropped their weapons and made a run for the car. The woman who'd been doing the loading appeared with two familiar bottles: Molotov cocktails. She didn't bother lighting them, she just rolled them towards me so slowly they wouldn't trigger my Ancile, then she used a blast to smash them and some simple pyromancy to set the petrol on fire. As the flames shot up, I saw her grab the Artefacts round her neck and wind up for something big. I flattened myself against the fence and started to inch away from the flames. The vegetation had been badly neglected and was just waiting for some petrol to turn itself into a merry forest fire.

The Mage jogged forward a few steps and aimed to my right. With a clap of thunder, a cherry tree and three fence panels blew away. The Range Rover started forwards. The woman mounted the running board and hauled herself inside. The momentum of the vehicle slammed her door closed, narrowly missing her fingers. The vehicle gathered speed and brushed the edge of the fire as it headed for the new gap.

There was nothing I could do except watch. When I got my firearms accreditation, the rules had been very clear: you only open fire on vehicles if there is an immediate threat to life. I lowered my gun and jogged to see where it was going.

In the field, Saffron had moved to put herself in the way of the Range Rover. Stupid Girl. Stupid, stupid girl. Richmond had realised this, and launched himself at her, just in time to push Saffron out of the way and have his leg sideswiped by the car. I'm sure they heard him scream at the Hare and Hounds.

The Range Rover bumped over the field, through the gate and on to the road.

Saffron had been sent sprawling, and crawled over to Richmond to check on him. He was giving her a great mouthful of abuse for what she'd done, and what she'd forced him to do. Impacts like the one he'd suffered can sometimes be deadly, sometimes you can get off lightly. I ran over to have a look. For the second time today, I saw a man who'd need an orthopaedic surgeon. Shit.

Vicky appeared through one of the gaps in the fence. She was carrying the two machetes that had been dropped by the bodyguards.

'How's Xavi?' I shouted.

'Bad. He got nearly a full grenade's worth. We were lucky – these weapons have a toxic coating. No wonder they dropped them rather than risk cutting themselves in the car.'

'Get out quick, Vicky, before the emergency services come. Are you okay to drive?'

'I'll manage. I didn't go in the house, and I was able to blow most of the gas away from me.'

'Take Xavi to Reading. It's the nearest A&E. He must have treatment. Go!'

She ran back through the gap, skirting the now growing fire. And was that smoke coming from the house, too?

I turned my attention to Richmond and Saffron.

'Who drove?' I said.

'Why the fuck does that matter,' said Richmond.

'I did,' said Saffron.

'Good. Where's your car, Dom? And give me the keys.'

'Are you going to leave me here?'

'Don't worry. I'm here to support, and that's what I'm doing. Where's the car?'

'Hare and Hounds.'

'Keys. We need them before we move you, or they might get trapped underneath you.'

He rolled a few inches and groaned. 'Right hand coat pocket.'

'Get them, Saff. You've got smaller fingers.'

'Right.' She unzipped the pocket and fished out the keys.

'Good. We're going to get you in my car in a second. I just need to check your pelvis.'

The last time I'd done this was for poor Diarmuid Driscoll. Vicky had driven the Volvo into him. Deliberately. I think Richmond had come off worse. I felt his pelvis and lifted his thigh a little. It moved as freely as you'd expect. If it hadn't, then it really would be an ambulance job.

'Saff, get him sitting up. I need to arrange the car.'

I went back to the Volvo, and found a terrified dog shivering underneath the driver's side. 'Out you come, boy. It's safe now.' I took two seconds to rub his coat and transfer a little Lux, then popped the boot open.

The back of a Volvo XC70 is big and long. Even longer when I pushed the rear passenger seat down. I moved Scout's dog basket and shifted as much of the gear as I could to leave a narrow channel. I grabbed the picnic blanket and put it down for a pillow.

Leaving the boot door up, I reversed the car as close to Richmond as I could get and left the engine running. 'Saffron, we're going to lift under his shoulders. Dom, pull your left knee up and get ready to push with your left leg. This is going to hurt. On three…'

He couldn't help but moan and hiss with the pain, but he was up. I took as much weight as I could under his right shoulder and Saffron did the same with his left. We turned and eased him back to the gaping boot of the car, then I eased him down into a sitting position, facing out and as far in as I could manage.

I went round to the door by his head and got my hands under his shoulders. I held him as tightly as I could. 'This is going to hurt even more,' I said. 'On three, Saffron is going to lift your leg and I'm going to pull you in. It may take two heaves. You can rest then. OK?'

The reality was starting to bite on both their faces. The enormity of Dom's injury was written in his dilated pupils and guilt was scrawled all over Saffron's compressed lips. 'One…'

His screams easily drowned out the sound of distant fire engines, but not the smoke alarms from inside Lilac Cottage. The overgrown bungalow was now well ablaze. I shut the door and went round to the boot, where Saffron was hovering, wondering what to do. 'Go straight home, get someone you trust, and come back for Dom's car. Take it back to Cherwell Roost.' She nodded and ran off across the grass towards the churchyard.

I shut the boot, got Scout on to the front passenger seat and drove as slowly as I dared out of the field. At the smashed gate, I turned left and took the back way out of the village. One more turn, and we were just A.N.Other vehicle on the A4.

'Where are we going?' said Richmond.

'On to the A34. I'm going to stop at the services. Just five minutes, that's all. Then I can give you some morphine.'

'I'd like that.'

It was closer to ten minutes before we got to the services. It was late enough that most of the car park was empty. I did not need any concerned citizen spotting my cargo. I got Richmond some water and a strong dose of Oxycontin. I stood next to his open door and lit a cigarette.

'Get a bloody move on,' he said.

'In a second. I'm going to have to call the Boss in a minute, and you need to know what's happening first. Also, a few minutes of peace will let the morphine kick in. That was one of the bravest things I've ever seen, Dom. Throwing yourself in front of that Range Rover was truly heroic. I mean that.'

'Stupid bitch. Karma, I suppose, for getting into such a mess. You haven't said *I told you so*. Get it over with.'

'I didn't tell you, did I? I didn't get the chance. You did your best, and no one died. Focus on that while I drive us to the John Radcliffe.'

'That's miles away. You sent Xavi to Reading.'

'You need to be in the same hospital as Morris Chandler. Besides, you live in Oxford. Someone might visit.'

'Why are you bothering with Chandler?'

I crushed out my cigarette. 'Because he's our only hope of finding them before they disappear or attack some soft target. Make yourself comfy.'

The text message I'd sent from the Hare & Hounds before this debacle unfolded was to Hannah, telling her to alert Thames Valley Police to a potential operation on their patch. I dialled her number, knowing that she'd probably be dealing with the fallout from Lilac Cottage already.

'Conrad! What's happened? Is everyone okay?'

'All alive. Dom's got a broken leg and Xavi's been teargassed. Haigh's gang all escaped.'

'Baruch Hashem. I've got the control room on hold. Where are you? I need to provide cover.'

'Vicky's going to Reading. We're on our way to the John Radcliffe.'

'Good. I'll call you back.'

Richmond was somewhere between asleep and unconscious when we got to the hospital. An armed police officer was lurking in the background, and the counter-terrorism inspector from this morning was leaning against the ambulance entrance. A team of paramedics rushed out of the building to attend to Richmond, ignoring me completely because Hannah had given the control room all the details already.

I stepped away from the Volvo and nodded to the inspector.

He pointed to the back of the car. 'You look better than he does, but there's not a lot in it.'

'It has been a long day.'

'And they got away again?'

'Yes. Last time, though. They're running out of places to hide.'

'It'll be off my patch, at least.'

I turned to look at him. 'Why do you say that?'

'They have a base, right?' I nodded. 'This Lilac Cottage place will be somewhere between their base and whatever their target was. That puts their base outside Thames Valley.'

That was a very good thought. I mulled over it for a second and watched them doing something to Richmond's leg before they moved him.

The inspector looked at his armed officer. 'This guy is the night-shift personal protection officer for Chandler. Who needs guarding most?'

'For tonight, Dom Richmond. I'll take Chandler myself. How is he, by the way?'

'Still deeply sedated. Ruptured spleen. They don't want him moving for at least twenty-four hours.'

There was a lot of activity by the back of the car. They put some sort of collapsible stretcher under Richmond and were able to lift him on to the gurney with a lot less pain than I'd managed. He called out to me and waved his hand.

The paramedics ignored him and got ready to move the trolley. 'Clarke,' he said, 'Tell me one thing you'd have done differently.'

Where to start? I gave him the one thing that would show up his lack of experience rather than his incompetence. 'Attack at night. The police make dawn raids. The Army does it at 02:00.'

He nodded, and the gurney disappeared through the huge doors into the hospital. The armed officer detached himself from the shadows and followed at a discreet distance.

I went to say goodbye to the inspector. 'I looked you up,' he said. 'Out of curiosity. I was amazed to find that you're a Special up north, as well as the other stuff. There was a name I recognised on your firearms certificate.'

'Smithy?'

'One and the same.'

'So naturally you gave him a call.'

'I did. He said, "Good bloke. Knows his stuff. Whatever you do, steer well clear of his weird shit." Did Richmond get too close?'

'Dom? No. He's in it up to his neck. Chandler was the one who got too close. You're still at a safe distance.'

'Goodnight, Clarke.'

20 — Friendly

'Arrf! Woof! Arrf!' said Scout. There was a Mage coming. Hopefully Saffron, and hopefully the nurse wasn't passing outside the door. I limped over and took a defensive position (after scratching Scout's ears).

Saffron slipped quietly into the room carrying two large Costa Coffee cups. 'Good morning, sir. How are you?'

The last time Saffron had walked into the ward, she'd been radiant from a job well done. Not today. Then again, I very rarely look radiant at six o'clock in the morning.

'Did you get any sleep?' I said. 'You're going to be here for a long time.'

'A bit.'

'Let's go into the corridor.'

I gave Scout the treat he'd earned, and we slipped out of the room. I accepted the coffee gratefully: my own little treat for being a good boy. I'd kept awake for the first few hours by moving around the building and going outside to check on Scout. At three o'clock, I'd smuggled him into the ward and made him a bed behind the door. Two nurses and one doctor had completely failed to spot him, which was bizarre. I'm beginning to suspect that Scout might have a lot more magick than I do.

'How's Dom?' was her first question. It got her a bonus point with me, because she was itching to apologise and grovel, yet she'd forced herself to ask about Dom first.

'Double fracture of the lower right leg. His knee's bad, too, but the on-call surgeon was their best, according to the theatre sister. He did them both at the same time. He'll be out of it until noon. After that, I'm hoping they'll move him into a double room with Chandler, then he can take over guard duty.'

'From his bed?'

'Why not? All he has to do is sense them coming and alert the armed protection officer. Until then, it's over to you.'

Her shoulders slumped. 'All I wanted to do last night was talk to someone about it. I was on the verge of quitting, just so I could go over to the Roost and talk to Mum. That's another thing Hannah didn't mention: the isolation.'

'Why did you do it? What were you hoping to achieve, standing in the way of the car like that?'

'I wasn't thinking. I just thought I had to do something.'

Physical contact between senior officers and junior ranks of the opposite sex is frowned upon for good reasons, but if this wasn't an exceptional circumstance, I don't know what is. I put down my coffee and put both hands on her shoulders. 'Saffron, you haven't had years of training for operations. Even then, split second decisions aren't easy. Try to remember this: Team at risk, do something. Team not at risk, do nothing.'

She nodded.

'Repeat after me. Team at risk…'

'Team at risk, do something. Team not at risk, do nothing.'

'Good.' I dropped my hands and picked up my coffee. 'In other news, Xavi is very sore but suffered no lasting effects, there is no trace of Eilidh Haigh or her gang, and I am now going home. Barring emergencies, I'll see you on Monday.'

'Monday? What about Eilidh?'

'She can wait. Until Chandler is fit to be interviewed, we have nothing, and nothing comes from nothing. I'm off to face a female foe of a different kind. One that I'm related to.'

'Vicky said your mother was nice. Odd, but nice.'

'And so she is. Somehow, she also gave birth to my sister. Have a good weekend.'

'Here they come,' said Myfanwy. 'Is that a bottle of Champagne your sister's carrying?'

I turned to face the Inkwell. Carole Thewlis and Rachael were heading our way with big smiles on their faces. 'Two bottles,' I said. 'Raitch would never buy one in case she has to go back to the bar. Saves the effort.'

'She does know we have our first match tomorrow,' sniffed Jules Bloxham. 'That's a lot of Champagne.'

'Not for Rachael,' I said.

Our little group stood up to greet the new arrivals. Normally Juliet would be well away from us, but Myfanwy had made a point of inviting her so that all the women's team who went to the pub were together. Some had stayed for a quick one and gone, and you may raise an eyebrow if I tell you that apart from Jules, all the stopouts were all from Team Elvenham: Mina, Myfanwy, Erin, Nell and Ben.

Carole and Rachael had changed after their drive from London and looked relaxed and happy together. They also looked like that Champagne wouldn't be their first drink of the evening. I know that their friendship has had its ups and downs, some of which I got blamed for, and it was good to see Rachael with someone from outside the world of high finance.

After a perfunctory kiss, Rachael handed off one of the bottles of Champagne to me and said, 'Open that, would you?' So much for the grand reunion: she was much more interested in meeting Mina and Myfanwy. I relieved Carole of the tray of glasses and moved out of the line of fire.

Mina pre-empted things by going for the full Namaste, and that's one of the things I love about her – she knows when to use her *otherness* to put people at a disadvantage. She even followed it up by saying, 'I'm so glad to finally meet Conrad's sister.'

She also tag-teams well with Myfanwy, who stuck out a hand before Rachael could respond. 'And I'm Myfanwy.'

While Rachael was shaking hands with Myfanwy (she didn't have a lot of choice, did she?), Mina gave Carole a full hug. 'So good to see you again. You must be so excited! Ellenborough Hall looks *lovely* on the website. I only wish that Conrad would take me there.'

They hadn't planned it like that. They didn't need to. I haven't seen my sister's nose put so firmly out of joint since she was a teenager, and Rachael had now been firmly demoted to the category of *guest*. It was up to her to earn her way back up the social ladder. I popped the champagne and everyone turned to look when Scout made his presence felt.

Carole made a huge fuss of the manic mutt, and even Rachael was forced to join in, and then it was time for them to say hello to Jules and Ben. Myfanwy completed the circle by introducing Erin, and we all sat down to a glass of the Inkwell's finest fizz.

'To the bride-to-be,' I said. I wasn't going to toast a man who'd done everything he could to avoid me, but Carole deserved her moment.

Carole responded with, 'To Clerkswell Ladies,' and followed that up with, 'and how are the plans? Have we interrupted vital preparations?'

Juliet looked at the new arrivals. She would have heard that Rachael and I didn't get on, and she wasn't about to miss out the chance to enrol them in Team Bloxham. 'No point,' she said. 'We were arguing about whether to have a nickname, like Western Storm.'

'Who are they?' said Rachael, shoving me brutally away from the end of the bench so that she could be in full view of everyone and cross her legs elegantly. Unlike the other women, Rachael's jeans were ripped and her trainers looked like they'd come out of the box this evening.

'Western Storm are the Gloucestershire women's T20 Super League team,' said Myfanwy. 'We're not up to their standard. Yet. I think we should stick to Clerkswell Ladies.'

'And I still say we should re-open the vote on that and switch to Clerkswell Women. We don't want to be defined by social stereotypes.' That was Nell. She can be a bit right-on at times, but I wasn't going to argue.

Rachael shook back her hair and said, 'Well, looking at you lot, I think the right name is the Clerkswell Coven.'

Myfanwy and Erin buried their noses in their Champagne flutes, as did Mina. She also added a muttered comment, 'That would seal our reputation: the Witches of Clerkswell.'

'I think it's a good idea,' said Nell. Everyone else looked at her as if she were mad. 'Witches were persecuted for *being* women. The idea of witchcraft is transgressive. It's women asserting their solidarity. I think it's a good name.'

Jules looked worried. 'Just imagine what Allington would do. Twitter would be full of old women with warts on their noses.'

Nell whipped out her phone. She quickly found three very affirming, positive memes of witches. 'We can put the fear of God into them.'

'Oh you must go for it!' said Rachael.

'We'll put it to the team tomorrow,' said Jules. 'And strictly unofficial to start with.'

Rachael raised her glass again. 'To the Clerkswell Coven.'

There was no sign of it getting cooler as the sun disappeared. The heatwave had become very sticky, to the point where rain would provoke wild street parties.

'Don't you need to take Scouty for a walk?' said Rachael. She leaned down to rub his ears. Rather too vigorously for his taste, probably because Rachael had drunk most of the second bottle herself. The ones with children, Nell and Jules, had gone first, and Carole and Ben left shortly after to talk to their parents. Myfwanwy and Erin had gone to put some supper out and leave Rachael, Mina and I to enjoy the last of the daylight.

Rachael looked across the meadow to Elvenham. 'Have you got champers in the cellar, Conrad?'

'Yes, but you'd be drinking it on your own. Some of us have a game tomorrow.'

'Spoilsport.' She looked at Mina. 'He was always telling me No when I was little.'

'He spends a lot of time doing that. He means well, though.'

Rachael drained her glass. 'Let's go home while he walks the dog.'

Mina uncurled herself from the bench and waited for Rachael to stand up, moving nimbly to put her arm round her and pretend it was sisterly bonding rather than structural support. I waited until they were on their way and lit a cigarette. 'C'mon boy. Let's take a turn round the churchyard.'

Rachael had done her best to win over the Clerkswell Coven by being the life and soul, and she can be great company. I'm not sure what the group made of her, really, because they could all see that she'd drunk too much and were too polite to point this out.

I opened the gate to the churchyard and Scout made a beeline for Thomas Clarke's grave. My eleven times great-grandfather had been haunting the family home since 1622, or thereabouts, and had only recently been laid at peace with Alice. Scout could feel the magick still lingering and to him, that plot of ground is as much Home as is Elvenham. I took him the long way round the church to the lychgate and the road to Elvenham. The solitary street light by the church flickered into life as I closed the gate behind me.

'Poor woman,' said Mina, handing me a plate before I'd got into the kitchen. It was piled high with snacks and treats. 'She's gone to where the tennis court was. Try to get her to eat something. She needs to soak up that alcohol. And take that water bottle from the fridge.'

Scout looked at the table. Mina took two sausage rolls off the tray and showed them to him, then she handed them to me. He almost bit my ankles as we walked up to find Rachael.

My sister was never going to win at Wimbledon, but for three teenage summers, she took out all of her frustration on that tennis court and in junior competitions. I still wonder whether Miss Parkes had done her a favour by getting her into that girls' boarding school, no matter that it led to a first in maths from Oxford and a fast-track to the City of London. Rachael had gone to that school a year ahead of her peers, not that any other girl from Clerkswell had ever gone there. And now the tennis court was gone.

The new garden, as designed by Myfanwy, was still a work in progress, and a lot of the beds had gaps in them. The hard landscaping was done, though, and I found Raitch on the three-seater wooden swing, rocking gently. It was my turn to budge her along. Away from the village, it was already nearly dark, especially by the well.

'Have you brought anything to drink?' she said.

'Here. Have some water.'

'Spoilsport.' She drank, then drank again. 'Is that food for me?'

I tossed Scout the first of his sausage rolls. 'Apart from his portion.'

She grabbed a samosa and bit into it. 'Mmm. Delicious. Did Mina make these?'

'Tesco's Finest. Mina's are much better. Samosas were one of the few things her mother taught her to make. She hasn't been able to face the deep fat fryer since she came back from India.'

'Shit. I'd forgotten about that.' She slapped her hands on the swing and it twisted on the long chains. 'How bloody crass of me. She's lost her mother, and I turn up swigging Champagne. What must she think of me?'

'What do you think of her?'

'Strong as steel and sharp as flint. I'm surprised she hasn't cut you.'

That was disturbing. I could take the questionable judgement, but they way it echoed the Gnome's gift was quite peculiar. Coincidence? Had to be. I threw Scout his other sausage roll, and he turned to look at Rachael. He knew he wouldn't get any more from me.

Rachael took another samosa. 'Then again, you are a bit of a rough diamond, Conrad. You don't cut easily.'

'You should see my leg. That cut easily enough.'

'Always a joke, brother. Always a joke. And the biggest fucking joke of all is this garden.' She waved the half-eaten samosa around. 'Not that it isn't lovely. It's great, and so's Myvvy.' She took another bite while she tried to remember what her point was. 'You didn't have to leave home, did you? All those years in the RAF, all the girlfriends, all the secret missions. None of them mattered, did they? Your heart was always here, and you could come back to reclaim it, and when you did, you just rubbed me out like a rough sketch and inked over the top. It's so not fucking fair that you get this and I have to find my own way.'

'Would it make you happy if I gave you the key and walked away? You could pay me by bank transfer and never have to see Mina, Myvvy or me again unless you sent us an invitation.'

'Would you do that for me?'

'You haven't answered my question.'

'What question? You just made made me an offer.'

'I asked you a question: would it make you happy if I gave you the key?'

She didn't answer. She put some motion into the swing for a second. 'Will I ever grow up, do you think? I'd love to know.'

Scout gave up watching Rachael and went to sniff round the well. He goes there all the time, drawn by the latent magick.

'Maybe you have. Maybe you just haven't noticed.'

'Maybe. This swing's making me feel sick. Take me home.'

We paused by the stables. 'Basket, Scout. Good boy.'

He trotted off to his bed, and Rachael said, 'Why do you make the poor thing sleep out there?'

'He's a working dog. Like me. We know our place. You don't need to grow up, Rachael, you just need to find your place.'

'Woof woof! *Find my place*? Why should I have a place I have to fit into? You'll be joining the Tory party next.'

'I am not joining any party that would have Stephen Bloxham as a member. Ditto the Freemasons.'

We arrived at the house. 'You'd better show me to my room. I don't want to disturb anyone by staggering about.'

I kissed Mina outside the pavilion and handed over her cricket bag.

'Wish me luck,' she said.

'You'll be fine. You're a good wicket keeper.'

'I know that. I'm talking about getting changed. It's time they saw my mark, and not just the one on my arm.'

'What are you going to say? I can't think of any rational explanation for having a huge swastika tattoo on your chest.'

'I shall say nothing. Nell will ask Myvvy, and Myvvy will say that she thinks it was something to do with being a widow at my mother's funeral. Nell will then tell everyone else. Everyone else will then Google it and see that it really is a Hindu holy sign. They will then politely try to ignore it.'

I shook my head in admiration. 'Good luck.'

Ben had already kissed Myfanwy, and we wandered out to check the state of the wicket, both for the Ladies' match and the Men's game later. 'How's Rachael?' said Ben. 'She looked a bit the worse for wear last night.'

'Rachael has been in hiding since she got up to go to the bathroom at two o'clock.'

'Eh?'

'She went into her old room and climbed in to bed with Erin.'

'Oooh. I thought Myfanwy's room used to be Rachael's.'

'It is. Erin was on the camp bed. I'm sure Myfanwy will give you the gory details when she's not focused on being vice-captain.'

We stared at the wicket for the Ladies' game. It was dry as concrete and hadn't been watered nearly as much as the others. 'Good luck to them on that,' said Ben dubiously.

Our game was a proper league match of 40 overs. The women were only playing 12 overs for their first outing, and the rules had been bent to allow batsmen to retire at will and resume their innings later. And before you say anything, the team had made their own decision to say "batsman" rather than "batter" or (Odin forbid) "batswoman". Jules had already won the toss and elected to bat first.

Today's opposition was from Bishop's Cleeve. Their first team was over-subscribed, and they jumped at the chance to have a knock-about for some of their reserve players. We returned to the pavilion and waited with a couple of dozen friends and family for the teams to emerge, .

'Here they come.'

The opposition came out to a smattering of polite applause, followed by a big roar from Ben when he saw Myfanwy. Juliet Bloxham led the team, of course, and Stephen cheered her, too, until she gave her husband a filthy look and he calmed down. As she passed, Myvvy gave Ben a big grin. 'Let's hear it for the Witches,' she said. 'It was unanimous: the Clerkswell Coven are here.'

Ben is the batting coach, for the obvious reason that I can't bat very well. I watched our innings and drew the equally obvious conclusion: the Clerkswell Coven weren't going to win this match. There were some positives, though. Jules showed real sticking power and was undefeated. Myfanwy has real promise and helped provide some comedy when she struck the Witches' only boundary – a four through the covers. That was on the other side of the ground, and there were no humans anywhere near the boundary. Scout was there, though, and he dashed round to intercept the ball. The amazing thing was that he waited until it had crossed the rope before trying to pick it up. Poor mite: his jaws aren't big enough yet. Still, he gave it a good lick, and forced the umpire to get a new ball.

'You'll be paying for that,' said Ben.

'I know. I think there are training issues to address.'

Mina batted okay for a few balls until the Bishops' fast bowler came back on and she tried to duck a bouncer and backed into the stumps. Erin was out first ball, though according to Jules it was a wicked delivery.

When the Coven took the field, Ben and I were both keeping our fingers crossed when Emily Ventress measured her run-up. If Clerkswell Ladies were going to have any hope of competing, they needed Emily to perform. Her first ball was well wide, but that wasn't what bothered me. The umpire was having a quiet word with her and pointing to her feet. Oh dear.

The next ball was on target, but the umpire had no choice. 'No-ball!' he announced. It didn't get any better: she bowled two more no-balls, and the legal deliveries were short and slow. One of them was whacked for six. At the end of the over, I whistled loudly and waved her off the field. She was brushing tears from her eyes before she'd got to the boundary; a substitute took her place, and I drew her away for a quiet word.

'You're just too springy, Emily,' I said.

'What?'

'You're young, you're growing and you bounce. Now we're in a match, you put an extra spring into your last two steps because you want to do well.'

She kicked the roller. 'That's the point. Doing well. That's the point.'

We only had a couple of minutes to come up with a solution, and I was getting desperate. 'When you go back on, tell Mina to move to the right a little. When you're running up, look into her eyes until you're two steps from the wicket.'

'Look into Mina's eyes?'

'They're quite hypnotic, I find.'

She pulled a face. 'Euw. That's gross.'

'Just try it for a couple of deliveries. We can work on something else in training.'

In the next over, Emily nearly had a hat trick, and Erin took two catches in the slips. I breathed a huge sigh of relief.

The rest of the innings was less encouraging. Mina did well, and Juliet played a good individual game, but her field placings were mystifying and the general level of fielding showed a lot of room for improvement. Oh, and yes, they lost.

They still got a big round of applause when they came off, and I was going in for a hug when Stephen Bloxham said those dreaded words.

'If I could have your attention for a moment?' As he said this, he held up a large jute bag.

What on earth?

'First of all, well done. I won't keep you a moment longer than necessary, but as club chairman and sponsor of the Ladies' team, I thought it would be good to start a new tradition. We're all looking forward to the men competing for the Clarke-Briggs trophy against Allington in a fortnight, so I got in touch with the Allington women's team, and I'm proud to announce a new trophy: the Bloxham-Hardy trophy for the women's game.'

With a flourish, he pulled a silver cup out of the bag. The Clarke-Briggs trophy is modest, battered and old. The Bloxham-Hardy trophy was gaudy, shiny and brand new. I couldn't fault the idea as such, though the motives are open to question. A lot of the crowd looked at me to see what I thought, and I held my hands up to applaud and said, 'Excellent!'

Myfanwy was standing next to Jules, and she was the only one who heard their captain mutter, 'Bloody stupid Stephen. May as well put Allington's name on it now.'

There was an hour and a half before the men's game, and Mina wanted to go home for a shower. I waited until Juliet's post-mortem had finished and the team started to emerge.

'Well done, love. You were brilliant.'

'That's a lie and you know it.'

'It was not. Until today, Clerkswell did not have a women's cricket team. Now it does. That's brilliant.'

'Hmmph. And what were you doing making that child stare at me? Most disconcerting.'

'You must admit it worked.'

She smiled. 'It does feel very good. Do you know what the real highlight was? I took my top off shortly after we'd voted on the nickname. Myfanwy pretended not to have seen the mark before. She pointed at me and made sure everyone could hear her when she said, "We are not having that as our logo. No way." That definitely broke the ice.'

We got a shock when we got back to Elvenham: Rachael had not only done the washing up from breakfast, she'd left two cards on the table, still in the paper bag from the village shop. Nell does not stock a vast range of cards, and the one addressed to Mina, Myfanwy and me must have been their most expensive *Thank You* card. Inside, Rachael had written, "You deserve better. All of you."

'That is very sad,' said Mina. 'You never told me your sister had such high levels of self-loathing. She could almost be Indian.'

'It's got worse over the last six months. I hope she gets a fresh start in Frankfurt.'

The other card was addressed to Erin, who appeared a few minutes later to collect her stuff. She wasn't staying for the men's game. She opened the card and burst out laughing. The outside had a sad-face emoji with stick-on googly eyes and *I'm (very) Sorry* underneath. Inside, Rachael had written, "This won't happen again, Erin. I've discovered that I prefer brunettes. Sorry."

'Erin, tell Conrad what happened at the crease,' said Mina.

Erin (who's blond) looked embarrassed. 'I was so focused on not using magick against that first ball that I forgot to move my feet. I kicked myself all the way back to the pavilion. Now that really won't happen again.'

Mina kissed me and headed for the shower. Erin moved her bag to the hall, then came back and put the kettle on. 'Do you want a cuppa?'

'Please. Good catch by the way.'

'Thanks. That's not what I wanted to talk to you about. Do you remember Eliza and Karina?'

Erin's circle of Mages, the Arden Foresters, had come to grief in the affair of the Phantom Stag. In the fallout, Karina had been sentenced to undertake a pilgrimage from Glastonbury to St Brigid's Well in Kildare, Ireland. On foot. Eliza had been cast out of the circle as she went into labour.

'Of course I remember them. I take it there's news.'

'Yeah.' Erin was still wearing her team shirt. It wasn't nice having to stare at *Bloxham Buildings* as the sponsor. They also appeared to be very itchy. She pulled at the seam under her arm. 'Karina's back. She completed the pilgrimage walk. She's spending some time with Oma to decide whether she wants to ask for permission to re-join the Foresters. Oma said that the whole group must decide in the end, but I have a veto. If I say no, Karina will disappear.'

Karina had been a party to the murder of Erin's best friend, a tragedy for which Erin seemed to have paid a high price: the Foresters had blamed her in some way, and that's why she was renting one of my stables. 'How do you feel about it?' I asked.

She made the tea and sat back down. 'I want to see her. I want to know what she has to say. If I think she's really sorry, I'll tell her that she can come back on one condition. She has to serve in the King's Watch for three years.'

'Whoa, Erin. Where did that come from?'

'Saffron. I've heard how much of a difference she's made already, and Karina is much more developed as a Mage. Karina's a good kid, really. The King's Watch is right up against it at the moment, and you need all the help you can get.'

We are up against it. The Nine of Wands hasn't finished with us yet. We do need all the help we can get. 'Do you think Karina will take the Oath of Allegiance?'

'Her choice. Take the Oath or ship out.'

Erin does tend to see things in black and white.

'The Constable may not have her. It's not my decision.'

'I know. All she has to do is apply and stick it out for three years if you take her. I think she'll jump at the chance.'

'Perhaps. What about Eliza?'

'You heard there were complications with the delivery?' I nodded. 'She and the baby were in hospital for ages. When she left the hospital, she got into a taxi and hasn't been seen since. There's a For Sale sign up outside her house. I thought you should know.'

'Thanks, Erin. That's useful. Are you thinking of moving yourself? Nearer to Clerkswell, perhaps?'

'I might. I do like it here, and Myfanwy's amazing. The only problem is that she nabbed the last half way decent bloke in the village. All the other single men aren't really single, they're divorced with children. Or they're children themselves.'

'There's only one solution. You'll have to dye your hair and take your chances with Rachael. You could do a lot worse.'

'In your dreams, Conrad.'

'My dreams do not involve my sister. On that score, you have my word.'

'Oh yeah. That would not be healthy, would it? How do you think the boys' team will do today?'

'Nice change of subject. We've got an incentive now: do better than the girls or we'll never live it down.'

We did do better than the girls. Ben decided to play both Stephen and me, given how dry the pitch was. We both took four wickets, and it was a great team victory. I conceded fewer runs than he did, which was personally very satisfying. In the interests of balance, I should point out that he scored more, too. A lot more. That doesn't make the Bloxham-Hardy trophy any less vulgar, though.

21 — Triangulation

We met in the now very familiar surroundings of the John Radcliffe car park on Monday morning. An immaculate Bentley Mulsanne swept into the turning circle and Saffron hopped out. She went slightly red when she saw me watching. 'I didn't think you'd be here yet,' she said.

'Didn't want me to see the chauffeur dropping you off?'

'I wish. That was my uncle at the wheel. Where are the others?'

'They got held up on the M40, but they won't be long. Good weekend?'

She laughed. 'Not as good as yours, by the sound of it. Erin text me to say that she'd had a close encounter with your sister.'

'It's a good job that only the magickal world will hear about this.'

We swapped weekend stories for a couple of minutes, until Vicky's TT appeared. She had the top down and her passenger was grinning all over her face. Xavi was having an extra couple of days to recover from the tear gas, and Vicky had brought Ruth Kaplan up from London. We'd decided that Ruth should take part in the interview because she'd done all the leg-work on identifying the bodyguards, and Morris Chandler would be facing charges in the mundane court sooner or later, and it would be good to have a real police officer's input.

Ruth looks like Hannah's younger sister, not her twin, and that's mostly down to the ageing effects of Hannah's major trauma. I still don't know how old they are, exactly. We found a wall to hide behind, more for shade than privacy, and got down to business. 'Don't go too far away,' I said to Vicky and Saffron. 'We might not even get in. Where are you going?'

'Total tourist, me,' said Vicky. 'Last week was my first visit to Oxford. Saffron says she's gonna show me the sights.'

'There's buses every ten minutes,' said Saff. 'We can be back in no time. Neither of us want to hang around here unless we have to.'

We discussed the interview strategy as a team, then the younger members left us to it. 'How's Hannah?' I asked.

Ruth looked away. 'I don't know. She spent Shabbos alone and she didn't say much at Friday night dinner. If she had hair, she'd be going grey.'

I looked at Ruth's full length bob. After the TT, it would need a good brush. 'No need to rub it in. Did you get all the data analysed?'

'What little there was. The Haighs of Dumbarton definitely know more than they're letting on. They've washed their hands of Eilidh in public, but I can't believe that none of them have had contact with her in the last year.'

'Is there no way to put more pressure on them?'

'Where would we start? Dan McCabe can't drag the whole clan off the street. He's done his best, but you know what these families are like.'

We both turned to look at the bus stop, where Saffron was disappearing inside a double decker. Mmm. If the Haighs are anything like the Hawkins, I'm not surprised the Scottish Watch got nowhere. 'Let's see if Chandler can help us out.'

The personal protection officer was happy enough to go for a break when Ruth showed her police inspector's warrant card. The medical team were less impressed.

'Mr Varcik hasn't been out of bed yet. He's certainly not fit to be interviewed under caution,' said the ward sister. She looked like she'd been here before. I suppose a lot of trauma patients must be of interest to the police.

'We're going to switch to his real name from today,' I said. 'Poor Kristoff's family need to grieve in public, and Mrs Chandler should be able to visit her husband.'

That did not amuse the ward sister. Having to amend all those records would not be easy. 'No,' she said. 'You may not use the hospital as a police station.'

Yesterday, when Myfanwy was working in the village shop, she'd given Mina a shopping list and sent us on a trip to a garden centre outside her zone of confinement. While we were there, I picked up a little something of my own. A few little somethings.

'We'll just have a word with Mr Richmond, then.'

The sister snorted. 'Good luck with that. He's the most morose and obstreperous patient I've seen in a long time.'

She opened the door to the double room and went to check Chandler's charts. Dom Richmond's bed had its curtains drawn. Was he being grumpy or having a pee? The curtains swished back, and an auxiliary nurse left with a cardboard bedpan. I've been there. It's no fun.

Richmond's right leg was swathed in bandages from mid-thigh to ankle. At least he didn't have pins sticking out of it. 'How are you?' said Ruth.

'As well as can be expected. This is the calm before the storm of physiotherapy.' He turned to me. 'Have you come to gloat, Clarke?'

'No. I rang the Boss, and she said you had a sweet tooth, so I bought these.' I put the large box of artisan chocolates on his cabinet and said, 'Anything untoward over the weekend?'

He looked at the chocolates, and some of the frown lines relaxed. 'No. Not a scintilla of magick on this floor of the hospital while I was awake.'

The ward sister decided we weren't about to pester her other patient and went back outside.

'Have you tried talking to Chandler?'

'He lost it when they wheeled him in here and I told him who I was. It's not been easy to talk to Chandler with the armed officer on guard, not that I wasn't grateful for his presence. Or hers. A woman volunteered for the night shift on Saturday so that her ex-husband would have to look after the kids and spoil his night out with his new girlfriend.'

'Let me guess,' said Ruth. 'Her ex-husband is on the same force and couldn't argue.'

'Now you know why I'm still single,' said Richmond. 'One of the reasons, anyway. I heard you having a free and frank exchange of views with the ward sister. What's your plan?'

I reached into the garden centre bag and pulled out my other purchase. This was supposed to be a three-bed high dependency ward, so there was a big gap in the middle. I raised my voice and called over to the other side. 'How are you feeling today, Mr Chandler?'

He couldn't help but look over, and he couldn't help but see the garden gnome. Did you know you can now buy zombie gnomes? It was horrible. 'Present for you,' I added. 'Would it be okay to have a word?'

He looked scared. 'I told you everything.'

'No you didn't. You were bleeding inside and out when we spoke. Now we need to have a proper chat.'

The ward sister came back in when she heard the raised voices. 'Is everything all right, Kristoff? Sorry. Morris?'

The sudden change of name shocked Chandler even more. He glanced at the zombie gnome. 'I'll talk to them.'

'Are you sure?'

He couldn't bring himself to speak and nodded in submission. The sister shook her head and left us to it.

I got a chair for Ruth and plonked myself on the other side of the bed. Chandler no longer looked as if he'd just crawled out of a vehicle fire with a broken leg, which was good. On the other hand, major surgery takes a lot out of you, as does a ruptured spleen. At least he'd managed to shave this morning.

'Start from the beginning,' I said. 'How did Eilidh Haigh recruit you?'

'It was Eve who recruited me. I only found out later that Eilidh had tapped her up first.'

Ruth shuffled her notes and showed Chandler a picture of Eve Maguire holding a trophy and wearing the elaborate outfit of a Kendo fighter. Eve had tried to stab me with a toxic spear, something I very much wish to discuss with her at the earliest opportunity.

'That's her. You know she's married to Marissa, right?'

Another shuffling. There were no wedding snaps on social media, but Ruth had a photograph of a slight woman, a few years older than Eve Maguire. She was a Spanish triathlete. According to statements from Eve's brother, she'd met Marissa at a Pride event in Manchester. Eve worked cash-in-hand as a bouncer in Birmingham, where she was a colleague of Chandler's. Marissa didn't seem to be employed anywhere.

'What happened?' I said.

'You know we all went to the Temple Gym in Sandwell, right?'

'Yes.'

'We were a tight crew there. Everyone knew everyone and there was always someone there to push you, to spar with you or just listen. Eve did her Kendo practice at a dojo in Birmingham, but she did all her training with us, especially after she met Marissa.' His eyes disappeared into the past and summoned a smile of regret. 'It ain't the swankiest gym, but the owner was one of us. He invested loads of the profit into new machines.'

'And then Eilidh came along.'

'Yeah. Eve said that Eilidh walked in one day and they got talking. She offered Eve a shedload of money to work for her, and more if Eve recruited any others. Eve and Marissa quit their jobs and signed up on the spot.'

Ruth had spread all of the bodyguards' photos across her lap. She tapped Eve's picture again. 'Haigh didn't walk off the street and pick Eve at random, did she?'

Chandler moved his shoulders a fraction. Shrugging would be difficult with abdominal stitches. 'I don't know. I suppose not. She said it was for a local job, so I suppose she'd done some research. Eve had a Just-Giving page to try and raise money to go to the world championships. Could be that.'

Ruth gestured at the other bodyguards' pictures and records. Morris Chandler was an amateur MMA fighter (not a very good one). Owen Holt had served briefly in the Army and was a friend of the fifth member, a former Royal Marine known as Eggers. It was Eggers that I'd seriously wounded and whom Eilidh had finished off.

'How did it get from Eve to you?' said Ruth.

'Eve started by sounding me out, then moved on to Eggers. Anything that Eggers did, Owen did, too. Once she had five in total, she introduced us to Eilidh, and we started having training sessions in private. Eilidh gave Eve the money to book this parish hall, and that's where we worked on the routines.'

During the ambush, Owen and Eggers had flanked Eve Maguire to protect her. She had been armed with a spear. It nearly worked.

Ruth glanced at me to take over. 'Morris, you're not stupid. You must have known that you were being trained for something deadly.'

He looked away. 'Maybe. Yeah. She said we were going to be bodyguards in Scotland. You know she's Scottish, right? Rich family. Showed us all these pictures, and they checked out online. It was only after we went to camp that it got really serious.'

'Tell me what happened.'

'It was a Friday in May. Eilidh said we needed to go to a final training camp. Told us to pack for the weekend and to leave our phones behind and not to tell anyone where we were going. I told the missus we were going on a stag weekend.' He'd been happy to talk so far, and I could tell from the way he slowed his voice that this was going to be the hardest part for him. He swallowed hard. 'She took us to this place in Shropshire. She blacked out the windows of the minibus when we left the M54 so we had no idea where we were going. I know how she did it now. When we got to the farmhouse, it was pitch black. She gave us these new combat outfits. Proper gear. We felt dead special, then she took us into a field and showed us the magick. I nearly shit meself.'

'How did you feel about what she showed you?' said Ruth.

'Like it was all me dreams come true all at once. I just wish the missus had been there to see it. She gave us those magick shields. Made us shoot a gun at her, then at each other. When those bullets bounced off, I felt like a god, I'll tell you.'

'What did she say about it?'

'She did a proper number on us. Made us swear an oath of loyalty and never to reveal secrets on pain of death and all that stuff. I wish I'd listened properly. Everyone thought it was like being in a film but real. The only one who took it in his stride was Eggers. He said it just meant there was more ways to die and asked for a pay rise.'

'You did actually get paid?' said Ruth, ever the copper.

'Yeah. Bank transfer. We all had to open new bank accounts before we got paid.'

She made a note. 'Have you any idea where the farmhouse was?'

'No. We had to stay inside during the day and we trained all night. On the Monday, we moved to a hotel in Birmingham. Eilidh let my wife come to see me. That's when she must have got pregnant. You know what happened on the Tuesday.'

That was the day of the ambush on Niði's dock. Ruth nodded to me again. 'Was Marissa the one working the boat on that day?'

'Yes. She didn't join in the combat training. She did first aid and stuff.'

'Had you met Irina or the Fae before that day?'

'The what?'

'The Fae. The other one in Irina's boat.'

'Oh. The queer one. Eilidh called him a fairy, and I just thought she was being homophobic. There's fairies? Really?'

'Fae. Doesn't matter. Had you seen him before?'

'Her. No. That Tuesday was the first and last time.'

'How did Eilidh explain shooting Eggers?'

'The oath. Tell no secrets. She said you'd torture him until he told you everything, then you'd hunt us down and kill us and our families.'

'So why did you run and start shouting my name?'

'Eilidh didn't say nothing about there being magickal police. She never mentioned you or the King's Watch until after the business at the dock. It was a big shock, I'll tell you, when you started talking about arresting people.'

'How did she explain that? I've read your files. None of you are career criminals, so breaking the law doesn't come naturally.'

'She said you were witchfinders and that you wanted to suppress all magick. When Eve said that didn't stack up with what you said, she claimed it was all a conspiracy against women. That got Eve and Marissa on her side again. You see, Eve had her nose put out of joint when Eggers was put in charge.'

'How did Owen feel about all this, and what changed your mind?'

'Owen thought whatever Eggers told him to think. After Eggers was gone, Eilidh flirted so much with Owen that he was like her little puppy. I'd had enough at that point, especially when the missus posted on Facebook that she was pregnant. Eilidh had used your last name, and that Gnome used your first name, so I looked you up. We were allowed on the internet. A bit. I looked you up, and it said you were RAF, so I thought I might be able to trust you. The way that Gnome stood by you, he obviously trusted you as well.'

He shifted slightly in the bed and took a drink of water. 'You were the only wizard whose name I knew. I reckoned if I could get to you before they caught up with me, I'd have a chance.'

'Go back to the ambush,' said Ruth. 'What happened after that?'

'We were in two Range Rovers. Irina and Eilidh drove us down to a service station on the M40 and made us all get in one of them. They did the magick thing again, and the next thing I knew, we was at the cottage.'

'That was weeks ago. What have you been doing?'

'Going mad. We didn't leave the house for three days, then Irina and the other two wizards showed up. The South African bloke and Jane Jones. I told you about them.'

'You did. What difference did they make?'

The door opened and an important looking doctor came in, followed by three younger doctors who all looked like they wanted to be just as important as him one day. The ward sister brought up the rear.

'Consultant,' said Chandler. 'Saved my life.'

'And my knee,' added Richmond.

'Out. All of you,' said the consultant. 'You can come back in an hour if you want.'

It was a week since I'd bonded permanently with Scout. He can spend longer spells away from me without suffering, and I'd thought about leaving him at home. Perhaps next time. I collected him and a can of cold Diet Pepsi from the car park and went for a walk up to the helipad before I called the Boss.

'What's Ruth doing?' was her first question after I'd filled her in.

'She's sending the West Midlands counter-terrorism unit to pick up Mrs Chandler. If Chandler's wife hands over the details of that bank account, she'll be allowed to visit her husband in hospital.'

'Good. Do you believe him?'

'So far, yes, and Ruth agrees. She called it confession syndrome.'

'Ah. Yes. The tricky part is working out what they're not saying. Good work. How's Dom?'

'Frustrated. Guilty. Bored.'

'I know all that. How is he medically?'

'We'll find out when the consultant's finished with them.'

'Keep me posted.'

Even Scout was running out of energy. I drank my Pepsi and sent a few texts. Mina had told me only to call her in an emergency because she had to get back to her work for the Cloister Court. Vicky found time to reply. She and Saffron were having a great time, apparently. I finished my break and headed back to the ward.

Dominic Richmond had some good news for us when Ruth and I got back to the ward. 'We've both been passed fit to be moved from a high dependency ward. Can I suggest that we be transferred to a private hospital. The police can pay for him, the Watch can pay for me. That way, the armed guard can be stood down and I'll keep an eye on him until the crisis is over.'

Chandler himself wasn't there to argue. He was on his way back from an MRI scan, and a couple of phone calls sorted out the principle. When they wheeled him in, I let Richmond break the news. Chandler seemed quite pleased with that, and pathetically grateful for the proper cup of tea I'd bought him from a concession downstairs.

While Richmond was speaking, I'd taken a closer look at Chandler. He had a sort of ratty beard that covered some healing acne. Of course. Why didn't I think of that before?

'When did Eilidh cut off your supply of steroids?' I said.

He went bright red. 'I don't know what you mean.'

'Yes you do. It takes a long time for the effects to fade, Mr Chandler. Who was the dealer at the gym? Don't lie to me, because I'll be following this up.'

'It was Marissa. She could get hold of them dead easy in Spain. She was starting to build up a network all across the west midlands.'

'How did Eilidh deal with the withdrawal, Chandler?'

'That's why she brought the South African guy up. He gave me something for it. Helped a bit. And it was about then that she made the golden triangles to go with our magick shields. They helped, too.'

Saffron had tried – and failed – to analyse the effects of the Artefact we'd taken from Chandler. I'd told her not to take any risks, because they could easily be booby-trapped. We might need to get Auntie Heidi on to that.

'Tell me about the South African and Jane Jones.'

'Johnno, we called him. We were in the cottage for a couple of days under lock and key, pretty much. I was starting to get itchy, you know? Then those two turned up and Eilidh let us off the leash a bit. We did training on the common above the village, and later we went into Banbury. That's how I worked out the escape route. Johnno wasn't about much, but Jane moved in more or less full time.'

This was all very interesting, but it didn't tell me anything about them as Mages. Or even as people. Ruth showed him the photograph of Willem van der Westhuesen, and he confirmed that this was "Johnno."

'Describe Jane Jones to me.'

'In her forties, maybe a bit older. Savage temper. Long brown hair. Sour face. Posh voice, a bit like yours. It was when they arrived that Eilidh told us about the gold. Jane brought some with her. You could feel the magick coming off it. She said that if we did a couple more jobs, we could walk away set up for life. We started proper training after that. She said we were going to be part of a raid on somewhere called the First Mine.'

I shivered inside. If Eilidh and her gang had joined the assault, I'd be dead. And so would Saffron, Lloyd and Mina. No wonder Hannah banned her from active operations: we'd escaped with the skin of our teeth on that one.

I breathed out slowly. 'But you didn't, did you? Why not?'

'Those three Gnomes turned up. There was a huge row that we could hear upstairs. We had to have the windows open because it was so hot. The Gnomes wouldn't let Eilidh come with them when they tried to get the gold. Eilidh told us not to worry, because we'd have 'em when they came out. Then she got a phone call while we were out training. She went ballistic and called Irina all the names under the sun, because Irina was supposed to tip us off about the raid.'

'That was the end of June. Two weeks ago. What were you up to after that?'

'We didn't find out until two days after you killed all the Gnomes. I can remember what happened when Eilidh finished on the phone: Eve Maguire and Jane Jones both looked at her and said, "They'll be coming for us next."'

'And how did Eilidh react to that?'

'She said, "There's one place left. We go for the vault."'

I could feel Ruth tense up across the bed. Even Richmond sat up a bit straighter.

'Tell us about this vault.'

'Nothing to tell. I got out before she started the detailed planning. She said she needed to go and do some work at the forge. That was the first time it was mentioned.'

'What work?'

He looked guilty again. 'You remember that spear that Eve used?'

I fixed him with a stare. 'The one with the toxic coating. The one that would have killed me with a single nick. Yes, you could say that I remember it.'

'She said it takes a hell of a lot of work to make those, which is why we only had the one with us. She wanted to make more, but that meant going away, and that's why she brought Jane Jones in.'

'Did she ever make any short trips to the forge? If so, how long was she away?'

'Hard to say. She went to loads of places. About an hour was the shortest, I reckon.'

We were running out of things to ask. I had one last question. 'You were with her a long time. What's Eilidh like as a person? What floats her boat? Give us a general impression.'

'You know what, she'd have fitted right in at the Temple Gym. Driven, she is. Whatever it takes. We lads used to talk a bit. Eggers, me and Owen. Eve and Marissa were always more on their own. After we lost Eggers, me and Owen used to wonder what it was like to be one of you wizards, and whether we could join. Owen said, "Not if it means turning into Eilidh." All she does is tinker with bits of magick and run. She and Marissa used to go out every day. At least once.'

He was flagging again. I looked at Ruth, and she shook her head, as did Richmond. Chandler was nearly asleep when we got up and thanked him for his time. I paused on the way out to tell the ward sister that he'd confessed to steroid addiction. She frowned and muttered something to herself. 'Thank you for telling me. No wonder some of his results were odd. I'll make sure it gets addressed.'

'Where now?' said Ruth.

'Call an Uber. We can meet Vicky and Saffron for lunch.'

'I don't mind lunch. You call the Uber.'

I showed her my phone. 'I'll call your twin. You call the Uber.'

I do like the Inspector Morse bits of Oxford. We visited a lot when Rachael was a student and I was based in the UK for a short while. On a day like today, it was full of coach parties. I mean *really* full. It seems to be a rite of passage for Italian high school students, and don't get me started on the Chinese. Vicky said that they were on the Broad, outside Balliol College. It was so crowded that the only way of finding them was to say, 'Scout, find

Saff. Find her.' It took him a while, because they were actually on the other side of the road.

When I pointed this out to Vicky, she said, 'Howay, man, it's way too sunny and way too crowded over there. I saw you coming from miles off. I was gonna text you, but you put the bloodhound on the job.'

'You were going to text me from the other side of the road?'

'Aye.'

I shook my head. 'You've been away from me too long already. I pity Xavi.'

Ruth shook her head. 'And I pity Hannah. It's like a school outing being round you lot. Can we eat? The grown-up is hungry.'

'This way,' said Saffron.

I should have known what to expect when she led us down a back alley off Pusey Lane. There were only three buildings down there, and one of them was the Worcester Roost. 'Don't tell me. A cousin.'

'Once. She sold it ages ago. It's in mundane hands now, but most of the Mages in Oxford still come here. I bet you'll see Dom Richmond's name in the book somewhere.'

'And this is my treat,' said Vicky. 'I've had a great morning.'

'I'm glad someone's happy,' said Ruth. 'I didn't know there was quite so much sight-seeing and entertaining in the Watch.'

'It helps take our minds off the near-death experiences and trauma,' I replied. 'After you.'

We filed in to the hallway of an old private house, where a smiling woman welcomed us. Some of us. 'I'm sorry, we only allow assistance dogs,' she said.

'And Familiars,' said Saffron. 'It's in your lease. I checked. If you give us the private room, no one else will know.'

At that point, Scout wagged his tail and did the little moan that usually gets him attention. The woman's smile disappeared and she grabbed some menus with an aggressive jab into the holder. She must be a cat person. Shame.

Lunch was delicious (and very expensive). It also relaxed us enough to toss round ideas without getting het up, which was how the breakthrough came about. We were about to throw in the towel when I said, 'I'm surprised that Chandler didn't have a complete psychotic episode locked up with two mad runners and coming down from steroid abuse.'

Saffron had read all the notes, and knew that Marissa was a triathlete. 'Who's the other runner, and what's wrong with running?'

'Eilidh herself, and I've always found it a bit pointless. Runners can get a bit obsessive. Unlike cricketers.'

'What! Cricket's even worse than running. All those bloody statist...' I could almost see the lightbulb come on over her head. 'Of course!' She picked up her fork to emphasise what she was about to say. 'When Eilidh went off the grid, she had to get a complete new identity, including a new phone and new email. If she's a fanatical runner, I'll bet she kept her running app. Losing all that data would break her heart. It'll have her routes, her dates and times. If we could hack that, we'd have her on toast.'

I was half way out of my seat. I'd made everyone leave their phones on the side-table. On the way over, I held up my hand to high-five my partner. 'Saffron, I could kiss you.'

She high-fived back and said, 'Please don't. Where are you going?'

I grabbed my phone and called the Earth Master, aka my Mage friend Chris Kelly. 'Chris, did you ever go running with Eilidh Haigh and if so, what app did she use? Oh, and sorry I haven't been in touch about that dinner invitation. I'll explain.' He told me, and I disconnected.

Saffron was staring at me. 'You're having dinner with Baldy Kelly? On his own, I hope.'

'No, with his wife. And Mina, of course. Why is that a problem?'

Vicky and Ruth were fiddling with their empty plates. 'Oh, no reason,' said Saffron. 'What did he say.'

'He never went running with her, but they did talk about it in the common room. She uses something called *Laufstrasse*. Run-street. Two more calls and we're home.'

'I bet I know who he calls first,' said Vicky.

'The Boss,' said Saffron.

'I agree,' said Ruth.

'Nah. I bet he calls his mother.'

'Correct, Vic,' I said, thumbing the contact.

While I waited for the connection, Vicky said, 'She used to work for GCHQ. She knows who to call next.'

22 — Second Nature

Of course, it wasn't that simple. How do I know? Because the man from GCHQ said, 'It's not that simple.'

There had been more than two phone calls. At least twelve that I know of, and plenty of emails, too, before the Cloister Court granted a warrant and the man from GCHQ suggested that we meet in the Inkwell because his quiz team often came there. All I knew about him was that he wasn't part of the world of magick.

He'd nodded to the landlord's husband (another GCHQ toiler) and accepted a half of Inkwell Bitter before we adjourned to a shady corner and he gave me the bad news.

Dealing with the security services is always a matter of negotiation, so I smiled at him and said, 'According to Mother, you can get pretty much everywhere on the net.'

'It's technically not difficult,' he said dismissively. 'We could be in like a shot if there was something important at stake.'

'Such as?'

'"Is the home secretary's mistress having an affair?" Something like that.' He slurped his beer. 'This is nice.'

'And you're a wind-up merchant.'

'Not really. I just try not to get too po-faced about these things. Let me explain.'

'Please do.'

'Laufstrasse is 100% German. If we were to hack their servers and get found out, there would be an almighty stink. You've got authority for our help, but not that much authority.' He held up a hand to forestall any complaints. 'I didn't say it was impossible, I just said that it wasn't simple. What I can't do is get your target's data. What I *can* do is get you access to her account.'

'What's the difference?'

'We did a bit of data sniffing, and your target is still using her old email address as the UserID. Now, she hasn't used that email account or the original phone in over a year, so we've cloned both of them for you. You've definitely got authority for that.'

'Good to know.'

'What you do is this: send a request to re-set the password. Laufstrasse will respond to the request, you re-set the password and you're in business. With any luck, your target will just think it's a blip when she can't access the app with her old password.'

I shook my head. 'She'll know. She'll know exactly what's going on.'

'That's the best I can do, I'm afraid.'

'I'll take it.'

He finished his beer and grinned. 'Give my regards to your mother.'

We shook hands and he left me to finish my pint. I'd hoped for a lot more and feared a lot worse. I could work with this.

I took my drink outside and found an empty table. Somehow, despite the heat, Scout managed to scamper over and jump up at me. I don't know why Duracell chose a bunny to front their ad campaign: nothing has more pointless energy than a young border collie. He'd been very good today, so I let him win at stick-wrestling. I looked over the meadow towards Wales. There was definitely a warm, wet front approaching. About time.

When a family from out of the village arrived, Scout lost interest in me and went to pester them. I think the Spirit that became Scout must have been an actor in a previous life: he schmoozed that family like a West End veteran.

I left them to it and opened my case. I took out Ordnance Survey map 185 for north Hampshire and spread it over the table. A very rough pair of lines in pencil showed the radius of half an hour's drive from Lilac Cottage and the likely zone for Eilidh Haigh's forge.

I know that area very well, because just east of map 185 is where my second home used to be – 7 Squadron at RAF Odiham. I lit a cigarette and did some calculations until Hannah rang.

'Can you talk?'

'Yes, he was only here long enough to wet his whistle and disappoint me. I've had longer and more fulfilling speed dates.'

'Hashem give me strength. I do not want to know about your love-life. So?'

I told her what he'd had to say, and she finished by asking my thoughts.

'I have a plan, ma'am. You won't like it.'

'I know I won't like it. I also know that it will be insane and that it will be our only option. Which bit will I like least?'

'The bit where we call up the reserves. I need Desirée as well as Vicky, Saffron and Xavi. We should all fit nicely in a Puma.'

'Don't tell me that's a helicopter. Do not tell me you want to fly in a bunch of Mages.'

'Of course not, ma'am. I won't be flying, I'll be a passenger.'

'Why? Why not go in on the ground? Like normal people?'

'Because I know that area. Eilidh has had a base there for over a year. She knows the net is closing in. She'll be ready to run, and if we go in over the ground, she'll know we're coming in plenty to time to get out. This time, she'll leave the bodyguards behind, and if she takes her Range Rover over the fields, we'll never catch her. I don't want her to get away a third time. If we go in by air, at night, we can hit them hard.'

I heard her sigh. That meant she'd given in on the principle. After that, it was just a question of details. I lit another fag and outlined my plan.

'My god it's huge. How do you handle something that size?'

'Please tell me we're not going in one of those.'

The Chinook helicopter is big. Very big. As tall as Lilac Cottage and much, much longer. Seeing a row of them is even more impressive. The only one not to be thoroughly impressed was Desirée. She was still getting over the issue of her combat uniform and the fact that people really do salute each other on an RAF base.

'Ours is round the back. Much smaller,' I said.

'Not that much,' said Vicky. 'You know, I swore I'd only ever get in a helicopter with you if Hannah ordered me.'

'I remember. Just be thankful I'm not the pilot.'

'At least we won't have to worry about getting decapitated by the rotors,' said Xavi. 'Just the teargas and the toxic weapons.' He does have a good line in morbid humour.

'And I still don't see why we're practising this,' said Saffron. 'How hard can it be to get out of a helicopter?'

'Let's find out, shall we?'

As we got closer, they realised that the step-bar to get in is quite high off the ground, and the cargo space is a lot higher. Troops in full kit are not allowed to jump out unless ordered.

'Oh,' said Saffron. 'Fair enough. Who's going to be first out?'

'Who do you think?'

She turned to Vicky. 'Please tell me he did this to you as well. I hate it when he puts me on the spot.'

'Aye, he did do it. Not usually in public, though.'

Saffron looked at me until she realised, yet again, that I was serious. She rubbed her chin and took her red beret off for the hundredth time. 'The fastest.'

'Correct. In the real drop, I will go last because my bad leg might slow you down. Now watch me.' I got in and out a couple of times, pointing out the hand holds and where to put your feet. 'Your turn.'

I made Saffron do it twelve times before she cracked and said, 'What am I doing wrong?'

'You didn't listen when I explained it. If you had, you'd know that you're an inch too short to do it that way. You need to put both feet on the rail.'

'But I can do it easily!'

The hurt, bewildered expression on her face was almost more than I could bear, and definitely more than Vicky could stomach. 'Take it easy, pet. He can be a pain at times, but just do it, eh? Sometimes, he really does know what he's talking about. Conrad brought me back from the dead, remember?'

'Sorry, sir,' said Saffron. The thirteenth time, she executed the manoeuvre perfectly.

We left the officers' mess at 01:30 and jogged across the base to one of the hangars. We didn't jog for exercise, we jogged because it was starting to rain, and judging from the size of the raindrops against the halogen lights, it was going to be a complete downpour. Desirée had asked what would happen if it rained. She was not impressed when I told her that we'd get wet.

Vicky pulled me to one side when we reached the shelter of the hangar. 'Are you sure this guy can fly in the rain?'

A couple of months ago, she'd have been taking Xanax and been of limited use. Now, she was just very nervous. Definitely progress.

'Dave has flown into much worse. He's very good, and he rates his co-pilot as being even better. We couldn't be in safer hands.'

'Aye, well, we'll see about that.'

We'd gone in to the hangar via a side entrance. Through one of the main doors at the front, we could see our ride for the night squatting on the tarmac. Dave and Sophie had only just flown in from their base in Oxfordshire, and the chopper was warmed up and ready to go. I wanted this over as fast as possible.

There was a very limited group of people in on this. The aircrew, an air traffic controller and the 7 Squadron CO were gathered round a bench by the entrance. The ATC had a big laptop open and ready. We'd rehearsed this part a couple of times. As far as we could. We only had one shot to get it right, and now was the time.

I introduced the aircrew to my team and passed the phone to Saffron. It was her idea, and she could be the one who spoke. She'd been practising, too, and now knew everything there was to know about Laufstrasse. On the nod, she clicked on the Password Reset button and switched to email.

'I hate this bit,' she said. 'All I want to do is keep refreshing the screen, even though I know it doesn't do any ... it's in!'

Her thumbs moved like lightning as she worked through the screens, and her face creased into a frown until she broke into a grin. 'We've got her! She was out running at 1900 tonight. And there are hundreds of routes all starting and finishing at a place she's called *The Forge*. Talk about serving it up on a plate. Right, the co-ordinates are ...'

She reeled off the location, and the ATC typed them into the laptop. He peered at the screen and shook his head. 'Check those. You've put her in the middle of a wood.'

'Damn,' I said. 'I'm afraid Lieutenant Hawkins will be right.'

The ATC wasn't having it. 'This satellite overlay is only 48 hours old. That is a solid wood. There must be a mistake.'

'Check it, Hawkins,' I said. 'Just to be sure.'

She did check it, and the screen still showed a wood. Dave and Sophie did not look happy. I wouldn't have looked happy in their shoes. The CO was holding himself back for now. I pulled my lip and asked for the phone.

I held it next to the laptop and compared the two. The wood was shaped (appropriately) like a triangle pointing south. All of Eilidhs' runs started in the lower part and seemingly crossed a field to the narrowest of public roads. I turned to Xavi as the team's expert on occulting. 'Correct me if I'm wrong, Metcalfe, but I think the upper part of the wood is real enough, with this lower, mini-triangle being screened, and that there's an access road just there.'

He repeated my comparison. 'Almost certainly, sir. If you look at the field, those white lines are where the tractor's been, and they don't circle round the lower wood. If you join those lines, they go straight through.'

I pointed to the top of the field on the far side, next to where I reckoned the real wood was located. 'Drop us there. Unless I see differently, we'll go through the wood rather than over the fence.'

'The wood's more likely to be Warded,' said Vicky.

'And it will give us cover. Unpicking the Wards is your job. Any other thoughts?'

The Mages in the hangar all shook their heads.

The CO was looking very dubious. 'Are you sure about this, Clarke? It seems very unlikely.'

'That's the plan, sir.'

'Then good luck.' We shook hands and he stepped back from the table.

The ATC shrugged and tapped his laptop. 'I've sent the flight plan through to the Puma. I'll just do you a manual copy.' He jotted down the information on a form and passed it to Sophie.

'Let's go,' said Dave.

'One kilometre,' said Sophie over the intercom.

I was the only Mage who heard her, because I was the only one wearing a helmet. The aircrewman also heard her and shuffled towards the door. I made a sign for the others to get back and got ready to be really stupid.

The aircrewman pulled back the door and I stuck my head out into the downpour. I barely had time to register the headlights of vehicles on the A34 before we were past it and back into the night. I could see the ground, just, but that was it. I brought up the night vision device and peered around. I also put every ounce of Lux I could muster into penetrating the Glamours surrounding the target.

'Two hundred metres,' said Sophie.

The wind was buffeting me, the rain was lashing into the open door, and we were very nearly over our target. Aah, there we go. Who's been a busy girl, then?

Eilidh's forge stood out like a beacon to the near-infrared goggles, and I could see three buildings exactly where the GPS tracker said they should be. And the wood behind them. Sometimes things do work out.

Which immediately made me worry that something bigger would go wrong. 'Target located. Land as planned.'

'I don't have eyeball,' said Sophie.

'Put us down anyway,' I replied.

'Sir,' said Dave. He slowed down and prepared to land. I backed away from the door and urged everyone forward, giving them a thumbs-up to show the plan hadn't changed. Yet.

The Puma dropped quickly on to the ground in a textbook landing, and the aircrewman waved Saffron forward. She executed a perfect dismount and disappeared in completely the wrong direction. Marvellous.

I grabbed Xavi's shoulder and pointed to where the wood bordered the meadow. He nodded and ducked way too low under the blades, but at least he was on his way. Desirée and Vicky followed him, and I took off the helmet. I chucked it to the aircrewman and swung out of the door.

Saffron and Xavi were supposed to get to the wood and check it for Wards. Xavi seemed confident that it was clear and had already gathered the other two around him. By the time I limped up, the Puma was back in the air and Saffron had realised her mistake.

'Sorry sir.'

'My fault. I should have briefed you. It's a lesson for all of us, though. Did any of you feel anything while we were in the air or since?'

They all said no. The rain was coming straight down in rods, which was deeply unpleasant but would have done a good job of minimising the noise of the chopper. I fished a baseball cap out of my combats and put it on. I wiped the rain off my face and turned to look at the wood. A great hedge of mature hawthorns separated us from the plantation, and the spiky hedge was interlaced with some wire fencing.

'What have we got?' I said. 'Xavi?'

'Nothing in the ground or anchored to the trees. Saff, could you look at the fence?'

She moved up to the wire and hovered her hands over it. She turned back with alarm on her face. 'There's an integrity and magick circle running through it. If any of us touch the metal or cut the wire, it will go off like a fire alarm in a gunpowder factory.'

'What about the wooden post holding it up?'

She checked again. 'That's clear.'

'Good. Do you reckon you could do a vault with one hand on the wood?'

Only Saffron reckoned she could do that. It was a big ask, but I'd seen her on the assault course, and she'd been working out since. I had to trust her.

'We only need one,' I said. 'The rest of us can be helped over.'

We dumped the kit over first, then quickly linked hands and boosted four of us over. Saffron measured out a run-up, and I had a flashback to Mrs Clarke's folly. 'Stop!'

Saffron walked back to the fence. 'What's wrong?'

'Don't run up. Stand to the side, next to the fence, and use the pole as a pivot. If you run up, there's too much of a risk of missing it in the dark.'

She nodded and stepped back. She flexed her knees, grabbed the post with her left hand and swung up. With a grunt, her legs cleared the top strand of wire and she flopped into the soaking grass. There were no fireworks. 'Good work,' I said. 'Xavi, Vicky, you two lead. Head off that way and circle gradually to the left. It's safe enough to use torches in here.'

Because we weren't following a path, there was a lot of bramble and undergrowth to clear, and going was much slower than I wanted. It was already 02:45, and there could easily be someone in there with an alarm set for 04:00.

We did find a path, and Vicky pulled on Xavi's sleeve before he could step on it. 'You should look at this, Conrad. I think there may be a Ley line under here. Just a feeling, like.'

I took off my pack and dug out my dowsing rod. I hadn't used it in a while, mostly because I didn't want another face-to-face encounter with the Spirit of Madeleine. The last time we'd met was during the *Wings over Water* trip to the East Riding. I now had a lot of unanswered questions about Maddy that worried me a lot. I edged towards the path and closed my eyes. I gripped the rod and sank into its weird world of water. For once, the rain was an advantage.

Whenever I use the rod, I get a sense of Maddy. Sometimes it's just a feeling – like being in a lift in the dark, and knowing that someone else is in there with you. Sometimes, like tonight, it's a full-on illusion.

The skies cleared, the sun rose, the trees disappeared and the dowsing rod in my hand turned into a punt pole. I looked down, and there was Maddy, sitting in the love seat of a punt in all her Edwardian finery. Today's outfit was a very fetching cream muslin gown with a broad-brimmed sun hat. It was very hot here. I moved the punt pole, and she shook her head violently, waving her hand in a warning. I stopped and looked where she was pointing.

Our punt wasn't on the water, it was still on the bank, and now I knew why: there was no peaceful water to launch into. If I'd punted forward, we'd have launched on to a river of molten lava. I jerked back and opened my eyes. 'Good call, Vic. That path has a booby-trap of epic proportions.'

'What now?' said Vicky.

I backed away from the path until the sensation of heat died down. 'Keep going parallel to the path and don't get any closer. We're not far from their compound now.'

Another twenty metres took us to the edge of the wood and a much more imposing fence. We could also now see the target properly.

With the naked eye, they were just black shapes. I brought up the night vision goggles and scanned the yard. We'd arrived nearest the forge itself. Eilidh hadn't adapted a farm building, she'd had one built specially using a steel skeleton and prefabricated panels. It would do the job, though. Our end of the forge had the chimney, also of steel. No wonder I could see it from the air.

I scanned right. Nearest the fence was a small building that could have been a lambing shed or fertiliser store. The doors were closed and padlocked. In front of it stood the familiar Range Rover Sport, last seen bouncing over the meadow in Stockcross. That left the old farmhouse.

It must be very crowded in there. Instead of a rambling stone building, the heart of the compound was two traditional stone cottages knocked into one, with barely any height to the upper storey and dormer windows. Tricky, but I saw no reason to change the plan. Provided we could get through the fence.

'This is serious,' said Xavi. 'We're not going to be vaulting that.'

He was right. The fence around the compound was made of ten feet high wire squares, and full of magick. Even I could feel it. I looked along the line of the fence and saw a gate where it met the path through the wood. That would be even worse. 'Any chance of de-activating it?' I asked.

Vicky, Xavi and Saff conferred for a second. 'Not in less than two or three hours,' concluded Vicky.

I looked at the fence again. There was a six inch gap underneath, presumably to let the local wildlife have a free passage without triggering false alarms. Scout would love that, if I hadn't left him at Elvenham. He's not ready for field work yet, but he did give me an idea. Sort of.

'Vicky, what about the posts? Could we cut through them at the base?'

She checked it out. 'Aye. Reckon so. Then what? The fence would break, wouldn't it?'

'Not if we did three posts. The sections are wide enough for the central one to lie flat if we're careful. Desi, can you sing a song and put pressure on the fence if the other three weaken the posts?'

She stood up straight. 'I can try.'

'Good. When the fence falls down, we play hopscout.'

'You what?' said Vicky.

'You're mad,' said Saffron. 'Those squares are only big enough for me. With your bad leg, you'll get your enormous feet trapped and trigger the alarm.'

'Worst case scenario, you're all through and I trigger the alarm. We're still inside, aren't we? I'm open to alternatives.' No one had anything better to hand, so we split up and got ready.

Desirée's magick is very rare in England, though more common in Wales and Ireland. Druids have always used Bards to enhance magick, and Desi was adapting it to her own heritage of Africa via the Caribbean. She raised her arms and started to intone the twenty-third psalm. I stood well behind her.

'… *He leadeth me to still waters…*' I could feel the magick building as Desi wove ribbons of air around her. I looked at the others, crouched by the posts and ready to use blades of sharpened air. When Desi was nearly ready to burst, I gave the signal and with a howling like dentists' drills, they cut through the wood and then flung themselves flat. It was a good job I'd moved us right behind the forge. Any nearer the house, and one of the crew inside would have woken up.

Desi pushed her arms forward and directed the force of magick against the posts. Two moved, but one held firm. I could see the wire stretching, and was about to stop the procedure until it gave with a crack and two panels of fence lay down. Vicky gave a thumbs-up and Desi lowered her arms.

23 — Lost in Translation

I was one third of the way over the fallen fence when my leg went into spasm. I had my weight on my right leg. Just. Moving my left leg was not an option; I couldn't even lift it off the ground.

'Conrad? Are you OK?' said Vicky.

'No. I need a hand. Specifically, I need a shoulder.'

They all wanted to do it, which was nice, but was also eating up valuable time. They argued for about ten seconds, their voices too low for me to hear, until Vicky spoke up. 'I'm doing it. I've done it before.'

'But…'

'Aye, I'm the least co-ordinated and weakest, but I'm the one who's been there before, so shut up and keep watch round the corner, okay?'

She put her pack down and studied the chessboard of wire squares. I needed to take about three more steps to get over the edge, and my left leg was vibrating. 'Now would be good, Vic.'

'Aye, give us a minute. I'm gonna back in to you, save trying to turn round.'

It took her shorter legs four strides, and I'm sure her boot was within millimetres of the wire at one point. When she got in range, I planted my hand on her shoulder and she braced herself. I got my left leg off the ground and forward. Now the hard part – she had to take all my weight while I flipped my right leg up.

She groaned and swayed. She held firm, and my right leg was now in front again. We only had to do it twice more. After the next attempt, Vicky swore and said, 'I canna do that again. We'll need to get someone else in.'

'Sod that. I really am going to hop.'

Without giving her time to argue, I hopped once. Twice. A third time, and I collapsed on to the wet grass. Vicky took two steps and threw herself next to me. 'I am not doing that again in a hurry,' she moaned.

I got up and held out my hand. 'Thanks, Vic. That was very well done.' She took my hand and I hauled her upright.

'I can't say I've missed the threat of imminent death, but you're more fun than Xavi. Let's get on with it.'

We took it in turns to peer round the corner of the forge using the night vision equipment. I'd only brought one set, because they're not easy to use, and the same went for respirators. Vicky had told me in detail that she'd been blindsided at Lilac Cottage because they'd made a trap in the hallway and used magick to stop them blowing the gas away. We knew the other side had respirators, and I was going to give them a taste of their own medicine.

'Everyone ready?'

'Aye.'

'Yes.'

'Yes sir.'

'Sir.'

'Go!'

Saffron sprinted towards the Range Rover. Xavi and Desi headed for the cottage, with Vicky behind them. I picked up the riot gun and followed suit.

As soon as Xavi entered the ground between the buildings, security lights burst into life. They were bright, and made targets of us all. I cringed, but no fire came from the farmhouse.

Xavi, Vicky and Desi stopped in front of the building and wound up their magick. On Vicky's count, they blasted the two upper windows and one of the lower ones, the force of their magick blowing the glass and curtains into the room. At the same time, the Range Rover's alarm sounded above the rain as Saffron sliced through one of the front axles. I raised the riot gun and fired tear gas cannisters through the windows.

We had rehearsed what to do next. Vicky went round the side, to meet Saffron at the back and cut off their exit that way. Desi and Xavi moved to the fourth, unbroken window and I drew the Hammer. Xavi blew in the window and gave Desi a hand to go through the gap. I shone a torch into the room and shouted 'King's Watch! Lie down!' at the top of my voice.

In the light, a very scared looking man half out of his sleeping bag immediately dropped down again and put his hands on his head. Desi shone her own torch around and looked for more of them, while Xavi boosted himself into the room and scrambled to get the suspect in restraints. And remove his magick. This was Willem, the Master. One Mage down, two to go. And three bodyguards.

'Secure,' said Xavi.

'Kitchen through that way,' said Desi. 'I'm letting Vicky in.'

I shone my torch on the door to the hall. 'Xavi, watch the door.'

He stepped into the middle of the room and hurled an armchair out of the way. I moved back from the window and tried to listen. Yes. Screams from upstairs. I changed position and shouted, 'King's Watch! Stay where you are.'

I looked back through the window as the door to the living room burst open and an unknown female Mage came barrelling through towards Xavi before I could fire a safe shot. This would be Jane Jones.

Xavi stood his ground and deployed his Badge of Office, a long, pointed dagger. If Jones had one of those toxic blades, this could end very quickly. He did the sensible thing and took two steps back.

I tried to shine my torch in her eyes, and got enough of her face for Xavi to recognise her. 'Miss Daines?' he said. He lowered his dagger, just enough for the woman to sense an opening. She lunged at him with a knife of her own, violet magick swirling around the blade.

Xavi took a step to the side, and she missed. There was a crash from the back of the room. Neither Xavi nor the woman looked up. I did, and I saw Desi and Vicky move quickly to cut off the woman's escape route.

'King's Watch. Drop your weapon,' said Vicky.

The woman took a step back, but didn't surrender. She looked at the odds against her and glanced over her shoulder. I now had a clear shot, if I wanted it.

'It's Miss Daines. Magick teacher from my school,' said Xavi. 'Her blade's not toxic,' he added.

'But you are,' said the woman. 'You're a pack of toxic bastards. Stick this.'

She charged at Xavi, and Vicky dived at her. They collided, and Vicky knocked her over. She'd grabbed for the woman's right arm and missed. The Mage swung her arm round and stabbed Vicky in the back. Xavi's blade flickered with light and he dived himself, bringing his dagger down on the woman's neck. He sliced through her throat and blood sprayed out of the wound.

'I surrender,' said a naked man in the doorway. He was simultaneously trying to hold up his hands up and protect his eyes. It was time to take charge.

'Xavi. Secure that man. Desi, put Vic in the recovery position and do not touch that knife. It needs to stay in her back. Understand? Good. Where's Saffron?'

'Don't know,' said Desi as she tried to move her friend away from the dead woman. Vicky was struggling to breathe, but she was breathing, and her legs were moving. Good signs for now.

The naked man was now face down. He must be the other former member of Temple Gym. 'Owen,' I said. 'Which room are Eve and Marissa in? Where are they?'

'Upstairs on the right,' he said. 'I need water on my eyes. I'm going blind.'

'Desi, Xavi, secure both prisoners and deal with the other two upstairs. I need to find Saffron and Eilidh.'

'What about Vicky?' said Desirée.

Vicky struggled to get a breath. 'Do what he says, man. Quick.'

I left them to it and looked around the yard. Shit. There was a door open to the forge, and two women were facing off inside. I ran as fast as I could across the yard.

And slipped in the rain. I was carrying a loaded gun, and first priority was not banging my hand, which meant my left hip took a battering. That really hurt. It hurt so much I couldn't focus for a second. A vital second. The lights from the forge came in bars. Like the Nine of Wands. Mercedes had got it wrong, perhaps in translation. There hadn't been a betrayal, but there had been a stab in the back. Literally. What Mercedes had got right was this: *no matter how hard, you have to keep going.*

I forced down the pain from my hip. I got a grip and pushed myself up. Only another ten metres. I didn't run this time.

Saffron had out her chain, but I didn't fancy her chances. Eilidh had pulled on a pair of trousers, but she was otherwise naked. In her left hand was an iron bar of some sort which she was using to ward off Saffron's chain. Her right hand was covered in a thermal glove and held a single piece of metal, roughly blade shaped. From the way she was waving it, and the way Saffron was avoiding it, that had to be a toxic blade, fresh out of the fire.

I dodged into the room and moved to the left to get a clear shot at Eilidh, just as Saffron tripped.

Eilidh bent down to strike, and Saffron only managed to get her chain a few inches above her face to block the blow. Eilidh shifted and got her blade round the chain. I breathed in and brought up a small Silence, and then took aim and fired.

There was a burst of light around the pair as Eilidh's Ancile dissolved and the round hit her full in the back. Her arms spasmed and she dropped the blade, just missing Saffron. Then the whole of her body went rigid, her spine bent back at an impossible angle. And Saffron started screaming.

'No! Get her off! No!'

The rounds in my gun fire bullets that disrupt your Imprint. Eilidh was touching Saffron at several points, and Saffron could clearly feel it. I holstered my gun and moved over as Eilidh went limp and collapsed on top of Saffron. Saffron carried on screaming.

I pulled Eilidh off her, and Saffron curled into a foetal position. I knelt down as best I could and put my arms round her. 'Easy, Saff. Easy now. She's gone.' I remembered the transfer of Lux I'd performed to save Vicky's life, and tried to do the same, but I had nothing left. Saffron started twitching and choking.

Come on, Clarke. You're in a magickal workshop.

I don't know where the voice came from, or even if it was just in my head, but it didn't sound like me. Couldn't argue with the conclusion, though.

I put my left hand on the concrete floor and my right hand on Saff's neck. I felt heat in the ground. The heat of Lux. I drew on it and passed it through my right hand into Saffron, letting the Lux flow in time to my heartbeat. After a few seconds, she stopped twitching. A few seconds more and her muscles relaxed. I let go and turned her face towards me. 'Earth to Hawkins. Are you there?'

'Sod off. Sod off, sir. Ow. That hurts.'

'What hurts?'

'My neck. If you've burnt me like you burnt Vicky, I'll sue.'

'Some people have no gratitude.'

She uncurled a little. 'That was horrible. I felt her unravel. She started sucking the life out of me. Literally. I was sinking into a whirlpool. And then everything went black.'

'Can you sit up?'

She held out a hand, and I dragged her upright. 'Thank you, sir.' She shivered. 'After going through that, I think I can call you Uncle Conrad. I'm sure Vicky won't mind.'

'I hope she gets the chance. Are you okay to be left?'

'Yes.'

I couldn't afford any more time, so I jogged back into the rain and over the yard. Xavi was pushing two naked women ahead of him, none too gently. He hooked his foot under one of their legs and the woman fell sprawling into the mud. He did the same with the other one. Callous, but not unwarranted. So far, neither of them had been restrained.

'Easy, lieutenant,' I said. 'I'll assist. What's the status?'

'Good, sir. I'm out of restraints.'

I passed him two pairs and he set to work. 'They'd barricaded themselves in the bathroom, sir. I had to threaten to put teargas through the window before they came out. I decided to get them away from Captain Robson.'

'And you did the right thing. Better safe than sorry. Well done, Xavi.'

He looked up in fear. 'Saffron? Eilidh?'

'Safe and dead, in that order.' I looked over my shoulder and saw Saffron weaving slowly out of the forge. She straightened up and shivered when the rain hit her face. I called her over and said, 'Can you sort these two while Xavi I and check around. I don't think there are more, but we can't risk moving Vicky until we're sure.'

'Yes sir.'

It only took a couple of minutes to search the house and forge. Desi sat grim-faced as we moved from room to room. When Xavi gave me the last all-clear, I got out my phone. I'd thought about bringing a Personal Role Radio, but what's the point?

'We need an urgent medical evacuation,' I said as soon as Dave took the call. 'Shove a stretcher in the back of the Puma and land to the west of the wood. It's all clear here.'

'I loaded one when we got back. Just in case. We're on our way.'

I told Saffron and Xavi to follow the track and get the gate open. 'When the chopper lands, you two bring the stretcher in here. I don't want any complications from bringing mundane people on site. We'll all carry the stretcher out, and Desi, you go with her to the hospital.'

I bent down to look at Vicky. She had gone almost milk white and her breathing was very shallow, but her eyes were open. 'You'll be fine, Vic. It's all over. The chopper's on it's way.'

She managed a smile. 'I'm not deaf. Or dead. Yet.'

I stood up and turned my attention to our prisoners.

24 — *Master of None*

Desi and Saffron had put the three bodyguards into a small den while Xavi and I were searching the compound. The windows were blown in, and there was a lingering reek of teargas, but at least they were all out of the rain and had towels to cover the worst of their nakedness. All three were secured hand and foot. Owen had a damp cloth over his eyes.

I double checked their restraints, and was going to leave them when Owen said, 'My eyes. I need to get to a hospital.'

I paused in the doorway. 'You're going to jail, Mr Holt, not hospital. Lieutenant Metcalfe made a full recovery. I'm sure you will, too.'

'We're going to sell our stories,' said Eve. 'We're going to blow the world of magick wide open.'

I had a moment, so I went back and squatted in front of the women. Easier not to stare at their naked chests that way. 'No you're not. You're going to a mundane prison for attempted murder. You'll plead guilty and you'll say nothing about magick. To anyone. Ever. Understand?'

'What are you going to do to us?' said Marissa.

'Lieutenant Hawkins is going to share a video with you. It shows what happens when you drink the Forgetting potion. It's an old film. From the 1960s. The Forgetting potion used to be compulsory then. Now it's optional. Enjoy.'

I had to lean on the wall to get upright. My hip was killing me.

Back in the kitchen-diner, Desi was still holding Vicky's hand and talking to her. As one, we paused and looked at the shattered window. The rain was easing a little, and the roar of twin turbo engines throbbed past overhead. Good.

I bent down and touched her cheek. 'You'll be fine Vic, but not for a while. Where do you want to convalesce? London? Newcastle? Clerkswell?'

'I'll look after you,' said Desi.

Vic gave the slightest shake of her head. 'You'll be busy. Clerkswell. Myfanwy.'

'Desi, tell the chopper crew to go to the John Radcliffe. We've got a loyalty card there.'

'Yes sir. I will also ignore the joke, sir.'

I couldn't blame her for that. I nodded to show that I'd understood and stood up. Oww. That hurt.

Our magickal prisoner, Willem van der Westheusen, had been hooded, restrained and placed under a Silence. I dispelled the Work and pulled the hood off. Unlike the others, Willem had slept in his boxer shorts. He was

233

below average height, of slight build and wore a wary expression. I wasn't going to risk squatting again, so I righted a chair and sank into it.

I looked at him for a moment. He didn't look happy, but he wasn't scared. 'I thought the Master would have their own bedroom,' I said.

'Master? Who sold you that sack of shit?'

'You're the Apex of the Golden Triangle, and you're nicked.'

'I'm not the Master. Get real, Clarke.' He thought for a second. 'Was it Irina?'

'Why would she lie?'

'Because she's been shagging the real boss for years, that's why.'

Crap. It made sense: Irina had fingered Willem as the boss to protect the real mastermind. From her perspective, there was a very good chance that either we'd never find Willem or that he would be killed. I must admit, Willem didn't look like a powerful master of magick.

'Prove it,' I said.

'I've only been back in the country a couple of months. I've been helping Eilidh with a few potions and stuff.'

From across the room, Desi said, 'What about the toxic blades?'

Willem looked away.

There were voices outside. 'We'll come back to that,' I said. I put the Silence and hood back on Willem and went to help.

We passed the stretcher through the broken window. It was easier that way. We put it next to Vicky and gently eased her, face down, on to the stretcher. We covered her with a couple of thermal blankets and got ready to lift. Her last words before we picked up the stretcher were, 'Any jokes about me weight and I'll murder you. One day.'

It was a long walk to the chopper through the rain. As we got away from the artificial glare of the security lights, we could just make out the farm track. Dawn would be along soon.

The aircrewman was waiting and took one end of the stretcher from inside the bay. In seconds, he had it secured and was checking where it was safe to put straps round Vicky. Desi climbed on board and took a position where she could reach Vicky's hand. The aircrewman rolled the door closed and we backed off. None of us moved from the gate until the chopper had headed off. They went north, so Desi must have followed Vicky's wishes and sent them to Oxford.

This was the first time I've done that. In the past, it's always been me at the controls of the helicopter taking someone else's comrade to hospital. Now I know why the ones left behind always wave. The three of us did it in unison. It doesn't hurt anyone, does it?

I turned to Saffron and Xavi. 'Well done, you two. It was a bit hairy in there. How's your head, Saffron?'

'Throbbing. I don't think there's any lasting damage.'

'Good.'

I looked Xavi in the eye. He'd slit someone's throat tonight. There was blood on his combats. Those stains don't come out easily. 'Xavi? Are you okay?'

'I don't know yet.'

'I'm not surprised. We don't have a policy for compulsory counselling in the King's Watch, but there are people you can talk to. People in the world of magick. It's not a weakness to ask for help.'

He nodded. 'No. Yeah. I'm good for now.'

I started walking back along the path and they fell into step. The rain had just about stopped now, not that we could tell. We were all soaked right through and squelching. 'Here's the plan,' I said. 'You two are going to ransack the upstairs for dry clothes. We're going to be here for a while, I think. We also need to clothe our prisoners, but most importantly … ?'

'We need to put the kettle on,' said Saffron.

'Correct, Lieutenant Hawkins. Jump to it. I'm going to call the Boss before she gets a call from the John Radcliffe.'

Hannah had let herself into Merlyn's Tower at one o'clock and had been waiting for me to call. I pictured her behind her great Victorian desk, or sitting by the window looking for dawn over the Thames. She answered before I'd even heard the ringtone.

'Yes?'

'It's over. Vicky's on her way to hospital with a collapsed lung. No other casualties on our side. Haigh is dead, as is "Jane Jones". The bodyguards are secure, as is van der Westheusen.'

'How bad is Vicky?'

'Deep stab wound. Bad, but she got lucky. The knife missed her heart and spine.'

'Baruch Hashem. I shall give thanks.'

'As will I. There's a problem.'

'What?'

'Irina has played us. Van der Westheusen is not the Master. She lied to protect him. Willem says that Irina and the Master are lovers.'

Hannah groaned. 'Irina went for knee surgery today. I'll call you back.'

That was ominous. Very ominous. By the time I'd got to the farmhouse and started to strip off, Hannah was back on the phone. 'She's gone. Stephanie Morgan was guarding her. She was drugged and restrained, but not hurt, baruch Hashem. I need to get on to this. What do you need?'

'Help. Prisoner transport. Someone who knows what they're doing to search the compound.'

'I'll come up myself. Once I've put out an alert for Irina.' She took a deep breath. 'Well done, Conrad. These are not good times. I'll see you soon.'

Saffron handed me a cup of tea. 'Who's on breakfast duty?' she asked.

I stuck my head into the den. 'Is there another vehicle on site?' I asked.

Owen Holt spoke up. 'There's a Ferrari in the shed. Believe it or not. Someone could take me to hospital in that.'

'I'm afraid we have other priorities, Mr Holt. I'm hungry.'

Back at the John Radcliffe, Desirée had blocked the door to Vicky's room like Cerberus. She has fewer heads, but she's just as scary. 'You can go in with one condition. No jokes. Absolutely none. Are we clear?'

'Is that a medical prohibition or an aesthetic one?'

'See? You're at again. If she laughs, the pain is excruciating. You should know about pain.'

I held my hands up. 'No jokes. How is she?'

'Lucky. That's what she is. And awake. Just.'

She moved away from the door. I'd had word straight after the operation that it had been a success. We'd provided the standby trauma team with their only action of the night, and Vicky had been in surgery before I'd finished getting changed back at the Whitchurch compound. It's a good job they'd hung on to Eggers' kit. He was almost as tall as me.

Vicky actually looked quite well, considering. She looked better than she'd done the last time I'd had to visit her in hospital, a point she was well aware of.

'Hiya, Uncle C,' she said when I bent down to kiss her. 'You know what? Being stabbed is less unpleasant than dying. Not that I recommend it.'

'You'll change your mind when the anaesthetic wears off.'

'I can wait. How's things? Desi's not told me nowt. Says you cut her out of the loop. I don't believe her.'

'I may have told a white lie,' said Desirée.

I filled Vicky in on what had happened after she took flight in the chopper. I left out Xavi's trip to the all night café in a Ferrari. Too much comic potential. I did leave in the sight of Hannah trying to pick her way through the mud in a pair of linen trousers that were too long for her.

'Did Saff get a video?' said Vicky.

'If she did, she wouldn't share it with me, would she?'

The long and short of it was that the forge had already been stripped before we arrived. All the magick associated with the Reduction of gold had been moved earlier. We could even see marks on the floor where some of the heavy equipment had recently stood. There was no sign of Irina Ispahbudhan or the Master either. I did have something, though.

'According to Willem, who's been very keen to co-operate, the Master is based somewhere near Cambridge.'

'How does he know?'

'The Master kept complaining about the roadworks on the A14.'

236

I could see that her body really wanted to go to sleep. Her mind had other ideas. 'What's the plan?'

'A few days off. Check Saffron and Xavi for signs of aftershock, then head out on the hunt.'

'Good.' She pointed to her wound. 'Who did this to me? Please don't tell me it was Xavi's old teacher.'

'Pretty much. She was at his school on a fixed term contract. It wasn't renewed when they found out she'd been sacked from her previous job.'

'What for? Stabbing the students?'

'Inappropriate relationships.'

Vicky made a disgusted face.

'Not with the kids. Apparently there were no complaints about her teaching. It was the company she kept outside school. Teachers are not supposed to have relationships with the Fae. Not that close, anyway.'

She perked up. As did Desirée. This was news to her as well. 'Any connection to the Codex?'

I shook my head sadly. 'Willem says she never gave anything away. Hannah's looking into it, but I'm guessing it will be another dead end.'

'No one plays the long game quite like the Fae,' said Vicky.

'And Dwarves,' I added.

'Aye. Have you spoke to Myvvy?'

'She's getting your room ready right now.'

Desi interrupted her. 'Not that you're going anywhere until Saturday at the earliest, and that's if your parents don't kidnap you first. I think it's time for both of us to leave.'

'One more thing, lieutenant.'

'Ooh, this sounds good,' said Vicky. 'Are you gonna put her on a charge for insubordination?'

'Far from it.'

'Hey, you cannat give her a medal. Not unless I get one, too.'

'Sorry, Vic, no gongs for this one. I do have something for Desirée, though.' I took out a small box and passed it over. 'The Constable asked me to present you with these. You've earned them.'

Desi opened the box and saw two pips. She was now a (first) lieutenant, the same rank as Xavi and Saffron.

Vicky reached out and patted her hand. 'Absolutely, pet. Absolutely.'

Desi looked at the pips for a long while. So long that Vicky drifted off to sleep. She finally looked up at me. 'I'm not sure that this is what Jesus wants for me.'

It was my turn to be silent. I had a dozen comebacks on the tip of my tongue and I suppressed them all. It was tough for her. I know exactly what the Allfather wants because I have his number in my Contacts list. If Jesus has a number, he hasn't yet shared it with Desi. Poor kid.

I stood up and stretched. There was an audible crack from my back when I did a twist. 'Hannah wants me to be part of the solution,' I said. 'I'm happy with that.' I looked down at Vic who was now well out of it. 'If Vicky does come to Clerkswell, Desi, the room next to hers is yours. You know that, don't you?'

She nodded and closed the box. I thought she was going to hand it back for a second. Instead, she put it on the bed and slipped to her knees. She looked up at me. 'I'm going to pray for a while. For Victoria, for the Watch and for guidance.'

'Goodnight. And well done. Your presence saved lives today. That's a fact.'

She nodded, and I left the room.

Mina pulled the quilt more closely around her and leaned in to me. I wrapped my arm around her and rested it on her back. I put my foot down and jogged the swing into life. It rocked gently and we enjoyed a moment of peace. Over to the left, the sun had already disappeared, not that we'd seen much of it today. Another warm front was on its way, and the weekend's cricket was in serious doubt.

That was a good job, because my left hip had stiffened to the point of immobility. It would get better in a few days, I'm sure, but this was more pain than a man my age should feel. And if I kept going, as the Nine of Wands demanded, would there be an end? And if there was an end, would it be a Happy Ever After ending where Mina and I got married, or would it be a posthumous VC and a military funeral?

Perhaps it was time to think seriously about applying for the Deputy Constable's job. It would mean living in Chester, and that would be a huge wrench for all of us. On the other hand, it would take me out of the field before my body broke in half.

I didn't hear him coming until Scout bounded up to the swing and barked.

'Shut up,' said Mina. 'I'm enjoying this.'

He lay down and gave her a hangdog look. I took pity on him and shuffled a little so that I could stretch out my right hand. He crawled forwards until I could scratch his ears. It wasn't as warm as Spain, but this was pretty much my idea of Paradise, and both our phones were in the house. For a while, at least, we could enjoy it.

I stopped scratching Scout's ears and let the swing come to rest. I would do anything to make Mina happy and look after her, and the tattoo on her chest showed (if I needed proof) that she'd do the same for me. Love does that to you.

And if it did it for us, it would do it for anyone, including the Master and Irina. Perhaps we wouldn't be going to Cambridge next week. Suddenly, I had a plan.

25 — *The Hypocritic Oath*

One day soon I'm going to get a summons to the Cherwell Roost. I can't believe that the extended Hawkins clan won't want to have a closer look at me, given that their youngest is in my tender care. I'm sure they'll dress it up as a dinner invitation, and they'll probably include Mina as well. The way that Bertie Hawkins went on the defensive as soon as the post of Peculier Auditor was created tells me that they have an interest in her, too. Will I go? Of course. Mina would never forgive me if I didn't.

Until that day arrives, Saffron is determined to keep me away from the place, which is why I picked her up from the Peartree Services on Tuesday morning rather than from her home, which would have been quicker and easier for both of us.

The rain had been and gone, and the sun was back with a vengeance. Saff was waving a large cappuccino in my direction and didn't object when I wanted to have a nicotine break before we set off. 'How's Vicky?' was her first question.

'How are you? No lasting ill effects?'

She looked down at her bottle of Diet Pepsi. 'A couple of nightmares on Saturday. Might have been the cheese.'

'Were they a reprise? Did you go back to the whirlpool?'

'Not really. One of them had a train in it. Eilidh was trying to get on the train, but it was leaving the station.'

'Good.'

'Eh?'

'I made a couple of calls. Someone who knows what they're talking about said that if you have a repeat of the actual experience, you might need to see a Necromancer. It sounds like you don't.'

She shivered in the hot sun. 'No thank you very much. Necromancers are creepy bastards, the lot of them.'

'Including Xavi?'

She smiled. 'I'm trying to steer him towards Occulting. Much more wholesome, if deadly boring. You never said how Vicky was? Enjoying the Welsh cooking?'

'Eventually. The hospital wouldn't sign her off until Monday. Something to do with the pleural sutures. She's doing well. Her parents came down and wanted to take her back to Newcastle.'

'That's parents for you.'

I shook my head. 'Jack and Erica love their daughter very much. Unfortunately, they can't afford to stay in hotels indefinitely, and Erica has both her clients and her own mother to worry about.'

'Oh.'

I waited another second, just to make sure she'd got the message. 'That's why we're having a party this weekend. It was Myfanwy's idea.'

She tipped her head to the side. 'A party? Will Vic be up for that?'

'It's the double header against Allington. The cricket? Jack and Erica are coming down for a long weekend and staying at Elvenham. My parents are flying over, too, and staying at the Inkwell. Cricket on Saturday for those who care for it and a big do on Sunday. Xavi and Desi are coming down, and so is Francesca Somerton. Erin will be there, too. You're more than welcome.'

'Are you sure?'

'Yes. It won't be the most exciting event in your social calendar, but my parents would like to meet you.'

'Thanks. Can I skip the cricket and come on Sunday?'

'Of course. Shall we go?'

We climbed in and I started the engine. The aircon whined and the satnav told me that we would arrive at our destination in fifty minutes.

'I have never been to Milton Keynes in my life,' said Saffron. 'Never had a good reason.'

'Strangely, neither have I. There aren't many places in England I haven't dropped in on at one time or another, but never Milton Keynes. It'll be an adventure.'

'I doubt it.'

'We'll see.'

Saffron gave me her sceptical look and shrugged. 'If it's a private hospital, they may have better coffee. We can hope.'

During the journey, Saffron filled me in on some of the more detailed findings from the magickal analysis of the Whitchurch compound and the full interrogation of Willem van der Westheusen. Hannah herself had conducted that, and although I'd read the transcripts, not a lot of it made sense.

One mystery that had been cleared up was the toxic blades. Something that powerful should either be in every Mage's armoury or as rare as hen's teeth. The truth was somewhere in between.

The original toxic blade was something knocked up by the Dwarves during the middle kingdom of Ancient Egypt, and yes, they are very very rare. At some point in the nineteenth century, a variant had been created which substituted a Herbal reduction for Gorgon's blood (Gorgons being very elusive, if not extinct).

As with most impersonations of Dwarven craft, the copy is not as good and has side effects. The formula and method that Eilidh was using took nearly a week to make and had a half-life of twenty-four hours, which was why the machetes we'd picked up at Lilac Cottage were inert before they could be analysed.

By the time Saffron had explained that in terms I could understand, we were within a mile of the Milton Keynes Oak Tree Hospital. The Oak Tree Health group specialises in treating complex orthopaedic injuries. They have close relationships with a number of Premier League football clubs. Mages do like to have the best of everything.

'Why are we here?' said Saffron.

'Didn't you read the reports I sent you?'

'Of course. You must have some clout to get the counter-terrorism people jumping like that.'

'We can thank Morris Chandler. If he hadn't caused a big stink with the mundane police by crashing his car and having a shootout, they wouldn't have bothered.'

'Right. So we know that Irina hasn't left the country on any plane, train or scheduled ferry.'

'As close to certain as we can be. You can't hide an injury like that. Not for long. I should know.'

She gave me a funny look. 'How's that?'

'When I was on crutches, I had to escape from the police. I hid in a horse box.'

I grinned at her. I'd said that to see how much of my murky past had leaked out into the wider magickal community. From the look on her face, not a lot. Quite comforting, really. I parked the car (no parking charges at private hospitals), and grabbed the files.

'What's the strategy?' said Saffron as we entered the building.

'Carrot and stick.' I showed my ID to reception, and we were ushered into the director's office. The surgeon joined us shortly after the PA had served coffee.

The director of Oak Tree Milton Keynes was clearly a woman on the up, judging by the streamlined office and well-pressed suit she was wearing. The aircon in the hospital was good, but it hadn't stopped her hair frizzing badly at some point. Probably when she cycled to work, judging by the helmet peeking out from a cupboard. The surgeon was like most surgeons: brisk, authoritative and convinced that this was not a good use of his time.

The director came straight to the point. 'I've agreed to a meeting so we can put an end to this. Why on earth should we talk to you without an order from the high court?'

'Because this way we can avoid an enquiry into your security, or lack of it.'

She frowned. 'This patient was your responsibility. You said she wasn't under formal arrest, and that you'd have someone to keep an eye on her. I'm not even sure that any crime has been committed.'

'Other than Miss Morgan being drugged.'

'Which is regrettable, but not down to us. Miss Morgan failed to search the patient and then allowed the patient access to her drink. If you find Irina, you can arrest her for assault or whatever.'

It was time to up the ante. I lifted my case on to my lap and made sure the director could see the front. Dad bought it for me when I first got my wings, and it's a Victorian adjutant's case, battle scarred and made of high quality leather that's been oiled and cherished for over a hundred and forty years. As well as the imposing crossed sabres on the front, Dad added a gold-tooled RAF insignia. People are always impressed when they see it, and inclined to take the piece of paper I pulled out more seriously as a result.

'I agree with what you say,' I acknowledged. 'However, that leaves out your failure to maintain CCTV properly, your failure to check the credentials of the ambulance crew and failure to discharge your patient correctly. What if the patient was a vulnerable adult? Those are the sort of questions a CQC enquiry would ask.'

The director didn't take this in her stride, but neither did she cave in. 'We would be prepared to co-operate fully. We don't believe that your team would be so happy to do that. All my attempts to find out which agency you really work for have been stonewalled.'

I didn't care for the woman, but she'd earned my respect. She'd called my bluff perfectly. There was one issue that I could push, though. 'Then show me the paperwork.'

That got her on the defensive. The Master (assuming it was him) had handed over a blank piece of paper, Enscribed to resemble authorised paperwork from the Oak Tree clinic in London. I pushed home the advantage. 'There wouldn't need to be a full CQC enquiry for that. I could just raise it with your head office. So far we haven't told them that you handed over a patient without any authority whatsoever.'

I let that sink in for half a second before getting out the (metaphorical) carrot. 'There's another reason you should help us find her. Until we do, you won't be able to give her the bill.'

The director visibly stiffened, and even the surgeon showed an interest for the first time.

'This booking was made by the Home Office. The bill is your responsibility.'

I took out a blank CD. 'We recorded the conversation. Our officer very clearly states that the booking was on behalf of Miss Ispahbudhan and that she would settle the bill. I believe the amount was around £28,000.' I turned to Saffron. 'Could you afford to lose that, Lieutenant Hawkins?'

'No, sir, I couldn't.'

I turned back to the director. 'If you co-operate, and if we find her, you can get her to settle the bill. And the co-operation will be completely off the record.'

'You don't have a hidden recorder? Nothing like that?'

'I don't. That's not how we work.'

She looked at the surgeon. 'Are you happy to talk?'

'What do you want to know?'

'What was your diagnosis? What procedures did you do? What are the indications for recovery? What further treatment, including drugs, will Miss Ispahbudhan require in the short term? Verbal answers are all we need.'

He rubbed his chin. Did he want to cause a stink or just get back to work and forget all about it? After all, surgeons get quite proprietary about their patients.

They also like to show off. 'Do you know much about orthopaedic surgery?'

I don't like doing this, but sometimes it saves a lot of time. I rolled up my left trouser leg and let him have a good look at the scars. I couldn't believe what happened next. The man actually reached over and took my leg in his hands. Waaay too much. I gritted my teeth and let him have a good feel.

'Where was this done?'

'Queen Elizabeth's, Birmingham.' I added the name of the surgeon, too.

He let my leg go. 'You were lucky. You got one of the best, there. Shame about the post-op care.'

'It was badly infected during rehab.'

'You've got good definition in your calf muscles. Don't lose it.'

He wiped his hands on a handkerchief and looked over my shoulder, accessing his mental case notes. 'The trauma to the patient's knee was horrific. I wouldn't like to meet the person who did that on a dark night. Not only was there a comminuted fracture of the patella, the ACL was snapped clean off.'

Saffron couldn't help herself. 'Mina did all that?'

I gave her a hard stare. 'Go on, doctor.'

'We had no choice. We had to open the knee right up. It took all day to knock it back into shape. She was barely fit to be moved along the corridor, never mind transported off site. She was on a lot of painkillers, obviously, as well as VTE drugs.'

'VTE?'

'Venous thromboembolism. Deep vein thrombosis to the layman. Her pregnancy was a complicating factor. She wasn't high risk, but she should be taking them for at least a week. And by now she really, really needs an MRI scan and X-Rays. If something has gone wrong with the operation, we only have a short window to correct it.' He looked at the director. 'And that's not all. Any consultant would also need to see the pre-operative scan results.'

That sounded promising. 'They weren't taken with her notes?' I asked.

The director shook her head. 'Online only. No paper copies, and before you ask, our online security is better than most banks.'

I gave her a sceptical look.

243

'Seriously. Supposing the league's top striker comes in here after a match, every newspaper and betting website, to say nothing of their rivals, is going to want to know the prognosis. Believe me, Mr Clarke, hacking by newspapers has not stopped, it's just been outsourced.'

I turned back to the surgeon. 'Try to imagine you're a humble private GP.'

He gave a self-deprecating wave of the hand. 'Whether it's me or a GP, we're all doctors.' The director gave him a sideways look and rolled her eyes. I'm surprised this man's ego fitted into a normal operating theatre.

'Thank you,' I said with a grateful smile. 'If someone came to you with a patient with those needs, a demand for total discretion and an unlimited supply of money, how would you arrange her treatment?'

He laughed. 'I would find an NHS registrar who has just got married and needs the money. Then I would book her into one of the little private clinics under a false name to get the MRI done. So long as they have a doctor's certificate authorising the procedure, they won't ask any questions.'

'Would this imaginary registrar not want her pre-op scans?'

'Yes, if they wanted to do the job properly. Money would trump that.'

'And are these clinics regulated?'

He leaned over the director, invading her personal space and taking a pen and notepad without asking. He wrote something down and handed it over. 'That website brokers scans at all the private facilities. Ignore the Oak Tree ones and other big players.'

'Thank you.'

He stood up, regardless of whether I'd finished. 'I'll give you a tip: don't ring them up. They'll never co-operate. Send someone round and ask to see their radiological logs. No facility in the UK would dare operate without proper logging. The computers won't let them. Those logs will tell you what was scanned.' Something passed over his face for a moment. 'If you do find her, look after her. I'd hate to see all my work go to waste.'

We parked round the corner from the hospital and sauntered over Great Ouse bridge to Linford Park so that I could give Scout a run around and we could plan our next move.

'Are all orthopaedic surgeons like that?' said Saffron. 'If some total stranger felt my leg up like he did, I'd kick them in the bollocks.'

'You know the old joke about the difference between God and a surgeon?'

She shook her head. 'That joke must be so old I've never heard it.'

'God knows he's not a surgeon. They all have a bit of that in them.'

'Now I know why you got changed in the other room at Whitchurch. I'd keep those scars hidden, too. I'm surprised you didn't show him a picture of Mina and threaten him with her.'

'I was saving that as a last resort. How do you reckon we should proceed?'

Most of the local schools had broken up for the summer holidays. The play area in Linford Park was teeming with unleashed energy. It was too noisy and too busy for us, and there was no way I could let Scout roam around there, so we headed into the formal park area and found a shady tree to lean against. When no one was looking, I slipped Scout's lead and let him explore.

'Let me check out that website first,' said Saffron. I handed her the surgeon's note and lit a cigarette while I waited. 'There's about forty in England,' she concluded. 'How much support will we get from the police?'

'We don't have much good will left. This would be our last shot if we asked them to help.'

She stared at her phone for a few seconds. 'Is that where we are? I always thought Milton Keynes was much closer to London than that.' She looked at me. 'We should have asked the surgeon what the furthest distance she could travel was.'

'We should. Her surgery was more complex than mine, if smaller scale. I could have coped with a couple of hours, max. It was the early hours of the morning. They could get a long way in two hours with no traffic. Assuming they avoid Hampshire because that's where the forge was, and Cambridge because that's where the Master's base is, where does that leave?'

She shrugged me a big peasant shrug. 'I haven't a clue. You'd have to explain it all to me.'

'You're right, and we haven't got time for a geography lesson. Lend me your phone.'

I studied the interactive map for a minute. 'Here's the plan. We get Eddie and Oscar to cover the ones in London. That leaves one for Rick and one for old Piers Weatherill. You and I can cover the other five.'

'Good. Where do we start?'

I heard Scout bark from down the track and looked up. He was standing at a safe distance from some sort of Rottweiler and making a fool of himself. The huge fighting dog looked disdainfully at Scout and moved on, pulling its owner behind it. I nearly jumped when I saw the woman's jet black hair and painfully thin frame. Then she lifted her head, and the resemblance disappeared. It wasn't who I thought it was, but the illusion made me think. There may be love involved in this, but that's only a part. I put Saffron's phone down for a second and called Lloyd Flint. When he'd answered my question, I knew where we were going.

Myfanwy and I have been teaching Scout to follow whistle commands. I gave the *come here* signal (a descending fifth) and heard the answering bark. 'We're starting in a place called Tettenhall, just west of Wolverhampton,' I told Saffron.

We stood up as Scout bounded back. I clipped him back on the lead. 'It's a two hour drive, but it feels right. After all, Bertie did say that Staffordshire was the wild west of magick.'

'Wolverhampton,' said Saffron. 'Another place I've never been.'

'It's got a very good all-weather racecourse. Can you ring the Boss? Manic Mutt doesn't like it if I use the phone when he's on the lead.'

'No problem. That's the trouble with dogs – they rule your life.'

26 — *Bedside Manor*

Hannah wanted us to turn round and go to Coventry and Evesham before heading to Tettenhall, and that was the real reason I'd got Saffron to ring her. It's much easier to flannel via a third party. The Boss didn't make it a direct order, so we sailed up the M1 while the rest of the team jumped into action. By the time we passed Wolverhampton Racecourse, three clinics had already been eliminated from our enquiries.

'Reminds me a bit of Cheltenham,' I said as we drove out of town towards the suburb/village of Tettenhall. Saffron had been giving me potted nuggets about it ever since she'd finished with the Constable. If I said that Tettenhall was almost unique in having two village greens, that gives you some idea of the place.

'How on earth does this remind you of Cheltenham?' she said.

'Big houses set back on the road to somewhere else. Do you want to handle the receptionist?'

'Only if it's a man and he's really hot. Or old. You're much scarier on first encounter than I'll ever be. Of course, once we get to know you, you're even scarier.'

'Ha ha. How long to become Sammi?'

She groaned. 'Do I have to? In this heat?'

'Yes, you do. You're going to scope the reception out and look for anyone keeping watch. Now find somewhere nice for a sandwich that has somewhere for you to get changed.'

'The Two Greens.'

'That's a place? As well as a claim to fame?'

'Turn left, just there.'

The old coaching road from London to Holyhead runs through Tettenhall. We left the (upper) green area and followed it out of the village. The Mercia Wholistic Clinic was about a mile down the road.

'Drive past and drop me up the road,' said Saffron/Sammi. 'I need to get in character. And bring up a few personal deflectors.'

'No problem. What are you going to do?'

'Walk in, look around. If anyone asks, I'm waiting for my sister, who wants to book an appointment. Then I'll walk out and stand by the door. I'll text you from there.'

That was a well-worked plan, and I told her so. Then I added, 'Whatever you do, don't attempt the local accent.'

''Oo do you fink I aam? Leave it out and drop us 'ere.'

I drove a bit further and parked in a pub car park. It didn't look nearly as nice as the Two Greens. I got the All Clear text a few minutes later.

You couldn't miss "Sammi" as you approached the clinic. She was standing next to the main door in such a way that any visitor would have to enter her personal space to get past, and any watchers would be drawn to look at her. She was staring at her phone and twirling her hair as I limped up to the door. She wasn't actually chewing gum, but she was moving her lips in a way that suggested she was having trouble reading the long words on the screen in front of her. Without acknowledging my presence, she moved a few inches to one side when the automatic door opened for me.

The reception area was decorated in soothing pastels and adorned with a mixture of impressionist prints and special offers. The Mercia seemed to think that "Wholistic" meant performing cosmetic surgery on the Whole person. Until today I had no idea that there were three different potential operations to correct bunions, and that was just the first option for better looking feet.

I took a roundabout route to the reception desk to give Saffron time to saunter in behind me while the receptionist's attention was focused on the approaching 6' 4" (nearly) bald man. I put on an especially serious face and leaned over the desk. I laid down a business card and flashed my ID. 'Conrad Clarke, National Security. Have you seen this woman? She has a foreign accent.'

Before the receptionist could take up my card, I covered it with a photograph of Irina. She took one look at the picture and her eyes flashed to one of the corridors leading off the reception area. Bingo.

'I need to see the manager. Immediately, and if they're on holiday, I need to see the most senior person on site.'

You've met Mina. You know I don't like playing on racial stereotypes without good reason. The receptionist was white, so I added Irina's foreign accent to go with her picture as an eastern woman. Couple that with the words "National Security" and you'll know why the receptionist picked up the photograph and said, 'I'll take you straight through.'

When her back was turned for one second, I pointed my arm down the relevant corridor. Saffron nodded and turned to face one of the posters.

We walked through a small admin area which was clearly not designed for prospective clients. No doubt the expensive consulting rooms are elsewhere. At the end was an open door to a small office for the Chief Executive and Clinical Director. Judging by the single desk, they were clearly one and the same person, in the shape of a man with gelled hair and a healthy tan.

The receptionist stopped in the doorway and looked at my card before speaking. 'This is Squadron Leader Clarke. He's come about Miss Soraya and he says it's a matter of national security.' She put my card and the photograph on the director's desk and stepped out.

'Come in, come in,' said the director. 'Shut the door behind you. What's going on?'

I shut the door and flipped over Irina's picture. 'This is her real name and details. Where is she and what treatment is she receiving right now?' In the tiny gap after I'd finished speaking, before he could bring up his guard, I showed him my ID badge.

'What do you want her for?'

'She's under arrest. She escaped from a secure medical facility on Thursday night.'

'Not on her own, she didn't. She's in a bad way.'

I said nothing. It worked.

'She had an MRI this morning. There's a surgeon coming to see her in half an hour. I checked the MRI results myself, just to be sure, and it's not good.'

I nodded sagely. 'Is it the comminuted fracture or the ACL?'

He looked surprised. 'The ACL. She'll need to go under the knife again, and the sooner the better. Won't be here, though.'

'Thank you. You've been most helpful. Is there anyone else in her room?'

'Her boyfriend came in with her and left before the scan. What are you going to do? Do I need to see a warrant for her arrest?'

'No warrant needed. She's escaped from custody, so I can just walk in. I'd prefer to do it quietly for obvious reasons. We'll take her away in a private ambulance.' My phone pinged. I checked the message. 'My colleague has the room under observation.'

He shot out of his chair and went to a monitor on another desk. He pressed a button, and live CCTV images flickered into life. 'Where are they?'

'I don't know. Could you take me there immediately.'

I moved so that he could get to the door but couldn't get back behind his desk. He nodded and led me back to reception and then down the corridor. We passed the expensive consulting rooms and came to a wide corridor with a nurse's station to the left and half a dozen recovery rooms on each side. The right hand end was a pair of double doors to the car park that had yellow hatching in front of them.

'This way,' said the director. He stopped and pointed to one of the rooms.

'One second,' I said. I touched the Hammer and brought up my Ancile. When I did so, the director caught a glimpse of the gun. I covered it with my jacket, and said, 'I won't be needing it, I'm sure. Thank you for your help. I'll take it from here. If the surgeon turns up, tell him to wait.'

'Right. Yes. I'll be in my office or in reception.' He paused. 'What if the boyfriend shows up?'

'My colleague will deal with him.'

When he'd gone, I took out the Hammer and pushed open the door.

Irina Ispahbudhan was a sorry sight when I opened the door. She looked a lot worse when she recognised me and saw the gun. She jerked upright on the bed, and did something to her leg that made her flop back down again with a strangled cry.

I checked the room for any surprises, such as the Master lurking in a corner. The only surprise I got was from the window, where Sammi winked at me. I moved to the bed and levelled the gun at her chest. Tears were forming and spilling at the corner of her eyes, wrecking the makeup she must have spent a long time applying this morning. She'd never made much of an effort for the Gnomes, and she'd dyed the grey out of her hair, too.

'Do you have any Artefacts?'

She shook her head. 'Can't take them in the scanner. I thought I was safe in here.'

I checked her for magickal hot-spots, then moved to the window and cracked it open as far as it would go. Saffron hopped over the flowerbed and came to listen.

'All good here. The Master came earlier and may come back, so watch the car park. Have you heard back from the Boss?'

'All sorted. About an hour.'

'Good.'

I went back to the bed. 'You are safe in here, and you'll be just as safe in the Undercroft. There's an ambulance on the way.' I holstered the gun. 'And if you tell me where I can find your boyfriend, we can let you go back to Oak Tree. According to the clinical director here, your knee's just about shot, I'm afraid.'

She cried and cried. I took some tissues from the nightstand and pressed them into her hand. I stepped back and opened the door, keeping one eye on Irina in case she did something really stupid. I held up my ID and shouted to the nurse. 'Sorry to bother you, what's the procedure for room service?'

'I'll sort it. What do you want?'

'Two teas. One with sugar.'

While I waited, and to give Irina time to pull herself together, I called Vicky. I'd just finished updating her when the director himself appeared with the teas, putting himself in harm's way to protect his staff. I bet he's a good boss. I thanked him and took the teas to the nightstand, then pulled up a chair.

'Yours has got sugar in it,' I said.

'You're all the bloody same. Tea. Nothing but tea for the pain. Sod off.'

'Can't do that, I'm afraid. You don't have to drink the tea, but you do have to talk to me.' I took a sip. 'Actually, you should drink the tea. It's good, for a hospital, which is where you need to be, for your sake and the baby's. You have to think about him first.'

'What do you know about it?'

'I don't know if you'll make a good mother; that's for certain. Believe me, Irina, I really want to give you the chance to find out. As things stand, they're not looking good.'

'I'll recover. One way or another.'

I shook my head. 'We did a deal. I kept my side of the bargain. You broke yours. You lied about the Master. You assaulted a Bailiff. You absconded. All bets are off, I'm afraid.'

'What do you mean?'

'I mean that you could find yourself giving birth by C-Section and never even holding your child before its taken away. Not once . And then you could find yourself in a Limbo Chamber for three years. I think they send the rescued babies – that's what they call them, by the way – I think they send the rescued babies abroad. We have a reciprocal deal.'

'Empty threats,' she said. Her eyes contradicted her. She was rattled, and nearly ready to give in. 'I'm not saying anything until I've seen a lawyer, and definitely not here. You said it yourself, I need medical attention.'

I held her gaze until she broke it and reached for the tea. 'Your boyfriend has abandoned you, Irina. You won't see him again.'

She slammed down the tea, slopping it over the surface. 'He's not my boyfriend!' She scrabbled in the nightstand and brought out an old tin. 'He's my husband. I had to take these off for the scanner, now I'm putting them back on. See?'

She twisted the tin lid and took out a set of rings: engagement, wedding, eternity, all in rose gold with emeralds for the stones. Nice. I was more interested in the tin.

Granddad Enderby was a Lincolnshire countryman turned Lincolnshire mechanic after serving in the tank regiment. He was pleased as punch when his daughter got into grammar school and thrilled beyond words when she got into Cambridge. He was less thrilled by her choice of husband, but he came round in the end. I can remember him walking up to the well at Elvenham not long before he died, trailing a cloud of thick, rich and spicy pipe smoke behind him and telling my father that it was going to be a good year for tomatoes. He filled his pipe from a tin exactly like the one Irina kept her wedding bands in, and the only other person I've ever known to do that was the Geomancer who set up the Dragon's Nest in Wales.

When Vicky and I headed in to stop the Dragon Brotherhood, three people escaped. They weren't part of the Brotherhood, but they'd enabled it and they knew where the magick had come from. When Helen Davies and I searched their abandoned vehicle, the same smell permeated the air. No wonder the Master wanted to keep himself well away from us.

Irina tried to shove her rings on to fingers that had swollen since she last wore them regularly. I put my hand on hers to hold her back. 'Stop. You'll make it worse. I've got the message.'

She stopped trying and gripped the rings in her hand. She was clearly devoted to him, but I got the feeling she was protesting a little too much.

I mopped up the spilt tea and settled down again. 'I spoke to Lloyd this morning. He says that Wesley gave you a token when you were made clan counsel. He reckons that you and your husband could use it to get into the First Mine. If you were willing to take a few risks.'

'So?'

'What does that say? For the chance of getting into the mine, he's moved you out to this place, damaged your knee and risked his child. For what? For gold? Come on, Irina. What does that say about the man?'

'It's *our* gold! We made it, and it's ours.'

'Then why didn't you just walk away with it? You could have been in and out of the First Mine and we'd have shrugged. Why did you attack me? Why put yourselves on the wanted list?'

She started crying again. 'Because of her.'

'Which her?'

'The Fae. She forced Ivan and Eilidh to attack you for that diamond. We had no choice.'

'You're doing well, Irina. What's Ivan's family name?'

A look of pure horror spread across her face. I hadn't tricked her out of giving her husband's name, she'd got so worn down she couldn't cope any more. She started shaking her head, pressing her lips together.

'One more name, Irina, and you can go. Just one more name and I'll walk out of that door and take Saffron with me. You and Ivan can leave the country in peace and raise your child somewhere safe. Just tell me the name of the Fae and I'll go.'

She shifted on her pillow and grabbed a ladies' handkerchief. It was edged with flowers and looked hand-sewn. The initials in the corner were in Arabic. An heirloom? A piece of juvenile craft work? She shoved it in her mouth and bit down. The message couldn't be clearer, neither could the sliver of black that had peeped out from under her pillow. I was going to search her, but she'd saved me the trouble.

'Excuse me, Irina, I'll just take that.'

I grabbed her left hand and used it to pin down her right. It only took a second to slip the phone out from the pillow. I pressed the button and the screen came up. It wasn't even locked. I let go her hands and stepped back. It was a brand-new Samsung Galaxy. Very expensive. There were only two contacts in the book: Ivan and Isaac.

My heart lurched in my chest and the screen went out of focus for a second. I stumbled back to the window and shouted for Saffron. Then I shouted again.

She bounded along the path, with Scout hard on her heels. 'Sir? What's up?'

'The Master was here this morning. He'd use a Glamour, yes, but what about his car? He was in here with Irina for some time.'

'Change the number plates, probably. It's mega-hard to change the appearance of cold iron when you're not in it.'

'I need you to check the CCTV. Come back in here when you've finished and tell me what car he was driving.'

'Sir.' She looked down. 'Scout, stay.' Then she sprinted back towards reception.

Irina had retreated into herself completely. I forced myself not to pace and checked the messages and browser history on the phone. There was a heartbreaking exchange between Irina and Ivan where she told him what the clinical director had said to her, and she'd lapped up his promises to get her the best surgeon in Paris. Bastard. There was nothing on the log for Isaac.

Saffron slipped into the room and closed the door softly. 'He was driving a big black Mercedes saloon. One of the really expensive ones. Scout was sniffing about all over where he'd parked, and he never barked once, so there's no residual magick there from a Glamour.'

My heart squeezed itself and all my ribs compressed. This was bad. Very bad. 'Go and get all your kit out of the car. I need to get off. This is bad, Saff, and you'll have to stay with Irina until she's under lock and key. I'll tell you why when you get back from the car.'

As soon as she'd gone I went and towered over Irina. 'Your husband is a bastard. A first rate shit. I hope there's someone with me when I catch him, because otherwise I may kick him to death. Not for my sake, or Vicky's. For Carole. And as for you, how could you go along with that? How could you let him seduce her and propose to her?'

She cowered back in to the pillows for a second until I'd finished, then she took the handkerchief out of her mouth. 'She is nothing but a cheap tart. He's not the first man to use his PA as cover.'

'PA? Is that what he told you? Carole Thewlis is a professional woman. Ben was right, she deserves so much more than your slippery shit of a husband.'

I wheeled away in disgust and called Mina.

'Hi. Hang on, let me save this,' she said. 'Done.'

'Where's Vicky?' I said.

She heard the urgency in my voice. 'Lying down in her room.'

'Get Myvvy and Erin and get up to her. Get Myvvy to find out where Ben is. There's a big problem. I'll call Vicky in a minute and explain it to her.'

'Are you OK?'

'I am. Myfanwy won't be when she hears what's been going on.'

'I'm on it, Conrad. Love you.'

Saffron returned with her rucksack and her holdall.

I passed her Irina's phone. 'We've identified the Master. Real name Ivan. Also known as Isaac Fisher.'

Her mouth opened in shock. 'As in the fiancé of Ben's sister? Are you sure?'

'Yes. Irina confirmed it. If he texts, can you pretend to be Irina and forward any messages to me. Can you fill in Hannah and get Ruth to try tracking both of those numbers. I need to get on the road to Clerkswell. We don't want a hostage situation to develop. They've tried just about every other shitty trick in the book.'

'Right. The director said something while I was looking at the CCTV. He said the driver of the private ambulance complained about the roadworks on the M5.'

'That's good to know. Well done. There's one more job before I go.'

I stood with my back to Irina and showed Saffron the restraints. She nodded and we moved quickly to tie Irina to the bed. She didn't put up a fight.

'Take care, sir.'

'And you.'

I jogged out of the room and through the double doors. Scout left his post guarding the window and scampered along. The Nine of Wands was definitely not finished with me yet.

27 — *The Master*

Myfanwy swore loudly and longly in Welsh when I broke the news. Vicky had put me on speaker, and when Myfanwy had run out of steam, Mina's smaller voice broke through. 'Conrad, I know you're sure, but are you sure sure?'

A small part of me inside smiled. 'Yes, I'm sure. Irina admitted it.'

Vicky spoke up. 'Where are you and what the fuck are we gonna do?'

'I'm on my way to Clerkswell. It'll take over an hour, but unless I hear otherwise, I think he's in our neck of the woods.'

'What makes you think that?'

'Irina was taken to Tettenhall by private ambulance, and it went up the M5. Where's Ben? Where's Carole?'

Myfanwy spoke up. 'Ben's standing in a field of Barley near Tibberton, wherever that is. He's also wondering whether I've gone mad. Carole is in Amsterdam.'

'Tell him to get to Elvenham as soon as he can. Just tell him it's urgent.'

Vicky said, 'I hate to say this, Conrad, but can Saffron cope on her own if he turns up?'

'We've restrained Irina. I'm going to call Saff in a second and tell her to move Irina to a different room. I'll also tell her to run if Fisher turns up.'

'You'd better make that a direct order,'

'Don't worry, Vic, I will. I'll keep you posted.'

I rang off and gave it a few minutes before I called Saffron. She sounded a little worried and a very much up for it when I gave her the orders. She also said that Hannah was going to put her wig on.

'What on earth for?'

'She said, and I quote, "So that I can tear out my hair at Conrad Clarke and all his works." She also sounded a bit pleased. I think.'

'That's about right. You get on with the relocation.'

'Will do.' She paused. 'When our ambulance turns up, where should I take her?'

'Get hold of Xavi. He can be at the Oak Tree Milton Keynes waiting for you. I loathe and detest Irina Ispahbudhan, but if she doesn't get remedial surgery soon, she may never walk again without crutches. I did actually once say that I wouldn't wish that on my worst enemy, and Irina is not top of that list.'

'Right. I'll get on to it.'

I disconnected and focused on the road. I'd opted to miss out the M5 roadworks and take the old road down to Worcester. At this time in the afternoon, it should be twenty minutes quicker. As I crossed the boundary into Worcestershire, I had a vision of the Nine of Wands shoving a lorry into the crash barrier ahead of me and blocking the road. It's a good job I don't have any skill in Divination, or I'd really worry. Then my phone rang: Ruth Kaplan.

'I've got some news. Good news for a change.'

'Tell me.'

'The number for "Ivan" is switched off. The number for "Isaac" however is very much active. It's pinging off a mast just north of Tewkesbury. Do you want me to authorise a hack? We might get the geolocation.'

'Too risky. Just let me know the minute it moves or goes dark.'

'Will do. Are you going to tell Hannah, or shall I?'

'I'll do it. Thanks, Ruth.'

Hannah was waiting for my call and gave thanks when I told her the news. 'What's your plan?'

'We've got a tiny window, ma'am. If we don't move now, we could lose him forever. He'll soon find out his cover is blown and he'll scarper.' I took a deep breath. 'I know you're not going to like this, but I want to use Ben, Erin and Mina as spotters. We know that Fisher isn't hiding his car. Four pairs of eyes will be better than one. Don't worry, I'll only move in if I can do it safely.'

'Don't worry? You want to take one and half civilians and a woman who threatened Vicky with a shotgun?'

'I'll tell Mina you said she was half a civilian. I trust them. I don't see a better plan.'

'Mina, reluctantly, but yes. Erin if you say so. Mr Thewlis, I'm not sure about.'

'If he finds out I've arrested Fisher and that Myfanwy knew about it first, it will cause a lot of problems you don't need.'

'Why should it cause me problems. Remember that your problems are not necessarily my problems.'

'You'll need to find Myfanwy somewhere else to live. You don't need that.'

'I don't. You're right, Conrad. Catching Fisher could lead us straight to the Fae who's behind all this. Hashem guide you.'

Knowing that Tewkesbury was the target area would save nearly half an hour. I called Mina and told her to to grab some maps and head for the Starbucks roadhouse just east of Junction 9 on the M5. Then I told her to pass the phone to Erin.

'You don't have to do this,' I said. 'You're not in the Watch.'

'No,' she replied. 'But I'm Myfanwy's friend. I owe her.'

'Good. Tell her to divert Ben. Mina has the directions, and I'll break the news to him. I should have come up with a cover story by the time I get there.'

Erin laughed. 'Selling oil secrets to the Chinese. That always goes down well in films. Oh, hang on. Hold that thought. Russia might be a better option. I'll explain when I see you.'

She had a point. Oil secrets it is. Oh yes, and the fact that he's already married. Once I told Ben that, he wouldn't care about the rest.

The mast where Fisher's phone was pinging wasn't one of the main ones in Tewkesbury. Good job, too. It was located north of the town on the plain between the rivers Avon and Severn. That still left a lot of ground to cover, though. I was contemplating this when Ben's battered pickup arrived.

Mina, Erin and I were grouped round the Volvo's bonnet. Scout would have joined in, too, if we'd let him. Before we'd got the map out, Erin showed me something on her phone. She's a very clever woman, is Erin.

I went up to Ben's car and pointed to the passenger seat. He popped the door locks, and I climbed in.

'What's this all about, Conrad? It looks like you're planning an operation over there.'

'We are. Have a look at this.'

I showed him the smartphone that Mina had given me. Hannah had made available an image from the UK Border Agency, and thanks to Erin's lucky guess, we now had chapter and verse on Isaac Fisher.

'Who's this Ivan Rybakov?'

'Rybakov means "Fisher" in Russian. Scroll down.'

He found the picture. 'Fucking hell. You mean that Isaac Fisher is really this Russian bloke?'

'Look at the next of kin.'

'Nooo. Please tell me this is a wind-up. Or that he's divorced.'

'Sorry, he's very much still married. Going to be a father.'

He stared at the phone, hoping it would miraculously change. It didn't. 'How do you know all this, Conrad? And why am I discussing it here?'

'Because his wife is in custody. We'd very much like him to join her. Espionage. Carole knows a lot of things the Russian oil industry would like to find out.'

'He's been using her this whole time?'

'He told his wife that Carole was his PA.'

'The bastard. The epic bastard. The fucking little shit. I'll murder him.'

'Not if he gets away, you won't.'

'What do you mean?'

'He knows we're on to him. If you promise not to lay a finger on him, you can help track him down.'

'Seriously? What about the police? What about MI5? Isn't that your mob?'

I shook my head. 'We deal with non-terror related threats to national security, and we're pretty thin on the ground. If there's no threat to life, the police won't lift a finger. Do you think I'd drag Mina and Erin into this if I had a choice?'

'Can't I just thump him the once? Kick him in the goolies?'

'No. It's hands off or I'll take your car keys and leave you here.'

He actually hesitated. Long enough that I reckoned he had a spare set of keys somewhere. 'If that's the deal, then yes. What do you want from me?'

'Come out and I'll explain.'

The plan was simple: the other three were going to drive around the lanes while I waited at a caravan park in the middle of the search zone and scrubbed locations off the map. That way, I could be sure that we hadn't missed anything.

Phase one was a drive-by of roadside properties, looking for the Mercedes. Where the houses were down a drive, my team would make a note and go back during phase two. If he moved before then, I could get to Junction 9 ahead of him and cut him off.

The best news came in before we left Starbucks: Saffron was safely in the ambulance and Xavi was already in place at Milton Keynes.

After that, things got very frustrating. Phase one took forty minutes, and at the end we had fifty properties where a car could be out of sight, including another, larger caravan park. Ben had also made the mistake of taking a call from Carole, and though he hadn't spilt the beans, she was now very suspicious. If I were her, I'd be ringing my fiancé and starting to ask questions.

Scout was looking worried, poor thing. He does rather take his cue from me when it comes to moods, which can be quite disturbing at times. He'd even gone off treats, and that's almost unheard of.

We were twenty minutes into phase two when Erin called. 'Got him,' she said.

'Where?'

'The lodge at Waterbury Manor. It's a good quarter of a mile from the road.'

'Got it. Any chance he saw you?'

'No. He doesn't know my car, and Waterbury Manor is a hotel. There are vehicles going along all the time. I've pulled in to a gate round the corner from the lodge. If he moves, he has to pass me.'

'Brilliant. I'll be there in ten.' I folded up the map, and Scout was already standing by the back door wagging his tail. 'Are you ready for some action, boy?'

'Awrf.'

When we got to the location, it was clear that Scout wasn't the only one ready for action.

The drive to Waterbury Manor swept away from the road through an imposing pair of stone gateposts. Beyond the gates, two cars and a pickup were waiting. Hannah would never believe this wasn't my doing.

I got out of the Volvo and slammed the door. 'Erin! What the fuck are you playing at?'

She looked at the gravel, and Mina grabbed my arm. 'It wasn't her fault. I made her.'

'And me,' said Ben. 'We made each other promise to text when we found something. Looks like he's bought himself a love-nest. Mina said she injured his wife. I bet he was going to install her here, not half an hour from Clerkswell. Do you think he was going to go through with the wedding?'

'Not now, Ben, we don't have time. Erin, describe the approach to the lodge.'

'It's about three hundred metres, round that bend. The lodge is on the right, set back a bit. The lake is behind it, so there's no escape that way. I saw a conservatory on the back, with the doors open. I bet he's working in there or in the garden.'

'Good.'

I looked up the road. It skirted a field full of sheep, with a substantial fence separating them. The field undulated at such an angle that Fisher's saloon would never cross it. Even better. I closed my eyes and tried to let my shoulders relax. I took three even breaths and shook my fingers. One more breath and I opened my eyes.

'Ben, this is too dangerous for you.'

'What about Erin? Don't tell me she's a secret ninja.'

'Close enough. I want you in your pickup with the engine running. If Fisher's car comes towards you, block the road and get the hell out. If he slips past us, you're crucial. Got that?'

He nodded.

'Good. Erin, you're going to run down to the lake and follow the shore round to the lodge and cut off his escape on foot. Mina, you drive past in the Volvo and be ready to block access to the hotel. Scout and I are going jog up the road thirty seconds later. Any questions?' They shook their heads. 'Have your phones out, get ready and go on my signal.'

I waited until Ben's back was turned before I took the Anvil out of the car and strapped the sword on my back. Once in place, he wouldn't see it. I did let him have a good look at the Hammer, though. I took it out of the holster and carried it in my right hand. I put the Bluetooth earpiece in and waited until they nodded. I raised my arm and waved them off.

Erin shot over the road and vaulted the fence smoothly enough to make Saffron jealous, if she were here. Mina drove off, and I counted to thirty. 'Come on, Scout. Let's find the Mage.'

The lodge slowly revealed itself as I got nearer the bend. I also got my first clear look at the lake, and saw that Erin was catching up. She saw me and slowed to a walk. I told you she was bright. Behind her on the water, a few small sailing dinghies competed with a couple of jet skis that shouldn't be on a body of water that small.

The lodge was definitely original. No reproduction building would be that small. There couldn't have been more than three rooms in the original, and only one of those upstairs. A downstairs extension had been added at the rear, and I could just make out the glass panels of the conservatory attached to it. I kept to a steady pace and Scout gave his first bark.

The lodge was separated from the drive by a privet hedge with a gap for Fisher to get his car in. It was lucky for us that the plot was too small to hide the car. I jogged through the gap, past the car and down the side of the building. I heard the rattle of diesel behind me and glanced over my shoulder. Mina had parked the Volvo over the gap and was getting out. I ran.

Scout ran, too, and let out a flurry of angry barks when he got round the corner. An astonished middle aged man was sitting at a table under a parasol, smoking his pipe, working at his laptop and wondering what the mad dog was doing. He looked up and looked down the barrel of the Hammer.

'King's Watch! Don't move, Fisher. Stay very still. Hands in the air. Slowly.'

He'd frozen in place, still seated, pipe smoking in the ashtray. Fisher might be the Master, but he wasn't the active type.

'Hands in the air! Do it now!'

I closed the distance as he slowly raised his hands. Fear spread across his face as he realised just how deep in the shit he was. To my right, Erin splashed through the shallow waters as she rounded the fence. Mina came round the corner behind me and stopped. I reached into my pocket and got out the wirecutters. I dropped them on the ground so that I could keep both hands on the gun.

'Mina, pick up the clippers. Get ready to remove his Artefacts.'

She swooped gracefully on the wirecutters, and I saw a set of restraints ready in her other hand.

'Stand up slowly, Fisher. Keep your hands in the air at all times. Do not lower them. Then back away from the table.'

He struggled to push the chair back without using his hands and his knees banged the table. With little grace, he overbalanced and landed on his side.

'Don't move. Stay still. Hands on your head.' He complied, after a fashion. 'Go, Mina, and don't get between us. I need a clear shot at all times.'

She danced round to the left and crawled up to Fisher. Her nimble fingers had the Artefacts off him and the restraints in place just as Erin arrived. Mina hopped back and swept her hair up with a grin.

'Erin, check him for any Artefacts, phones, anything.'

260

'Clear of magick. No phones either.'

'Would you like to help Mr Fisher back into his chair? We need to have a word.'

They moved the chair well away from the table and out into the sun, then they used as much force and arm twisting as they could to get him into it.

I lowered the gun, but didn't put it in the holster, nor did I lower my Ancile. Since I'd come round the corner, he'd been a target. Now I looked at him as a human being. He wasn't in the best shape for a man of his age, which looked about fifty. His shirt was soaked with sweat and now grubby from being manhandled on the floor. He had slightly more hair than me, but not much. His face was a strong one, and he definitely had a notable chin. His eyes were still a little glazed, possibly from the shock of having his Artefacts removed.

'Isaac Fisher, by the authority vested in me by the Peculier Constable, I am arresting you for breaching the King's Peace. You will answer the charge in the Cloister Court.'

His eyes came back into focus and he shifted in the chair. 'My name is Rybakov. Ivan Petrovich Rybakov.' His voice was deep, so deep it rumbled in his chest. 'How did you find me?'

'You shouldn't have given Irina that phone. She's safe, by the way. We'll look after her. And your child. Mina, call Ben and tell him to stand down.'

He struggled in the chair. 'Not Ben. Keep him away from me.'

Erin pushed his shoulder down and spoke straight into his ear. 'Watch Captain Clarke will keep Ben at spitting distance. I mean that literally, you piece of shit. I hope you suffer for what you've done to Carole.'

He leaned away from her. 'My phone is switched off. How did you find it?'

'You've been using your Isaac phone all day. We traced that.'

He slumped in his chair as if Ben had thumped him in the stomach. 'Irina, Irina, why did you do it? Why did you put that number in the phone?'

'Because she loves you,' said Mina. 'I don't know why, but she does. A good job for us, though.'

Ben appeared and stopped when he saw Fisher. His hands curled into fists and the tendons flexed in his jaw. Erin left Fisher's side and went up to Ben. She placed her hand on his arm. 'Don't,' she said. 'For Carole and Myfanwy's sake, leave it to Conrad.'

'The question is,' I said, 'do you love Irina at all? Do you care about the child she's carrying? I made her an offer, and I'll make you the same one: give up the Fae and you can see her tonight. You can leave the country and start a new life.'

He looked down and shook his head.

I walked a bit closer. 'Do you know what's going to happen to her? Shall I spell it out?'

Scout had been keeping a close eye on Fisher. He stood up and looked at the lake. Then Erin looked, then Mina. What?

I stepped back and glanced at the water. A jet ski was heading our way. Fast.

Scout charged towards the lake. What the hell? The jet ski revved up and beached at the end of the garden. A woman wearing a bright red wetsuit jumped off the machine. As soon as her feet hit the ground, Scout went ballistic, barking his magick bark as if the world were about to end. I took out the SIG and passed it to Mina. 'Cover Fisher.'

The woman was beautiful. You could see every curve under the red neoprene, and she moved with the grace of a ballerina. I was getting a very, very bad feeling about this, as was Erin. She gripped Ben's arm and stammered, 'By the Goddess, no.'

The woman bent down and said, 'Who's a clever boy, then? Nice doggy.' She put her finger to her lips and Scout went quiet. A pain shot through my head, behind my right ear. I could see him barking, but no noise came out. The woman ran up the garden, bare feet barely touching the grass. She stopped about three metres away and brushed impossibly dry hair behind her ears. Diamond studs winked in her earlobes and a great diamond ring glittered on the third finger of her left hand.

'Is this the part where you tell me that Ivan is under your protection?' Her voice was too sweet, like sugar in your tea when you don't expect it.

'He is. Don't come any closer.'

'Sorry, but Ivan is foresworn. He's mine. Excuse me.'

Two steps took her to Fisher. He shrank back in utter terror. I raised the Hammer and aimed at the woman.

She put her hands on her hips and pouted. 'Shame on you, Ivan. You've been very disappointing.' She shook her head. 'Ivan Rybakov, you are in default and I claim the debt. So mote it be.'

She reached her left hand up and stroked his chest for a second, then plunged it in and ripped out his heart. Lux swirled around her, silver lights and tiny fireworks flared off her body. I fired my gun.

And the bullet exploded into a silver mist when it hit her wetsuit. It didn't even leave a mark.

She took a deep breath. 'Ooh, that hurt. Don't do it again. I don't want to hurt you.' She sniffed the heart, still dripping with blood. 'Good. I'll enjoy that later. Sorry to interrupt.'

She turned and ran back to the jet ski. She dragged it effortlessly off the grass and into the water. With a graceful twitch of her leg, she swung on board and raced back across the lake. As she disappeared, I saw her lift her left hand to her mouth and take a bite from Isaac Fisher's heart.

28 — Entangled

The first priority was my team. Behind me, Ben was throwing up into the bushes, with Erin holding his shoulders. Scout ran back to me with his tail between his legs and curled up on my feet with a whimper. I felt my lower legs go cold as he took Lux from them, except for my titanium tibia. That got hotter. I bent down to scratch his ears and checked on Mina.

She had retreated when the Fae approached Fisher. A good job, too, because there had been a fair bit of blood spatter. She walked over to me, face rigid, and offered me my gun back. I stood up and took it. She wrapped herself round me and gripped me with all her strength. I bent down and kissed the top of her head.

'Conrad,' she whispered, 'I have seen my brother murdered, and my husband. I have seen my face after it was smashed and I have seen a Gnome decapitated. None of them were as bad as what she did to Fisher. I want you to promise me something. I want you to give me your word that you will never offer yourself in a bargain with the Fae. Not even to save my life. Or anyone's life.'

What could I do? 'I promise, love.'

She gave me an extra squeeze and stood back.

Ben was also standing up. 'Did you see anything, Ben?' I asked.

Erin answered. 'It's my fault. I was holding him when it happened, so he saw everything.'

'What was that … thing?' said Ben. He didn't wait for an answer. 'This is your world, isn't it Conrad? This nightmare stuff. Please tell me that Myfanwy is not one of those things.'

'She's not. She's as human as you or I, Ben. So's Erin and Vicky, and Saffron. We just live in a slightly different world, that's all.'

'You didn't always, did you?'

'No, I didn't. The others have.'

Erin had kept her hand lightly on his back. He started to sway again. 'Let's get inside,' she said. 'We don't need to keep looking at Ivan, do we?' She guided him gently through the open doors of the conservatory and eased him into a seat. Mina, Scout and I followed.

'Erin, did you recognise her?'

'Him. No. I've never met him before, and I've never seen so much Fae magick outside a sídhe, either. He was dripping in Quicksilver like he'd bathed in it. I doubt I'd recognise him again. I'm not Vicky.'

Damn. Double Damn.

'Mina, you're an officer of the Cloister Court. Bear witness that I declare Ben to be Entangled in the world of magick through no action of Myfanwy.'

'Noted.'

'What does that mean?' said Ben.

'It means that you need to have a very long conversation with Myfanwy.'

'Is it over between us?'

'I hope not. I'll get Erin to run you home in a bit. I don't want you driving today.' I moved to the doorway and lit a cigarette, keeping my back firmly to the chair outside where Fisher was still tied, then I thought of something. I went and scooped up Fisher's laptop from the table and passed it to Mina. 'Can you find some flight times from Frankfurt to Amsterdam, leaving in about an hour. Book Rachael a ticket, then call her and present it as a fait accompli. She can break the news to Carole.'

'What's the story going to be?'

'He was married. His wife has been arrested and Fisher has fled from justice. Tell her they were involved with the Russian mafia. In a couple of weeks, I'll tell Carole that he's been murdered by his associates.' Ben had been following the conversation. 'Is that OK?'

'I should tell her myself. She deserves to know the truth.'

'She needs a friend, and Rachael's a good friend. She does not need to know about magick. Sorry, but that's one of the rules.'

He nodded his acceptance, and Mina sat down to open the laptop. I crushed out my cigarette. 'Erin, I'm going to do a quick search of the lodge. Can you put the kettle on?'

'I'd prefer a proper drink, but I'll make do with tea. And biscuits.'

In the upstairs room, I found a bed with blood on the sheets and a whole pile of medication that had been prescribed for Irina. There was no sign of any magick anywhere beyond a few sigils on the doorframes. It would need to be searched properly at some point. I did find something else, though, in a case under the stairs. It was heavy, and I carried it carefully into the conservatory. Mina was still talking to Rachael.

'No, Conrad can't come to the phone. He's busy. You have to trust me, Rachael ... Yes, if I'm lying, I promise I will get you tickets for Centre Court. Men's *and* women's final. Now go, you have a plane to catch.'

She rolled her eyes. 'It's a shame Ben is taken. Carole would make a much nicer sister-in-law. No offence, Conrad.'

'None taken. His parents are a bit boring compared to mine, though. No offence, Ben.'

He managed his first smile. 'It's true, though.'

Erin appeared with tea and several packets of biscuits. She'd already found a bowl of water for Scout. We all tucked in.

Once my sugar levels were restored, I took a moment to think about what to do next. 'Mina, I need to get to Milton Keynes. You can guess why.'

'The death knock. I don't envy you that.'

'I'd like you to come. We can stop at Clerkswell for a minute so that you can get changed.'

'Of course I'll come. I don't think I should see Irina, though.'

'No. That's settled. Erin, you take Ben first. Mina, you follow. I need to lock up and tidy the garden.'

Ben sat up. 'I should help you with that. Tidying the garden, I mean. He's a big bloke. What are you going to do? Please tell me you don't carry body bags in your car.'

'Thanks, Ben. I could do with a hand. And yes, I'm afraid I do carry body bags in the car. Before we do that, there's something I need to share with you, and I don't mean socially.'

I opened the box and put six 1Kg gold bars on the table. 'These are worth about £30,000 each.' Everyone's eyes boggled. It's not often you see that much gold around. Unless you're well in with the Gnomes, of course. I tapped each bar in turn. 'Saffron, Mina, Erin, Ben, me. I want the last one to go to Carole. We'll call it Fisher's contribution to the cancellation of the wedding. I'll sell it and say that he'd put it in an account under her name.'

'That's theft,' said Ben. 'You can't.'

'It's called plunder, Ben. Myfanwy will explain. I'll get a letter from my boss if you want, but as the Watch Captain, it's up to me where it goes. You've earned this. Oh, and don't walk in to a pawn shop with it. You'll have the mundane police on to you.'

'Mundane?'

'One of the many things Myvvy will have to explain. If you let her.' I tossed the keys to Fisher's Mercedes on to the table. 'Anyone want his car?' There were no takers. 'Then I'll sell it. The house, by the way, goes to his wife. When she gets out of jail. I think it's time to go now. Ben, are you sure about helping me?'

'No, but I will. That's not a burden you should carry on your own.'

The Oak Tree hospital director had been waiting outside for Irina and had given her a big smile when she arrived. She'd also given Irina the bill and refused to admit her until she'd paid it, and paid in advance for the remediation work. As soon as the bank transfer was complete, they'd whisked her into theatre. The clinic in Wolverhampton had forwarded the MRI results by email, so they knew what to do.

The surgeon had used a local anaesthetic this time. I'd made Saffron leave the in-room security to Xavi and ordered her to stay outside after I'd told her what had happened. Informing Irina is my job.

Mina came up to the room with me and took Saffron away for a break. At least she'd had the chance to change out of her Sammi persona. I took a moment and walked in.

Irina locked eyes with me as soon as I'd closed the door. 'They found him, didn't they?'

'Yes.'

She closed her eyes for a moment. When she opened them, the bleak future was easy to read. 'Did they do it in person? The full pound of flesh?'

'I'm afraid so. It was quick.'

She gave the hollowest of laughs. 'You don't understand, do you? It's not just the flesh. They suck all your Lux into it first. They collapse your soul and squeeze it into your heart before they pull it out. They say it's anything but quick from the inside.'

I shivered. My brain couldn't quite process that.

'I'm sorry, Irina. No one should suffer like that. If I ever catch up with the creature that did it, I will bring them to justice.'

'No you won't, as your Peculier Constable will tell you. Ivan entered into the bargain freely. A bargain covered by Fae law.'

Xavi was looking a bit green at this point. 'Wait outside for a bit,' I said, and he made a sharp exit. I pulled up a chair and sat down.

'How did it happen? What led him to that?' I asked.

'He owed them money. He bought the scrolls from them to make Reduced Gold, but he couldn't get it going fast enough. He needed an Artificer, and Eilidh didn't come on board until it was too late. The Fae demanded a service in return, and that service was to stop you getting the diamond. There was a penalty clause. If he was arrested, they could take his heart. He knew what he was getting in to.'

'Help me get them, Irina. Help me get them before they destroy any more lives.'

'He kept me out of it. Deliberately. I don't know which ones he dealt with.' She sighed, a deep sigh from somewhere around her heart. 'At least you will leave me alone now. Before you go, tell me: how did you find Ivan? He was so careful.'

I passed her the phone. 'I couldn't have done it without your help, Irina. If you hadn't put Isaac's number into there, we'd have been stuck. Call it karma for spraying me with acid.'

She looked like she wanted to be sick.

I stood up and moved the chair. 'I really am very sorry for your loss, Irina, but not as sorry as I am for Carole or for Eggers' children, or Vicky or Dom Richmond.'

I let Xavi back in to the room and went to find Mina and Saffron.

Mina gave me a kiss after Saffron had gone back upstairs. 'How bad was it?'

'Very.'

She nodded. 'I have some good news. Myvvy and Ben are engaged. Wedding planned for when she's released. You are best man. Announcement on chief bridesmaid to follow, but no announcements to anyone yet.'

'What?'

'Only you, Vicky, Erin and I know about this. They're not going to go public until after the 20th of September. The date that Carole was going to get married.'

'Of course. I hope it works out for them.'

'So do I.'

I took her in my arms. 'It feels weird, love. We're talking about their wedding, but there's the small matter of Pramiti in the way of ours.'

'Our wedding will happen before Myvvy's. I am sure of this. Of course, it will have to be in Clerkswell, or Myvvy wouldn't be able to come.'

'I'm sure that the Cloister Court would give her a day off for that. Let's face it, neither of us want the ceremony to be in St Michael's do we?'

She took hold of the lapels of my jacket and stepped back half a pace so that she wouldn't have to strain her neck to look up. 'I'm so proud of what you did and what you've done. Soon it will be time to deal with Pramiti, but not yet. Let's go home and focus on the weekend. Surely you deserve to enjoy the cricket and your family.'

'Not my decision. It's up to the Nine of Wands.'

'Don't say that. We are the masters of our destiny in this life, if not the next. Don't lose sight of that.' She pulled me down for a kiss. 'We really are very, very lucky.'

29 — All's Fair in Love and Cricket

The last time the kitchen had been this full was for Mum and Dad's leaving do. Today, they were conspicuous by their absence.

'I still can't believe we got to stay here and your Mam and Dad had to slum it in the pub,' said John Robson, Vicky's father.

'All the rooms at the Inkwell are en-suite,' said Vicky. 'Do you blame them?'

She was looking brighter today. A little. Every so often she'd take a deeper breath than usual, and the pain flashed across her face in waves. I had pushed for John and Erica to stay here, so that they could spend time with Vicky without her having to leave the house. I also knew that my parents wanted to keep their distance and put off the inevitable: meeting Myfanwy and seeing what she's done to the gardens. That could wait.

The room was in two halves. The cricketing party were putting their stuff together at one end and the spa group were lingering by the Aga. John Robson was floating between the two – his wife and daughter were going to a very nice spa hotel in Cheltenham, along with my mother, while John was coming to the cricket, and my dad was going to take him under his wing. Desirée Haynes completed the luxury group.

Myfanwy took a dirty plate towards the sink, where Erica Robson intercepted her. 'I've told you, pet, that I'll deal with all this. We're not going for ages yet, and you'd better get a shift on.'

Mina and Erin were all packed and ready. Myfanwy wiped her hands on her jeans and went to pick up her bag. Sounds broke out around the room, like a data version of the dawn chorus. At least three people had just received a message. Vicky, Desi, Myvvy and Erin all reached for their mobiles.

Erin won the race. 'Ooh, the Earl of Tintagel's just died.'

I put my bag down and looked at Mina. 'I told the Boss we were not to be disturbed. Whatever's happened, Rick can deal with it.'

'Calm down, man,' said Vicky. 'He's died of cancer and old age.'

'So what's the big deal?'

'There's going to be a contested election for the King of Wessex,' said Erin. She saw my face and added, 'You don't know what I'm talking about, do you?'

'And he doesn't need to,' said Myfanwy. 'He's got more important things to worry about. Like Emily's bowling, for example? Let's go.'

The cricketing party left to loud wishes of good luck from the others.

'You know the real reason I'm coming with youse lot?' said John as we loaded the car.

'Too girly for you at the spa?'

'Naa. I can handle that. It was your mam. She said I had to keep an eye on your dad, what with me being sober. She's one of the few people who doesn't pussy-foot around the fact that I'm a recovering alcoholic.'

'My mother is not known for her tact and diplomacy. Thanks, John.'

The girls filed in to the dressing room, and Ben joined me to inspect the wicket. He looked a lot happier than the last time I'd seen him.

'How's it going, Ben? It's tough to get your head round.'

He nodded. 'You're not joking. The strangest thing is that nothing's really changed. Myfanwy's still bonkers.'

So that was it: Ben had adjusted to the world of magick as if it were the least important thing about Myfanwy. He's probably right. 'How's Carole? Where's Carole?'

He looked up at me. 'Angry. Hurt. Mortified. Mostly angry, though. She's still in Amsterdam, but Rachael's spending the weekend with her. Carole says that Rachael has called you all the names under the sun, and says it's all your fault because you won't talk to her about it.'

'Sounds normal. And there was me thinking we were building an adult relationship.'

'There's going to be a lot of awkward questions soon.' He shrugged. A real countryman's shrug that spoke of generations of farmers who were dependent on the weather, but could do nothing to control it. 'What do you reckon to this wicket, then?

I turned my attention to the grass, or lack of it. The middle of a cricket pitch is called the square, and inside that, 22 yard strips are laid out for the wicket. There were two games today, and the stumps had already been put in for the ladies' game. The groundsman had allocated them a pretty dry section that had been used already this season. A greener strip had been reserved for our game later.

'I'm going to swap them,' said Ben decisively. 'Our men are much better spin bowlers than Allington's.'

'It's a risk,' I said, 'and our fast bowlers won't thank you.'

'Tough. Grab the stumps and move them before anyone notices.'

There was quite a crowd when the girls came out of the pavilion, Clerkswell in the lead because they were fielding first. A big cheer went up, and I'm sure one of the boyfriends at the back shouted, 'Come on the Coven!' Even Scout joined in and barked aggressively at the Allington players.

Emily Ventress bowled well, and if she'd been allowed more than five overs, Allington Ladies might have been in serious trouble. As it was, they posted a respectable score and it was up to the Clerkswell batsmen to chase it.

Juliet Bloxham opened the batting, and was making slow but steady progress when her partner was bowled, and that brought Myfanwy to the crease. For a split-second, I worried that their enmity might hold them up, until I stared in disbelief. Had I just seen Jules Bloxham *giving Myfanwy a high-five*? I had.

They rattled along brilliantly, and the Allington captain was panicking. She tossed the ball to a new bowler and whispered in her ear. Two balls later, Juliet was out, and our number 4 followed suit at the end of the over. Mina's turn next.

They scored a few runs, and Myfanwy grabbed a single to get the strike in the next over. Their new bowler ran in and bowled an absolute corker. I don't know how Myvvy blocked it, but she did, and then I noticed Mina rubbing her left arm and looking very puzzled. She was not happy.

The Allington bowler walked back to her mark, and Mina followed her. The whole of Mrs Clarke's Folly stared as my girlfriend marched up to the bowler and started to berate her. No one moved until Mina lifted her finger and jabbed it at the other woman's chest, at which point the umpire and the Allington captain lurched into action.

Before they could get there, Mina had said her piece and turned back towards the wicket. The Allington skipper spoke to her teammate, and got a shake of the head in reply.

'What the hell was that all about?' said Ben.

'We'll find out in a second.'

The Allington bowler started her run-up, much more slowly, and bowled a long hop to Myfanwy, who promptly smashed it through the covers for four runs. Meanwhile, the bowler had pulled up and started massaging her hamstring.

'Did Mina do that?' said Ben. 'Or Myfanwy?'

'In a manner of speaking.'

The bowler limped off the pitch without bowling another ball. As she got closer to the boundary, she gave me an evil look. Scout barked loudly as she passed his shady spot by the pavilion steps.

'That Allington bowler,' I said, 'she's a Mage of some sort. Mina detected magick in use and called her out.'

'Bloody hell. Does it happen often?'

'No.'

The Clerkswell Coven wrapped up the match shortly afterwards.

'I have two awards to make,' said Stephen Bloxham.

'Hurry up,' said his wife, 'or you'll be fined for starting the men's game late.'

'Right. First, the man of the match award goes to the top scorer from either team, Myfanwy Lewis.'

I don't think I've ever seen her so happy. Well, perhaps. The morning after her first night with Ben, maybe, or when she re-started Vicky's heart. Even when she realised that the award was just the match ball, she was still thrilled.

The second presentation was real enough, and Stephen handed over his gaudy, tasteless trophy to his wife. Juliet Bloxham is reserved, precise and always elegant, a pose she maintained until the cup was in her hands. At that point, Erin elbowed her in the ribs and said, 'Hold the bloody thing up, Jules, I want to bask in the applause.'

'Do we have to have that thing sitting on a chair?' said Mother. 'Do we have enough chairs?'

The Clarke-Briggs Cup, back in Clerkswell after a ten year spell of imprisonment in Allington, had pride of place at the party. The women's trophy was over at the Manor, in Juliet's custody, but the men's cup was with our captain, and Ben was with Myfanwy. Sitting next to the trophy were two cricket balls with messages scrawled on them in silver ink: *Man of the Match – Myfanwy Lewis; Man of the Match – Conrad Clarke.* What made it even more special was that the team had voted for my award. Even Stephen Bloxham.

'Yes, dear,' said Dad.

'Yes what? Yes that we have to have it on display or yes that we have enough chairs.'

'Yes to both.'

Mother sniffed and turned her back on the trophy. 'Conrad, be of some use, will you? You can't let your guests think that the women are doing all the work.'

It's amazing. In Spain, Mother behaves like a normal person, but twenty minutes at her old home and she's treating me like I'm thirteen again. 'Just going for more punch,' I said.

She trailed after me towards the kitchen. The real reason she was acting strangely is that she's very awkward unless she has something to do, and Myfanwy, Mina and Erin were doing fine on their own. Behind us, Dad drifted over to the swing, where Vicky was propped up on cushions, surrounded by a guard of honour. Desi saw him and shuffled along the new rustic bench to make room. In seconds, the whole group was laughing at one of his stories, probably about me.

Myfanwy was running round the kitchen table doing three things at once. I dodged past her and started to fill my flagons from the vat of punch. Mother leaned against the worktop and watched her. Myfanwy put the last of the tartlets on a server and stood back to admire her handiwork. She wiped her forehead and breathed out.

'I don't know you do it, dear,' said Mother. 'The gardens have never looked so good in all of history, and this is a magnificent spread.'

'Thank you, Mrs Clarke. Sorry. Thank you, Mary. I was so worried you wouldn't like what I've done outside.'

Mother shook her head. 'Superb. You have real vision. Please let me do something to help.'

'All done. Can you whistle? It's time to get them in. I don't want to leave this out in the sun, so if you could chivvy everyone to come and load up their plates, that would be great.'

Mother perked up and strode out of the kitchen with purpose.

'Thank the gods for that, Conrad, I was so worried.'

'About what?'

'About your mother. Everyone in the village has been saying how odd she is. I think she's lovely.'

'And so do I, but I'm biased. Where's Mina and Erin?'

'Nipped out to the shop for a couple of bits. Sounds like them back now.'

It took a long while for everyone to get served, even with Mother taking charge of the queue and forcing people back outside once they'd loaded their plates. Mina and I went last, and took our food to couple of chairs in the shade of an old oak tree that had been spared Myfanwy's cull. It gave us a good view of the proceedings. Scout joined us and sat in front, staring hopefully at our plates. We ignored him.

Two of the party had stayed outside and had their food brought to them. One was Vicky, on the swing, the other was Miss Parkes, ensconced under a giant parasol. As people went to sit down, it was noticeable that my father and Ben both avoided Miss Parkes, while Mother and Myfanwy were more than happy to sit next to her. Then again, they'd never been in her class.

'Would it be tempting fate to say that this is Paradise regained?' said Mina.

'Yes, but do it anyway.'

'Perhaps not. Seeing Mary and Erica together does remind me that I'm the only one under forty without a mother.'

I put my arm round her shoulder and kissed her head.

She took a bite of Myfanwy's quiche. 'This is good. Perhaps I could find a new mother. One I could safely invite to events like this.'

'Surely she wasn't that bad.'

'You have no idea, Conrad.' She sighed. 'Myfanwy has already taken Miss Parkes. I know. I could ask Francesca Somerton to adopt me.'

'You could do a lot worse.'

People started drifting back to the kitchen for cake, and Vicky had to take a comfort break. She'd been in the middle of a conversation with Saffron, and the two of them were nearly at the house when they looked up at the sound of crunching gravel, followed shortly by a car horn from round the front. Who the hell was that?

'We'll go,' shouted Vicky. 'I need the exercise.'

Scout barked his Mage bark and trotted off after them. Mina and I looked at each other.

'Rick?' she said. 'A surprise visit from Hannah?'

I put my plate down. 'Unlikely. My money's on Bertie, Saffron's cousin. I'd better go and see for myself.'

I wasn't worried. There are Wards and defences on the house now, and no one starts an attack by blowing a car horn. There was a slight delay when I stood up and had to hop around on my good leg, and by the time I'd crossed the lawn, Vicky and Saffron were coming back with a young woman I didn't recognise at first.

She was lifting a cabin case over the grass, and I heard Vicky saying that she could take her big case through the front door later. There was a puzzled and slightly annoyed look on Vicky's face, and on the other side of the newcomer, Saffron looked as if she were about to burst with gossip and devilment. Various members of the party had stopped what they were doing and drifted over to see what all the excitement was about.

Our visitor was walking along with her head turned behind her, staring at the house, and when she turned to look at the gathering, she put her hand to her mouth and went bright red. It was Sofía, daughter of the Spanish tarot reader. What on earth was she doing here?

Vicky was giving me a strange look, a hurt look, as if I'd said or done something to upset her. 'Why didn't you tell me about your other sister, Conrad?'

Oh. Oh shit.

Vicky's eyes widened. 'Ohmygod sorry. You didn't know, did you?'

I was looking at Sofía. 'I don't think she knew either.'

Vicky pivoted and gasped, and immediately doubled over clutching her wound. Erin moved to catch her, and I heard footsteps behind me as her parents came to the rescue.

Sofía was oblivious. She was staring at me as if I were the Angel of Death come to pay an early visit. Mina arrived, and Sofía broke eye contact to blink and take a step back. Mina stepped forward and put her arm round Sofía. I turned to look behind, to see just how many people had heard.

Everyone, I think. And everyone was trying desperately hard not to look at my parents. They were standing, together, in the middle of a semi-circle. Dad looked upset, and very concerned. He lifted his arm in a gesture of sympathy towards Sofía, then dropped it. Mother was looking down and looking guilty. Everyone says I have Dad's eyes, and now that I thought about it, so does Sofía, so why does Mother look guilty?

'Why don't you go into the house?' said Myfanwy.

'*Nueve de varitas,*' said Sofía. The Nine of Wands.

It looked like the last word was going to go to a playing card, but Mina had other ideas. She gently pulled the case from Sofía's fingers and pushed her

273

towards the back door. 'Come with me. You must be desperate to freshen up after the journey.'

John was leading Vicky back to the swing, and Myfanwy shooed everyone else, leaving Mum and Dad alone. 'Let's go in,' said Mum. 'This may take some time.'

Conrad, Mina and the whole gang's story continues in Eight Kings, the Sixth Book of the King's Watch, available from Paw Press. You can also find out what happened to Conrad and Woody at Draxholt in:

Wings over Water – A King's Watch Story
Turn over for more...

The first Four King's Watch Novellas are now available in paperback under the title:

Tales from the Watch

Including:

Phantom Stag

Wings over Water

Ring of Troth

French Leave

Wings over Water

The second King's Watch novella is now available from Paw Press on Amazon.

In this story, Conrad is whisked from his training course in Shropshire to deal with a haunted former airfield in Yorkshire. Conrad, RAF Veteran, reckons he can deal with a few old airmen. How hard can it be? Very.

Find out what's buried under Draxholt in *Wings over Water* and…

Now Available

PAW PRESS

Eight Kings

The Sixth Book of the King's Watch
by

Mark Hayden

The King is dead.

Long live the Queen…?

There hasn't been a Mage-King of Wessex in over a thousand years. Everyone thinks the title is as dead as its last owner.
Lord Mowbray has other ideas. He has the charter, he has the votes, and he has a candidate: his son.
The Daughters of the Goddess don't agree. What's wrong with a Queen of Wessex?
The Great and the Good from the world of magick gather at Lord Mowbray's mansion in Cornwall to sort it out.
Conrad is (rightly) worried about security. Saffron is worried about disgracing her family. Scout is worried about dinner, and Mina is most worried of all: what will she wear?
When a murderer strikes, Conrad has to draw on all his resources to stop a tragedy turning into an all-out war.

And why not join Conrad's elite group of supporters:

The Merlyn's Tower Irregulars

Visit the Paw Press website and sign up for the Irregulars to receive news of new books, or visit the Facebook page for Mark Hayden Author and Like it.

Author's Note

The *King's Watch* books are a radical departure from my previous five novels, all of which are crime or thrillers, though very much set in the same universe, including the *Operation Jigsaw Trilogy*. Conrad himself refers to it as being part of his history.

You might like to go back the *Jigsaw* trilogy and discover how he came to the Allfather's attention. As I was writing those books, I knew that one day Conrad would have special adventures of his own, and that's why the Phantom makes a couple of guest appearances.

Other than that, it only remains to be said that all the characters in this book are fictional, as are some of the places, but Merlyn's Tower, Earlsbury and the First Mine are, of course, all real places, it's just that you can only see them if you have the Gift…

I started writing this book in February 2019. Less than two months before that, I was seized with the worst flare-up of my bad back that I've ever had. I had to be helped into the house, it was that bad. As I type this, on the day of publication, I am pain free. That trajectory of recovery wouldn't have been so fast or so complete without the expertise of Suzanne Wells, physiotherapist extraordinaire of the Lakeland & Lunesdale clinic. For once, it is literally true that this book wouldn't have been written without her help.

Nor could it have been written without love, support, encouragement and sacrifices from my wife, Anne. It just goes to show how much she loves me that she let me write the first Conrad book even though she hates fantasy novels. She says she now likes them.

As ever, Chris Tyler's friendship is a big part of my continued desire to write.

Thanks,
Mark Hayden.

Printed in Great Britain
by Amazon